GN00738546

A BIGGLES OMNIBUS

Captain W E Johns

LEOPARD

This edition first published in 1995 by Leopard Books
An imprint of the Random House Group
20 Vauxhall Bridge Road
London SW1V 2SA

Copyright © W. E. Johns (Publications) Ltd 1994
Biggles Learns to Fly © W. E. Johns (Publications) Ltd 1935
Biggles Flies East © W. E. Johns (Publications) Ltd 1935
Biggles in the Orient © W. E. Johns (Publications) Ltd 1945

All rights reserved. No part of this publication may
be reproduced, stored in a retrieval system, or
transmitted in any form or by any means, electronic,
mechanical, photocopying, recording or otherwise,
without the prior permission of the copyright owner.

ISBN 0 7529 0129 X

Printed and bound in Great Britain by
Mackays of Chatham PLC, Chatham, Kent

CONTENTS

Biggles Learns to Fly
5

Biggles Flies East
205

Biggles in the Orient
439

BIGGLES
LEARNS TO FLY

Author's Note

The printing of this book is the answer to those who have asked when and where Biggles learned to fly. It was written many years ago, while the events were fresh in the author's mind, long before there was any talk of Hitler and a Second World War. The sons of some of the boys who read it then now fly jets. Time marches on—and in aviation it has marched very fast indeed. But this was the beginning, and the beginning of Biggles.

To readers of the modern Biggles books these early adventures may seem strange, both in the terms used and in the style of conversation. But Biggles was very young then. So was the Air Service. In fact, there was no air service. Fighting planes were flown by officers seconded from the Army (the R.F.C.) and the Navy (Royal Naval Air Service).

When Biggles (and the author) learned to fly, aeroplanes and equipment, by modern standards, were primitive. Combat tactics, as they are understood to-day, were unknown. Every pilot had his own method and, if he lived long enough, picked up a few tricks from the old hands. Once in the air he could more or less do as he pleased, for he was out of touch with the ground except by simple visual signals.

Communication between aircraft, or between pilot and gunner, was also by hand signals. Crossed fingers meant an enemy aircraft. First finger and thumb in the

7

form of a circle meant British aircraft. Thumbs up meant all was well. Thumbs down—well, not so good. One also signalled the approach of enemy aircraft by rocking one's wings.

As the reader may guess, the writer's own experiences were much the same as those described herein. A few flights, and off you went solo. A few hours solo, and off you went to war, to take your luck. Casualties, of course, were grim; but all the same, happy-go-lucky were those days that have now become history. The mystery is that anyone survived, for apart from the risks of battle, structural failure was common, and there were no parachutes. On the other hand, the machines being slow, and made of wood, wire and fabric, one had a better chance in a crash than in the modern high-performance fighter.

The word 'Hun', as used in this book, was the common generic term for anything belonging to the enemy. It was used in a familiar sense, rather than derogatory. Witness the fact that in the R.F.C. a hun was also a pupil at a flying training school.

Chapter 1
First Time Up!

One fine late September morning in the war-stricken year of 1916, a young officer, in the distinctive uniform of the Royal Flying Corps, appeared in the doorway of one of the long, low, narrow wooden huts which, mushroom-like, had sprung up all over England during the previous eighteen months. He paused for a moment to regard a great open expanse that stretched away as far as he could see before him in the thin autumn mist that made everything outside a radius of a few hundred yards seem shadowy and vague.

There was little about him to distinguish him from thousands of others in whose ears the call to arms had not sounded in vain, and who were doing precisely the same thing in various parts of the country. His uniform was still free from the marks of war that would eventually stain it. His Sam Browne belt still squeaked slightly when he moved, like a pair of new boots.

There was nothing remarkable, or even martial, about his physique; on the contrary, he was slim, rather below average height, and delicate-looking. A wisp of fair hair protruded from one side of his rakishly tilted R.F.C. cap; his eyes, now sparkling with pleasurable anticipation, were what is usually called hazel. His features were finely cut, but the squareness of his chin and the firm line of his mouth revealed a certain doggedness, a tenacity of purpose, that denied any suggestion of weakness. Only his hands were small and white, and might have been those of a girl.

His youthfulness was apparent. He might have reached the eighteen years shown on his papers, but his birth certificate, had he produced it at the recruiting office, would have revealed that he would not attain that age for another eleven months. Like many others who had left school to plunge straight into the war, he had conveniently 'lost' his birth certificate when applying for enlistment, nearly three months previously.

A heavy, hair-lined leather coat, which looked large enough for a man twice his size, hung stiffly over his left arm. In his right hand he held a flying-helmet, also of leather but lined with fur, a pair of huge gauntlets, with coarse, yellowish hair on the backs, and a pair of goggles.

He started as the silence was shattered by a reverberating roar which rose to a mighty crescendo and then died away to a low splutter. The sound, which he knew was the roar of an aero-engine, although he had never been so close to one before, came from a row of giant structures that loomed dimly through the now-dispersing mist, along one side of the bleak expanse upon which he gazed with eager anticipation. There was little enough to see, yet he had visualized that flat area of sandy soil, set with short, coarse grass, a thousand times during the past two months while he had been at the 'ground' school. It was an aerodrome, or, to be more precise, the aerodrome of No. 17 Flying Training School, which was situated near the village of Settling, in Norfolk. The great, darkly looming buildings were the hangars that housed the extraordinary collection of hastily built aeroplanes which at this period of the first Great War* were used to teach pupils the art of flying.

A faint smell was borne to his nostrils, a curious aroma that brought a slight flush to his cheeks. It was one common to all aerodromes, a mingling of petrol, oil, dope**, and burnt gases, and which, once experienced, was never forgotten.

Figures, all carrying flying-kit, began to emerge from other huts and hurry towards the hangars, where strange-looking vehicles were now being wheeled out on to a strip of concrete that shone whitely along the front of the hangars for their entire length. After a last appraising glance around, the new officer set off at a brisk pace in their direction.

A chilly breeze had sprung up; it swept aside the curtain of mist and exposed the white orb of the sun, low in the sky, for it was still very early. Yet it was daylight, and no daylight was wasted at flying schools during the Great War.

He reached the nearest hangar, and then stopped, eyes devouring an extraordinary structure of wood, wire, and canvas that stood in his path. A propeller, set behind two exposed seats, revolved slowly. Beside it stood a tall, thin man in flying-kit; his leather flying-coat, which was filthy beyond description with oil stains, flapped open, exposing an equally dirty tunic, on the breast of which a device in the form of a small pair of wings could just be seen. Under them was a

* The First World War 1914–18. Principal contenders, the Allies: Britain, France, Russia, Italy, Serbia, Belgium, Japan (1915), Romania (1916), USA (1917). Against the Central Powers: Germany, Austria-Hungary, Turkey and Bulgaria (1915).
** Liquid similar to varnish, applied to the fabric surfaces to stiffen and weatherproof them.

tiny strip of the violet-and-white ribbon of the Military Cross.

To a fully fledged pilot the figure would have been commonplace enough, but the young newcomer regarded him with an awe that amounted almost to worship. He knew that the tall, thin man could fly; not only could he fly, but he had fought other aeroplanes in the sky, as the decoration on his breast proved. At that moment, however, he seemed merely bored, for he yawned mightily as he stared at the aeroplane with no sign of interest. Then, turning suddenly, he saw the newcomer watching him.

'You one of the fellows on the new course?' he asked shortly.

'Er—er—yes, sir,' was the startled reply.

'Ever been in the air?'

'No, sir.'

'What's your name?'

'Bigglesworth, sir. I'm afraid it's a bit of a mouthful, but that isn't my fault. Most people call me Biggles for short.'

A slow smile spread over the face of the instructor.

'Sensible idea,' he said. 'All right, Biggles, get in.'

Biggles started violently. He knew that he had come to the aerodrome to learn to fly, but at the back of his mind he had an idea that there would be some sort of ceremony about it, some preliminary overtures that would slowly lead up to a grand finale in which he would take his place in an aeroplane before the eyes of admiring mechanics. And now the instructor had just said 'Get in!' as if the aeroplane were a common motor-car. Mechanics were there, it is true, but they were getting on with their work, taking not the slightest notice of the thrilling exploit about to be enacted. Only one, a corporal, was standing near the nose of the machine looking round the sky with a half-vacant expression on his face.

In something like a daze, Biggles donned his flying-kit. It was the first time he had worn it, and he felt that the weight of it would bear him to the ground. Stiffly he approached the machine.

'Look out!'

He sprang back as the shrill warning came faintly to his ears through the thick helmet. The instructor was glaring at him, his face convulsed with rage.

'What are you trying to do?' he roared. 'Break my propeller with your head? Come round to the front!'

'Sorry, sir,' gasped Biggles, and hurried as fast as his heavy kit would permit to the front of the machine. He raised his foot and clutched at a wire to help him up.

'Not there, you fool! Take your foot off that wing before you burst the fabric!' shouted the instructor from his seat.

Biggles backed away hastily—too hastily; his foot caught in one of the many wires that ran in all directions. He clutched wildly at the leading edge of the lower 'plane to save himself, but in vain, and the next instant he had measured his length on the ground.

The instructor looked down at him with such withering contempt that Biggles nearly burst into tears. The corporal came to his assistance. 'Put your left foot in that hole—now the other one in there—now swing yourself up. That's right!'

To Biggles the cockpit seemed hopelessly inadequate, but he squeezed himself into it somehow and settled down with a sigh of relief. Something struck him smartly on the back of the head, and he jumped violently.

'Strap in,' said a hard voice, 'and keep your hands and feet off the controls. If you start any nonsense I'll lam you over the back of the skull with this!'

With some difficulty Biggles screwed his head round to see what 'this' was. A large iron wrench was thrust under his nose; at the same moment the machine began to move forward, slowly at first, but with ever-increasing speed.

Something like panic seized him, and he struggled wildly to buckle up the cumbrous leather belt that he could see on either side of him. It took him a minute to realize that he was sitting on it. 'If he loops the loop or something I'm sunk!' he muttered bitterly, as he fought to pull it from under him. The machine seemed to lurch suddenly, and he grabbed both sides of the cockpit, looking down as he did so. The hangars were just disappearing below.

The next few minutes, which seemed an hour, were a nightmare. The machine rose and fell in a series of sickening movements; every now and then one of the wings would tip up at an alarming angle. He was capable of the one thought only: 'I shall never fly this thing as long as I live—never. I must have been crazy to think I could.'

Woods, fields, and houses passed below in bewildering succession, each looking like its fellow. Had the pilot told him they were over any county in the United Kingdom, he would have believed him.

'We must have gone fifty miles away from the aerodrome,' he thought presently; but the nose of the machine tilted down, and he saw the hangars leaping up towards him. For a moment he really did not believe they were the hangars; he thought it was a trick of the imagination. But there was a sudden grinding of wheels, and before he really grasped what was happening, the machine had run to a standstill in exactly the same spot from which it had taken off. He surveyed the apparent miracle with wonderment, making no effort to move.

'Well, how did you like it?' said a voice in his ear.

Biggles clambered awkwardly from his seat and turned to the speaker. The instructor was actually smiling.

'Grand!' he cried enthusiastically. 'Top hole.'

'Didn't feel sick?'

'Not a bit.'

'It's a wonder. It's bumpy enough to make anyone sick; we shall have to pack up flying if it doesn't get better. Let's go and mark your time up on the board. Enter up your log-book. "First flight. Air experience five minutes." '

'Five minutes!' cried Biggles incredulously. 'We were only up five minutes? I thought we were at least half an hour.'

The instructor had stopped before a notice-board headed ' "A" Flight,' below which was a list of names.

'What did you say your name was?' he asked, a frown lining his forehead.

'Bigglesworth, sir.'

'What flight are you in?'

'Flight? I don't know, sir.'

'You don't know?' snarled the instructor. 'Then what the dickens do you mean by wasting my time? What were you loafing about here for? These are "A" Flight sheds.'

Biggles stepped back quickly in his nervousness; his

heel struck a chock, and he grabbed wildly at a passing officer to save himself from falling.

'Hi! Not so much of the clutching hand!' growled a voice. 'This is a flying ground, not a wrestling school.'

'Sorry!' cried Biggles, aghast, detaching himself.

'Your name isn't Bigglesworth, by any chance, is it?' went on the officer, a short, thick-set man with a frightful scar on his face that reached from the corner of one eye to his chin.

'Why, yes, sir,' replied Biggles hesitatingly.

'Then what are you doing down here? You're in my flight, and you've kept the class waiting.'

'I've been flying, sir,' protested Biggles.

'You've been what?'

'He's right!' grumbled the first instructor. 'He was down here, so I naturally thought he was one of my fellows. I wish you'd look after your own pupils!'

Biggles waited for no more, but hurried along the tarmac to where a little group of officers—all pupils, judging by their spotless uniforms—stood at the door of a hangar.

'Where have you been?' cried one. 'Nerky's been blinding you to all eternity!'

'Nerky?'

'Captain Nerkinson. We call him Nerky because he's as nerky as they make 'em! He's crashed about ten times, so you can't blame him. Look out, here he comes!'

'Well, don't let us waste any more time,' began the instructor. 'Gather round this machine while I tell you something about it.'

The pupils formed a respectful semi-circle round the machine he had indicated.

'This aeroplane,' he began, 'is called a Maurice

16

Farman Shorthorn, chiefly because it hasn't any horns, short or otherwise. Some people call it a Rumpity. Others call it a birdcage, because of the number of wires it has got. The easiest way to find out if all the wires are in their places is to put a canary between the wings; if the bird gets out, you know there is a wire missing somewhere.

'Always remember that if this machine gets into a spin, it never gets out of it; and if it gets into a dive, the wings are apt to come off. Presently I shall take you up in it, one at a time; if anybody doesn't like it, he has only to say so, and he can transfer to the infantry.'

His voice trailed away to a whisper as a faint whistling sound reached their ears. All eyes were staring upwards at a machine that was coming in to land. It was a Rumpity, and it seemed to be descending in short jerks, as if coming down an invisible staircase; the pilot could seen sitting bolt upright in his seat.

A deep groan burst from the instructor's lips, as if he had been suddenly smitten with a violent pain.

'That's Rafferty, I'll bet my hide!' he muttered. 'I thought I'd cured him of that habit. Watch him, everybody, and you'll see the answer to the question why instructors go mad!'

Everybody on the tarmac was watching the machine, Biggles with a curious mixture of fear and fascination. A motor-truck, with a dozen mechanics carrying Pyrene fire-extinguishers hanging on to it, was already moving out on to the aerodrome in anticipation of the crash.

The pilot of the descending machine continued to swoop downwards in a series of short jerks. At the last moment he seemed to realize his danger, and must have pulled the joystick back into his stomach, for the machine reared up like a startled horse and then slid back, tail first, to the ground. There was a terrific crash of breaking woodwork and tearing fabric, and the machine collapsed in a cloud of flying splinters. The pilot shot out of his seat as if propelled by an invisible spring, and rolled over and over along the ground like a shot rabbit. Then, to the utter astonishment of everybody, he rose to his feet and rubbed the back of his head ruefully. A shout of laughter rose into the air from the spectators.

Captain Nerkinson nodded soberly.

'You have just seen a beautiful picture,' he said, 'of how not to land an aeroplane!'

18

Chapter 2
Landed—But Lost

A week later, a Rumpity landed on the aerodrome, and Captain Nerkinson swung himself to the ground. Biggles, in the front cockpit, was about to follow, but the instructor stopped him.

'You're absolutely O.K.,' he said, 'except that you are inclined to come in a bit too fast. Don't forget that. Off you go!'

'Off I what?' cried Biggles, refusing to believe his ears.

'You heard me. You're as right as rain—but don't be more than ten minutes.'

'I won't—by James I won't, you can bet your life on that!' declared Biggles emphatically. He took a last lingering survey of the aerodrome, as when a swimmer who has climbed up to the high diving-board for the first time looks down. Then, suddenly making up his mind, he thrust the throttle open with a despairing jerk and grabbed at the weird, spectacle-like arrangement that served as a joy-stick in the Rumpity.

The machine leapt forward and careered wildly in a wide circle towards the distant hedge. For a moment, as the machine started to swing, Biggles thought he was going to turn a complete circle and charge the hangars; but he kept his head, and straightened it.

The tail lifted, and he eased the joy-stick back gently. To his surprise the machine lifted as lightly as a feather, but the needle on the air-speed indicator ran back alarmingly. He shoved the joy-stick forward again with a frantic movement as he realized with a heart-palpitating shock that he had nearly stalled through climbing too quickly. Settling his nose on the horizon and holding the machine on an even keel, he soon began to gather confidence.

A nasty 'bump' over the edge of a wood brought his heart into his mouth, and he muttered 'Whoa, there!' as if he was talking to a horse. The sound of his own voice increased his confidence, so from time to time he encouraged himself with such comments as 'Steady, there! Whoa, my beauty!' and 'Easy does it!'

Presently it struck him that it was time he started turning to complete a circuit that would bring him back to the aerodrome. He snatched a swift glance over his left shoulder, but he could not see the hangars. He turned a little farther and looked again. The aerodrome was nowhere in sight. It had disappeared as completely as if the earth had opened and swallowed it up. Perspiration broke out on his brow as he quickened his turn and examined every point of the compass in quick succession; but there was no aerodrome.

It took him another few seconds to realize that this miracle had actually taken place.

'No matter,' he muttered. 'I've only got to go back the way I came and I can't miss it.' In five minutes he was looking down on country that he knew he had never seen before.

His heart fluttered, and his lips turned dry as the full shock of the fact that he was completely lost struck him. Another 'plane appeared in his range of vision, seeming to drift sideways like a great grasshopper in that curious manner other machines have in the air, and he followed it eagerly. It might not be going to his aerodrome, but that did not matter; any aerodrome would suit him equally well. His toe slipped off the rudder-bar, and he looked down to adjust it.

When he looked up again his machine was in an almost vertical bank; he levelled out from a sickening side-slip, with beads of moisture forming inside his goggles. He pushed them up with a nervous jerk, and looked around for the other machine. It had gone. North, south, east and west he strained his eyes, but in vain. His heart sank, but he spotted a railway line and headed towards it.

'It must be the line that goes to Settling,' he thought, and he started to follow it eagerly. He was quite right — it was; but unfortunately he was going in the wrong direction.

After what seemed an eternity of time, a curious phenomenon appeared ahead. It seemed as if the land stopped short, ending abruptly in space, so to speak. He pondered it for a moment, and had just arrived at the conclusion that it was a belt of fog, when something else caught his eye, and he stared at it wonderingly. The shape seemed familiar, but for a moment or two he could not make out what it was. It looked like a ship, but how could a ship float in fog? Other smaller ones came into view, and at last the truth dawned on him. He was looking at the sea. It seemed impossible. As near as he could judge by visualizing the map, the coast was at least forty miles from Settling.

'This is frightful!' he groaned, and turned away from the forbidding spectacle. A blast of air smote him on the cheek, and objects on the ground suddenly grew larger. He clenched his teeth, knowing that he had side-slipped badly on the turn. He snatched a quick glance at the altimeter, and noted that it indicated four hundred feet, whereas a moment before the needle had pointed to the twelve hundred mark.

'Good heavens, this won't do!' he told himself angrily. 'What was it Nerky had said? "Never lose your head!" That was it.' He pulled himself together with an effort and looked at his watch. He had been in the air an hour and a half, and Nerky had told him not to be more than ten minutes.

He wondered how much longer his petrol would last, realizing with fresh dismay that he did not know how much petrol had been in the tanks when he started. The light was already failing; presently it would be dark, and what hope would he have then of finding his way? He remembered that he had a map in his pocket, but what use was that if he did not know where he was? He could only find that out by landing and asking somebody.

'It's the only way!' he told himself despairingly. 'I might go on drifting round in circles for the rest of my life without finding the aerodrome.'

He began to watch the ground for a suitable field on which to land.

He flew for some time before he found one. It was an enormous field, beautifully green, and he headed the machine towards it. At the last moment it struck him that there was something queer about the grass, and he pulled up again with a jerk, realizing that he had nearly landed on a field of turnips.

Another quarter of an hour passed, and another large field presented itself; it looked like stubble, which could do the machine no harm; but he approached it warily. Only when he was quite sure that it was stubble did he pull the throttle back. The sudden silence as the engine died away almost frightened him, and he watched the ground, now seeming to come towards him, longingly.

In the next few seconds of agonizing suspense he hardly knew what he did, and it was with unspeakable relief and surprise that he heard his wheels trundling over solid earth. The machine stopped, and he surveyed the countryside, scarcely able to believe that he was actually on the ground.

'I've landed!' he told himself joyfully. 'Landed without breaking anything! How did I do it? Good old aeroplane!' he went on, patting the wooden side of the cockpit. 'You must have done it yourself—I didn't. But the thing is, where are we?'

He stood up in the cockpit and looked around. Not a soul was in sight, nor was there any sign of human habitation.

'I would choose the only place in England where there aren't any roads, houses or people!' he thought bitterly. 'If I've got to walk to the horizon looking for somebody, it will be pitch dark before I get back. Then I should probably lose myself as well as the aeroplane!' he concluded miserably.

He sprang up as the sound of an aero engine reached his ears. It was a Rumpity, and, what was more, it was coming towards him. It almost looked as if the pilot intended landing in the same field.

'Cheers!' muttered Biggles. 'Now I shall soon know where I am!'

He was quite right; he was soon to know.

The Rumpity landed. The pilot jumped to the ground and strode towards him; there seemed to be something curiously familiar about his gait.

'Can it be?' thought Biggles. 'Great jumping fish, it is. Well, I'm dashed!'

Captain Nerkinson, his brows black as a thunder-cloud, was coming toward him. 'What game d'you think you're playing?' he snarled.

'Game?' echoed Biggles, in amazement. 'Playing?'

'Yes, game! Who told you you could land outside the aerodrome?'

'I told myself,' replied Biggles truthfully. 'I wanted to find out where I was. I lost myself, and I knew I had got so far away from the aerodrome that I—'

'Lost! What are you talking about? You've crossed the aerodrome three times during the last hour. I saw you!'

'I crossed the aerodrome?'

'You've just flown straight over it! That's why I chased you.'

'Flown over it!' Biggles shut his eyes, and shook his head, shuddering. 'Then it can only be a few miles away,' he exclaimed.

'A few miles! It's only a few yards, you young fool— just the other side of the hedge!'

Biggles sank down weakly in his seat.

'All right, let's get back,' went on the instructor. 'Follow close behind, and don't take your eyes off me.'

He hurried back to his machine and took off. Biggles followed. The leading machine merely hopped over the hedge and then began to glide down again at once, and Biggles could hardly believe his eyes when the aerodrome loomed up; it did not seem possible that he could have missed seeing those enormous sheds.

He started to glide down in Captain Nerkinson's wake. He seemed to be travelling much faster than the leading machine, for his nose was soon nearly touching its tail. He saw the instructor lean out of his seat and

24

look back at him, white-faced. He seemed to be yelling something.

'He thinks I'm going to ram him,' thought Biggles. 'And so I shall if he doesn't get out of my way; he ought to know jolly well that I can't stop.'

The instructor landed, but he did not stop; instead, he raced madly across the ground towards the far side of the aerodrome, Biggles following close behind.

'I'm not losing you,' he declared grimly.

Captain Nerkinson swung round in a wide circle towards the sheds, and then, leaping out of the machine almost before it had stopped, sprinted for safety.

Biggles missed the other machine by inches; indeed, he would probably have crashed into it but for half a dozen mechanics, who, seeing the danger, dashed out and grabbed his wings.

'Are you trying to kill me?' Captain Nerkinson asked him, with deadly calm. He was breathing heavily.

'You said I wasn't to lose you.'

'I know I did, but I didn't ask you to ram me, you lunatic!'

The instructor recovered himself, and pointed to the hangar. 'Go and enter up your time,' he said sadly. 'If you stick to the tails of the Huns as closely as you stuck to mine, you should make a skyfighter.'

Three days later a little group collected around the notice-board outside the orderly-room.

'What is it?' asked Biggles, trying to reach the board.

'Posting,' said somebody.

Biggles pushed his way to the front and ran his eye down the alphabetical list of names until he reached his own, and read:

2nd Lieut. Bigglesworth, J., to No. 4 School of Fighting, Frensham.

The posting was dated to take effect from the following day.

He spent the evening hurriedly packing his kit, and, in company with four other officers who had been posted to the same aerodrome, caught the night train for his new station.

It was daylight the following day when they arrived, for although the journey to the School of Fighting, which was situated on the Lincolnshire coast, was not a long one, it involved many changes and delays. A tender met them at the station and dropped them with their kits in front of the orderly-room.

Biggles knocked at the door, entered, and saluted.

'Second-Lieutenant Bigglesworth reporting for duty, sir,' he said smartly.

The adjutant* consulted a list. 'The mess secretary will fix you up with quarters, Bigglesworth,' he said. 'Get yourself settled as soon as you can and report to "A" Flight—Major Maccleston.' He nodded, and then went on with his work.

Biggles dumped his kit in the room allotted to him, and then made his way to the sheds, where he was told that Major Maccleston was in the air.

He was not surprised, for the air was full of machines—Avros, B.E.s, F.E.s, Pups, and one or two types he did not recognize. Most of them were circling at the far side of the aerodrome and diving at something on the ground. The distant rattle of machine-guns came to his ears.

* An officer responsible for assisting the Commanding Officer with correspondence and paperwork.

26

Later on he learned that the far side of the aerodrome ran straight down into the sea, a long, deserted foreshore, on which old obsolete aeroplanes were placed as targets. Scores of officers stood on the tarmac, singly or in little groups, waiting for their turns to fly.

A Pup* taxied out to take off, and he watched it with intense interest, for it was the type that he ultimately hoped to fly. An F.E. was just coming in to land, and he stiffened with horror, knowing that a collision was inevitable.

He saw the gunner in the front seat of the F.E. spring up and cover his face with his arms; then the Pup bored into it from underneath with a dreadful crash of splintering woodwork. For a moment the machines clung together, motionless in mid air; then they broke apart, each spinning into the ground with a terrible noise which, once heard, is never forgotten. A streak of fire ran along the side of one of them, and then a sheet of flame leapt high into the air. An ambulance raced towards the scene, and Biggles turned away, feeling suddenly sick. It was the first real crash he had seen.

A flight-sergeant was watching him grimly. 'A nasty one, sir,' he said casually, as if he had been watching a football match in which one of the players had fallen. 'You'll soon get used to that, though,' he went on, noting Biggles' pale face. 'We killed seven here last week.'

Biggles turned away. Flying no longer seemed just a thrilling game; tragedy stalked it too closely. He was glad when an instructor landed, turned out his passen-

* Sopwith Pup. A single seat fighter with one fixed machine-gun synchronised to allow the bullets to pass between the propeller blades.

27

ger, and beckoned him to take his place. Biggles took his seat in the cockpit, noting with a thrill that it was fitted with machine-guns.

'We're going to do a little gunnery practice,' said the instructor, and took off.

Three days later, Biggles was called to the orderly-room.

'What's up?' he asked a sober-faced officer, who was just leaving.

'Heavy casualties in France,' was the reply. 'They're shoving everybody out as fast as they can.'

Biggles entered and saluted. The adjutant handed him a movement order and a railway warrant.

'A tender will leave the mess at six forty-five to catch the seven o'clock train,' he said. 'You will proceed direct to France via Newhaven and Dieppe.'

'But I haven't finished my tests yet, sir!' exclaimed Biggles, in surprise.

'Have you got your logbook and training transfer-card?'

Biggles placed them on the desk.

The adjutant filled in the tests which had not been marked up, signed them, and then applied the orderly-room stamp.

'You've passed them now,' he said, with a queer smile. 'You may put up your "wings"!'

Biggles saluted, and returned to the aerodrome in a state of suppressed excitement. Two thoughts filled his mind. One was that he was now a fully fledged pilot, entitled to wear the coveted 'wings', and the other that he was going to France.

The fact that he had done less than fifteen hours' flying, dual and solo, did not depress him in the least.

Chapter 3
The Boat for France

There are some people who say that the North Pole is the most desolate spot on the face of the globe. Others give the doubtful credit to the middle of the Sahara Desert. They are all wrong.

Without the slightest shadow of doubt the most dismal spot on the face of the earth is that depressing railway terminus known as Newhaven Quay, on the south coast of England, where the passenger for the Continent gets out of a train, walks across a platform, and steps on to the cross-Channel boat. At normal times it is bad enough, but during the First World War it was hard to find words to describe it.

So thought Biggles, who crouched rather than sat on a kit-bag in a corner of the platform. His attitude dripped depression as plainly as the dark silhouette of the station dripped moisture.

He was not alone on the platform. At intervals along the stone slabs, dark, ghostly figures loomed mysteriously, in ones and twos, and in little groups. At the far end, a long line of men in greatcoats, with unwieldy-looking bundles on their backs, filed slowly into view from an indistinguishable background. The only sounds were vague, muffled orders, and the weird moaning of the biting north-east wind through the rigging of a ship that rested like a great vague shadow against the quay. Not a light showed anywhere, for German submarines had been reported in the Channel.

Once, a low laugh echoed eerily from the shadows, and the unusual sound caused those who heard it to turn curiously in the direction whence it came, for the occasion of the departure of a leave-boat for France was not usually one for mirth.

Biggles moved uneasily and seemed to sink a little lower into the greatcoat that enveloped him. He did not even move when another isolated figure emerged slowly from the pillar behind which it had been sheltering from the icy blast, and stopped close by.

'Miserable business, this messing about doing nothing,' observed the newcomer. His voice sounded almost cheerful, and it may have been this quality that caused Biggles to look up.

'Miserable, did you say?' he exclaimed bitterly. 'It's awful. There isn't a word bad enough for it. I'm no longer alive—I'm just a chunk of frozen misery.'

'They say we shall be moving off presently.'

'I've been hearing that ever since I arrived!'

'They say it's a U-boat in the Channel that's holding us up.'

'What about it? Surely to goodness it's better to drown quickly than sit here and freeze to death slowly. Why the dickens don't they let us go on board, anyway?'

'Ask me something easier. Is this your first time over?'

Biggles nodded. 'Yes,' he said grimly, 'and if it's always like this, I hope it will be the last.'

'It probably will be, so you needn't worry about that.'

'What a nice cheerful fellow you are!'

The other laughed softly. 'I see you're R.F.C. What squadron are you going to?'

'I've no idea. My Movement Order takes me as far as the Pool* at St Omer.'

'Splendid! We shall go that far together: I'm in Two-six-six.'

Biggles glanced up with fresh interest. 'So you've been over before?' he queried.

'Had six months of it; just going back from my first leave. By the way, my name's Mahoney—we may as well know each other.'

'Mine's Bigglesworth, though most people find that rather a mouthful and leave off the "worth." You fly Pups in Two-six-six, don't you?'

'We do—they're nice little Hun-getters.'

'I hope to goodness I get to a scout squadron, although I haven't flown a scout yet.'

'So much the better,' laughed Mahoney. 'If you'd been flying scouts they'd be certain to put you on bombers when you got to France. Fellows who have been flying two-seaters are usually pitched into scout squadrons. That's the sort of daft thing they do, and one of the reasons why we haven't won the war yet. Hallo! It looks as if we're going to move at last.'

A gangway slid from the quay to the ship with a dull rattle, and the groups of officers and other ranks began to converge upon it.

'Come on, laddie; on your feet and let's get aboard,' continued Mahoney. 'Where's the rest of your kit?'

'Goodness knows! The last I saw of it, it was being slung on to a pile with about a thousand others.'

'Don't worry. It will find you all right. How much flying have you done?'

* A depot to which officers were posted until assigned to an active service squadron.

31

'Fifteen hours.'

Mahoney shook his head. 'Not enough,' he said. 'Never mind, if you get to Two-six-six, I'll give you a tip or two.'

'You can give me them on the journey, in case I don't,' suggested Biggles. 'I've been waiting for a chance to learn a few things first-hand from someone who has done it.'

'If more chaps would take that view there would be fewer casualties,' said Mahoney soberly, as they crossed over the narrow gangway.

Two days later a Crossley tender pulled up on a lonely, poplar-lined road to the north of St Omer, and Biggles stepped out. There was nothing in sight to break the bleak inhospitality of the landscape except three many-hued canvas hangars, a cluster of wooden huts, and three or four curious semi-circular corrugated iron buildings.

'Well, here you are, Biggles,' said Mahoney, who had remained inside the vehicle. 'We say good-bye here.'

'So this is One-six-nine Squadron,' replied Biggles, looking about him. 'My word! I must say it doesn't look the sort of place you'd choose for a summer holiday!'

'It isn't. But then you're not on a holiday!' smiled Mahoney. 'Don't worry; you'll find things cheerful enough inside. It's too bad they wouldn't let you go to a scout squadron; but F.E.'s* aren't so bad. They can fight when they have to, and the Huns know it, believe me. I suppose they're so short of pilots that they are just bunging fellows straight to the squadrons where

* Two-seater biplane with the engine behind the pilot, the gunner just in front of him. See cover illustration.

32

pilots are most needed. Well, I must get along; Two-six-six is only seven or eight miles farther on, so we shall be seeing something of each other. Come over to our next guest night. Remember what I've told you—and you may live until next Christmas. Cheerio, laddie!'

'Cheerio!' replied Biggles, with a wave of farewell as the car sped on to its destination. He picked up his valise and walked towards a square wooden building near the hangars, which he rightly judged to be the squadron office. He tapped on the door, opened it in response to a curt invitation to enter, and saluted briskly.

'Second-Lieutenant Bigglesworth, sir,' he said.

An officer who sat at a desk strewn with papers, rose, came towards him, and offered his hand. 'Pleased to meet you, Bigglesworth,' he said. 'And if you can fly, everyone here will be more than pleased to see you. We are having a tough time just at present. I'm Todd—more often known as "Toddy"—and I'm simply the Recording Officer. The C.O. is in the air, but he'll want a word with you when he gets back. You'll like Major Paynter. Wing 'phoned us that you were on the way, so you'll find your quarters ready in Number Four Hut. Get your kit inside, and make yourself comfortable; then go across to the mess. I'll be along presently. By the way, how many hours' flying—solo—have you done?'

'Nearly nine hours.'

Toddy grimaced. 'What on?' he asked.

'Shorthorns and Avros.'

'Ever flown an F.E.?'

'Not solo. I had a flight in one at Frensham, but an instructor was in the other seat.'

33

'Never mind; they're easy enough to fly,' answered Toddy. 'See you later.'

Biggles departed to his quarters. The work of unpacking his kit occupied only a few minutes, and then he made his way slowly towards the officers' mess*. He was still a little distance away, when the sound of an aero-engine made him glance upwards. An aeroplane was heading towards the aerodrome, a type which he did not recognize. But, unwilling to betray his ignorance before possible spectators in the mess, he paid no further attention to it and continued on his course. He then noted with some surprise that Toddy was behaving in a very odd manner. The Recording Officer began by flinging open the door of the squadron office and racing towards the mess. When he had reached about half-way, however, he appeared to change his mind, and, turning like a hare, took a flying leap into a sort of hole.

Biggles next noticed the faces of several officers at the mess window; they seemed to be very excited about something, waving their arms wildly. It did not occur to him for a moment that the signals were intended for him. The first indication he received that something unusual was happening was a curious whistling sound; but even then the full significance of it did not strike him. The whistle swiftly became a shrill howl, and thinking he was about to be run down by a speedy car, he jumped sideways. The movement probably saved his life, for the next instant the world seemed to explode around him in a brilliant flash of flame. There was a thundering detonation that seemed to make the very earth rock, and he was flung violently to the ground. For

* The place where officers eat their meals and relax together.

a moment he lay quite still, dazed, while a steady down-pour of clods, stones, and loose earth rained about him.

The steady rattle of machine-guns in action pene-trated his temporarily paralysed brain, and he rose unsteadily to his feet. He noted that the aeroplane had disappeared, and that a little crowd of officers and mechanics were racing towards him.

'What the dickens was that?' he asked the officers who ran up.

The question seemed to amuse them, for a yell of laughter rose into the air.

Biggles flushed. 'Do you usually greet new fellows like that?' he inquired angrily.

There was a renewed burst of laughter.

'Jerry* does, when he gets the chance. Our friends over the Line must have heard that you had arrived, so they sent their love and kisses,' replied a tall, good-looking officer, with a wink at the others. 'Don't you know an L.V.G.** when you see one?' he added.

'An L.V.G.! A Hun!' cried Biggles.

The other nodded. 'Yes. Just slipped over to lay the daily egg. You're lucky,' he went on. 'When I saw you strolling across the aerodrome as if you were taking an airing in the park, I thought we should be packing up your kit by this time. You're Bigglesworth, I suppose; we heard you were coming. My name is Mapleton, of A Flight. This is Marriot—Lutters—Way—McAngus. We're all A Flight. The others are in the air. But come across to the mess and make yourself at home!'

'But what about that L.V.G.?' cried Biggles. 'Do you let him get away with that sort of thing?'

* Slang: Germans
** A German two-seater, the product of Luft Verkehrs Ges'ellschaft.

'He's half-way home by now; the best thing we can hope for is that the Line archies* give him a warm time. Hallo, here comes the patrol! What—'

A sudden hush fell upon the group as all eyes turned upwards to where two machines were coming in to land. Biggles noticed that Mapleton's face had turned oddly pale and strained. He noticed, too, for the first time, that there were three stars on his sleeves, which indicated the rank of captain.

'Two!' breathed the man whom Captain Mapleton had named Marriot. 'Two!' he said again. And Biggles could feel a sudden tension in the air.

'Come on!' said Mapleton. 'Let's go and meet them. Maybe the others have stayed on a bit longer.'

Together they hurried towards the now taxi-ing machines.

The events of the next few minutes were to live in Biggles' mind for ever. His whole system, brought face to face with the grim realities of war, received a shock which sent his nerves leaping like a piece of taut elastic that has been severed with scissors. He was hardly conscious of it as the time, however, when, with the others, he reached the leading machine. He merely looked at it curiously. Then, instinctively, he looked at the pilot, who was pushing up his goggles very slowly and deliberately.

One glance at his face and Biggles knew he was in the presence of tragedy. The face was drawn and white, but it was the expression on it—or, rather, the absence of expression on it—that made Biggles catch his breath. There was no fear written there, but rather a look of weariness. For perhaps two minutes he sat thus, staring

* Anti aircraft gun batteries close to the front line of battle.

36

with unseeing eyes at his instrument-board. Then, with a movement that was obviously an effort, he passed his hand wearily over his face and climbed stiffly to the ground. Still without speaking he began to walk towards the mess, followed by two or three of the officers.

A low, muttered exclamation made Biggles half-turn to the man next to him. It was Lutters.

'Just look at that kite!' Lutters said. 'The Old Man* must have been through hell backwards.'

'Old Man?' ejaculated Biggles questioningly.

'Yes—the C.O. There must be two hundred bullet holes in that machine; how it holds together beats me!'

Biggles' attention had been so taken up with the pilot that he had failed to notice the machine, and now he caught his breath as he looked at it. There were holes everywhere; in several places pieces of torn canvas hung loosely, having been wrenched into long, narrow streamers by the wind. One of the interplane struts was splintered for more than half its length, and a flying wire trailed uselessly across the lower 'plane.

He was about to take a step nearer, when a cry made him look towards the second machine. Two mechanics were carefully lifting a limp body to the ground.

'You'd better keep out of the way,' said McAngus brusquely, as he passed; but Biggles paid no attention. He knew that McAngus was right, and that the sight was hardly one for a new pilot; but the tableau drew him irresistibly towards it.

When he reached the machine they had laid the mortally wounded pilot on the ground. His eyes were

* Slang for the person in authority, Commanding Officer, often shortened to C.O.

open, but there was an expression in them that Biggles had never seen before.

'Jimmy—how's Jimmy?' the stricken man was muttering; and then: 'Look after Jimmy!'

Biggles felt himself roughly pushed aside.

It was the C.O., who had returned. 'Get him to hospital as fast as you can,' he told the driver of the motor-ambulance which had pulled up alongside. Then, 'How's Mr Forrester?' he asked a mechanic, who was bending over the front cockpit of the machine.

'I'm afraid he's dead, sir,' was the quiet reply.

'All right—get him out!' said the C.O. briefly.

Biggles watched two mechanics swing up to the forward cockpit of the F.E. Slowly, and with great care, they lifted the body of the dead observer and lowered it into waiting hands below.

Biggles caught a glimpse of a pale, waxen face, wearing a curious, fixed smile, and then he turned away, feeling that he was in the middle of a ghastly dream, from which he would presently awaken. He was overwhelmed with a sense of fantastic unreality.

Again the drone of an aero-engine rose and fell on the breeze, and at the same instant a voice cried: 'Here's another!' He swung round and stood expectant with the others as the machine reached the aerodrome, roared low over their heads as it came round into the wind, and then landed. A large white letter U was painted on the nose.

'It's Allen and Thompson!' cried several voices at once.

The machine taxied up quickly. The observer leaped out as soon as it stopped, and started buffing his arms to restore the circulation. The pilot joined him on the ground, flung open his flying-coat and lit a cigarette.

Biggles saw there were several bullet-holes in this machine, too, but neither pilot nor observer paid any attention to them. In fact, the pilot, a stockily built, red-faced youth, was grinning cheerfully, and Biggles stared in amazement at a man who could laugh in the shadow of death.

'Love old Ireland!' observed Thompson, the observer. 'Isn't it perishing cold! Give me a match, somebody. What a day!' he went on. 'The sky's fairly raining Huns. The Old Man got a couple—did he tell you? Poor Jimmy's gone, I'm afraid, and Lucas. We ran into the biggest bunch of Huns over Douai that I ever saw in my life.'

He turned and walked away towards the mess, the others following, and Biggles was left alone with the mechanics, who were now pulling the machines into the hangars with excited comments on the damage they had suffered. He watched them for a few minutes, and then, deep in thought, followed the other officers towards the mess, feeling strangely subdued. For the first time he had looked upon death, and although he was not afraid, something inside him seemed to have changed. Hitherto he had regarded the War as 'fun'. But he now perceived that he had been mistaken. It was one thing to read of death in the newspapers, but quite another matter to see it in reality.

He was passing the squadron office when Toddy called him. 'The C.O. wants to have a word with you right away,' he said.

Several officers were in the room when Biggles entered, and he felt rather self-conscious of his inexperience; but the C.O. soon put him at ease.

'I'm afraid you've come at rather a bad moment,' he began, shaking hands. 'I mean for yourself,' he

39

added quickly. 'We hope it will be a good one for us. I'm posting you to A Flight; Captain Mapleton will be your flight-commander. We like to keep pilots and observers together, as far as we can, but it's not always possible. I believe Way is without a regular pilot, isn't he, Mapleton? So Bigglesworth might pair off with him.'

Captain Mapleton nodded. 'Yes, sir,' he said. 'He's my only observer now without a regular pilot.'

'Good! Then your Flight is now up to establishment,' continued the major, turning again to Biggles. 'Don't let what you've seen to-day depress you. It was an unfortunate moment for you to arrive; that sort of thing doesn't happen every day, thank goodness!' He hesitated and went on, 'I want you always to remember that the honour of the squadron comes first. We are going through rather a difficult time just now, and we may have a lot of uphill work ahead of us, so we're all doing our best. Trust your flight-commander implicitly, and always follow his instructions. In the ordinary way I should give you a week or two to get your bearings before letting you go over the Line, but we've had a bad run of casualties, and I need every officer I can get hold of. It's rather bad luck on you, but I want you to do the best you can in the circumstances. Study the map and the photographs in the map-room; in that way you will soon become acquainted with the area. All right, gentlemen, that's all.'

As the officers filed out, a deeply tanned, keen-eyed young officer tapped Biggles on the arm. 'I'm Mark Way,' he said. 'It looks as if we shall be flying together, so the sooner we know each other the better.'

'That's true,' said Biggles. 'Have you been out here long?'

'Nearly three months,' replied Mark simply. 'But I saw a bit of active service with the infantry before I transferred to the R.F.C. I came over with the New Zealand contingent; my home is out there.'

'Sporting of you to come all this way to help us. Who have you been flying with?'

'Lane.'

'Where is he now?'

Mark gave Biggles a sidelong glance. 'He's gone topsides,' he said slowly. 'He died in hospital last week—bullet through the lungs.'

Biggles was silent for a moment, feeling rather embarrassed.

'You'll like Mapleton,' went on Mark. 'He's a good sort. By the way, we call him Mabs; I don't know why, but he was called that when I came here. Marble is his observer—his real name is Mardell, but Marble is a good name for him. He's as cold as ice in a dog-fight,* and knows every inch of the Line. They're a jolly good pair, and I'd follow them anywhere. Allen is O.C.** B Flight. It's best to keep out of his way; he's a bad-tempered brute. Perhaps it isn't quite fair of me to say that, because I don't think he means to be nasty; he's been out here a long time, and his nerves are all to pieces. Rayner has C Flight. He's all right, but a bit of a snob, although personally I think it's all affectation. His brother was killed early in the war, and all he really thinks about is revenge. He's got several Huns. He takes on Huns wherever he finds them, regardless of numbers, and he gets his Flight into pretty hot water; but they can't complain, because he's always

* An aerial battle rather than a hit-and-run attack.
** Officer commanding B Flight

41

in the thick of it himself. I don't think his luck can last much longer. I wouldn't be his observer for anything! Marriot and McAngus are the other two pilots in A Flight. Conway flies with Marriot, and Lutter is Mac's observer; they're a good crowd. Hallo, here comes Mabs. What does he want?'

'Bigglesworth,' began the flight-commander, coming up, 'I don't want to rush you, but I'm taking a Line patrol up this afternoon. I think it will be pretty quiet, or I wouldn't let you come, even if you wanted to. But the fact is, everybody has been flying all hours, and it will mean extra flying if someone has to make a special journey to show you the Lines. And it isn't as if we were flying single-seaters; you've always got Mark with you to put you right if you get adrift. So if you care to come this afternoon it will serve two purposes. You'll get a squint at the Line and a whiff of archie, and it will give McAngus a rest. He's looking a bit knocked up.'

'Certainly I'll come,' replied Biggles quickly.

'That's fine! I thought you wouldn't mind. It's all for your own good, in the long run, because the sooner you get used to archie the better. But for goodness' sake keep close to me. You keep your eye on him, Mark. We take off at three o'clock, but be on the tarmac a quarter of an hour before that, and I'll show you our proposed course while the engines are warming up.'

Chapter 4
Battle

It was under a cold, grey sky, that Biggles sat in his cockpit the same afternoon, waiting for the signal to take off. He had made one short flight over the aerodrome immediately after lunch to accustom himself to his new machine, and he had satisfied himself that he was able to fly it without difficulty. The F.E.2b. was not a difficult machine to fly; it had no vicious habits, which was, perhaps, the reason why those who flew it were unstinted in its praise.

The patrol was made up of three machines. Captain Mapleton, of course, was leading. Marriot and his gunner, 'Con' Conway, were on the right, and Biggles, with Mark Way in the front seat, on the left.

The machine was fitted with two machine-guns, one firing forward and the other backwards over the top 'plane, both operated by the gunner. A rack containing drums of ammunition was fitted to the inside of the cockpit.

Biggles felt a thrill of excitement run through him as the flight-commander's machine began to move forward; he heard Marriot's engine roar, and then the sound was drowned in the bellow of his own as he opened the throttle. Together the three machines tore across the damp aerodrome and then soared into the air, turning slowly in a wide circle.

A quarter of an hour later they were still over the aerodrome, but at a height of seven thousand feet, and Biggles, who had settled down into the long turn, dashed off at a tangent as the leader suddenly straightened out and headed towards the east. A sharp exclamation from the watchful Mark warned him of his error, which he hastened to rectify, although he still remained at a little distance from the other two machines.

'Try to keep up!' yelled Mark, turning in his seat and smiling encouragingly. 'It's easier for everybody then.'

Biggles put his nose down a little to gain extra speed, and then zoomed back into position, a manœuvre which Mark acknowledged with an approving wave. For some time they flew on without incident, and then Mark began to move about in his cockpit, looking towards every point of the compass in turn, and searching the sky above and the earth below with long, penetrating stares.

Once he reached for his gun, and caused Biggles' heart to jump by firing a short burst downwards. But then Biggles remembered that Mark had said he would fire a burst when they reached the Line, to warm the guns, which would reduce the chance of a jam.

Following the line of the gun-barrel, he looked down and saw an expanse of brown earth, perhaps a mile in width, merging gradually into dull green on either side. Tiny zig-zag lines ran in all directions. Must be the Lines, he thought, with a quiver of excitement, not unmixed with apprehension, and he continued to look down with interest and awe.

'Hi!'

He looked up with a guilty start; Mark was yelling at him, and he saw the reason—he had drifted a good hundred yards from his companions.

'My hat!' he mused. 'I shall never see anything if I can't take my eyes off them without losing them.'

But Mark was pointing with outstretched finger over the side of the cockpit, and, following the line indicated, he saw a little group of round, black blobs floating in space. Automatically he counted them; there were five—no, six. He blinked and looked again. There were eight. 'That's queer!' he muttered, and even as the truth dawned upon him there was a flash of flame near his wing-tip, and a dull explosion that could be heard above the noise of the engine.

The swerve of the machine brought his heart into his mouth, but he righted it quickly and looked around for the other two. They had disappeared. For a moment he nearly panicked, but Mark's casual nod in the direction of his right wing restored his confidence, and, peering forward, he perceived them about fifty yards or so to his right. He turned quickly into his proper place, receiving a nod of approval from his gunner as he did so.

The black archie bursts were all around them now, but Mark did not appear to notice them; he had reached for his gun and held it in a position of readiness. Suddenly he tilted it up and fired a long burst: then, as quick as lightning, he dragged it to the other side and fired again.

Biggles nearly strained his neck trying to see what Mark was shooting at, but seeing nothing but empty air decided that he must be warming up his guns again. He looked across at the machine on his right, and noticed that Conway was shooting, too. As he watched him he ceased firing and looked down over the side of his cockpit for a long time; then he looked across at Mark and held up his fist, thumb pointing upwards.

'There seems to be a lot of signalling going on!' thought Biggles. 'I wonder what it's all about?'

The time passed slowly, and he began to feel bored and rather tired, for it was the longest flight he had ever made. This seems a pretty tame business, he pondered. I should have liked to see a Hun or two, just to get an idea of what they look like. 'Hallo!'

Mark was standing up again, trying to point his gun straight down, and for the first time he seemed to be excited. Casually Biggles leaned over the side to see what it was that could interest his gunner to such an extent. There, immediately below him, not fifty yards away, was a large green swept-back wing, but that which held his gaze and caused his lips to part in horrified amazement were the two enormous black Maltese crosses, one on each end. His skin turned to goose flesh and his lips went dry. He saw a man standing in the back seat of the machine pointing something at him; then, for no reason that he could discover, the man fell limply sideways, and the green wing folded up like a piece of tissue paper. It turned over on its side and the man fell out.

In a kind of paralysed fascination Biggles watched the brown, leather-clad body turning slowly over and over as it fell. He thought it would never reach the ground.

He was brought to his senses with a jerk by a shrill yell. The other two machines were turning—had nearly completed the turn. He swung round after them in a frantic bank, skidding in a manner that made Mark clutch at the side of his cockpit. He could see no other German machines in sight, so he decided that the time allotted for their patrol had expired.

'My word, now he has decided to go home, he is

certainly going in a hurry!' thought Biggles, as the leading machine nearly stood on its nose as it dived full out towards the ground. He thrust his joy-stick forward, and with difficulty restrained a yell of delight.

The shriek of the propeller, the howl of the wind in the wires, seemed to get into his blood and intoxicate him. He wondered vaguely why Mark was looking back over his shoulder instead of looking where they were going and enjoying the fun, and he was almost sorry when the flight-commander pulled out of the dive and commenced to glide down.

He watched the ground closely, noting such landmarks as he thought he would be able to recognize again, until the aerodrome came into view, when he concentrated on the business of landing.

A green Very light* soared upwards from the leading machine, and then dropped swiftly; it was the 'washout' signal, meaning that the machines were to land independently. He allowed the others to land first, and then, with exultation in his heart, he followed them down and taxied up to the hangars.

Mark gave him a queer smile as he switched off the engine. 'Pretty good!' he said cheerfully. 'That's one on the slate for me on Lane's account.'

'You mean that green Hun underneath us?' cried Biggles. 'My gosh! It gave me a queer feeling to see that fellow going down.'

'Great Scott, no! Conway got him. I got the blue-and-yellow devil.'

'What!' exclaimed Biggles, in amazement. 'What blue-and-yellow devil?'

---

* A coloured flare fired as a signal, from a special short-barrelled pistol.

'Didn't you see him diving down on us from in front? He was after you.'

'No, I didn't, and that's a fact,' admitted Biggles soberly. 'I didn't see you shoot at him.'

'I couldn't at first, because I was busy plastering the black fellow who was peppering us from underneath.'

Biggles blinked and shook his head. 'Black, blue, green! How the dickens many of them were there?' he muttered, in a dazed voice.

'Seven altogether. We got three of them between us.'

Biggles sat down limply. 'And I only saw one!' he groaned. 'What on earth would have happened to me if I'd been alone?'

Mark laughed. 'Don't worry, you'll soon get the hang of spotting 'em,' he said. 'You saw that mob coming down on us at the finish?'

Biggles shook his head, eyes wide open. He couldn't speak.

'You didn't? You ought to have seen those—there must have been more than a dozen of 'em. Mabs spotted them the instant they shoved their ugly noses out of the mist, and like a sensible fellow he streaked for home.'

'Thank goodness he did!' muttered Biggles weakly. 'And I thought he was merely hurrying home!'

'That's just what he was doing,' observed Mark dryly. 'But let's go and get some tea—I can do with it!'

Chapter 5
Plots and Plans

Biggles landed his F.E. after a short test flight and glanced in the direction of the sheds, where Mabs and the rest of the flight were standing watching him.

A week had elapsed since his first never-to-be-forgotten flight over the Lines. He had done at least one patrol every day since, and was already beginning to feel that he was an old hand at the game. He had picked up the art of war flying with an aptitude that had amazed everyone, particularly his flight-commander, who had reported to Major Paynter, the C.O., that young Biggles seemed to have a sort of second sight where enemy aircraft were concerned.

He jumped down now from the cockpit and with a brief 'She's running nicely!' to his fitter, walked quickly towards the flight shed, where the others were apparently waiting for him.

'Come on!' announced Mabs, with a curious smile. 'There's a little party on, and we knew you wouldn't like to be left out.'

'You're right!' agreed Biggles. 'What's it about? I like parties.'

'You may not like this one,' said Mabs. 'Stand fast while I get it off my chest. You know, of course, that headquarters have been shouting for days about a report they want making on the railway junction and sidings at Vanfleur?'

'You mean the show that Littleton and Gormsby went on?'

'That's right. As you know, they didn't come back. Neither did Blake nor Anderson, who went yesterday. Both the other flights have had a shot at it, and now it's our turn. The Old Man says I'm not to go, otherwise I shouldn't be here telling you about it. That means that either you or Marriot or McAngus will have to go.'

'I'd already worked that out,' replied Biggles. 'Nothing wrong with that, is there?'

'Nothing! I'm just telling you, that's all. You can settle amongst yourselves who's going, or if there's any argument about it I shall have to detail someone for the job. I'm not going to ask for volunteers, because you'd all volunteer on principle, and nothing would be decided. But there's two things you've got to remember. In the first place, it's no use going all the way to Vanfleur and coming back without learning something. It means counting every wagon and truck in the siding, and noting any dumps in the vicinity. In other words, the information has got to be correct. It's no use guessing or imagining things, because incorrect information is misleading, and does more harm than good. The other thing is, it's going to be a stick show for the man who goes. Vanfleur is forty miles over the Line, if it's an inch. You don't need me to tell you that there are more Hun scouts at Douai than any Boche* aerodrome on the front. Rumour says that Richthofen** and his crowd have just moved to Douai, and maybe that's

---

* Derogatory term for the Germans.
** Manfred Von Richthofen 'the Red Baron' – German ace who shot down a total of 80 Allied aircraft. Killed in April 1918.

why the other fellows didn't get back. Well, there it is. Tell me in five minutes who's going.'

'I'll go!' said Biggles promptly.

'No, you don't!' replied Mabs quickly. 'I'm not letting anyone commit suicide just because he thinks it's the right thing to do. I suggest you toss for it—odd man goes—that's the fairest way, and then whatever happens there can be no reproaches about it.'

Biggles took a coin from his pocket and the others did the same. 'Spin,' he said, and tossed the coin into the air. The three coins rang on the concrete.

'Heads,' said Biggles, looking at his own coin.

'Tails,' announced Marriot.

'Same here,' said McAngus.

'That means I'm the boob!' grinned Biggles. 'When do I start?'

'When you like—the sooner the better. I should think first thing in the morning might be the best time,' suggested Mabs.

'Why do you think that?'

'Well, that's the time these shows are usually done.'

'That's what I thought—and the Huns know that as well as we do. I'll go this afternoon, just by way of a change, if it's all the same to you. What do you think, Mark?'

'Suits me!'

'That's that, then!' said Mabs. 'You'd better come with me and tell the Old Man you're going. He'll want to have a word with you first. And you'd better come along, too, Mark.'

The C.O. looked up from his desk when they entered the squadron office. 'Ah, so it's you, Bigglesworth, and Way. I had an idea it might be.' He rose to his feet and walked over to them. 'Now look here, you fellows,' he went on. 'There isn't much I can say, but remember that these shows are not carried out just for the fun of it, or to find us jobs of work. They are of the greatest possible importance to H.Q., as they themselves are beginning to admit.' He smiled whimsically, recalling the days when the military leaders had laughed at the idea of aeroplanes being of practical value for reconnoitring. 'I want you to pay particular attention to the rolling stock in the sidings,' he resumed. 'Also, have a good look at these places I've marked on the map. Study the last set of photographs we got of the area—you'll find them in the map-room. You know what to look out for; make a note of any alterations in the landscape.

'If you see a clump of bushes growing where there were none last week, when the photos were taken, it probably means that it is a camouflaged battery. Watch for "blazes" on the grass, caused by the flash of the guns, and cables leading to the spot. You will not be able to see telephone wires, of course, but you may see the shadows cast by the poles, or a row of dots—the newly turned earth at the foot of each pole. You may see a track joining the dots—the footmarks and beaten-down grass caused by the working party. It's easier still to pick out an underground cable. If the trench has not been filled in, it shows as a clear-cut line; if it has been filled in, it reveals itself as a sort of woolly line, blurred at the edges. If you see several such lines of communication converging on one spot it may mean that there is an enemy headquarters there.

'Quantities of fresh barbed wire means that the enemy is expecting to be attacked, and has prepared new positions upon which to retire. On the other hand, new trenches, saps, dug-outs, and, more particularly, light railways, means that he is preparing an offensive. But there, you should have learned about these things by now so there's no need for me to go over them again. When have you decided to go?'

'After lunch, sir,' replied Biggles.

'I thought you'd start in the morning: that's the usual time.'

'Yes, sir; that's why we decided to go this afternoon.'

The C.O. frowned, then a smile spread over his face. 'Good for you!' he said, nodding approval. 'That's the worst of being out here a long time; we get into habits without knowing it. Little points like the one you've just mentioned have been staring us in the face for so long that we can't see them. All right, then. Good luck!'

'Come on, Mark!' said Biggles, when they had left the office. 'Let's get the machine ready. Then we can sit back and think things over until it's time to go.'

It was exactly two o'clock when they took off. The distance to their objective was, Mabs had said, a full forty miles, and as they expected to be away at least three hours, they dared not start later, as it began to get dark soon after four.

For twenty minutes Biggles climbed steeply, crossing and recrossing the aerodrome as he bored his way upwards, knowing that the higher they were when they crossed the Lines the less chance there would be of their being molested; so he waited until the altimeter was nearly on the eight thousand feet mark before striking out for the Lines.

A few desultory archie bursts greeted them as they passed over, and for the next half-hour they had the sky to themselves. It was a good day for their purpose from one point of view, but a bad day from another aspect.

Great masses of wet clouds were drifting sluggishly eastwards at various altitudes—6,000, 8,000 and even at 10,000 feet—and while this might afford cover in the event of their being attacked, it also provided cover for prowling enemy scouts to lie in wait for them. Again, while it concealed them from the gunners on the ground, it limited their range of vision and prevented them from seeing many of the landmarks they had decided to follow. Moreover, if their objective was concealed by cloud, they would either have to return with their mission unfulfilled, or they would have to descend very low, a dangerous performance so far over enemy territory. Nevertheless, Biggles had decided that unless enemy interference made the project hopeless, he would go down to a thousand feet, if necessary, rather than return with a blank report, which, rightly or wrongly, would be regarded as failure by headquarters.

They were now approaching the objective, and Biggles began to hope that they might achieve their object without firing a single shot. But the atmosphere rapidly thickened, and he realized with annoyance that a blanket of mist hung over the very spot they had come so far and risked so much to view. He shut off his engine and began a gentle glide.

'I'm going down!' he roared to Mark, who stood up in his seat, guns ready for action, scanning the atmosphere anxiously in all directions.

At six thousand feet they sank into the billowing mist, and Biggles turned his eyes to his instruments, every nerve tense. 5,000—4,000—3,000 feet, and still there was no break, and he knew he would never be able to climb up through it again without losing control of the machine. He hoped desperately that he would find a hole, or at least a thin patch, in the cloud, after their work was accomplished. At two thousand feet he emerged into a cold, cheerless world, and looked about anxiously for the railway line. 'There it is!' he yelled, pointing to the right, at the same time opening up his engine and heading towards it. Mark had seen the junction at the same instant, and, leaving his guns, grabbed his note-book and prepared to write.

Whoof, whoof, whoof, barked the archie; but the enemy gunners were shooting hurriedly, and the shots went wide. Other guns joined in, and the bursts began to come closer as the gunners corrected their aim. But Biggles kept the machine on even keel as he watched the sky around them, while Mark counted the railway trucks, jotting down his notes as well as his cold hands and the sometimes swaying machine would permit.

Biggles made a complete circuit around the railway junction, which was as choc-a-bloc with traffic as only a railway junction of strategical importance could be in time of war.

Four long trains were in the station itself; two others—one consisting of open trucks, carrying field artillery—stood in a siding, with steam up and ready to move. Shells were being loaded in the other from a great dump.

'Have you finished?' yelled Biggles.

'Go round once more!' bellowed Mark.

Biggles frowned, but proceeded to make another circuit, twisting and turning from time to time to dodge the ever-increasing archie and machine-gun bullets. Wish I had a bomb or two, he thought, as he eyed the great ammunition dump. But there, no doubt the bombers will arrive in due course, when we've made our report.

Without warning the archie stopped abruptly. Mark

dropped his pencil, shoved his writing-pad into his pocket, and grabbed his gun. 'Look out!' he yelled.

But Biggles had already seen them—a big formation of straight-winged planes sweeping up from the east. There was no need to speculate as to their nationality.

'What a mob!' he muttered, and swung round for home. But an icy hand clutched his heart as he beheld yet another formation of enemy machines racing towards the spot from the direction of the Lines. They were cut off.

We stayed too long, he thought bitterly. The people at the station must have rung up every squadron for miles, and they're not going to let us get our report home if they can prevent it. 'Well, I can't fight that lot!' he muttered desperately, and, turning his nose to the north-west, raced away in the only direction open to him.

Fortunately there was a lot of broken cloud on the horizon, apart from a big mass overhead, and this, he hoped, would help him to throw the wolves off his trail.

Mark suddenly crouched low behind the gun that fired backwards over the top 'plane, and began firing in short, sharp bursts. Biggles winced as a bullet bored through his instrument-board with a vicious thud. He began side-slipping gently to and fro to throw the enemy pilots off their mark—a tip that had been given him on the boat coming over. A faint rattle reached his ears above the noise of the engine. They're overtaking us, he thought. Mark signalled frantically to him to climb. He put his nose down for an instant to gather speed, and then zoomed upwards. The cold, grey mist enveloped them like a blanket.

'Must be twenty of 'em—Albatripes*!' yelled Mark.

* Albatros, German single seater fighter with two fixed machine guns.

But Biggles was busy fighting to keep the machine on even keel. The bubble of the inclinometer* was jumping from one side to the other in a most alarming way, and the needle of his compass was swinging violently. 'It's no use—I'll have to go down!' he yelled. A blast of air struck him on the side of the face, and he knew he was side-slipping; he rectified the slip, but, as usual in such cases, he overdid it, and the draught struck his other cheek. He shot out of the cloud with one wing pointing straight to the ground.

He picked the machine up while Mark clambered to his feet, searching the atmosphere behind them. Biggles, snatching a glance behind him, saw enemy machines scattered all over the sky to the south-east, still effectually barring their return. No sooner did the lone F.E. appear than they turned in its direction and began overhauling it.

'I don't know where we're getting, but I can't face that lot,' shouted Biggles, still heading north-west. 'We must be miles off our course.'

The black-crossed machines were closing the gap between them quickly, so he pushed his nose down and raced towards the low clouds, now only a short distance away. He reached them just as a burst of fire from the rear made the F.E. quiver from propeller-boss to tail-skid, and he plunged into the nearest mass of white, woolly vapour in something like a panic. He came out on the other side, banked vertically to the left, and plunged into another.

And so he went on, twisting and turning, sometimes through and sometimes around the clouds. He dived

* An instrument similar to a spirit level, for showing the angle of the aircraft relative to the ground

57

below them and then zoomed up again through them. He knew he was hopelessly lost, but even that, he decided, was better than facing the overwhelming odds against them.

Mark, still standing up, was examining the sky behind them; then he held up his fists, thumbs pointing upwards.

'O.K.! We've lost them!' he bellowed.

Biggles breathed a sigh of relief and began to glide down through the cloud, hoping to pick up some outstanding landmark that might be recognized from his map. The F.E. emerged once more into clear air, and he looked down anxiously. He stared, blinked, and stared again as a dark green expanse of foam-lashed water met his horrified gaze.

There could be no mistake. He was looking down at the sea. The clouds, as so often happens, ended abruptly at the coast-line, which revealed itself as a white, surf-lashed line just behind him. In front of him the sky was a clear, pale blue as far as he could see.

He thought quickly, feeling for his map, guessing what had happened. In their long rush to the northwest they had actually reached the Belgian coast, so he turned to the south, knowing that sooner or later they were bound to reach France again.

Mark, too, examined his map as Biggles began following the coast-line.

'We shall be all right if the petrol holds out, and if it doesn't get dark before we can see where we are,' he shouted, and then settled back in his seat, to resume the eternal task of watching the sky for enemy machines. Slowly the blue of the sky turned to misty grey with the approach of dusk, and Biggles came lower in order not to lose the coast-line.

Suddenly Mark sprang to his feet and swung his gun round to face the open sea. Biggles, following the line of the gun, saw an Albatros diving on them out of the mist. Something, it may have been pure instinct, made him glance in the opposite direction—a second Albatros was coming in on their left, the landward side. Two scouts, evidently working together, were launching a dual attack.

The events of the next thirty seconds followed each other so swiftly that they outraced Biggles' capacity for thinking. Mark was shooting steadily at the first scout, which had now opened fire on them; Biggles was watching the second, which was also shooting. The pilots of both enemy scouts, evidently old hands at the game, thrust home their attack so closely that Biggles instinctively zoomed to avoid collision; but they both swerved at the last moment in the same direction. They met head-on just below and in front of the F.E. with a crash that made Biggles jump. At the same instant his engine cut out dead, and a pungent, almost overpowering stench of petrol filled his nostrils. Automatically he put his nose down towards the shore. Out of the corner of his eye he saw the fragments of the two German scouts strike the water with a terrific splash.

Chapter 6
Late for Dinner

In the now failing light the coast-line, although fairly close, was not much more than a dark, indistinct mass, with a strip of pale orange sand, lashed with white foam, running along the edge.

We shall never reach it!' thought Biggles, as he glanced at his altimeter. It registered one thousand feet.

Mark was standing up, calmly divesting himself of his leather coat and flying-boots. He tore off the two top pages of his writing-pad and folded the precious report carefully into a leather wallet, which he thrust into his breeches pocket.

He lifted the guns off their mountings and tossed them overboard, and Biggles knew that he did this for two reasons. Firstly, to prevent them falling into the hands of the enemy, and secondly, to lighten the machine, and thus give them a better chance of reaching the shore.

Then Mark looked at Biggles, and, cupping his hands round his mouth, shouted: 'Get your clothes off. It looks as if we shall have to swim for it!'

With some difficulty, first holding the joy-stick with one hand and then the other, Biggles managed to get his coat off and throw it overboard. Cap, goggles and sheepskin flying-boots followed.

At the last moment, just as he thought they might reach the beach, a slant of wind caught them and they dropped swiftly. He held the machine off as long as he could, but as it lost flying speed it wobbled and then flopped bodily into the water. A wave lifted the doomed F.E. like a feather and rushed it towards the beach; then, as it grated harshly on the sand, they jumped clear and struck out for the shore.

Half drowned, Biggles felt a wave roll him over and over. It dropped him on all fours on solid ground, and he dug his fingers into the sand as he felt the backwash sucking him back again. Mark, who was heavier, grabbed him by the collar and clung to him desperately until the wave had receded. Crawling, swaying, stumbling and falling, they managed to reach the beach, gasping and spitting out mouthfuls of sea-water.

'My hat, isn't it cold!' muttered Biggles through chattering teeth.

'Come on, get on your feet—they'll be here any minute. They must have seen us come down!' snapped Mark; and at a reeling gait in their water-logged clothes they hurried towards the wide sand dunes which line that part of the Belgian coast.

'What's the hurry?' panted Biggles.

'The Huns will be here any minute—we're still the wrong side of the Lines!'

Hardly had they plunged into the bewildering valleys of the dunes than they heard the sound of harsh, guttural voices coming towards them.

'Down!' hissed Mark, and they flung themselves flat in the coarse, scrubby grass that grew in patches on the sand. It was now nearly dark, so there was still just a chance that they might escape observation.

Biggles clenched his teeth tightly in order to restrain their chattering, which he thought would betray them, while the voices passed not more than ten yards away and receded in the direction of the shore.

For twenty minutes or more they lay while dark figures loomed around them, going towards or returning from the beach. One party came so close that Biggles held his breath, expecting to feel a heavy boot in the small of his back at any moment.

'What are we going to do? I shall freeze to death if we stay here much longer!' he whispered as the footsteps receded.

'So shall I if it comes to that,' muttered Mark. 'I'm dead from the feet up. But our only chance is to lie still and hope that they'll think we were drowned. They must have seen the two Albatripes attack us, and for all they know we might have been wounded. There are bound to be people on the beach for some time watching for the bodies of those two Boche pilots. We shall have to put up with the cold for a minute or two while people are moving about. When it gets a bit darker we'll crawl to the top of a dune and see if we can see what's going on.'

Another quarter of an hour passed, and at last it was really dark, except for the feeble light of a crescent moon low in the sky. With a whispered 'Come on!' Mark began crawling up the sloping side of the nearest sand dune, and Biggles followed, glad to be moving at last. Side by side they reached the top, and, raising their heads slowly, peered round. Not a soul was in sight except on the beach, where a small group of figures could just be made out watching the remains of the F.E being pounded to pieces by the surf. Some debris had evidently been salved, for it lay in a pile just beyond the reach of the waves.

'They must think we were drowned or there'd be

more activity,' breathed Mark. 'Our only chance now is to work our way along the coast. It might be better if we waited a bit longer, but we can't do that or we shall be frozen to death. Anyway, we've got to be round the wire before morning or we shall certainly be spotted.'

'Wire—what wire?' asked Biggles.

'The barbed wire between the Lines. I'm not absolutely certain but I think I saw it as we came down; I was on the look-out for it. If I'm right, it's only about a mile farther along. Confound those two Huns; in another five minutes we should have been well over the Lines.'

'Shall we be able to get through the wire, do you think?' asked Biggles.

'We shall not. I hear they have tightened things up a good deal along here lately, owing to escaped prisoners working their way back along the coast. Somebody told me they've got little bells hung all along the wire, and you can't touch it without ringing them. In any case, we should need rubber gloves because the Huns are electrifying their wire. No, I'm afraid we shall have to go round it.'

'Round it!'

'Yes, by swimming round it. It's been done before and it's our only chance.'

Biggles groaned. 'Fancy having to get into that water again! I'd sooner face the biggest formation of Huns that ever took the air. I had no idea water could be so cold. I nearly joined the Navy once; I'm thundering glad I didn't!' he grumbled.

'Don't grouse—we're lucky to be alive!' muttered Mark. 'Come on, now, no noise!'

Crouching and crawling, they began to wind their

way through the dunes, taking a peep over the top whenever an opportunity presented itself in order to keep direction, which lay parallel to the shore. Sometimes they were able to walk a few yards, but on other occasions they had to worm their way like snakes across open spaces. Once they had to lie flat as a squad of troops, evidently a working party, passed within a few yards of them.

At last Mark raised himself up and peered forward. 'I think I can see the wire just ahead,' he breathed, 'but we can't get any farther along here. There must be a trench just in front, because I can hear people talking. We'd better get down to the water.'

'Lead on,' breathed Biggles. 'I can't be any colder than I am already!'

Dragging themselves along on their stomachs, often stopping to listen, they wormed their way to the water's edge.

'How far can you swim?' whispered Mark.

'I don't know,' admitted Biggles. 'I've never found it necessary to find out.'

'You'll have to chance it, then. I can swim pretty well any distance, but not when it's as cold as this. I was brought up by the sea. If you feel your strength giving out, hang on to my collar and we'll get round— or sink together. We shall have to get out just beyond the breakers, and then swim parallel to the coast. As soon as we see our own wire we'll come ashore. If we don't see it, we'll swim as far as we can. But the Lines can't be very far apart—come on!'

They plunged into the icy water and struck out through the blinding spray. Biggles paid little or no attention to the direction, but simply fixed his eyes on the black head bobbing in front of him and followed it.

How long they swam he did not know, but it seemed to be an eternity and he was just about to call out that he could go no farther when Mark turned shorewards. Biggles made one last despairing dash through the surf, and then lay panting and gasping like a stranded fish.

Mark seized him by the collar and dragged him out of the reach of the waves. 'Get up!' he snapped.

'Wait—a minute—let me—get—breath!' panted Biggles.

Mark dragged him roughly to his feet. 'Run!' he said. 'We shall have to start our blood moving, or we shall both be down with pneumonia. I think we're round both lots of wire; if we aren't then we're unstuck, that's all about it.'

Without waiting for any more he set off at a steady trot along the sand, Biggles reeling behind him, their clothes squelching and discharging water at every step.

'*Halte la**!'

They pulled up with a jerk as the challenge rang out.

'Friend—ami!' yelled Biggles desperately, but joyfully, for he knew the language was not German.

'*Attendez!*' called the voice, and they heard the jangle of military equipment. A dark figure, closely followed by several others, loomed up in the darkness in front of them, rifles and bayonets held at the ready.

'You do the talking!' growled Mark. 'I can't speak the lingo!'

'*Je suis—nous ont—Anglais*', began Biggles in his best French. '*Aviateurs—aviateurs Anglais.*'

There was a sharp intake of breath, and a flashlight

---

* French: halt! wait! I am—we have—English. Aviators. English aviators.

stabbed the darkness. The figures closed around them and they were hurried a short distance into a trench, and then into a dugout, where an officer in a blue uniform sat writing.

Quickly, in a strange mixture of English and broken French, Biggles told his story to the Belgian officer. He eyed them suspiciously at first, but at the end of the story he made a brief telephone call which seemed to satisfy him.

The dripping clothes were stripped off the two airmen, blankets were produced, and boiling soup, in great basins, thrust into their hands.

An hour later a British staff officer stepped into the dugout.

'Who are you?' he asked curtly, obviously suspicious. But suspicion quickly gave way to friendliness as the two airmen told their story.

Mark handed over his report, which, although wet, was still legible. 'I wish you'd get that back as quickly as you can, sir,' he said. 'We've been through some trouble to get it!'

'You can bring it yourself,' the officer told him. 'I have a car waiting a little way back. But you'll have to borrow some clothes if our Belgian friends can provide them. You can't put those wet ones on again!'

Dinner was in progress when Biggles and Mark, attired in mixed Belgian uniforms, arrived at their aerodrome. They opened the mess door, and amid dead silence, with all eyes on them, they marched stiffly to the head of the table, where the C.O. sat, and apologized for being late for dinner.

The C.O. stared at them, while a babble of voices broke out, punctuated with laughs, that finally swelled into a roar in which everyone joined. Mark, who had seen such a scene before, knew that the laughter was simply the British way of expressing relief after they had been given up for lost.

But Biggles turned a pained face to the room.

'What's the joke?' he cried hotly. 'Do you think we're all dressed up for the fun of it?'

A fresh burst of laughter greeted his words.

'Everyone's glad to see you back, that's all!' said the C.O. 'And that's the chief thing. Did you get a report on the junction?'

'Yes, sir,' replied Mark.

'That's splendid! Sit down and have your dinners. You can tell us all about it afterwards!'

Chapter 7

A Daring Stunt

'I'm not going to pretend that I know much about it, but it seems to me that if the Huns are going to mass their squadrons—as apparently they are—we shall have to do the same or else be wiped out.' Biggles, having ventured an opinion for the first time since he joined the squadron, glanced up, half-expecting a remark about his inexperience.

'He's right!' exclaimed Mabs emphatically. 'I've been saying the same thing for the last month. Richthofen, they say, has grouped three squadrons together, including all the best pilots in the German Air Force. And, whether he has or not, we know for a fact that he's sailing up and down the Lines with thirty triplanes* tagged on behind him. Who's going to face that bunch? Who's going to take on that little lot, I'd like to know? What chance has an ordinary Line patrol of three planes got if it bumps into that pack?'

'Rot!' snapped Captain Rayner, of C Flight. 'The more the merrier! Dive straight into the middle of them and the formation will go to pieces. It will take them all their time to avoid collision.'

'Don't kid yourself!' declared Captain Allen of B Flight. 'They've got this game weighed up nicely. They

---

* Fokker aeroplane with three wings and two forward-firing machine guns. Often referred to as a tripe or tripehound.

didn't wait for us to bump into them this morning—they bumped into us and we jolly soon knew about it!'

There was silence for a moment, due to the fact that B Flight had lost two machines that very morning through the menace they were discussing.

'I think it's a logical conclusion that if we start sending big patrols of twenty or thirty machines against them they'll start flying in fifties or more. Whatever we do, they will maintain numerical superiority, and at the finish formations will be flying in hundreds. A nice sort of game that will be!' declared Marriot disgustedly.

'Well, it may come to that some day, but if it does I hope I'm not here to see it,' observed Allen coldly. 'I—'

The ante-room door opened and an orderly appeared. 'Major Paynter's compliments, and will all officers please report to the squadron office at once?'

There was a general move towards the door.

The Major was in earnest conversation with Toddy, the Recording Officer, when they arrived, but he broke off and turned to face them as they entered.

'Well, gentlemen,' he said, 'I've some news for you, though whether you'll regard it as good or bad I don't know. Will all those officers who have had any experience of night-flying please take a pace to the front?'

Mabs, a pilot of B Flight, and a pilot and observer of C Flight stepped forward.

'That's worse than I expected,' said the Major. 'Never mind; this is the position. Whether we like it or not, Wing have decided to carry out certain operations that can best be done at night. As you know, enemy scout squadrons have been concentrated opposite this sector of the Front, and our machines have neither the performance nor numerical strength of theirs. In these circumstances we are going to try to cripple them on the ground. It is thought that night raids will adversely affect their morale, to say nothing of the damage we may cause on their machines or aerodromes. It's proposed to carry out the first raid on a very big scale; other squadrons will participate and keep the ball rolling all night. In order to put as large a number of machines in the air as possible, this squadron will take part in the raid, which will be on Douai Aerodrome, the headquarters of the Richthofen group.

'Fortunately, our machines are well adapted for night-flying, so for the next two nights I shall want all officers to put in as much practice in the air as possible. It's up to everyone to make himself proficient in the new conditions. Flares will be put out, and lectures will be arranged, which must be attended by all officers on the station. Has anyone any questions to ask?'

'I take it that the attack will be in the form of a bomb raid, sir?' said Biggles.

'We shall attack with all arms—heavy bombs, Cooper bombs, baby incendiaries*, and machine-guns. Naturally, it is in our own interest to make a good job of the show; if things go according to plan, we shall meet with less opposition when we resume daylight patrols. That's all.'

'Well, that's the answer to the question!' observed Mark brightly, when they were outside.

'What question?'

'The thing we were talking about in the mess when

---

* Heavy bombs 112lb and Cooper bombs 20lb were both carried under the aircraft. Baby incendiaries (sometimes abbreviated as BI's) were fire bombs thrown by hand from the cockpit—a dangerous game.

the C.O. sent for us—the big Boche formations. We're going to swipe them on the ground!'

'Well, it may be all right,' replied Biggles thoughtfully, 'but we could have wiped them out in daylight shows if it comes to that. I'm thinking that there is one thing the staff people may have overlooked.'

'What's that?'

'You don't imagine for one moment that the Huns will take this night-strafing business lying down, do you? If I know anything about 'em they'll soon be showing us that it's a game two can play. You mark my words, they'll be over here the next night, handing us doses of our own medicine—in spoonfuls. I hope I'm mistaken, but I reckon things will be getting warm-ish here presently!'

'Well, the staff won't mind that; they won't be here,' observed Mark bitterly. 'I must say I don't fancy being archied at night; the flashes look ghastly. I've been told that they are a nice bright orange when they are close to you, and a beautiful dull crimson when they're some distance away.'

'We shall soon be able to see for ourselves whether your information is correct,' returned Biggles. 'As long as they're not pink with blue spots on 'em I don't mind!'

The weather on the night decided for the first raid was all that could be desired, considering the time of the year. There was no wind, and a new moon shone brightly in a clear, frosty, star-spangled sky, against which the hangars loomed as black silhouettes.

By the C.O.'s orders not a light gleamed anywhere, for every step was being taken to prevent information of the impending raid from reaching the enemy through the many spies whose duty it was to report such operations.

An engine roared suddenly in the darkness, and the end machine of a long line that stood in front of the hangars began to waddle, in the ungainly fashion of aeroplanes on the ground, towards the point allocated for the take-off; a dark red, intermittent flame, curled back from the exhaust-pipe.

'There goes Mabs,' said Biggles, who, with Mark his gunner, was standing by their machine.

The planes were to leave at five-minute intervals, which gave each aircraft a chance to get clear before the next one took off, and so lessened the chances of a collision either on the ground or in the air.

'Marriot goes next, and then McAngus, so we've got a quarter of an hour to wait,' went on Biggles. 'It's going to be perishing cold if I know anything about it,' he remarked, glancing up at the frosty sky. 'But there, we can't have it all ways. We shall at least be able to see where we are, and that's a lot better than groping our way in and out of clouds; that's bad enough in the day-time! Hallo! There goes Marriot!'

A second machine taxied out and roared up into the darkness.

'Mabs has got to the Line—look!' said Mark, pointing to a cluster of twinkling yellow lights in the distant sky. 'That's archie!'

Lines of pale green balls seemed to be floating lazily upwards.

'Look at the onions,' he added, referring to the well-known enemy anti-aircraft device commonly known as flaming onions.

A third machine taxied out and vanished into the gloom.

'Well, there goes McAngus; we'd better see about getting started up,' said Biggles tersely.

They climbed into their cockpits, and mechanics ran to their wings and propeller.

'Switch off!'

'Off!'

The engine hissed and gurgled as the big propeller was dragged round to suck the gas into the cylinders.

'Contact!' cried the mechanic.

'Contact!' echoed Biggles.

There was a sharp explosion as the engine came to life; then it settled down to the musical purr peculiar to the Beardmore type.

For a few minutes they sat thus, giving the engine time to warm up; then Biggles opened the throttle a trifle and pointed to his right wing—the signal to the mechanics that he wanted it held in order to slew the machine round to the right. While a machine is on the ground with the engine running all orders are given by signals, for the human voice would be lost in the noise of the engine; even if it was heard, the words might not be distinguished clearly, and an accident result.

With his nose pointing towards the open aerodrome, Biggles waved both hands above his head, the signal to the mechanics to stand clear. The F.E. raced across the aerodrome, and then roared up into the starry night.

He did not waste time climbing for height over the aerodrome, but headed straight for the Lines, climbing as he went. Peering below, he could see the countryside about them almost as plainly as in day-time; here and there the lighted windows of cottages and farms stood out brightly in the darkness; far ahead he could see the

73

track of the three preceding machines by the darting flashes of archie that followed them.

A British searchlight flashed a challenge to him as he passed over it, but Mark was ready, and replied at once with the colour of the night—a Very light that first burnt red and then changed to green. 'O.K.—O.K.,' flashed the searchlight in the Morse code, and they pursued their way for a time unmolested.

Biggles crouched a little lower in his seat as the first archies began to flash around them. It reached a crescendo as they crossed the Line, augmented by the inevitable flaming onions that rose up vertically from below like white-hot cannon-balls; but the turmoil soon faded away behind them as they sped on through the night over enemy territory, the Beardmore engine roaring sullen defiance. From time to time he peered below to pick up his landmarks, but for the most part he stared straight ahead, eyes probing the gloom for other machines.

The planes, of course, carried no lights, and although the chances of collision were remote, with machines of both sides going to and fro all the time, it was an ever-present possibility. In night raids it was usual for the machines taking part to return by a different route, or at a higher altitude to the one taken on the outward journey, and while machines adhered to this arrangement, collision was impossible.

Biggles was, of course, aware of this, but he kept an anxious eye on his line of flight in case an enemy machine had decided to take the same route as himself, but in the opposite direction, or in case Marriot or McAngus had got off their course.

Mark suddenly rose to his feet and pointed with outstretched finger. Far away, almost on the horizon,

74

it seemed, a shaft of flame had leapt high into the air; the sky glowed redly from the conflagration, and Biggles knew that one of the machines preceding him had either reached its destination and set fire to the hangars, or had itself been shot down in flames.

The fire, however, served one good purpose, for it acted as a beacon that would guide them direct to their objective. It continued to blaze fiercely as they approached it, and presently the crew of the F.E. were able to see that it was actually on Douai Aerodrome. It looked like one of the hangars. Keeping on a line that would bring him right over it Biggles throttled back and began gliding down.

Orders had stated that machines should descend as low as five hundred feet, if necessary, to be reasonably sure of hitting the target; but the thrill of the game was in his blood, and he no longer thought of orders. At five hundred feet he shoved the throttle open wide, and, pushing the stick forward, swept down so low that Mark, in the front seat, stared back over his shoulder in amazement.

The instant he opened his throttle an inferno seemed to break loose about the machine. Anti-aircraft guns and even field-guns situated on the edge of the aerodrome spat their hate; machine-guns rattled like castanets, the tracer bullets cutting white pencil lines through the darkness. Out of the corner of his eye Biggles saw Mark crouch low over his gun and heard it break into its staccato chatter.

He grabbed the bomb-toggle as the first hangar leapt into view, and, steadying the machine until the ridge of the roof appeared at the junction of his fuselage and the leading edge of the lower plane, he jerked it upwards—one, two.

Two 112-pound bombs swung off their racks, and the machine wobbled as it was relieved of their weight. Straight along over the hangars the F.E. roared, while Mark stood up and threw the baby incendiaries overboard.

When they came to the end of the line, Biggles zoomed up in a wide turn and tore out of the vicinity, twisting and turning like a wounded bird. Only when the furious bombardment had died away behind them did he lean over the side of his cockpit and look back at the aerodrome. His heart leapt with satisfaction, for two hangars were blazing furiously, the flames leaping high into the sky and casting a lurid glow on the surrounding landscape.

A body of men was working feverishly to get some aeroplanes out of one of the burning hangars; a machine that had evidently been standing outside when the attack was launched had been blown over on its back; several figures were prone on the ground, and one man was crawling painfully away from the heat of the fire.

'Well, that should make things easy for the others; they can't very well miss that little bonfire!' mused Biggles with satisfaction. Shells started bursting again in the air on the far side of the aerodrome, and he knew that Captain Allen, in the leading machine of B Flight, was approaching to carry on the good work.

'If our people are going to keep that up all night, those fellows down there will have nasty tastes in their mouths by the morning!' called Biggles, smiling; but the next instant the smile had given way to a frown of anxiety as a new note crept into the steady drone of the engine.

Looking back over his shoulder his heart missed a

beat as he saw a streamer of flame sweeping aft from one of the cylinders. Mark had seen it, too, and was staring at him questioningly, his face shining oddly pink in the glow.

Biggles throttled back a trifle and the flame became smaller, but the noise continued and the machine began to vibrate.

'It feels as if they've either blown one of my jampots* off or else a bullet has knocked a hole through the water jacket,' he yelled. 'If it will last for another half-hour, all right! If it doesn't, we're in the soup!'

With the throttle retarded he was creeping along at a little more than stalling speed, so he tried opening it again gently. Instantly a long streamer of fire leapt out of the engine, and the vibration became so bad that it threatened to tear the engine from its bearers. With a nasty sinking feeling in the pit of his stomach he snatched the throttle back to its original position, and shook his head at Mark as the only means he had of telling him that he was unable to overcome the trouble.

The noise increased until it became a rattling jar, as if a tin of nails was being shaken. A violent explosion behind caused him to catch his breath, and he retarded the throttle still farther, with a corresponding loss of speed. He had to tilt his nose down in order to prevent the machine from stalling, and he knew that he was losing height too fast to reach home.

He moistened his lips and stared into the darkness ahead, for it had been arranged that a 'lighthouse' should flash a beam at regular intervals to guide the bombers back to their nest. Watching, he saw a glow on the skyline wax and wane, but it was still far away.

* Slang: engine cylinders

He looked at his altimeter; it registered two thousand five hundred feet. Could he do it? He thought not, but he could try.

The rattle behind him and the vibration grew rapidly worse; it became a definite pulsating jolt that threatened to shake the machine to pieces at any moment. But he could see the Lines in the distance now, or rather, the trench system, where the patrols on either side were watching or trying to repair their barbed wire.

Two loud explosions in quick succession and a blinding sheet of flame leapt from the engine and made him throttle right back with frantic haste.

'Well, if we're down, we're down!' he muttered savagely. 'But I'm not going to sit up here and be fried to death for anybody; the Huns can shoot us if they like when we're on the ground, and that's better than being roasted like a joint of meat on the spit.'

Looking behind him he could see flames from the engine playing on his tail unit, and he knew that if he tried to remain in the air it was only a matter of seconds before the whole thing took fire. He switched off altogether and began gliding down through the darkness, straining his eyes in an effort to see what lay beneath.

In the uncanny silence he could hear the reports of the guns on the ground, and even hear the rattle of machine-gun fire. A searchlight probed the sky like a trembling white finger, searching for him, and archie began to illuminate the surrounding blackness.

Mark, the ever-practical, was calmly preparing for the inevitable end, and even in that desperate moment Biggles wondered if there was anything that could shake Mark out of his habitual calmness. He picked up the machine guns, one after the other, and threw them overboard; the Huns would be welcome to what was left of them after their eight-hundred-foot fall. The ammunition drums followed. He tore up his maps, threw them into the air and watched them swirl away aft.

Biggles felt in the canvas pocket inside the cockpit, then took out his own maps, ripped them across, and sent the pieces after Mark's. He thrust his loaded Very pistol into his pocket in readiness to send a shot into the petrol tank of the machine as soon as they were on the ground—providing they were not knocked out in the crash.

The destruction of his machine to prevent it falling into the hands of the enemy is the first duty of an airman who lands in hostile territory.

The sky around them became an inferno of darting flames and hurtling metal. Several pieces of shrapnel struck the machine, and it quivered like a terrified horse. Once the F.E. was nearly turned upside down by a terrific explosion under the port wing-tip. 400—300—200 feet ran the altimeter. Mark was leaning over the side staring into the blackness below them.

Biggles could distinguish nothing; the earth looked like a dark indigo stain, broken only by the flashes of guns and the intermittent spurts of machine-guns. He no longer looked at his altimeter, for he knew he was too low for it to be of any assistance; he could only keep his eyes glued below and hope for the best.

Suddenly, the shadow that was the earth swept up to meet him. He pulled the joy-stick back until the machine was flying on even keel. It began to sink as it lost flying speed, then staggered like a drunken animal. He lifted his knees to his chin, covered his face with his arms, and waited for the end. For a moment there was silence, broken only by the faint hum of the wires and the rumble of the guns.

Crash! With a crunching, tearing, rending scream of protest, the machine struck the ground and subsided in a heap of debris. The nacelle, in which the crew sat, buried its nose into the earth, reared up, then turned turtle.

Biggles soared through space and landed with a dull squelch in a sea of mud, but he had scrambled to his feet in an instant, wiping the slime from his eyes with the backs of his gauntlets.

'Mark—Mark!' he hissed. 'Where are you, Mark? Are you hurt, old man?'

'Hold hard, I'm coming! Don't make such a row, you fool!' snarled Mark, dragging himself clear of the debris and unwinding a wire that had coiled around his neck.

Rat-tat-tat-tat. Rat-tat-tat-tat.

A Very light soared upwards, and half a dozen machine-guns began their vicious stutter somewhere near at hand; bullets began splintering into the tangled wreck of the machine and zipping into the mud like a swarm of angry hornets.

'Come on, let's get out of this!' gasped Mark. 'Run for it; the artillery will open up any second!'

'Run! Where to?' panted Biggles.

'Anywhere—to get away from here!' snapped Mark, slithering and sliding through the ooze.

Whee-e-e—Bang! The first shell arrived with the noise of an express train and exploded with a roar like the end of the world. Biggles took a flying leap into a shell-hole and wormed his way into the mud at the bottom like a mole. He grunted as Mark landed on top of him.

'Why—the dickens—don't you look—where you're

going!' he spluttered, as they squelched side by side in the sludge; while the shell-torn earth rocked under the onslaught from the artillery.

'We're all right here,' announced Mark firmly. 'They say a shell never lands in the same place twice.'

'I wish I knew that for a fact,' muttered Biggles. 'This is what comes of night-flying. Night birds, eh? Great jumping mackerel, we're a couple of owls all right; an owl's got enough sense to stay—'

'Shut up!' snarled Mark, as the bombardment grew less intense, and then suddenly died away. 'Let's see where we are,' he whispered, as an eerie silence settled over the scene.

'See where we are? Have you any idea where we are?'

'Hark!'

They held their breaths and listened, but no sound reached their ears.

'I thought I heard someone coming,' breathed Mark. 'This is awful, not knowing which side of the lines we're on!'

They crept up to the lip of the shell-crater and stared into the surrounding darkness. A Very light soared upwards from a spot about a hundred yards away. Biggles, peering under his hand in the glare, distinctly saw a belt of barbed wire a few yards away on their left. Mark, who was looking in the other direction, gripped his arm in a vice-like clutch.

'Huns!' he whispered. 'There's a party of them coming this way. I could tell them by the shape of their helmets. Come on, this way!'

They started crawling warily towards the wire, but when they reached it, finding no opening, they commenced crawling parallel with it, freezing into a death-like stillness whenever a Very light cast its weird glow over the scene.

'Those Huns were coming from the opposite direction, so this should be our side,' muttered Mark.

'Don't talk,' whispered Biggles, 'let's keep going—this looks like a gap in the wire.'

By lying flat on the ground so that the obstruction was silhouetted against the sky, they could see a break in the ten feet wide belt of barbed wire, where it had evidently been torn up by shell-fire. They crawled through the breach, then paused to listen with straining ears.

'I can hear someone talking ahead of us; they must be in a trench,' whispered Mark.

'So can I; let's get closer,' whispered Biggles. 'Ssh—there it is! I can see the parapet. We shall have to go carefully, or we may be shot by our own fellows.' He raised himself on his hands and was about to call out—in fact, he had opened his mouth to do so—when a sound reached their ears that seemed to freeze the blood in their veins.

It was a harsh, coarse voice, speaking in a language they did not understand, but which they had no difficulty in recognizing as German. It came from the parapet a few yards in front of them.

A line of bayonets and then a body of men rose up in the darkness at the edge of the trench; there was no mistaking the coal-scuttle helmets.

Neither of the airmen spoke; as one man they sank to the ground, forcing themselves into the cold mud, and lay motionless. Heavy footsteps squelched through the mud towards them; a voice was speaking in a low undertone. Nearer and nearer they came, until Biggles felt the muscles of his back retract to receive the stab-

82

bing pain of a bayonet-thrust. He nearly cried out as a heavy foot descended on his hand, but his gauntlet and the soft mud under it saved the bones from being broken. The German stumbled, recovered, half-glanced over his shoulder to see what had tripped him; but, seeing what he supposed to be a corpse, turned and walked quickly after the others.

'Phew!' gasped Biggles, as the footsteps receded into the distance.

'Let's get out of this!' muttered Mark. 'They may be back any moment. Another minute and we should have walked straight into their trench. Hark!'

The hum of an F.E. reached their ears, and although they could not see it they could follow its path of flight by the archie bursts and the sound. It was coming from the direction of the German trench. It passed straight over them; the archie died away, and presently the sound faded into the night.

'That's one of our fellows going home, so it gives us our direction if we can only find a way through our own wire. If there isn't a gap, we're sunk; so we might crawl along this blinking wire to Switzerland!'

'Ssh!'

Once more the sound of footsteps reached them from somewhere near at hand, but they could see nothing.

'I can't stand much more of this!' growled Biggles. 'It's giving me the creeps. I've just crawled over some-body—or something that was somebody.'

Bang! They both jumped and then lay flat as another Very light curved high into the air; in its dazzling light Biggles distinctly saw a group of German soldiers, evidently a patrol, standing quite still, not more than fifty yards away. Suddenly he remembered something. He groped in his pocket, whipped out his own Very pistol, took careful aim, and fired. The light in the air went out at the same moment. The shot from Biggles' pistol dropped in the mud a hundred yards away, where it lay hissing in a cloud of red smoke that changed gradually to a ghastly, livid green.

'You fool, what are you at?' snarled Mark. 'I thought I was shot.'

'Didn't you see those Huns? I bet I've made them jump!'

'They'll probably make us jump in a minute!' retorted Mark.

'Would have done if I hadn't fired that Very light at 'em, you mean!' retorted Biggles. 'Nothing like getting in the first shot. Makes the other fellow scary. We've been walked over by one crowd and treated as bloomin' doormats. I don't want a second dose of that!'

'You'll get a dose of something else if those Huns poodle along here to inquire what the fireworks are for!' replied Mark.

'If!' jeered Biggles. 'I'll bet those chaps are legging it for home for all they're worth. An' I don't blame 'em. I'd do the same myself if I jolly well knew where home was.'

'You'll never live to see home again if you don't stop playing the silly ass!' growled Mark. 'And now shut up and listen. See if you can hear anybody talking in a language we understand.'

For some time the two airmen remained still, lying on the ground and listening intently for the sound of voices. But they could hear nothing save the occasional banging of rifles. At last Biggles grew impatient.

'Well, I'm not going to stay messing about here any longer!' he snapped. 'We'll settle things one way or the other. I will start to get light presently, and then we're

84

done for. I believe that's our wire just in front of us. What about letting out a shout to see if our fellows are within earshot?'

'The Huns will hear us, too.'

'I can't help that. Hold tight, I'm going to yell. Hallo, there!' he bellowed. 'Is anybody about?'

A reply came from a spot so close that Biggles instinctively ducked.

'What are you bleating abart?' said a Cockney voice calmly. 'You come any closer to me and I'll give you something to holler for. You can't catch me on that hop!'

Bang! A rifle blazed in the darkness, not ten yards away, and a bullet whistled past Biggles' head.

'Hi! That's enough of that!' he shouted. 'We're British officers, I tell you—fliers. We crashed outside the wire and can't get through. Come and show us the way!'

'Why didn't you say so before?' came the reply. 'You might 'ave got 'urt. 'Old 'ard a minute! But you keep your 'ands up, and no half-larks!'

Silence fell.

'He's either coming himself, or he's gone to fetch someone,' muttered Mark. 'We can't blame him for being suspicious. He must have been in the listening-post, which is where people shoot first and ask questions afterwards. The Huns get up to all sorts of tricks.'

'Where are you, you fellow?' suddenly said a quiet voice near them.

'Here we are!' answered Biggles.

'Stand fast—I'm coming.'

An officer, revolver in hand, closely followed by half a dozen Tommies wearing the unmistakable British tin helmets, loomed up suddenly in the darkness.

85

'How many of you are there?' said the voice.

'Two,' replied Biggles shortly.

'All right, follow me—and don't make a row about it.'

Squelching through the ooze, they followed the officer through a zigzag track in the wire. The Tommies closed in behind them. A trench, from which projected a line of bayonets, lay across their path, but at a word from their escort the rifles were lowered, and the two airmen half-slipped and half scrambled into the trench. The beam of a flash-lamp cut through the darkness and went slowly over their faces and uniforms.

'You look a couple of pretty scarecrows, I must say,' said a voice, with a chuckle. 'Come into my dugout and have a rest. I'll send a runner to headquarters with a request that they ring up your squadron and tell them you're safe. What have you been up to?'

'Oh—er—night flying, that's all. Just night flying!' said Biggles airily.

Chapter 8

The Dawn Patrol

Biggles opened his eyes drowsily as a hand shook his shoulder respectfully but firmly. At the back of his sleep-soaked mind he knew it was his batman* calling him.

'Come on, sir!' said the voice. 'It's six o'clock! Patrol leaves at half-past!'

Second-Lieutenant Bigglesworth (Biggles for short) stared at the man coldly. 'Push off!' he said, and nestled lower under the bedclothes.

'Come on, now, sir, drink your tea!' The batman held out the cup invitingly.

Biggles swung his legs over the side of the bed, shivering as the cold air struck his warm limbs, and took tea. 'What's the weather like?' he asked.

'Not too good, sir, lot of cloud about, but no rain as yet!' Satisfied that his officer was really awake, the batman departed.

Biggles stood up and pulled his sweater on. He glanced across the room at Mark Way, who had already been called, but was fast asleep again and snoring gently. He picked up his pillow and heaved it at the peaceful face of his flying partner.

Instead of hitting the slumbering Mark, it swept a row of ornaments from the shelf above his head. There was a fearful crash as they scattered in all directions.

* An attendant serving an officer. A position discontinued in today's Royal Air Force.

87

Mark leapt up in bed as if impelled by an invisible spring.

'What th—' he began, looking about him wildly.

Biggles, who was brushing his hair in front of a cracked mirror, side-stepped quickly to avoid the pillow as it came back, hurled by a vigorous arm. It caught the half-empty tea-cup and swept it into the middle of his bed. He looked at the marksman in disgust.

'Rotten shot!' he said. 'Your shooting on the ground is worse than it is in the air, and that's saying something!'

'Can't you fellows get up without making such an infernal din?' snarled an angry voice from the far end of the room. 'This place is like a madhouse when A Flight are on an early show. You two should save your energy; you'll need it presently, when Rayner gets going.'

'Rayner—what's Rayner got to do with me?' asked Biggles, in surprise, as he pulled on his sheepskin boots.

'Mapleton is going to have a tooth drawn this morning, so he has had to report sick. I heard him talking to the Old Man about it last night. Rayner is going to lead your show this morning.'

'I see,' said Biggles. 'Well, it'll be a change for him to find his Flight sticking to his tail instead of scattering all over the sky when a Hun heaves into sight.'

He ducked to avoid a cake of soap hurled by a member of C Flight, of which Captain Rayner was in command, and departed.

He hurried to the sheds and started the engine of his F.E.2b two-seater plane. Mark came out of the armoury carrying his gun, which he proceeded to test, and Captain Rayner appeared at the corner of A Flight hangar.

'It's right, then!' Biggles muttered to Mark. 'Mabs isn't doing the show—here's Rayner!'

'What about it?' grunted Mark, from the cockpit, where he was carefully arranging his ammunition drums.

'I suppose he'll try to show us what a hot-stuff merchant he is, that's all. And it's a bit too early in the morning for fireworks,' answered Biggles.

Captain Rayner climbed into his machine, looked around to see that the others were in place, taxied out on to the aerodrome, and roared into the air. The three other machines that were to form the dawn patrol took off behind him, heading towards the distant trenches of the western battlefront.

The grey light of early morning grew stronger, and before the Lines were reached the sun was shining brightly. A strong wind was blowing from the west, bringing with it masses of cloud like great white cauliflowers, gleaming with gold and yellow at the top, merging into dark blue and purple at the base. Here and there the ground was still obscured by long grey blankets of ground mist, through which the earth showed in pale greens and browns.

The patrol climbed for some time before approaching the Lines, the leader making his way towards one of the strips of blue sky that here and there showed through the mass of cloud. They entered the opening at five thousand feet, and then corkscrewed upwards, climbing steeply as though through a hollow tube to the top side of the cloud. Then the four machines levelled out and headed eastward.

Biggles, looking over the side, could see mile after mile of rolling white clouds, like great masses of cotton-wool, stretching away to the infinite distance where they cut a hard line against the blue sky. Below them, their four grey shadows, each surrounded by a complete rainbow, raced at incredible speed over the top of the gleaming vapour.

As far as he could see there were no other machines in the sky, although he was not quite certain if they had actually crossed the Lines yet. But Rayner seemed to be flying on a steady course, and Biggles could not help admiring the confident manner in which the leader flew. He seemed to know exactly where he was and what he was doing.

For some time they flew on, climbing gently, rounding mighty fantastic pyramids of cloud that seemed to reach to high heaven. Compared with them the four F.E.s were so small as to be negligible—'like gnats flying round the base of snow-covered mountains,' Biggles thought.

For twenty minutes or so Rayner headed straight into German territory, turning neither to right nor left, a proceeding which caused Mark to look round at his pilot with a sour grimace.

Biggles knew well enough what his gunner was thinking. The distance they had covered, with the wind behind them, could not be less than twenty miles; it would take them a long time to return with the wind in their teeth. He wished there were some gaps in the clouds so that he might see the Lines if they were in sight. They formed a barrier between the known and the unknown. On one side lay home, friends, and safety; on the other, mystery, enemies, and death!

From time to time round, whirling balls of black smoke stained the cloudscape; they increased in size, becoming less dense as they did so, and then drifted into long plumes before they were finally dispersed by the wind. Archie—otherwise anti-aircraft gunfire! Biggles eyed it moodily, for although he no longer feared it, he never failed to regard it with suspicion. After all, one never knew—

Mark stood up, and, with a reassuring smile at Biggles, fired a short burst downwards from his gun, to warm it up and make sure it was in working order. From time to time the other observers did the same.

Biggles was glad when at last Rayner changed his direction and began to fly north-west on a course nearly parallel with the Lines, a course that Biggles estimated would bring them back to the Lines some thirty miles above where they had crossed.

The clouds seemed to increase in size in their new direction, until they assumed colossal proportions. The patrol was now flying at nine thousand feet, but the summits of the clouds seemed to tower as far above them as the bases were below. Biggles had no idea that clouds could be so enormous.

They had been in the air for more than an hour, and so far they had not seen a single other machine, either friend or foe. Several times Mark stood up—as did the other gunners—and squinted at the blinding sun between his first finger and thumb.

'This is too tame to be true,' thought Biggles, as he wiped the frozen breath from his windscreen with the back of his glove, and worked his lips, which felt as if they were getting frostbitten in the icy wind. He noticed that Rayner was leading them to the very top of a stupendous pile of cloud that lay directly in their path.

'He's going over it rather than round it—got an idea there's something on the other side, I suppose,' thought Biggles, watching both sides of the gleaming mass.

The gunners were suspicious, too, for they all stood

up as the machines approached it, guns at the 'ready.' Mark looked round and grinned, although his face was blue with cold.

'Yes, this is where we strike the rough stuff!' said Biggles to himself. He did not know why he thought that. On the face of it, there was no more reason to suppose that this particular cloud would conceal enemy aircraft any more than the others they had already passed. It may have been the amazing instinct which he was beginning to develop that warned him. At any rate, something inside him seemed to say that hostile machines were not far away.

Rayner was immediately over the top of the cloud-pile now, and Biggles could see him, and his gunner, looking down at something that was still invisible to the others.

'There they are!' thought Biggles. And he no longer thought of the cold, for Rayner's machine was wobbling its wings. A red Very light soared into the air from the gunner's cockpit—the signal that enemy aircraft had been sighted.

Rayner was banking now, turning slowly, and the other three machines swam into the spot where the leader had been a few moments before.

Biggles looked over the side, and caught his breath sharply as he found himself looking into a hole in the clouds, a vast cavity that would have been impossible to imagine. It reminded him vaguely of the crater of a volcano of incredible proportions.

Straight down for a sheer eight thousand feet the walls of opaque mist dropped, turning from yellow to brown, brown to mauve, and mauve to indigo at the basin-like depression in the remote bottom. The precipitous sides looked so solid that it seemed as if a man might try to climb down them, or rest on one of the shelves that jutted out at intervals.

He was so taken up with this phenomenon that for a brief space of time all else was forgotten. Then a tiny movement far, far below caught his eye, and he knew he was looking at that which the eagle-eyed flight-commander had seen instantly.

A number of machines—how many, he could not tell—were circling round and round at the very bottom of the yawning crater, looking like microscopic fish at the bottom of a deep pool in a river. Occasionally one or more of them would completely disappear in the shadows, to reappear a moment later, wings flashing faintly as the light caught them.

They were much too far away to distinguish whether they were friends or foes, but Rayner seemed to have no doubt in the matter. A tiny living spark of orange fire, flashing diagonally across the void, told its own story. It was a machine going down in flames, and that could only mean one thing—a dog-fight was in progress in that well of mystery.

Then Rayner went down, closely followed by the others.

Biggles never forgot that dive. There was something awe-inspiring about it. It was like sinking down into the very centre of the earth. There was insufficient room for the four machines to keep in a straight dive, as the cavity was not more than a few hundred yards across, so they were compelled to take a spiral course.

Down—down—down they went. Biggles thought they would never come to the end. The wind howled and screamed through struts and wires like a thousand demons in agony, but he heeded it not. He was too engrossed in watching the tragedy being enacted below.

Twice, as they went down in that soul-shaking dive, he saw machines fall out of the fight, leaving streamers of black smoke behind them, around which the others continued to turn, and roll, and shoot. There were at least twenty of them: drab biplanes with yellow wings, and rainbow-hued triplanes—red, green, blue, mauve, and even a white one.

Soon the dawn patrol was amongst the whirling machines, and it was every man for himself.

Biggles picked out a group of triplanes with black-crossed wings that were flying close together. They saw him coming, and scattered like a school of minnows when a pike appears. He rushed at one of them, a blue machine with white wing-tips, and pursued it relentlessly. Mark's gun started chattering, and he saw the tracer-bullets pouring straight into the centre of the fuselage of the machine below him.

The Hun did not burst into flames as he hoped it would. Instead, it zoomed upwards, turned slowly over on to its back, and then, with the engine still on, spun down out of sight into the misty floor of the basin.

Biggles jerked the machine up sharply, and swerved just in time to avoid collision, with a whirling bonfire of struts and canvas. His nostrils twitched as he hurtled through its smoking trail.

Mark was shooting again, this time at a white machine. But the pilot of it was not to be so easily disposed of. He twisted and turned like a fish with a sea-lion after it, and more than once succeeded in getting in a burst of fire at them.

This was the hottest dog-fight in which Biggles had as yet taken part. One thought was uppermost in his mind, and that was—that he must inevitably collide with somebody in a moment. Already they had missed machines—triplanes, F.E.s, and Pups, which he now perceived the British machines to be—by inches. But the thought of collision did not frighten him.

He felt only a strange elation, a burning desire to go on doing this indefinitely—to down the enemy machines before he himself was killed, as he never doubted that he would be in the end. There was no thought in his mind of retreat or escape.

Mark's gun was rattling incessantly, and Biggles marvelled at the calm deliberation with which he flung the empty drums overboard after their ammunition was exhausted, and replaced them with new ones.

Something struck the machine with a force that made it quiver. The compass flew to pieces, and the liquid that it contained spurted back, half blinding him. Mechanically, he wiped his face with the back of his glove.

Where was the white Hun? He looked around, and his blood seemed to turn to ice at the sight that met his gaze. An F.E.—a blazing meteor of spurting fire— was roaring nosedown across his front at frightful speed!

A black figure emerged from the flames with its arm flung over its face, and leapt outwards and downwards. The machine, almost as if it was still under control, deliberately swerved towards the white triplane that was whirling across its front.

The Hun pilot saw his danger, and twisted like lightning to escape. But he was too late. The blazing F.E. caught it fair and square across the fuselage. There was a shower of sparks and debris, and then a blinding flash of flames as the triplane's tanks exploded. Then the two machines disappeared from Biggles's field of view.

For a moment he was stunned with shock, utterly unable to think, and it was a shrill yell from Mark that brought him back to realities. Where was he? What was he doing? Oh, yes, fighting! Who had been in the F.E.? Marriot? Or was it McAngus? It must have been one of them. A yellow Hun was shooting at him.

With a mighty effort he pulled himself together, but he felt that he could not stand the strain much longer. He was flying on his nerves, and he knew it. His flying was getting wild and erratic.

Turning, he swerved into the side of the cloud, temporarily blinding himself, and then burst out again, fighting frantically to keep the machine under control. Bullets were crashing into his engine, and he wondered why it did not burst into flames.

Where were the bullets coming from? He leaned over the side of the cockpit and looked behind. A yellow Hun was on his tail. He turned with a speed that amazed himself. Unprepared for the move, the Hun overshot the F.E. Next instant the tables were turned, Biggles roaring down after the triplane in hot pursuit.

Rat-tat-tat-tat! stuttered Mark's gun. At such short range it was impossible to miss. The yellow top wing swung back and floated away into space, and the fuselage plunged out of sight, a streamer of flame creeping along its side.

For a moment Biggles watched it, fascinated, then he looked up with a start. Where were the others? Where were his companions? He was just in time to see one of them disappear into the side of the cloud, then he was alone.

At first he could not believe it. Where were the Huns? Not one of them was in sight. Where, a moment or two before, there had been twenty or more machines, not one remained except himself—Yes, one; a Pup was just disappearing through the floor of the basin.

A feeling of horrible loneliness came over him and a doubt crept into his mind as to his ability to find his way home. He had not the remotest idea of his position. He looked upwards, but from his own level to the distant circle of blue at the top of the crater there was not a single machine to be seen. He had yet to learn of the suddenness with which machines could disappear when a dog-fight was broken off by mutual consent.

He had hoped to see the F.E. that he had seen disappear into the mist come out again, but it did not.

'I'll bet that Pup pilot knows where he is; I'll go after him,' he thought desperately, and tore down in the wake of the single-seater that had disappeared below. He looked at his altimeter, which had somehow escaped the general ruin caused by the bullets. One thousand feet, it read. He sank into the mist and came out under it almost at once. Below lay open country— fields, hedges, and a long, deserted road. Not a soul was in sight as far as he could see, and there was no landmark that he could recognize.

He saw the Pup at once. It was still going down, and he raced after it intending to get alongside in the hope of making his predicament known to the pilot. Then, with a shock of understanding, he saw that the Pup's propeller was not turning. Its engine must have been put out of action in the combat, and the pilot had no choice but to land.

As he watched the machine, he saw the leather-helmeted head turn in the cockpit as the pilot looked back over his shoulder. Then he turned again and made a neat landing in a field.

Biggles did not hesitate. He knew they were far over

hostile country—how far he did not like to think—and the Pup pilot must be rescued. The single-seater was blazing when he landed beside it, and its pilot ran towards the F.E., carrying a still smoking Very pistol in his hand.

Biggles recognized him at once.

'Mahoney!' he yelled.

The Pup pilot pulled up dead and stared.

'Great smoking rattlesnakes!' he cried. 'If it isn't young Bigglesworth!'

'Get in, and buck up about it!' shouted Biggles.

'Get in here with me,' called Mark. 'It'll be a bit of a squash, but it can be done.'

Mahoney clambered aboard and squeezed himself into the front cockpit with the gunner.

'Look out,' he yelled. 'Huns!'

Biggles did not look. He saw little tufts of grass flying up just in front of the machine, and he heard the distant rattle of a gun. It told him all he needed to know, and he knew he had no time to lose.

The F.E. took a long run to get off with its unusual burden, but it managed it. Fortunately, its nose was pointing towards the Lines, and there was no need to turn. The machine zoomed upwards and the mist enfolded them like a blanket.

For a few minutes Biggles fought his way through the gloom, then he put the nose of the machine down again, for he knew he could not hope to keep it on even keel for very long in such conditions. The ground loomed darkly below; he corrected the machine, and then climbed up again.

'Do you know where we are?' he yelled.

Mahoney nodded, and made a sign that he was to keep straight on.

Biggles breathed more comfortably, and flew along just at the base of the clouds. Suddenly he remembered the blazing F.E.

'Who was in that F.E.?' he bellowed to Mark.

'Rayner!' was the reply.

So Rayner had gone at last—gone out in one of the wildest dog-fights he could have desired. Sooner or later it was bound to happen, Biggles reflected, but it was tough luck on poor Marble, his observer.

Poor old Marble. Two hours before they had drunk their coffee together, and now—What a beastly business war was!

It must have been Marble whom he had seen jump. And Rayner had deliberately rammed the Hun, he was certain of it.

'Well, I only hope I shall have as much nerve when my time comes!' he mused. 'Poor old Rayner, he wasn't such a bad sort!'

Biggles pulled himself together and tried to put the matter from his mind, but he could not forget the picture. He knew he would never forget it.

An archie burst blossomed out just in front of him and warned him that they were approaching the Lines. Two minutes later they were in the thick of it, rocking in a wide area of flame-torn sky. The gunners, knowing to an inch the height of the clouds, were able to make good shooting, yet they passed through unscathed, letting out a whoop of joy as they raced into the sheltered security of their own Lines.

Mahoney guided the F.E. to his own aerodrome, which Biggles had seen from the air, although he had never landed on it, and after a rather bumpy landing, it ran to a standstill in front of No. 266 Squadron sheds, where a number of officers and mechanics were watching.

'I believe I've busted a tyre,' muttered Biggles, in disgust. But a quick examination revealed that the damage had not been his fault. The tyre had been pierced from side to side by a bullet.

There was a general babble of excitement, in which everybody talked at once. Biggles was warmly congratulated on his rescue work, which everyone present regarded as an exceptionally good show.

'Does anyone know what happened to the other two F.E.s?' asked Biggles.

'Yes, they've gone home,' said several voices at once. 'They broke off the fight when we did, and we all came home together!'

'Thank goodness!' muttered Biggles. 'I thought they had all gone west. How did the show start?'

'We saw the Huns down in that hole, and we went in after 'em; it looked such a nice hole that we thought it ought to be ours,' grinned Mahoney. 'There were seven of us, but there were more of them than we thought at first. We had just got down to things when you butted in. I didn't see you until you were amongst us. Which way did you come in?'

'Through the front door—at the top!' laughed Biggles.

'Well, it was a fine dog-fight!' sighed Mahoney. 'The sort of scrap one remembers. Hallo, here's the C.O.!' he added. 'Here, sir, meet Bigglesworth, who I was telling you about the other day. He picked me up this morning in Hunland after a Boche had shot my engine to scrap iron.' He turned to Biggles again. 'Let me introduce you to Major Mullen, our C.O.,' he said.

'Pleased to meet you, Bigglesworth,' said Major

100

Mullen, shaking hands. 'You seem to be the sort of fellow we want out here. I shall have to keep an eye on you with a view to getting you transferred to 266.'

'I wish to goodness you could fix that, sir,' replied Biggles earnestly. 'I shall not be happy until I get in a scout squadron—although I should be sorry to leave Mark,' he added quickly.

'Don't worry about me,' broke in Mark. 'My application's in for training as a pilot, so I may be leaving you, anyway.'

'Well, I can't promise anything, of course, but I'll see what can be done about it,' Major Mullen told him.

'What are you two going to do now?' asked Mahoney.

'I think we'd better be getting back,' answered Biggles.

'Won't you stay to lunch?'

'No, thanks. We'll leave the machine here, if you'll have that tyre put right and can lend us transport to get home. We'll come back later on to fly the machine home.'

'Good enough!' declared Mahoney. 'I'll ask the C.O. if you can borrow his car. I shan't forget how you picked me up. Maybe it will be my turn to lend a hand next time!'

'Well, so long as you don't ask me to squeeze into the cockpit of a Pup with you I don't mind!' laughed Biggles. 'See you later!'

Chapter 9
Special Mission

'Beg pardon, sir, but Major Paynter wishes to speak to you, sir.'

Biggles glanced up, folded the letter he was reading, and put it in his pocket. 'On the 'phone, do you mean?' he asked the mess waiter, who had delivered the message.

'No, sir, in his office. Mr Todd rang up to say would you go along right away.'

'All right, Collins, thanks.' Biggles picked up his cap as he went through the hall and walked quickly along the well-worn path to the squadron office. Two people were present in addition to the C.O. when he entered—one a red-tabbed staff-officer, and the other, a round-faced, cheerful-looking civilian in a black coat and bowler hat. Biggles saluted.

'Just make sure the door is closed, will you, Bigglesworth?' began the C.O. 'Thanks. This is Major Raymond, of Wing Headquarters.'

'How do you do, sir?' said Biggles to the staff officer, wondering why the C.O. did not introduce the civilian, and what he was doing there.

'I want to have a few words with you, Bigglesworth, on a very delicate subject,' went on the C.O. rather awkwardly. 'Er—I, or I should say the squadron, has been asked to undertake an—er—operation of the greatest importance. It is a job that will have to be done single-handed, and I am putting the proposition to you first because you have shown real enthusiasm in your work since you've been with us, and because you have extricated yourself from one or two difficult situations entirely by your own initiative. The job in hand demands both initiative and resource.'

'Thank you, sir.'

'Not a bit. Now, this is the proposition. The operation, briefly, consists in taking an—er—gentleman over the Lines, landing him at a suitable spot, and then returning home. It is probable that you will have to go over the Lines again afterwards, either the same night or at a subsequent date, and pick him up from the place where you landed him.'

'That does not seem diffi—'

Major Paynter held up his hand.

'Wait!' he said. 'Let me finish. It is only fair that I should warn you that in the event of your being forced down on the wrong side of the Lines, or being captured in any way, you would probably be shot. Even if you had to force-land in German territory on the return journey, with no one in the machine but yourself, it is more than likely that the enemy would suspect your purpose and subject you to rigorous interrogation. And if the enemy could wring the truth from you—that you had been carrying a Secret Service agent—they would be justified in marching you before a firing squad.'

'I understand. Very good, sir. I'll go.'

'Thank you, Bigglesworth! The gentleman here with Major Raymond will be your passenger. It would be well for you to meet him now, as you will not see him again in daylight, and you should be able to identify each other.'

Biggles walked over to the civilian and held out his hand. 'Pleased to meet you!' he said.

103

The spy—for Biggles had no delusion about the real nature of the work on hand—smiled and wrung his hand warmly. He was a rather fat, jovial-looking little man with a huge black moustache; in no way was he like the character Biggles would have expected for such work.

'Well, I think that's all for the present, Raymond,' went on the C.O. 'Let me know the details as soon as you can. I'll have another word with you, Bigglesworth, before you go.'

Biggles saluted as the staff officer departed with his civilian companion, and then turned his attention again to Major Paynter, who was staring thoughtfully out of the window.

'I want you to see this thing in its true perspective,' resumed the C.O. 'We are apt to think spying is rather dirty work. It may be, from the strictly military point of view, but one should not forget that it needs as much nerve—if not more—than anything a soldier is called upon to face. A soldier may be killed, wounded, or made prisoner. But a spy's career can only have one ending if he's caught—the firing squad! He does not die a man's death in the heat of battle; he is shot like a dog against a brick wall. That's the result of failure. If he succeeds, he gets no medals, honour or glory. Silence surrounds him always.

'And most of these men work for nothing. Take that man you've just seen, for instance. He is, of course, a Frenchman. In private life he's a schoolmaster at Aille, which is now in territory occupied by the enemy. He worked his way across the frontier into Holland, and then to France, via England, to offer his services to his country. He asks no reward. There's courage and self-sacrifice, if you like. Remember that when he's in your machine. His knowledge of the country around Aille makes his services particularly valuable. If he gets back safely this time—he has already made at least one trip—he will go again. And so it will go on, until one day he will not come back.

'As far as you're concerned as his pilot, you need have no scruples. Most of the leading French pilots have taken their turns for special missions, as these affairs are called. For obvious reasons, only the best pilots, those of proven courage, are chosen for the work. Well, I think that's all. I'll let you know the details, the date and time, later on. Don't mention this matter to anybody, except, of course, your flight-commander, who will have to know.'

Biggles bumped into Mapleton, his flight-commander, just outside the office.

'What's on?' asked Mabs quietly. 'Special mission?'

Biggles nodded.

'I thought so. For the love of Mike be careful! You've only got to make one bloomer at that game, and all the king's horses and all the king's men couldn't save you. I did one once, and that was enough for me. No more, thank you!'

'Why, did things go wrong?' inquired Biggles, as they walked towards the mess.

'Wrong! It was worse than that. In the first place, the cove refused to get out of the machine when we got there; his nerves petered out. He couldn't speak English, and I can't speak French, so I couldn't tell him what I thought of him. When I tried to throw him out he kicked up such a row that it brought all the Huns for miles to the spot. I had to get off in a hurry, I can tell you, bringing the blighter back with me. But some of these fellows have been over no end of times, and they have brought back, or sent back, information of the greatest importance. They have to carry a basket of pigeons with them, and they release one every time they get information worth while. How would you like to walk about amongst the Boche with a pigeon up your coat? It's only got to give one coo and you're sunk. The French do a lot of this business; most of the leading French pilots have had a go at it. Vedrines, the pre-war pilot, did several shows. When the War broke out the French expected great things of him, and when he just faded into insignificance they began saying nasty things about him. But he was doing special missions, and those are things people don't talk about.'

'Well, if my bowler-hatted bird starts any trouble I'll give him a thick ear!' observed Biggles.

'Oh, he'll be all right, I should think!' replied Mabs. 'The landing is the tricky part. The Huns know all about this spy-dropping game, and they do their best to catch people in the act by laying traps in likely landing-fields, such as by digging trenches across the field and then covering them up with grass so that you can't see them. When you land—zonk! Another scheme is to stretch wire across the field, which has a similar result.'

'Sounds cheerful! And there are no means of knowing whether a trap has been laid in the field that you have to land on?'

'Not until you land,' grinned Mabs.

'That's a fat lot of good!' growled Biggles. 'Well, we shall see. Many thanks for the tips!'

'That's all right. My only advice is, don't let them catch you alive, laddie. Remember, they shoot you as well as the fellow you are carrying if you're caught. They treat you both alike!'

'They'll have to shoot me to catch me!' replied Biggles grimly.

The hands of the mess clock pointed to the hour of nine when, a few evenings later, Biggles finished his after-dinner coffee, and, collecting his flying kit from its peg in the hall, strolled towards the door.

Mark Way, who had followed him out of the room, noted these proceedings with surprise. 'What's the idea?' he asked, reaching for his own flying kit.

'I've a little job to do—on my own. I can't talk about it. Sorry, old lad!' replied Biggles, and departed. He found Major Raymond and his civilian acquaintance waiting on the tarmac. In accordance with his instructions to the flight-sergeant, his F.E.2b had been wheeled out and the engine was ticking over quietly.

'Remember, he's doing the job for us, not for the French,' Major Raymond told him quietly. 'He's going to dynamite a bridge over the Aisne near the point that I told you about yesterday,' he went on, referring to a conversation on the previous day at which the details had been arranged. 'He's asked me to tell you not to worry about his return. He's quite willing for you to leave him to work his own way back across the frontier, although naturally he'd be glad if you would pick him up again later on.'

'How long will he be doing this job, sir?' asked Biggles.

'It's impossible to say. So much depends on the conditions when he gets there—whether or not there are guards at the bridge, and so on. If it is all clear, he might do the job in half an hour, or an hour. On the other hand, he may be two or three days, waiting for his opportunity. Why do you ask?'

'I was thinking that if he wasn't going to be very long, I might wait for him?'

The major shook his head. 'It isn't usually done that way,' he said. 'It's too risky!'

'The risk doesn't seem to be any greater than making another landing.'

'Wait a minute and I'll ask him,' said the major.

He had a quick low conversation with the secret agent, and then returned to Biggles.

'He says the noise of your engine would attract attention if you waited, and it would not be advisable for you to switch off,' he reported. 'All the same, he asked me to tell you that he'd be very grateful if you would pick him up a few hours afterwards—it would save him three weeks' or a month's anxious work getting through Holland. He suggests that you allow him as much as possible, in case he's delayed. If you'll return at the first glimmer of dawn he'll try to be back by then. If he's not there, go home and forget about him. He suggests dawn because it may save you actually landing. If you can't see him in the field, or on the edge of the field, don't land. If he is there, he'll show himself. That seems to be a very sensible arrangement, and a fair one for both parties.'

'More than fair,' agreed Biggles. 'If he's got enough nerve to dodge about amongst the Huns with a stick of dynamite in one pocket and a pigeon in the other, I ought to have enough nerve to fetch him back!'

'Quite! Still, he's willing to leave it to you.'

Biggles strolled across and shook hands with the man, who did not seem in the least concerned about the frightful task he was about to undertake. He was munching a biscuit contentedly.

108

'It is an honour to know you,' Biggles said. And he meant it.

'It is for *La France*,' answered the man simply.

'Well, I'm ready when you are!'

'*Bon*. Let us go,' was the reply. And they climbed into their seats.

Biggles noted with amazement that his passenger did not even wear flying kit. He wore the same dark suit as before, and the bowler hat, which he jammed hard on. He carried two bundles, and Biggles did not question what they contained; he thought he knew. Pigeons and dynamite were a curious mixture, he thought, as he settled himself into his seat.

He could hardly repress a smile as his eye fell on the unusual silhouette in the front cockpit. There was something queer about going to war in a bowler hat. Then something suspiciously like a lump came into his throat at the thought of the simple Frenchman, unsoldierly though he was in appearance, risking his all to perform an act of service to his country. He made up his mind that if human hands could accomplish it, he would bring his man safely back.

'I am ready, my little cabbage. Pour the sauce*!' cried the man. And Biggles laughed aloud at the command to open the throttle. There was something very likeable about this fellow who could start on a mission of such desperate peril so casually.

'Won't you be frozen?' asked Biggles.

'It is not of the importance,' replied the Frenchman. 'We shall not be of the long time.'

'As you like,' shouted Biggles, and waved the wing-tip mechanics away. The engines roared as he opened

* French slang for 'open the throttle'

109

the throttle, and a moment later he was in the air heading towards the Lines. In spite of the cold the little man still stood in his seat, with his coat-collar turned up, gazing below at the dark shadow of his beloved France.

Presently the archie began to tear the air about them. It was particularly vicious, and Biggles crouched a little lower in his seat. The spy leaned back towards him, and cupped his hands around his mouth. 'How badly they shoot, these Boche!' he called cheerfully.

Biggles regarded him stonily. The fellow obviously had no imagination, for the bombardment was bad enough to make a veteran quail.

'He can't understand, that's all about it! Great jumping cats, I'd hate to be with him in what he would call good shooting!' he thought, and then turned his attention to the task of finding his way to the landing-ground they had decided upon. For his greatest fear was that he would be unable to locate it in the darkness, although he had marked it down as closely as he could by means of surrounding landmarks.

He picked out a main road, lying like a grey ribbon across the landscape, followed it until it forked, took the left fork, and then followed that until it disappeared into a wood. On the far side of the wood he made out the unmistakable straight track of a railway line, running at right angles to it. He followed this in turn, until the lights of a small town appeared ahead. Two roads converged upon it, and somewhere between the two roads and the railway line lay the field in which he had been instructed to land.

He intended to follow his instructions to the letter, knowing that the authorities must have a good reason for their choice. Possibly they knew from secret agents who were working, or had worked, in the vicinity, that the field had not been wired, or that it had not even fallen under the suspicion of the enemy. He dismissed the matter from his mind and concentrated upon the task of finding the field and landing the machine on it.

He cut the engine and commenced a long glide down. He glided as slowly as he could without losing flying speed so that possible watchers on the ground would not hear the wind vibrating in his wires, which they might if he came down too quickly. The spy was leaning over the side of the cockpit, watching the proceedings with interest. Then, as Biggles suddenly spotted the field and circled carefully towards it, the Frenchman picked up his parcels and placed them on the seat with no more concern than a passenger in an omnibus or railway train prepares to alight.

Biggles could see the field clearly now—a long, though not very wide strip of turf. He side-slipped gently to bring the F.E. dead in line with the centre of the field, glided like a wraith over the tops of the trees that bounded the northern end, and then flattened out.

The machine sank slowly, the wheels trundled over the rough turf—with rather a lot of noise, Biggles thought—the tail-skid dragged, and the machine ran to a stop after one of the best landings he had ever made in his life. He sank back limply, realizing that the tension of the last few minutes had been intense.

'Thank you, my little cabbage!' whispered the Frenchman, and glided away into the darkness.

For a moment or two Biggles could hardly believe that he had gone, so quietly and swiftly had he disappeared. For perhaps a minute he sat listening, but he could hear nothing, save the muffled swish of his idling propeller. He stood up and stared into the darkness on

111

all sides, but there was no sign of life; not a light showed anywhere. As far as his late passenger was concerned, the ground might have opened and swallowed him up.

'Well, I might as well be going!' he decided.

There was no need for him to turn in order to take off. He had plenty of 'run' in front of him, and the engine roared as he opened the throttle and swept up into the night. He almost laughed with relief as the earth dropped away below him.

It had been absurdly easy, and the reaction left him with a curious feeling of elation—a joyful sensation that the enemy had been outwitted. 'These things aren't so black as they're painted!' was his unspoken thought as he headed back towards the Lines. He crossed them in the usual flurry of archie, and ten minutes later taxied up to his flight hangar and switched off. He glanced at his watch. Exactly fifty minutes had elapsed since he and his companion had taken off from the very spot on which the machine now stood, and it seemed incredible that in that interval of time he had actually landed in German territory and unloaded a man who, for all he knew, might now be dead or in a prison cell awaiting execution. He hoped fervently that the second half of his task might prove as simple. He climbed stiffly to the ground and met Mabs and Mark, who had evidently heard him land.

'How did you get on?' asked Mabs quickly.

'Fine! If I'd known you were waiting I'd have brought you a bunch of German primroses; there were some growing in the field.'

'You'd better turn in and get some sleep,' Mabs advised him.

'Yes, I might as well—for a bit.'

'For a bit? What do you mean?'

'I'm going over again presently to fetch my bowler-hatted pal back!'

Biggles condemned the spy, the authorities in general, and the Germans in particular, to purgatory when, at the depressing hour of five o'clock the following morning, his batman aroused him from a deep, refreshing sleep.

It was bitterly cold, and the stars were still twinkling brightly in a wintry sky; a thick layer of white frost covered everything and wove curious patterns on the window-panes. It was one of those early spring frosts that remind us that the winter is not yet finished.

'What an hour to be hauled out of bed!' he grumbled, half-regretting his rash promise to fetch his man. But a cup of hot coffee and some toast put a fresh complexion on things, and he hummed cheerfully as he strode briskly over the crisp turf towards the sheds. He had told the flight-sergeant to detail two mechanics to 'stand by,' and he found them shivering in their greatcoats, impatiently awaiting his arrival. 'All right, get her out,' he said sharply, and between them they dragged the F.E. out on to the tarmac. 'Start her up,' he went on, tying a thick woollen muffler round his neck and then pulling on his flying kit.

Five minutes later he was in the air again, heading towards the scene of action.

The sky began to grow pale in the east, and, following the same landmarks that he had used before, he had no difficulty in finding his way. The first flush of dawn was stealing across the sky as he approached the field, but the earth was still bathed in deep blue and purple shadows.

113

He throttled back and began gliding down, eyes probing the shadows, seeking for the field and a little man. He picked out the field, but the spy was nowhere in sight, and Biggles' heart sank with apprehension, for he had developed a strong liking for him. He continued to circle for a few minutes, losing height slowly, eyes running over the surrounding country. Suddenly they stopped, and remained fixed on the one spot where a movement had attracted his attention. Something had flashed dully, but for a second he could not make out what it was.

A fresh turn brought him nearer, and then he saw distinctly—horses—mounted troops—Uhlans*. A troop of them was standing quietly under a clump of leafless trees near the main road, not more than a couple of hundred yards away from the field. He saw others, and small groups of infantry, at various points around the field, concealing themselves as well as the sparse cover would permit.

His lips turned dry. No wonder the little man was not there. For some reason or other, possibly because the mission had been successful, the whole countryside was being watched. Yet, he reasoned, the very presence of the troops suggested that the little man had not been caught. If he had been taken there would be no need for the troops—unless they were waiting for the plane. Well, the little man was not there, so there was no point in landing. He might as well go home. He had no intention of stepping into the trap.

He was within two hundred feet of the ground, and actually had his hand on the throttle to open his engine again, when a figure burst from the edge of the field

* German cavalrymen

114

and waved its arms. Biggles drew in his breath with a
sharp hiss, for the Uhlans had started to move forward.
He flung the control-stick over to the left, and, holding
up the plane's nose with right rudder, dropped like a
stone in a vertical sideslip towards the field.

Never in his life had his nerves been screwed up to
such a pitch. His heart hammered violently against his
ribs but his brain was clear, and he remained cool and
collected. He knew that only perfect judgment and
timing could save the situation. The Uhlans were
coming at a canter; already they were in the next field.

With his eyes on the man he skimmed over the tops
of the trees, put the machine on even keel, and began
to flatten out. Then a remarkable thing happened—an
occurrence so unexpected and so inexplicable that for
a moment he was within an ace of taking off again. A
second figure had sprung out of the ditch behind the
man in the field and started to run towards him. The
new-comer wore a black coat and bowler hat. He did
not run towards the machine, but raced towards the
man who had been waving, and who was now making
for the F.E.

Up to this moment it had not occurred to Biggles
for one instant that the man who had been waving was
not his little man, and when the second figure appeared
his calculations were thrown into confusion. The man
in the bowler hat was the spy, there was no doubt of
that, for he was now close enough for his face and
figure to be recognized. Who, then, was the other?

The Frenchman seemed to know, for as he closed on
him he flung up his right hand. There was a spurt of
flame. The other flung up his arms and pitched forward
on to his face.

Biggles began to see daylight. The thing was an

artfully prepared trap. The first man who had showed himself was a decoy, an imposter to lure him to his death. The real spy had been lying in the hedge bottom, not daring to show himself with so many troops about, hoping that he, Biggles, would not land, which would have been in accordance with their plans.

From his position the spy had seen the decoy break cover, and knew his purpose. So he had exposed himself to warn his flying partner, even at the expense of his own life.

The knowledge made Biggles still more determined to save him, although he could see it was going to be a matter of touch-and-go. The decoy lay where he had fallen, and the little Frenchman, still wearing his bowler, was sprinting as fast as his legs could carry him towards the now taxi-ing machine.

But the Uhlans were already putting their horses at the hedge, not a hundred yards away. Shots rang out, the sharp whip-like cracks of cavalry carbines splitting the still morning air. Bullets hummed like angry wasps, one tearing through the machine with a biting jar that made Biggles wince.

'Come on!' he roared, unable to restrain himself, and he opened the throttle slightly.

The little man's face was red with exertion, and he was puffing hard. He took a flying leap at the nose of the F.E. and dragged himself up on to the edge of the cockpit. '*Voila*! We have made it, my little mushroom!' he gasped. And then, as Biggles jammed the throttle wide open, he pitched head first inside.

The Uhlans were galloping towards them, crouching low on the backs of their mounts, and spurring them to greater efforts. There was no time to turn. Biggles did the only thing possible. He shoved the joy-stick

116

forward and charged. He caught a glimpse of swerving horses and flashing carbines straight in front of him; then he pulled the stick back into his stomach, flinching from what seemed must end in collision.

He relaxed limply as the F.E. zoomed upwards, and shook his head as if unable to believe that they were actually in the air. For the last two or three minutes he had not been conscious of actual thought. He had acted purely on instinct, throwing the whole strain on his nerves.

A round, good-humoured face appeared above the edge of the forward cockpit. The spy caught his eye and grinned. '*Bon*! he shouted. 'That's the stuff, my little cabbage!'

Major Raymond was watching on the tarmac when they landed. His face beamed with delight when he saw they were both in the machine.

'How did it go?' he asked the little Frenchman quickly.

'*Pouf*! Like that!' said the spy. 'The bridge is no more, and, thanks to my little specimen here, I can now have my coffee at home instead of with the pigs-heads over the way.'

'Have a close call, Bigglesworth?' asked the major, becoming serious.

'We did, sir!' admitted Biggles. 'I think I shall fly in a bowler hat in future—they seem to be lucky!'

'Ah! But those Boches are cunning ones!' muttered the Frenchman. 'They hunt for me, but I am in the ditch like a rabbit. They know the aeroplane will come, so they find another man to make my little artichoke land. He lands—so. I think furiously. *La, la*, it is simple. I shoot, and then I run. My Jingoes, how I run! Pish.

117

We win, and here we are. I think we will go again some day, eh?' He beamed at Biggles.

'Perhaps!' agreed Biggles, but without enthusiasm. 'I've had all I want for a little while, though!'

'Pish!' laughed the spy. 'It was nothing! Just a little excitement to—how you say?—warm the blood.'

'Warm the blood!' exclaimed Biggles. 'When I want to do that I'll do it in front of the mess-room fire, thanks! Your sort of warm gets me overheated!'

Chapter 10
Eyes of the Guns

Biggles' face wore a curious expression as he gazed down upon the blue-green panorama four thousand feet below. The day was fine and clear, and recent rain had washed the earth until roads and fields lay sharply defined to the far horizon. Ponds and lakes gleamed like mirrors in the sun, and ruined villages lay here and there like the bones of long-forgotten monsters. At intervals along the roads were long, black caterpillars that he knew were bodies of marching men, sometimes with wagons and artillery. There was nothing unusual about the scene, certainly nothing to cause the look of distaste on the pilot's face. It was an everyday scene on the Western Front.

The truth of the matter was he was setting out on a task that he expected would be wearisome to the point of utter boredom. He had never been detailed for this particular job before, but he had heard a good deal about it, and nothing that was pleasant. The work in question was that known throughout the Royal Flying Corps by those two mystic syllables 'art obs'—in other words, artillery observation.

There were certain squadrons that did nothing else but this work—ranging the guns of our artillery on those of the enemy; sometimes, however, the target was an ammunition dump, a bridge, or a similar strategical point that the higher command decided must be destroyed.

119

It was by no means as simple as it might appear, and the crew of the machine told off for the task were expected to remain at their post until each gun of the battery for which it was working had scored a hit, after which, without altering the range, they might continue to fire shot after shot at the target until it was wiped out of existence.

If the pilot was lucky, or clever, and the battery for which he was spotting good at its work, the job might be finished in an hour—or it might take three hours; and during the whole of that period the artillery aeroplane would have to circle continuously over the same spot, itself a target for every archie battery within range, and the prey of every prowling enemy scout.

Whether the task was more monotonous for the pilot, who had to watch his own battery for the flash of the gun and then the target for the bursting shell, signalling its position by the Morse code, or for the observer, whose duty it was not to watch the ground (as might reasonably be supposed) but the sky around for danger while the pilot was engrossed in his work, is a matter of opinion.

In any case, Biggles neither knew nor cared, but of one thing he was certain; circling in the same spot for hours was neither amusing nor interesting. Hence the unusual expression on his face as he made his way eastwards towards the Lines, to find the British battery for which he was detailed, and the enemy battery which the British guns proposed to wipe out. This being his first attempt at art obs, he was by no means sure that he would be able to find either of them, and this may have been another reason why he was not flying with his usual enthusiasm.

Now, in order that the operation known as art obs

should be understood, a few words of explanation are necessary, although the procedure is quite simple once the idea has been grasped. Biggles, like all other R.F.C. officers, had been given a certain amount of instruction at his training school, but as he had hoped to be sent to a scout squadron, which never did this class of work, he had not concentrated on the instruction as much as he might have done.

Briefly, this was the programme, for which, as a general rule, wireless was used, although occasionally a system of Very lights was employed. Wireless, at the time of which we are speaking, was of a primitive nature. The pilot, by means of an aerial which he lowered below the machine, could only send messages; he could not receive them. The gunners, in order to convey a message to the pilot, had to lay out strips of white material in the form of letters. The target was considered to be the centre of an imaginary clock, twelve o'clock being due north. Six o'clock was therefore due south, and the other cardinal points in their relative positions. Imaginary rings drawn round the target were lettered A, B, C, D, E, and F. These were 50, 100, 200, 300, 400, and 500 yards away respectively.

When the gunners started work, if the first shell dropped, say, one hundred yards away and due north of the target, all the pilot had to do was to signal B 12. 'B' meant that the shell burst one hundred yards away, and the '12' meant at twelve o'clock on the imaginary clock face. Thus the gunners were able to mark on their map exactly were the shell had fallen, and were therefore able to adjust their gun for the next shot. As another example, a shell bursting three hundred yards to the right of the target would be signalled D 3, or three hundred yards away at three o'clock. In this way

121

the pilot was saved the trouble of tapping out long messages.

Briefly, while the 'shoot', as it was called, was in progress, the pilot continued to correct the aim of the gunners until they scored a hit. The first gun was now ranged on the target. The second gun was ranged in the same way, and so it went on until every gun in the battery was ranged on the target. Then they fired a salvo (all guns together) which the pilot would signal 'mostly O.K.', and thereafter the battery would pump out shells as fast as it could until the enemy guns were put out of action.

This is what Biggles had to do.

Approaching the Line, he quickly picked out the battery of guns for which he was to act as the 'eyes', and after a rather longer search he found the enemy battery, neatly camouflaged, and quite oblivious to the treat in store for it. He reached for his buzzer, which was a small key on the inside of his cockpit, and sent out a series of letter B's in the Morse code, meaning 'Are you receiving my signals?'

This was at once acknowledged by the battery, which put out three strips of white cloth in the form of a letter K—the recognition signal.

Biggles was rather amused, not to say surprised, at this prompt response. It struck him as strange that by pressing a lever in the cockpit he could make people on the ground do things. In fact, it was rather fun. He reached for his buzzer again, and sent K Q, K Q, K Q, meaning 'Are you ready to fire?' (All signals were repeated three times) Biggles, of course, could not hear his own signals; they were sent out by wireless, which was picked up on a small receiving set at the battery's listening-post.

The white strips of cloth on the ground at once took the form of a letter L, meaning 'ready.'

'G—G—G, buzzed Biggles. G was the signal to fire. Instantly a gun flashed, and Biggles, who was becoming engrossed in his task, turned his machine, eyes seeking the distant objective to watch the shell burst.

'Hi!'

The shrill shout from Mark Way, his observer, made him jump. Mark was pointing. Falling like a meteor from the sky was an Albatros, silver with scarlet wing-tips. The sun flashed on the gleaming wings, turning them into streaks of fire, on the ends of which were two large black crosses.

Biggles frowned and waved his hand impatiently. 'Make him keep out of the way!' he yelled, and turned back to watch the shell burst. But he was too late. A faint cloud of white smoke was drifting across the landscape near the target, but it was already dispersing, so it was impossible to say just where the shell had burst.

'Dash it!' muttered Biggles, turning and feeling for his buzzer. 'Now I've got to do it again.' G—G—G, he signalled.

There was a moment's pause before the gun flashed again, the gunners possibly wondering why he had not registered their first shot. Biggles turned again towards the target, but before the shell exploded the chatter of a machine-gun made him look up quickly. The Albatros had fired a burst at them, swung up in a climbing turn, and was now coming back at them.

'You cock-eyed son of a coot!' Biggles roared at Mark, as he turned to meet the attack. At this rate the job would never be done. 'And I'll give you something to fling yourself about for, you interfering hound!' he growled at the approaching Albatros. Curiously, it did not occur to him that their lives were in any particular danger, a fact which reveals the confidence that was coming to him as a result of experience. He was not in the least afraid of a single German aeroplane. However, he had still much to learn.

His windscreen flew to pieces, and something whanged against his engine. Again the Hun pulled up in a wonderful zoom, twisting cunningly out of the hail of lead that Mark's gun spat at him. He levelled out, turned, and came down at them again.

For the first time it dawned on Biggles that the man in the machine was no ordinary pilot; he was an artist, a man who knew just what he was doing. Further, he had obviously singled him out for destruction. Well, the battery would have to wait, that was all.

Biggles brought his machine round to face the new attack, pulling his nose up to give Mark the chance of a shot. But before he could fire, the Hun had swerved in an amazing fashion to some point behind them, and a steady stream of bullets began to rip through the wings of the British machine. Again Biggles turned swiftly—but the Hun was not there.

Rat-tat-tat-tat-tat—a stream of lead poured up from below, one of the bullets jarring against the root of the joystick with a jerk that flung it out of his hand.

'You artful swipe!' rasped Biggles, flinging the F.E. round in such a steep turn that Mark nearly went overboard.

'Sorry!' Biggles' lips formed the words, but he was pointing at the Hun, who had climbed up out of range, but was now coming down again like a thunderbolt, guns spurting long streams of flame. Mark was shooting, too, their bullets seeming to meet between the two machines. The Albatros came so close that Biggles could distinctly see the tappets of the other's engine working, and the pilot's face peering at them over the side of his cockpit. Then he swerved, and Biggles breathed a sigh of relief.

But he was congratulating himself too soon. The Albatros twisted like a hawk, dived, turned as he dived, and then came up at them like a rocket. To Biggles this manœuvre was so unexpected, so seemingly impossible, that he could hardly believe it, and he experienced a real spasm of fright. He no longer thought of the battery below; he knew he was fighting the battle of his life, his first real duel against a man who knew his job thoroughly.

During the next five minutes he learnt many things, things that were to stand him in good stead later on, and the fact that he escaped was due, not to his ability, but to a circumstance for which he was duly grateful. Twice he had made a break, in the hope of reaching the Lines. For during the combat, as was so often the case, the wind had blown them steadily over enemy country, but each time the enemy was there first, cutting off his escape. Mark had not been idle, but the wily German seldom gave him a fair chance for even a fleeting shot, much less a 'sitter*.'

The Hun seemed to attack from all points of the compass at once. Biggles turned to face his aggressor in a new quarter—the fellow was always in the most unexpected quarter—and dived furiously at him; too furiously. He overshot, and, before he could turn, the Hun was behind him, pouring hot lead into his engine.

* A target moving directly away from the gunner and therefore a relatively easy target.

He knew that he was lost. Something grazed his arm, and with horror he saw blood running down Mark's face. He crouched low as he tried to turn out of the hail of lead. The bullets stopped abruptly as he came round, glaring wildly. The Hun had gone. Presently Biggles made him out, dropping like a stone towards the safety of his own territory. He could hardly believe his eyes. He had been cold meat* for the enemy pilot, and he knew it. Why, then—But Mark was pointing upwards, grinning.

Biggles' eyes followed the outstretched finger, and he saw a formation of nine Sopwith Pups sweeping across the sky five thousand feet above them. He grinned back, trembling slightly from reaction.

'By gosh, that was a close one! I'll remember that piece of silver-and-red furniture, and keep out of his way!' he vowed, inwardly marvelling, and wondering how the Boche pilot had been able to concentrate his attack on him in the way that he had, and yet watch the surrounding sky for possible danger. He knew that if there had been a thousand machines in the sky he would not have seen them, yet the Hun had not failed to see the approaching Pups when they were miles away. 'Pretty good!' he muttered admiringly. 'I'll remember that!'

And he did. It was his first real lesson in the art of air combat. His pride suffered when he thought of the way the Hun had 'made rings round him,' and he was not quite as confident of himself as he had been, yet he knew that the experience was worth all the anxiety it had caused him.

* Slang: an easy victim

But what about the enemy battery? He looked down, and saw that he had drifted miles away from it.

He snorted his disgust at the archie that opened up on him the instant the Hun had departed, and made his way back to his original rendezvous. The calico 'L' was still lying on the ground near the battery. Although he did not know it, the gunners had watched the combat with the greatest interest, and were agreeably surprised to see him returning so soon after the attack.

G—G—G, he buzzed. The gun flashed, and the F.E. rocked suddenly, almost as if it had been shaken by an invisible hand.

Biggles started, and looked at his altimeter. In the fight he had, as usual, lost height, and he was now below three thousand feet. He knew that the great howitzer shell had passed close to him, so he started climbing as quickly as possible to get above its culminating point. The archie smoke was so thick that he had great difficulty in seeing the shell burst. It was a good five hundred yards short. F6—F6—F6 he signalled; and then, after a brief interval: G—G—G. He watched with interest for the next shell to burst, but it was farther from the mark than the first one had been.

'If they don't improve faster than that we shall still be here when the bugles blow "Cease fire!" ' he muttered in disgust.

The next shot was better, but it was a good four hundred yards beyond the mark and slightly to the right. D1—D1—D1 he tapped out as he turned in a wide circle and then back again towards the target on a course which, had he been a sky-writer, would have traced a large figure eight—the usual method of the artillery spotting 'plane, which allowed the pilot to see both his own battery and the target in turn. It also kept the archie gunners guessing which way he was going next.

An hour later Biggles was still at it, and the first gun had got no closer than two hundred yards to its mark. The fascination of the pastime was beginning to wear off; indeed it was already bordering on the monotonous. 'This is a nice game played slow,' he shouted. 'Why don't those fellows learn to shoot?'

He was falling into a sort of reverie, sending his signals automatically, when he was again brought back to realities by a yell from Mark. He looked round sharply, and fixed his eyes on a small, straight-winged machine that was climbing up towards them from the east. The German anti-aircraft gunners must have seen it, too, for the archie died away abruptly as they ceased fire rather than take the risk of hitting their own man. There was no mistaking the machine. It was the red-and-silver Albatros.

Biggles was not to be caught napping twice. He turned his nose towards home and dived, only pulling out when he felt he was a safe distance over the Lines. He turned in time to see his late adversary gliding away into a haze that was forming over the other side of the Lines.

Once more he returned to his post, and signalled to the gunners to fire, but even as the gun flashed, he heard the *rat-tat-tat-tat* of a machine-gun, and the disconcerting *flac-flac-flac* of bullets ripping through his wings.

'You cunning hound!' he grated, seething with rage as he caught a glimpse of the red-and-silver wings of his old adversary as it darted in from the edge of the haze in which it had taken cover. It was another tip in the art of stalking that he did not forget. At the moment he was concerned only with the destruction of his persistent tormentor, and he attacked with a fury that he had never felt before. He wanted to see the Albatros crash—he wanted to see that more than he had ever wanted to see anything in his life. Completely mastered by his anger, he made no attempt to escape, but positively flung the F.E. at the black-crossed machine. This was evidently something the Hun did not expect, and he was nearly caught napping.

Mark got in a good burst before the Hun swerved out of his line of fire. Biggles yanked the F.E. round in a turn that might have torn its wings off, and plunged down on the tail of the Albatros. He saw the pilot look back over his shoulder, and felt a curious intuition as to which way he would turn. He saw the Hun's rudder start to move, which confirmed it, and, without waiting for the Albatros actually to answer to its controls, he whipped the F.E. round in a vertical bank.

The Hun had turned the same way, as he knew he must, and he was still on its tail, less than fifty yards away. It was a brilliant move, although at the time he did not know it; it showed anticipation in the moves of the games that marked the expert in air combat. He thrust the stick forward with both hands until he could see the dark gases flowing out of his enemy's exhaust-pipe; saw the pilot's blond moustache, saw the goggled eyes staring at him, and saw Mark's bullets sewing a leaden seam across his fuselage.

The Hun turned over on to its back and then spun, Biggles watching it with savage satisfaction that turned to chagrin when, a thousand feet from the ground, the red-and-silver machine levelled out and sped towards home. The pilot had deliberately thrown his machine out of control in order to mislead his enemy—another trick Biggles never forgot.

'We've given the blighter something to think about, at any rate!' he thought moodily, as he turned to the battery.

The gunners were waiting for him, but, to his annoyance and disgust, the first shot went wide; it was, in fact, farther away from the target than the first one had been.

'This is a game for mugs!' he snarled. 'As far as I can see, there's nothing to prevent this going on for ever. Don't those fellows ever hit what they shoot at?'

He was getting tired, for they had now been in the air for more than three hours, and, as far as he could see, they were no nearer the end than when they started. The archie was getting troublesome again, and he was almost in despair when an idea struck him.

'H.Q. want that Hun battery blown up, do they?' he thought. 'All right, they shall have it blown up—but I know a quicker way of doing it than this.' He turned suddenly and raced back towards his aerodrome, sending the C H I signal as he went. C H I in the code meant 'I am going home.' He landed and taxied up to the hangars.

'Fill her up with petrol and hang two 112-pounder bombs on the racks—and make it snappy!' he told the flight-sergeant. Then he hurried down to the mess and called up on the telephone the battery for which he had been acting.

'Look here,' he began hotly, 'I'm getting tired, trying to put you ham-fisted—What's that? Colonel? Sorry, sir!' He collected himself quickly, realizing that he had made a bad break. The brigade colonel was on the other end of the wire. 'Well, the fact is, sir,' he went on, 'I've just thought of an idea that may speed things up a bit. The target is a bit too low for you to see, I think, and—well, if I laid an egg on that spot it would show your gun-layers just where the target is. What's that, sir? Unusual? Yes, I know it is, but if it comes off it will save a lot of time and ammunition. If it fails I'll go on with the shoot again in the ordinary way. Yes, sir—very good, sir—I'll be over in about a quarter of an hour.'

He put the receiver down, and, ignoring Toddy's cry of protest, hurried back to the sheds. Mark looked at him in astonishment when he climbed back into his seat. 'Haven't you had enough of it, or have you got a rush of blood to the brain?' he asked coldly.

'Brain, my foot!' snapped Biggles. 'I'm going to give those Huns a rush of something. I've done figures of eight until I'm dizzy. Round and round the blinking mulberry-bush, with every archie battery for miles practising on me. I'm going to liven things up a bit. You coming, or are you going to stay at home? Things are likely to get warmish.'

'Of course I'm coming!'

'Well, come on, let's get on with it.'

He took off, and climbed back to the old position between the batteries, but he sent no signal. He did not even let his aerial out. He began to circle as if he was going to continue the 'shoot,' but then, turning suddenly, he jammed his joystick forward with both hands and tore down at the German gunpits. For a few moments he left the storm of archie far behind, but as the gunners perceived his intention, it broke out again with renewed intensity, and the sky around him became an inferno of smoke and fire.

Crouching low in his cockpit, his lips pressed in a

straight line, he did not swerve an inch. It was neck or nothing now, and he knew it. His only hope of success lay in speed. Any delay could only make his task more perilous, for already the artillery observers on the ground would be ringing up the *Jagdstaffeln* (German fighter squadrons), calling on them to deal with this Englander who must either be mad or intoxicated.

He could see his objective clearly, and he made for it by the shortest possible course. Twice shells flamed so close to him that he felt certain the machine must fall in pieces out of his hands. The wind screamed in his wires and struts and plucked at his face and shoulders. A flying wire trailed uselessly from the root of an inter-plane strut, cut through as clean as a carrot by shrapnel, beating a wild tattoo on the fabric.

Mark was crouching low in the front cockpit, blood oozing from a flesh wound in his forehead, caused by flying glass.

It is difficult to keep track of time in such moments. The period from the start of his dive until he actually reached the objective was probably not more than three minutes—four at the most—but to Biggles it seemed an eternity. Time seemed to stand still; trifling incidents assumed enormous proportions, occurring as they did with slow deliberation. Thus, he saw a mobile archie battery, the gun mounted on a motor-lorry, tearing along the road. He saw it stop, and the well-trained team leap to their allotted stations; saw the long barrel swing round towards him, and the first flash of flame from its muzzle. He felt certain the shot would hit him, and wondered vaguely what the fellows at the squadron would say about his crazy exploit when he did not return.

The shell burst fifty feet in front of him, an orange

spurt of flame that was instantly engulfed in a whirling ball of black smoke. He went straight through it, his propeller churning the smoke to the four winds, and he gasped as the acrid fumes bit into his lungs.

He saw the gun fire again, and felt the plunging machine lurch as the projectile passed desperately close. He did not look back, but he knew his track must be marked by a solid-looking plume of black smoke visible for miles. He wondered grimly what the colonel to whom he had spoken on the telephone was thinking about it, for he would be watching the proceedings.

Down—down—down, but there was no sensation of falling. The machine seemed to be stationary, with the earth rushing up to meet him. At five hundred feet the enemy gun-crew, who could not resist the temptation of watching him, bolted for their dug-outs like rabbits when a fox-terrier appears. Perhaps they had thought it impossible for the British machine to survive such a maelstrom of fire. Anyway, they left it rather late.

Not until he was within a hundred feet of the ground did Biggles start to pull the machine out of its dive, slowly, in case he stripped his wings off as they encountered the resistance of the air. Mark's gun was stuttering, bullets kicking up the earth about the gunpits in case one of the German gunners, bolder than the rest, decided to try his luck with a rifle or machine-gun.

The end came suddenly. Biggles saw the target leap towards him, and at what must have been less than fifty feet, he pulled his bomb toggle, letting both bombs go together. Then he zoomed high.

Such was his speed that he was back at a thousand feet when the two bombs burst simultaneously; but the blast of air lifted the F.E. like a piece of tissue paper. He fought the machine back under control, and, without

133

waiting to see the result of the explosion, tore in a zigzag course towards his own battery.

At three thousand feet he levelled out and looked back. He had succeeded beyond his wildest hopes, and knew that he must have hit the enemy ammunition dump. Flames were still leaping skyward in a dense pall of black smoke.

With a feeling of satisfaction, he lowered his aerial. His fingers sought the buzzer key and tapped out the letters G—G—G. The British gun flashed instantly. The gun-layer was no longer firing blind, and the shot landed in the middle of the smoking mass.

O.K.—O.K.—O.K. tapped Biggles exultantly.

The second gun of the battery sent its projectile hurtling towards the Boche gunpits. It was less than one hundred yards short, but with visible target to shoot at it required only two or three minutes to get it ranged on the target. The others followed.

G—D—O, G—D—O, G—D—O, tapped Biggles enthusiastically, for G—D—O was the signal to the gunners to begin firing in their own time. The four guns were ranged on the target, and they no longer needed his assistance. With salvo after salvo they pounded the enemy gunpits out of existence, Biggles and Mark watching the work of destruction with the satisfaction of knowing their job had been well done.

Then they looked at each other, and a slow smile spread over Biggles's face. C H I, C H I, C H I (I am going home) he tapped, and turned towards the aerodrome. Instantly his smile gave way to a frown of annoyance. What were the fools doing? A cloud of white archie smoke had appeared just in front of him. White archie!

Only British archie was white! Why were they shoot-

134

ing at him? The answer struck him at the same moment that Mark yelled and pointed. He lifted up his eyes. Straight across their front, in the direction they must go, but two thousand feet above them, a long line of white archie bursts trailed across the sky. In front of them, always it seemed just out of their reach, sped a small, straight-winged plane, its top wings were slightly longer than the lower ones.

Two thoughts rushed into Biggles' mind at once. The first was that the gunners on the ground had fired the burst close to him to warn him of his danger, and the second was that the German machine was an Albatros. There was no mistaking the shark-like fuselage. Something, an instinct which he could not have explained, told him it was their old red-and-silver enemy. He was right—it was. At that moment it turned, and the sun revealed its colours. It dived towards the British machine, and the archie gunners were compelled to cease fire for fear of hitting the F.E.

There was no escape. Biggles would have avoided combat had it been possible, for he was rather worried about the damage the F.E. might have suffered during its dive. Mark glowered as he turned his gun towards the persistent enemy, and then crouched low, waiting for it come into effective range.

But the Hun had no intention of making things so easy. His machine had already been badly knocked about in the last effort, an insult which he was probably anxious to avenge, and intended to see that no such thing occurred again. At two hundred feet he started shooting, and Biggles pulled his nose up to meet him. From that position he would not swerve, for it was a point of honour in the R.F.C. never to turn away from a frontal attack, even though the result was a collision.

Just what happened after that he was never quite sure. In trying to keep his nose on the Hun, who was still coming down from above, he got it too high up, with the result that one of two courses was open to him. Either he could let the F.E. stall, in which case the Hun would get a 'sitting' shot at him at the moment of stalling—a chance he was not likely to miss—or he could pull the machine right over in a loop. He chose the latter course.

As he came out of the loop, he looked round wildly for the Hun. For a fleeting fraction of an instant he saw him at his own level, not more than twenty or thirty feet away, going in the opposite direction. At the same moment he was nearly flung out of his seat by a jar that jerked him sideways and made the F.E. quiver from propeller boss to tail skid. His heart stood still, for he felt certain that his top 'plane, or some other part of the machine, had broken away, but to his utter amazement it answered to the controls, and he soon had it on an even keel.

Mark was yelling, jabbing downwards with his finger. Biggles looked over the side of his cockpit. The Hun was gliding towards his own Lines.

There seemed to be something wrong with the Albatros—something missing; and for the moment Biggles could not make out what it was. Then he saw. It had no propeller! How the miracle had happened he did not know, and he had already turned to follow it to administer the knock-out when another yell from Mark made him change his mind—quickly. A formation of at least twenty Huns were tearing towards the scene.

Biggles waited for no more. He put his nose down for home and not until the aerodrome loomed upon the horizon did he ease the pace. He remembered his aerial,

136

and took hold of the handle of the reel to wind in the long length of copper wire with its lead plummet on the end to keep it extended.

The reel was in place, but there was no aerial, and he guessed what had happened. He should have wound it in immediately he had sent the C H I signal, and he knew that if he had done so he would in all probability by now be lying in a heap of charred wreckage in No Man's Land. He had forgotten to wind in, and to that fact he probably owed his life. When he had swung round after his loop, the wire, with the plummet on the end, must have swished round like a flail and struck the Boche machine, smashing its propeller!

The C.O. was waiting for them on the tarmac when they landed. There was a curious expression on his face, but several other officers who were standing behind him were smiling expectantly.

'You were detailed for the art obs show to-day, I think, Bigglesworth,' began Major Paynter coldly.

'That is so, sir,' said Biggles.

'Wing has just been on the telephone to me, and so has the commander of the battery for whom you were acting. Will you please tell me precisely what has happened?'

Briefly Biggles related what had occurred. The major did not move a muscle until he had finished. Then he looked at him with an expressionless face. 'Far be it from me to discourage zeal or initiative,' he said, 'but we cannot have this sort of thing. Your instructions were quite clear—you were to do the shoot for the artillery. You had no instructions to use bombs, and your action might have resulted in the loss of a valuable machine. I must discourage this excess of exuberance,' went on the C.O. 'As a punishment, you will return this afternoon to the scene of the affair, taking a camera with you. I shall require a photograph of the wrecked German battery on my desk by one hour after sunset. Is that clear?'

'Perfectly, sir.'

'That's all, then. Don't let it happen again. The artillery think we are trying to do them out of their jobs; but it was a jolly good show, all the same!' he concluded, with something as near a chuckle as his dignity would permit.

Chapter 11
The Camera

There was no hurry. Major Paynter, the C.O., had not named any particular hour for the 'show'. He had said that the photographs must be delivered to him by one hour after sunset and there were still five hours of daylight.

With Mark, Biggles made his way to the mess for a rest, and over coffee they learned some news that set every member of the squadron agog with excitement. Toddy, the Recording Officer, divulged that the equipment of the squadron was to be changed, the change to take effect as quickly as possible. In future they were to fly Bristol Fighters.*

It transpired that Toddy had been aware of the impending change for some time, but the orders had been marked 'secret,' so he had not been allowed to make the information public. But now that ferry pilots were to start delivering the new machines, there was no longer any need to keep silent. They might expect the Bristols to arrive at any time, Toddy told them, and A Flight, by reason of its seniority, was to have the first.

Biggles, being in A Flight, was overjoyed. He had grown very attached to his old F.E. which had given him good service, but it had always been a source of irritation to him, as the pilot, that the actual shooting

* Two-seater biplane fighter with remarkable manoeuvrability.

had perforce been left to Mark. In future they would both have guns, to say nothing of a machine of higher performance.

In the excitement caused by the news the time passed quickly, and it was nearly two-thirty when they walked towards the sheds in order to proceed with the work for which they had been detailed.

Biggles' shoulder had been grazed by a bullet in the morning's combat with the red-and-silver Albatros, but it caused him no inconvenience, and he did not bother to report it. Neither had Mark's wound been very severe, not much more than a scratch, as he himself said, and it did not occur to him to go 'sick' with it. It was a clean cut in his forehead about an inch long, caused by a splinter of flying glass. He had washed it with antiseptic, stuck a piece of plaster over it, and dismissed it from his mind. On their way to the hangars they met the medical officer on his way back from visiting some mechanics who were sick in their huts. They were about to pass him with a cheerful nod when his eyes fell on the strip of court-plaster on Mark's forehead. He stopped and raised his eyebrows. 'Hallo, what have you been up to?' he asked.

'Up to?' echoed Mark, not understanding.

'What have you done to your head?'

'Oh—that! Nothing to speak of. I stopped a piece of loose glass in a little affair with a Hun this morning,' replied Mark casually.

'Let me have a look at it.' The M.O. removed the piece of court-plaster and examined the wound critically. 'Where are you off to now?' he inquired.

'I've got a short show to do with Bigglesworth.'

'Short or long, you'll do no more flying to-day, my boy; you get back to your quarters and rest for a bit.

Too much cold air on that cut, and we shall have you down with erysipelas. I'll speak to the C.O.'.

'But—' began Mark, in astonishment.

'There's no "but" about it,' said the M.O. tersely. 'You do as you're told, my lad. Twelve hours' rest will put you right. Off you go!'

Mark looked at Biggles hopelessly.

'Doc's right, Mark,' said Biggles, nodding. 'I ought to have had the sense to know it myself. I'll bet your skull aches even now.'

'Not it!' snorted Mark.

'That's all right, doc, I'll find another partner,' asserted Biggles. 'See you later, Mark.'

He made his way to the Squadron Office and reported the matter to Toddy.

'You wouldn't like to take one of the new fellows, I suppose?' suggested Toddy, referring to two new observer officers who had reported for duty the previous evening. 'I think they're about somewhere.'

'Certainly I will,' replied Biggles. 'Someone will have to take them over some time, so the sooner the better. It's only a short show, anyway.'

Toddy dispatched an orderly at the double to find the new officers, and Biggles awaited their arrival impatiently. He had already spoken to them, so they were not quite strangers, but they were of such opposite types that he could not make up his mind which one to choose. Harris was a mere lad, fair-haired and blue-eyed, straight from school. He had failed in his tests as a pilot, and was satisfied to take his chances as an aerial gunner rather than go into the infantry. Culver, the other, was an older man, a cavalry captain who had seen service in the Dardanelles before he had transferred to the R.F.C.

141

They came in quickly, anxious to know what was in the wind. Briefly, Biggles told them and explained the position. 'Toss for it,' he suggested. 'That's the fairest way. All I ask is that whoever comes will keep his eyes wide open and shoot straight, if there is any shooting to be done.'

Harris won the toss, and with difficulty concealed his satisfaction, for although Biggles was unaware of it, he—Biggles—had already achieved the reputation of being one of the best pilots in the squadron.

'Good enough. Get into your flying kit and get a good gun,' Biggles said shortly. 'I'll go and start up.'

He was satisfied but by no means enthusiastic about taking the new man over. Few experienced pilots felt entirely happy in the company of men new to the job and who had not had an opportunity of proving themselves. It was not that cowardice was anticipated. Biggles knew what all experienced flyers knew; that a man could be as plucky as they make them when on the ground—might have shown himself to be a fearless fighter in trench warfare—but until he had been put to the test it was impossible to say how he would behave in his first air combat; how he would react to the terrifying sensation of hearing bullets ripping through spruce and canvas.

As a matter of fact, it was worse for an observer than it was for a pilot. It needed a peculiar kind of temperament, or courage, to stand up and face twin machine-guns spouting death at point-blank range; not only to stand up, but calmly align the sights of a Lewis gun and return the fire.

There was only one way to find out if a man could do it and that was to take him into the air. There were some who could not do it, in the same way that there were cases of officers who could not face 'archie.' And after one or two trips over the Line this was apparent to others, even if it was not admitted. And it needed a certain amount of courage to confess. But it was better for an officer to be frank with his C.O. and tell the truth, rather than throw away his life, and an aeroplane. Officers reporting 'sick' in this way were either transferred to ground duties or sent home for instructional work.

Biggles wore a worried frown, therefore, as he walked up to the sheds. He realized for the first time just how much confidence he had in Mark, and the comfort he derived from the knowledge that he had a reliable man in the observer's cockpit.

They took their places in the machine, and after Biggles had given Harris a reassuring smile he took off and headed for the strafed* German battery. He would gain all the height he needed on the way to the Lines, for he proposed to take the photographs from not higher than five thousand feet. A good deal of cloud had drifted up from the west, which was annoying, for it was likely to make his task more difficult. It would not prevent him reaching his objective, but the C.O. would certainly not be pleased if he was handed a nice photograph of a large white cloud.

He crossed the Lines at four thousand, still climbing, and zigzagged his way through the archie in the direction of the wrecked German battery. He noted with satisfaction that his new partner took his baptism of anti-aircraft fire well, for he turned and smiled cheerfully, even if the smile was a trifle forced. He was rather

* To strafe: to bombard a target with gunfire, artillery shells or machine-gun fire.

143

pale, but Biggles paid no attention to that. There are few men who do not change colour the first time they find themselves under fire.

The sky seemed clear of aircraft, although the clouds formed good cover for lurking enemy scouts, and he began to hope the job might be done in record time. He skirted a massive pile of cloud, and there, straight before him, lay the scene of his morning exploit. A grin spread over his face as he surveyed the huge craters that marked the spot where the enemy battery had once hidden itself; the job had been done thoroughly, and headquarters could hardly fail to be pleased.

After a swift glance around he put his nose down and dived, and then, swinging upwind, he began to expose his plates. In five minutes he had been over the whole area twice, covering not only the actual site of the battery, but the surrounding country. With the satisfaction of knowing that his job had been well done, he turned for home. 'Good!' he muttered. 'That's that!'

Swinging round another towering mass of opaque mist he ran into a one-sided dog-fight with a suddenness that almost caught him off his guard. A lone F.E. was fighting a battle with five enemy Albatroses.

Now, according to the rules of war flying, this was no affair of Biggles'. Strictly speaking, the duty of a pilot with a definite mission was to fulfil that mission and return home as quickly as possible; but needless to say, this was not always adhered to. Few pilots could resist the temptation of butting into a dog-fight, or attacking an enemy machine if one was seen. To leave a comrade fighting overwhelming odds was unthinkable.

Biggles certainly did not think about it. The combat was going on at about his own altitude, and although the F.E. had more than one opportunity of dodging into the clouds and thereby escaping, the pilot had obviously made up his mind to see the matter through.

Biggles' lips parted in a smile and he barged into the fight. Then, to his horror, he saw that his gunner was not even looking at the milling machines. He had not even seen them. It seemed incredible. But there it was. And Biggles, remembering his own blindness when he was a beginner, forgave him. Harris was gazing at the ground immediately below with an almost bored expression on his face.

'Hi!' roared Biggles, with the full power of his lungs. 'Get busy!'

Harris' start of astonishment and horror as he looked up just as a blue Albatros dashed across his nose was almost comical; but he grabbed his gun like lightning and sent a stream of lead after the whirling Hun.

Biggles dashed in close to the other F.E. to make his presence known. A swift signal greeting passed between the two pilots, and then they set about the work on hand.

The fight did not last many minutes, but it was red-hot while it lasted. One Albatros went down in flames; another glided down out of control with its engine evidently out of action. The other three dived for home. Biggles straightened his machine and looked around for the other F.E., but it had disappeared. He had not seen it go, so whether it had been shot down, or had merely proceeded on its way, he was unable to ascertain.

Harris was standing up surveying their own machine ruefully, for it had been badly shot about. Biggles caught his eye and nodded approvingly. 'You'll do!' he told himself; for the boy had undoubtedly acquitted

145

himself well. Then he continued on his course for the aerodrome.

He reached it without further incident and taxied in, eyes on a brand new Bristol Fighter that was standing on the tarmac. The photographic sergeant hurried towards him to collect the camera and plates, in order to develop them forthwith. Biggles jumped to the ground, and was about to join the group of officers admiring the Bristol when a cry from the N.C.O. made him turn.

'What's the matter?' he asked quickly.

'Sorry sir, but look!' said the sergeant apologetically.

Biggles' eyes opened wide as they followed the N.C.O.'s pointing finger, and then he made a gesture of anger and disgust. The camera was bent all shapes, and the plate container was a perforated wreck. There was no need to wonder how it had happened; a burst of fire from one of the enemy machines had reduced the camera to a twisted ruin.

He could see at a glance that the plates were spoilt. His journey had been in vain. Looking over the machine thoroughly for the first time he saw that the damage was a good deal worse than he had thought. Two wires had been severed and one of the hinges of his elevators shot off. The machine had brought him home safely, but in its present condition it was certainly not safe to fly.

'What's the matter?' asked Mapleton, his flight-commander, seeing that something was wrong.

Briefly, Biggles explained the catastrophe.

'What are you going to do about it?' asked Mabs.

'I'll have to do the show again, that's all about it!' replied Biggles disgustedly. 'The Old Man was very decent about this morning's effort. He's waiting for these photos; I can't let him down.'

'You can't fly that machine again today, that's a certainty.'

'So I see.'

'Would you like to try the Bristol?'

Biggles started. 'I'd say I would!'

'You can have it if you like, but for the love of Mike don't hurt it. It's been allotted to me, so it's my pigeon. She's all O.K. and in fighting trim. I was just off to try her out myself.'

'That's jolly sporting of you,' declared Biggles. 'I shan't be long, and I'll take care of her. Come on, Harris, get your guns—and get me another camera, sergeant; look sharp, it will soon be dark.'

In a few minutes Biggles was in the air again, on his way to the enemy battery for the third time that day. He had no difficulty in flying the Bristol, which was an easy machine to fly, and after a few practice turns he felt quite at home in it.

He noticed with dismay that the clouds were thickening, and he was afraid that they might totally obscure the objective. Twice, as he approached it, he thought he caught sight of a lurking shadow, dodging through the heavy cloud-bank above him, but each time he looked it had vanished before he could make sure.

'There's a Hun up there, watching me, or I'm a Dutchman,' he mused uneasily. 'I hope that kid in the back seat will keep his eyes skinned.' He shot through a small patch of cloud and distinctly saw another machine disappear into a cloud just ahead and above him. It was an Albatros, painted red and silver. 'So it's you, is it?' he muttered, frowning, for the idea of taking on his old antagonist with a comparatively

147

untried gunner in the back seat did not fill him with enthusiasm. With Mark it would have been a different matter.

He turned sharply into another cloud and approached the objective on a zigzag course, never flying straight for more than a few moments at a time. He knew that this would leave the watcher, if he were still watching, in doubt as to his actual course, but it was nervy work, knowing that an attack might be launched at any moment.

As he expected, he found the battery concealed under a thick layer of grey cloud, but he throttled back and came out below it at two thousand feet. Instantly he was the target for a dozen archie batteries, but he ignored them and flew level until he had exposed all his plates. He was feeling more anxious than he had ever felt before in the air, not so much for his own safety as for the safety of Mab's machine, so it was with something like a sigh of relief that he finished his task, jammed the throttle wide open, and zoomed upwards through the opaque ceiling.

The instant he cleared the top side of the cloud the rattle of a machine-gun came to his ears and the Bristol quivered as a stream of lead ripped through it. He whirled round just in time to see the red-and-silver 'plane zoom over him, not twenty feet away. Why hadn't Harris fired? Was he asleep, the young fool? With his brow black as thunder Biggles twisted round in his seat and looked behind him. Harris was lying in a crumpled heap on the side of his cockpit.

Biggles went ice-cold all over. The corners of his mouth turned down. 'He's got him!' he breathed, and then exposing his teeth, 'You hound!' he grated, and

148

dragged the Bristol round on its axis and in the direction of the Albatros, now circling to renew the attack.

If the Boche pilot supposed that the British machine would now seek to escape he was mistaken. Unknowingly, he was faced with the most dangerous of all opponents, a pilot who was fighting mad. A clever, calculating enemy, fighting in cold blood, was a foe to be respected; but a pilot seeing red and seething with hate was much worse. For the first time, the war had become a personal matter with Biggles, and he would have rammed his adversary if he could have reached him.

The pilot in the black-crossed machine seemed to realize this, for he suddenly broke off the combat and sought to escape by diving towards the nearest cloud. Biggles was behind him in a flash, eye to the Aldis sight. Farther and yet farther forward he pushed the control-stick, and the distance rapidly closed between them.

The Hun saw death on his tail and twisted like an eel, but the Bristol stuck to him as if connected by an invisible wire. A hundred feet—fifty feet—Biggles drew nearer, but still he did not fire. The glittering arc of his propeller was nearly touching the other's elevators. The cross-wires of the Aldis sight cut across the tail, crept along the fuselage to the brown-helmeted head in the cockpit.

Biggles knew that he had won and was filled with a savage exultation. He was so close that every detail of the Boche machine was indelibly imprinted on his brain. He could see the tappets of the Mercedes engine working, and the dark smoke pouring from its exhaust. He could even see the patches over the old bullet holes in the lower wings. His gloved hand sought the Bowden lever, closed on it, and gripped it hard. Orange flame darted from the muzzle of his gun and the harsh metallic clatter of the cocking handle filled his ears. The Albatros jerked upwards, the Bristol still on its tail. A tongue of scarlet flame licked along its side, and a cloud of black smoke poured out of the engine. The pilot covered his face with his hands.

Biggles turned away, feeling suddenly limp. He seemed to have awakened with a shock from a vivid dream. Where was he? He did not know. He saw the Hun break up just as it reached the lower stratum of cloud, and he followed it down to try to pick up some landmark that would give him his position. It was with real relief that he was able to recognize the road near where the wreck of the Albatros had fallen, and he shot upwards again to escape the ever-present archie.

For the first time since the fight began he remembered Harris, and raced for home. He tried to persuade himself that perhaps he was only wounded, but in his heart of hearts he knew the truth. Harris was dead. Four straight-winged 'planes materialized out of the mist in front of him, but Biggles did not swerve. The feeling of hate began to surge through him again. 'If you're looking for trouble you can have it!' he snarled, and tore straight at the Albatroses.

They opened up to let him go through, and then closed in behind him. He swerved round a fragment of cloud, and then, with the speed of light, flung the Bristol on its side with a sharp intake of breath. It was perhaps only because his nerves were screwed up to snapping point that he had caught sight of what seemed to be a fine wire standing vertically in the air.

Without even thinking, he knew it was a balloon cable. Somewhere above the clouds an enemy observation balloon was taking a last look round the landscape, or as much of it as could be seen, before being wound down for the night. Then an idea struck him, and he swerved in the opposite direction.

The leading Hun, with his eyes only on the Bristol was round in a flash to cut across the arc of the circle and intercept him, and Biggles witnessed just what he hoped would happen—the picture of a machine colliding with a balloon cable. It was a sight permitted to very few war pilots, although it actually happened several times.

The cable tore the top and bottom port wings off the Albatros as cleanly as if they had been sheared through with an axe. The machine swung round in its own length, and the pilot was flung clean over the centre section. He fell, clutching wildly at space. Biggles saw that the cable had parted, and that the other machines were hesitating, watching their falling leader. Then they came on again. They overtook him before he reached the Lines, as he knew they would. A bullet splashed into his instrument-board, and he had no alternative but to turn and face them.

With a steady gunner in the back seat he would have felt no qualms as to the ultimate result of the combat, but with his rear gun silent he was much worse off than the single-seaters, as he had a larger machine to handle. To make matters worse, the Lewis gun, pointing up to the sky in the rear cockpit, told its own story. The enemy pilots knew that his gunner was down, and that they could get on his tail with impunity.

The three Boche pilots were evidently old hands, for they separated and then launched an attack from three directions simultaneously. The best that Biggles could do was to take on one machine at a time, yet while he was engaging it his flanks and tail were exposed to the attacks of the other two.

Several bullets struck the Bristol, and it began to look as if his luck had broken at last. He fought coolly, without the all-devouring hate that had consumed him when he attacked the red-and-silver Albatros. These methods would not serve him now.

He tried to break out of the circle into which they had automatically fallen, in order to reach the shelter of the clouds, but a devastating blast of lead through his centre section warned him of the folly of turning his back on them. He swung round again to meet them. A shark-like aircraft, painted dark green and buff, circled to get behind him; the other two were coming in from either side. His position, he knew, was critical.

Then a miracle happened, or so it seemed. The circling Hun broke into pieces and hurtled earthwards. Biggles stared, and then understood. A drab-coloured single-seater, wearing red, white, and blue ring markings, swept across his nose. It was a Sopwith Pup. He looked around quickly for others, but it was alone.

Its advent soon decided matters. The black-crossed machines dived out of the fight and disappeared into the clouds. Biggles waved his hand to the single-seater pilot and they turned towards the Lines. The Pup stayed with him until the aerodrome loomed up through the gloom, and then disappeared as magically as it arrived.

Biggles felt for his Very pistol and fired a red light over the side. The ruddy glow cast a weird light over the twilight scene. He saw the ambulance start out almost before his wheels had touched the ground, and he taxied to meet it. Mabs and Mark were following it

152

at a brisk trot; the C.O. was standing in the doorway of the squadron office.

Mark, with a bandage round his head, caught Biggles' eye as two R.A.M.C men gently lifted the dead observer from his seat. Biggles did not look; he felt that tears were not far away, and was ashamed of his weakness. He taxied up to the sheds and climbed wearily to the ground.

'How did the Bristol go?' asked Mabs awkwardly.

'Bristol? Oh, yes—fine, thanks!'

The photographic sergeant removed the camera.

'See that the prints are in the squadron office as quickly as you can manage it,' Biggles told him.

'Lucky for me the doc made me stay at home,' observed Mark.

Biggles shrugged his shoulders. 'Maybe. On the other hand, it might not have happened if you'd been there.'

'How did it happen?' asked the C.O., coming up.

Briefly Biggles told him.

'Anyway, it's some consolation that you got the Hun,' said the C.O.

'Yes, I got him!' answered Biggles grimly.

'And the photos?'

'You'll have them in time, sir.'

'Cheer up, whispered Mark, as they walked slowly towards the mess. 'It's a beastly business, but it's no good getting down-hearted.

'I know,' replied Biggles. 'It's the sort of thing that's liable to happen to any of us—will happen, I expect, before we're very much older. But it was tough luck for Harris. He'd only been here about five minutes, and now he's gone—gone before he fully realized what he was up against. It's ghastly.'

'It's a war!' retorted Mark. 'Try to forget it, or we'll
have you getting nervy. The other Bristols will be here
in the morning,' he added, changing the subject.

'Mahoney, of 266, is on the 'phone asking for you,'
shouted Toddy, as they passed the squadron office. 'He
asked me who was in the Bristol, and when I told him
it was you he said he'd like to have a word with you.'

Biggles picked up the receiver. 'Hallo, Mahoney!' he
said.

'You'll be saying hallo to the Flanders poppies if you
don't watch your step, my lad!' Mahoney told him
seriously.

Biggles started. 'What do you know about it?' he
asked quickly.

'Know about it? I like that,' growled Mahoney, over
the wire. 'Is that all the thanks I get—?'

'Was that you in the Pup?' interrupted Biggles, suddenly understanding.

'What other fool do you suppose would risk being
fried alive to get a crazy Bristol out of a hole? You
ought to look where you're going. Have you bought the
sky, or something?'

'Why, have you sold it?' asked Biggles naïvely.

There was a choking noise at the other end of the
wire. Then: 'You watch your step, laddie! We want
you in 266. The Old Man has already sent in an application for your transfer, but it looks to me as if he's
wasted his time. You'll be cold meat before—'

'Oh, rats!' grinned Biggles. 'I'm just beginning to
learn something about this game. You watch your perishing Pup!'

'Well, we're quits now, anyway,' observed Mahoney.

'That's as it should be,' replied Biggles. 'Meet me

tonight in the town and I'll stand you a dinner on the strength of it.'

'I'll be there!' Mahoney told him briskly. 'Bring your wallet—you'll need it!'

Chapter 12
The 'Show'

Biggles had just left the fireside circle preparatory to going to bed when Major Paynter entered the officers' mess.

'Pay attention, everybody, please!' said the major, rather unnecessarily, for an expectant hush had fallen on the room. 'A big attack along this entire section of Front has been planned to come into operation in the near future. If weather conditions permit, it may start tomorrow morning. As far as this squadron is concerned, every available machine will leave the ground at dawn, and, flying as low as possible, harass the enemy's troops within the boundaries you'll find marked on the large map in the squadron office. Each machine will carry eight Cooper bombs and work independently, concentrating on preventing the movement of enemy troops on the roads leading to the Front. Every officer will do three patrols of two and a half hours each, daily, until further notice.

'The greatest care must be exercised in order that pilots and observers do not fire on our own troops, who will disclose their positions, as far as they are able, with Very lights and ground strips. Their objective is the high ridge which at present runs about two miles in front of our forward positions. These are the orders, gentlemen. I understand that all British machines not actually engaged in ground strafing will be in the air, either bombing back areas or protecting the low-flying

156

machines from air attack. I need hardly say that the higher command relies implicitly on every officer carrying out his duty to the best possible advantage; the impending battle may have very decisive results on the progress of the War. I think that's all. All previous orders are cancelled. Officers will muster on the tarmac at six-fifty, by which time it should be light enough to see to take off. Good night, everybody.'

A babble of voices broke out as the C.O. left the mess.

'That's the stuff!' declared Mark Way, enthusiastically.

Mabs eyed him coldly. 'Have you done any trench strafing?' he asked. 'I don't mean just emptying your guns into the Lines as you come back from an O.P.*, but as a regular job during one of these big offensives?'

Mark shook his head. 'As a matter of fact, I haven't,' he admitted.

Mabs grinned sarcastically. 'Inside three days you'll be staggering about looking for somewhere to sleep. But there won't be any sleep. You're going to know what hard work it is for the first time in your life. I was in the big spring offensive last year, and the Hun counter-attack that followed it, and by the time it was over I never wanted to see another aeroplane again as long as I lived. You heard what the Old Man said— three shows a day. By this time tomorrow you won't be able to see the ground for crashes, and those that can still fly will have to do the work of the others as well as their own.'

'You're a nice cheerful cove, I must say!' said Biggles.

* Offensive Patrol – actively looking for enemy aircraft to attack.

157

'Well, you might as well know what we're in for,' returned Mabs, 'and it won't come as a surprise! When you've flown up and down a double artillery barrage for a couple of hours you'll know what flying is.' He rose and made for the door. 'I'm going to hit the sheets,' he announced. 'Get to bed, officers of A Flight, please. It may be the last chance you'll get for some time!'

There was a general move towards the door as he disappeared.

'Tired or not, I've got an appointment with a steak and chips in Rouen tomorrow night,' declared Curtiss, of B Flight, yawning, little dreaming that he was going to bed for the last time in his life.

The tarmac, just before daybreak the following morning was a scene of intense activity. Nine big, drab-coloured Bristol Fighters stood in line in front of the flight sheds, with a swarm of air mechanics bustling about them, adjusting equipment and fitting Cooper bombs on the bomb racks. Propellers were being turned round and engines started up, while the *rat-tat-tat-tat* of machine-guns came from the direction of the gun-testing pits. Biggles' fitter was standing by his machine.

'Everything all right?' asked Biggles.

'All ready, sir,' was the reply.

'Suck in, then!' called Biggles, as he climbed into his cockpit. 'Suck in' was the signal to suck petrol into the cylinders of the engine.

Mark, his gunner, disappeared for a few moments, to return with a Lewis gun, which he adjusted on the Scarff mounting round the rear seat. A mechanic handed up a dozen drums of ammunition.

The engine roared into pulsating life, and Biggles fixed his cap and goggles securely as he allowed it to warm up. Mabs' machine, wearing streamers on wing-tips and tail, began to taxi out into position to take off. The others followed. For a minute or two they waddled across the soaking turf like a flock of ungainly geese. Then, with a roar that filled the heavens, they skimmed into the air and headed towards the Lines. They kept no particular formation, but generally followed the direction set by the leader. The work before them did not call for close formation flying.

A watery sun, still low on the eastern horizon, cast a feeble and uncertain light over the landscape, the British reserve trenches, and the war-scarred battle-fields beyond. Patches of ground mist still hung here and there towards the west, but for the most part the ground lay fairly clear. Signs of the activity on the ground were at once apparent. Long lines of marching men, guns, horses, and ammunition wagons were winding like long grey caterpillars towards the Front. A group of queer-looking toad-like monsters slid ponderously over the mud, and Biggles watched them for a moment with interest. He knew they were tanks, the latest engines of destruction.

The ground was dull green, with big bare patches, pock-marked with holes, some of which were still smoking, showing where shells had recently fallen. A clump of shattered trees, blasted into bare, gaunt spectres, marked the site of what had once been a wood. Straight ahead, the green merged into a dull brown sea of mud, flat except for the craters and shell-holes, marked with countless zigzag lines of trenches in which a million men were crouching in readiness for the coming struggle.

Beyond the patch of barren mud the green started again, dotted here and there with roofless houses and shattered villages. In the far distance a river wound like

159

a gleaming silver thread towards the horizon. Spouting columns of flame and clouds of smoke began to appear in the sea of mud; the brown earth was flung high into the air by the bursting shells.

It was a depressing sight, and Biggles, turning his eyes upwards, made out a number of black specks against the pale blue sky. They were the escorting scouts. In one place a dog-fight was raging, and he longed to join it, but the duty on hand forbade it. He nestled a little lower in his cockpit, for the air was cold and damp, so cold that his fingers inside the thick gauntlets were numbed. They had nearly reached the Lines now, so he turned his eyes to Mabs' machine, watching for the signal Very light that would announce the attack. It came, a streak of scarlet flame that described a wide parabola before it began to drop earthwards. Simultaneously the machine from which it had appeared roared down towards the ground. The open formation broke up as each pilot selected his own target and followed.

Biggles saw the welter of mud leaping up at him as he thrust the control-stick forward, eyes probing the barren earth for the enemy. Guns flashed like twinkling stars in all directions. He saw a Pup, racing low, plunge nose-first into the ground to be swallowed up by an inferno of fire.

Charred skeletons of machines lay everywhere, whether friend or foe it was impossible to tell. Lines of white tracer bullets streamed upwards, seeming to move quite slowly. Something smashed against the engine cowling of the Bristol and Biggles ducked instinctively.

Rat-tat-tat-tat! Mark's gun began its staccato chatter, but Biggles did not look round to see what he was shooting at; his eyes were on the ground. The sky above would have to take care of itself. The needle of his altimeter was falling steadily; five hundred feet, four hundred, yet he forced it lower, throttle wide open, until the ground flashed past at incredible speed.

He could hear the guns now, a low rumble that reminded him of distant thunder on a summer's day. He heard bullets ripping through the machine somewhere behind him, and kicked hard on right rudder, swerving farther into enemy country. He could still see Mabs' machine some distance ahead and to the left of him, nose tilted down to the ground, a stream of tracer bullets pouring from the forward gun.

Something tapped him sharply on the shoulder and he looked round in alarm. Mark was pointing. Following the outstretched finger he picked out a mud-churned road. A long column of troops in field-grey were marching along it, followed by guns or wagons, he could not tell which.

He swung the Bristol round in its own length, noting with a curious sense of detachment that had he continued flying on his original course for another two seconds the machine must have been blown to smithereens for a jagged sheet of flame split the air; it was too large for an ordinary archie and must have been a shell from a field-gun. Even as it was, the Bristol bucked like a wild horse in the blast.

He tilted his nose down towards the German infantry and watched them over the top of his engine cowling. His hand sought the bomb-toggle. There was a rending clatter as a stream of machine-gun bullets made a colander of his right wing; a wire snapped with a sharp twang, but he did not alter his course.

A cloud of smoke, mixed with lumps of earth, shot

161

high into the air not fifty yards away, and again the machine rocked. He knew that any second might be his last, but the thought did not worry him. Something at the back of his mind seemed to be saying: 'This is war, war, war!' and he hated it. This was not his idea of flying; it was just a welter of death and destruction.

The enemy troops were less than five hundred yards away, and he saw the leaders pointing their rifles at him. He drew level with the head of the column, and jerked the bomb-toggle savagely. Then he kicked the rudder-bar hard, and at the same time jerked the control-stick back; even so, he was nearly turned upside-down by the force of the explosions, and clods of earth and stones dropped past him from above.

He glanced down. The earth was hidden under a great cloud of smoke. Again he swept down, tore straight along the road, and released the remainder of his bombs. Again he zoomed upwards.

The air was filled with strange noises; the crash of bursting shells, the clatter of his broken wire beating against a strut, and the slap-slap-slap of torn fabric on his wings. Mark's gun was still chattering, which relieved him, for it told him that all was still well with his partner. He half-turned and glanced back at the place where he had dropped his bombs.

There were eight large, smoking holes, around which a number of figures were lying; others were running a away. It struck him that he was some way over the Lines, so he turned again and raced back towards the conspicuous stretch of No Man's Land, across which figures were now hurrying at a clumsy run. Nearer to him a number of grey-coated troops were clustered around a gun, and he sprayed them with a shower of lead as he passed.

He reached the Line, and raced along it, keeping well over the German side to make sure of not hitting any British troops who might have advanced. Burst after burst he poured into the trenches and at the concrete pill-boxes in which machine-guns nestled.

He passed a Bristol lying upside-down on the ground, and a scout seemingly undamaged. Mark tapped him on the shoulder, turned his thumbs down and pointed to his gun, and Biggles knew that he meant that his ammunition was finished.

'I'll finish mine, too, and get out of this!' he thought. 'I've had about enough.' He took sights on a group of men who were struggling to drag a field-gun to the rear, and they flung themselves flat as the withering hail smote them. Biggles held the Bowden lever* of his gun down until the gun ceased firing, then turned and raced towards his own side of the Lines.

Some Tommies waved to him as he skimmed along not fifty feet above their heads. Mark returned the salutation. The Bristol rocked as it crossed the tracks of heavy shells, and Biggles breathed a sigh of relief as they left the war zone behind them.

Five machines, one of which was Mabs' had already returned when they landed, their crews standing about on the tarmac discussing the 'show.'

'Well, what do you think of it?' asked the flight-commander as Biggles and Mark joined them.

'Rotten!' replied Biggles buffing his arms to restore circulation. He felt curiously exhausted, and began to understand the strain that low flying entails.

'Get filled up, and then rest while you can. We leave the ground again in an hour!' Mabs told them. 'The

---

* The 'trigger' to fire the machine-guns.

enemy are giving way all along the sector and we've got to prevent them bringing up reinforcements.'

'I see,' replied Biggles, without enthusiasm. 'In that case we might as well go down to the mess. Come on, Mark.'

Chapter 13
Dirty Work

For three days the attack continued. The squadron lost four machines; two others were unserviceable. The remainder were doing four shows a day, and Biggles staggered about almost asleep on his feet. Life had become a nightmare. Even when he flung himself on his bed at night he could not sleep. In his ears rang the incessant roar of his engine, and his bed seemed to stagger in the bumps of bursting shells, just as the Bristol had done during the day. Mabs had gone to hospital with a bullet through the leg, and new pilots were arriving to replace casualties.

On the fourth morning he made his way, weary and unrefreshed, to the sheds; Mark, who was also feeling the strain, had preceded him. They seldom spoke. They no longer smiled. Mark eyed him grimly as he reached the Bristol and prepared to climb into his seat. 'Why so pale and wan, young airman, prithee why so pale?' he misquoted mockingly.

Biggles looked at him coldly. 'I'm sick and I'm tired,' he said, 'and I've got a nasty feeling that our turn is about due. Just a hunch that something's going to happen, that's all,' he concluded shortly.

'You'll make a good undertaker's clerk when this is over, you cheerful Jonah!' growled Mark.

'Well, come on, let's get on with it. Personally, I'm beyond caring what happens,' replied Biggles, climbing into his seat.

He was thoroughly sick of the war; the futility of it appalled him. He envied the scouts circling high in the sky as they protected the flow-flying trench strafers; they were putting in long hours, he knew, but they did at least escape the everlasting fire from the ground. Above all he sympathized with the swarms of human beings crawling and falling in the sea of mud below.

He took off and proceeded to the sector allotted to the squadron, and where four of its machines now lay in heaps of wreckage. For some minutes he flew up and down the Line, trying to pick out the new British advance posts, for the enemy were still retiring; it would be an easy matter to make a mistake and shoot up the hard-won positions that a few days before had been in German hands.

Archie and field-guns began to cough and bark as he approached the new German front Line, and machine-guns chattered shrilly, but he was past caring about such things. There was no way of avoiding them; they were just evils that had to be borne. One hoped for the best and carried on.

The battle was still raging. It was difficult to distinguish between the British and German troops, they seemed so hopelessly intermingled, so he turned farther into German territory rather than risk making a mistake.

He found a trench in which a swarm of troops were feverishly repairing the parapet, and forced them to seek cover. Then he turned sharp to the right and broke up another working-party; there were no more long convoys to attack, but he found a German staff car and chased it until the driver, taking a corner too fast in his efforts to escape, overturned it in a ditch.

For some minutes he worried a battery of field-guns

166

that were taking up a new position. Then he turned back towards the Lines—or the stretch of No man's Land that had originally marked the trench system.

He was still half a mile away when it happened. Just what it was he could not say, although Mark swore it was one of the new 'chain' archies—two phosphorus flares joined together by a length of wire that wrapped itself around whatever it struck, and set it on fire. The Bristol lurched sickeningly, and for a moment went out of control.

White-faced, Biggles fought with the control-stick to get the machine on even keel again, for at his height of a thousand feet there was very little margin of safety. He had just got the machine level when a wild yell and a blow on the back of his head brought him round, staring.

Aft of the gunner's cockpit the machine was a raging sheet of flame, which Mark was squirting with his Pyrene extinguisher, but without visible effect. As the extinguisher emptied itself of its contents he flung it overboard and set about beating the flames with his gauntlets.

Biggles did the only thing he could do in the circumstances; he jammed the control-stick forward and dived in a frantic effort to 'blow out' the flames with his slipstream. Fortunately his nose was still pointing towards the Lines, and the effort brought him fairly close, but the flames were only partly subdued and sprang to life again as he eased the control-stick back to prevent the machine from diving into the ground.

The Bristol answered to the controls so slowly that his wheels actually grazed the turf, and he knew at once what had happened. The flames had burnt through to his tail unit destroying the fabric on his elevators, rendering the fore and aft controls useless. He knew it was the end, and, abandoning hope of reaching the Lines, he concentrated his efforts on saving their lives. He thought and acted with a coolness that surprised him.

He tilted the machine on to its side, holding up his nose with the throttle, and commenced to slip wing-tip first towards the ground. Whether he was over British or German territory he neither knew nor cared; he had to get on to the ground or be burnt alive.

A quick glance behind revealed Mark still thrashing the flames with his glove, shielding his face with his left arm. Twenty feet from the ground Biggles switched off everything and unfastened his safety belt. The prop stopped. In the moment's silence he yelled 'Jump!'

He did not wait to see if Mark had followed his instructions, for there was no time, but climbed quickly out of his cockpit on to the wing just as the tip touched the ground. He had a fleeting vision of what seemed to be a gigantic catherine wheel as the machine cart-wheeled over the ground, shedding struts and flaming canvas, and then he lay on his back, staring at the sky, gasping for breath.

For a ghastly moment he thought his back was broken, and he struggled to rise in an agony of suspense. He groaned as he fought for breath, really winded for the first time in his life.

Mark appeared by his side and clutched at his shoulders. 'What is it—what is it?' he cried, believing that his partner was mortally hurt.

Biggles could not speak, he could only gasp. Mark caught him by the collar and dragged him into a near-by trench. They fell in a heap at the bottom.

'Not hurt—winded!' choked Biggles. 'Where are we?'

Mark took a quick look over the parapet, and then jumped back, shaking his head. 'Dunno!' he said laconically. 'Can't see anybody. All in the trenches, I suppose.'

Biggles managed to stagger to his feet. 'We'd better lie low till we find out where we are!' he panted. 'What a mess! Let's get in here!' He nodded towards the gaping mouth of a dugout.

Footsteps were squelching through the mud towards them, and they dived into the dugout, Biggles leading. He knew instantly that the place was already occupied, but in the semi-darkness he could not for a moment make out who or what it was. Then he saw, and his eyes went round with astonishment. It was a German, cowering in a corner.

'*Kamerad! Kamerad**!' cried the man, with his arms above his head.

'All right, we shan't hurt you,' Biggles assured him, kicking a rifle out of the way. 'It looks as if we're all in the same boat, but if you try any funny stuff I'll knock your block off!'

The German stared at him wide-eyed, but made no reply.

There was a great noise of splashing and shouting in the trench outside; a shell landed somewhere close at hand with a deafening roar, and a trickle of earth fell from the ceiling.

Mark grabbed Biggles' arm as a line of feet passed the entrance; there was no mistaking the regulation German boots, but if confirmation was needed, the harsh, guttural voices supplied it. They both breathed

---

* German: Friend! Friend!

169

more freely as the feet disappeared and the noise receded.

'It looks as if we've landed in the middle of the war,' observed Biggles, with a watchful eye on the Boche, who still crouched in his corner as if dazed—as indeed he was.

'What are we going to do? We can't spend the rest of the war in here,' declared Mark.

'I wouldn't if I could,' replied Biggles. 'But it's no use doing anything in a hurry.'

'Some Boche troops will come barging in here in a minute and hand us a few inches of cold steel; they're not likely to be particular after that hullaballoo outside.'

Hullaballoo was a good word; it described things exactly. There came a medley of sounds in which shouts, groans, rifle and revolver shots and the reports of bursting hand-grenades could be distinguished.

'It sounds as if they're fighting all round us,' muttered Mark anxiously.

'As long as they stay round us I don't mind,' Biggles told him. 'It'll be when they start crowding in here that the fun will begin!'

Heavy footsteps continued to splash up and down the communication trench. Once a German officer stopped outside the dugout and Biggles held his breath. The Boche seemed to be about to enter, but changed his mind and went off at a run.

Then there came the sound of a sharp scuffle in the trench and a German N.C.O. leapt panting into the dugout. He glanced around wildly as the two airmen started up, and broke into a torrent of words. He was splashed with mud from head to foot, and bleeding from a cut in the cheek. He carried a rifle, but made no attempt to use it.

'Steady!' cried Biggles, removing the weapon from the man's unresisting hands. The Boche seemed to be trying to tell them something, pointing and gesticulating as he spoke.

'I think he means that his pals outside are coming in,' said Biggles with a flash of inspiration. 'Well, there's still plenty of room.'

'Anybody in there?' cried a voice from the doorway. Before Biggles could speak the German had let out a yell.

'Just share this among you, but don't quarrel over it!' went on the same voice.

'This' was a Mills bomb* that pitched on to the floor between them.

There was a wild stampede for the door; Biggles slipped, and was the last out. He had just flung himself clear as the dugout went up with a roar that seemed to burst his eardrums. He looked up to see the point of a bayonet a few inches from his throat; behind it was the amazed face of a British Tommy.

The soldier let out a whistle of surprise. More troops came bundling round the corner of the trench, an officer among them. 'Hallo, what's all this?' he cried, halting in surprise.

'Don't let us get in your way,' Biggles told him quickly. 'Go on with the war!'

'What might you be doing here?'

'We might be blackberrying, but we're not. Again, we might be playing croquet, or roller-skating, but we're not. We're just waiting.'

* Hand grenade.

171

'Waiting! What for?'

'For you blokes to come along, of course. I've got a date with a bath and a bar of soap, so I'll be getting along.'

'You'd better get out of this,' the other told him, grinning, as he prepared to move on.

'That's what I thought!' declared Biggles. 'Perhaps you'd tell us the easiest and safest way?'

The other laughed. 'Sure I will,' he said. 'Keep straight on down that sap* we've just come up and you'll come to our old Line. It's all fairly quiet now.'

'So I've noticed,' murmured Biggles. 'Come on, Mark, let's get back to where we belong.'

'What about the Bristol?' asked Mark.

'What about it? Are you thinking of carrying it back with you? I didn't stop to examine it closely, as you may have noticed, but I fancy that kite, or what's left of it, will take a bit of sticking together again. We needn't worry about that. The repair section will collect it, if it's any good. Come on!'

Three hours later, weary and smothered with mud, they arrived back at the aerodrome, having got a lift part of the way on a lorry.

Mabs, on crutches, was standing at the door of the mess. 'Where have you been?' he asked.

'Ha! Where haven't we!' replied Biggles, without stopping.

'Where are you off to now in such a hurry?' called Mabs after him.

'To bed, laddie,' Biggles told him enthusiastically. 'To bed, till you find me another aeroplane.'

---

* Part of the trench system to protect moving troops from enemy gunfire.

172

Chapter 14
The Pup's First Flight

When the time came for Biggles to leave his old squadron and say good-bye to Mark Way, his gunner, he found himself a good deal more depressed than he had thought possible; he realized for the first time just how attached to them he had become. Naturally, he had been delighted to join a scout squadron, for he had always wanted to fly single-seaters. The presence of his old pal, Mahoney, who was flight-commander, prevented any awkwardness or strangeness amongst his new comrades, and he quickly settled down to routine work.

The commanding officer, Major Mullen, of his new squadron, No. 266, stationed at Maranique, allowed none of his pilots to take unnecessary risks if he could prevent it. So he gave Biggles ten days in which to make himself proficient in the handling of the single-seater Pup that had been allocated to him.

Biggles was told to put in as much flying-time as possible, but on no account to cross the Lines, and he found that the enforced rest from eternal vigilance did him a power of good, for his nerves had been badly jarred by his late spell of trench strafing.

By the end of a week he was thoroughly at home with the Pup, and ready to try his hand at something more serious than beetling up and down behind his own Lines. He had noted all the outstanding landmarks around Maranique, and once or twice he accompanied

Mahoney on practice formation flights. His flight-commander had expressed himself satisfied, and Biggles begged to be allowed to do a 'show.'

His chance came soon. Lorton was wounded in the arm and packed off to hospital, and Biggles was detailed to take his place the following morning. But the afternoon before this decision took effect he had what he regarded as a slice of luck that greatly enhanced his reputation with the C.O., and the officers of the squadron, as well as bringing his name before Wing Headquarters.

He had set off on a cross-country flight to the Aircraft Repair Section at St Omer, to make inquiries for the equipment officer about a machine that had gone back for reconditioning, when he spotted a line of white archie bursts at a very high altitude—about 15,000 feet, he judged it to be.

He was flying at about 5,000 a few miles inside the Lines at the time, and he knew that the archie was being fired by British guns, which could only mean that the target was an enemy aircraft. It seemed to be flying on a course parallel with the Lines, evidently on a photographic or scouting raid.

Without any real hope of overtaking it he set off in pursuit, and, knowing that sooner or later the German would have to turn to reach his own side he steered an oblique course that would bring him between the raider and the Lines. In a few minutes he had increased his height to 10,000 feet, and could distinctly see the enemy machine. It was a Rumpler two-seater*. He had no doubt that the observer had spotted him, but the

* German two-seater biplane used for general duties as well as fighting.

machine continued on its way as if the pilot was not concerned, possibly by reason of his superior altitude.

Biggles began to edge a little nearer to the Lines, and was not much more than a thousand feet below the Hun, when, to his disgust, it turned slowly and headed off on a diagonal course towards No Man's Land.

The Pup was climbing very slowly now, and it was more with hope than confidence that Biggles continued the pursuit. Then the unexpected happened. The enemy pilot turned sharply and dived straight at him, but opened fire at much too great a range for it to be effective, although he held the burst for at least a hundred rounds. Biggles had no idea where the bullets went, but he saw the Hun, at the end of his dive, zoom nearly back to his original altitude, and then make for home at full speed. But he had lingered just a trifle too long.

Biggles climbed up into the 'blind' spot under the enemy's elevators, and although the range was still too long for good shooting, he opened fire. Whether any of his shots took effect he was unable to tell, but the Hun was evidently alarmed, for the Rumpler made a quick turn out of the line of fire. It was a clumsy turn, and cost him two hundred precious feet of height at a moment when height was all-important. Moreover, it did not give the gunner in the back seat a chance to use his weapon.

Biggles seized his opportunity and fired one of the longest bursts he ever fired in his life. The German gunner swayed for a moment, then collapsed in his cockpit. Then, to his intense satisfaction, Biggles saw the propeller of the other machine slow down and stop, whereupon the enemy pilot shoved his nose down and dived for the Lines, now not more than two or three miles away.

It was a move that suited Biggles well, for the Rumpler was defenceless from the rear, so he tore down in hot pursuit, guns blazing, knowing that the Hun was at his mercy. The enemy pilot seemed to realize this for he turned broadside on and threw up his hands in surrender.

Biggles was amazed, for although he had heard of such things being done it was his first experience of it. He ceased firing at once and took up a position on the far side of the disabled machine; he did not trust his prisoner very much, for he guessed that he would, if the opportunity arose, make a dash for the Lines—so near, and yet so far away. Biggles therefore shepherded him down like a well-trained sheep-dog bringing in a stray lamb.

He could not really find it in his heart to blame the enemy pilot for surrendering. The fellow had had to choose between being made prisoner and certain death, and had chosen captivity as the lesser of the two evils. 'Death before capture,' is no doubt an admirable slogan, but it loses some of its attractiveness in the face of cold facts.

The German landed about four miles from Maranique and was prevented by a crowd of Tommies from purposely injuring his machine. Biggles landed in a near-by field and hurried to the scene, arriving just as the C.O. and several officers of the squadron, who had witnessed the end of the combat from the aerodrome, dashed up in the squadron car. It was purely a matter of luck that Major Raymond, of Wing Headquarters, who had been on the aerodrome talking with Major Mullen, was with them.

He smiled at Biggles approvingly. 'Good show!' he said. 'We've been trying to get hold of one of these machines intact for a long time.'

Biggles made a suitable reply and requested that the crew of the Rumpler should be well cared for. The pilot, whose name they learnt was Schmidt, looked morose and bad-tempered—as, indeed, he had every cause to be; the observer had been wounded in the chest and was unconscious.

They were taken away under escort in an ambulance, and that was the end of the affair. Biggles never learned what happened to them.

The offensive patrol for which he had been detailed in place of Lorton turned out to be a more difficult business. It began quite simply. He took his place in a formation of five machines, and for an hour or more they cruised up and down their sector without incident, except, of course, for the inevitable archie. Then the trouble started around a single machine.

Several times they had passed a British machine— an R.E.8*—circling over the same spot, obviously engaged in doing a 'shoot' for the artillery, and Biggles was able to sympathize with the pilot. He watched the circling 'plane quite dispassionately for a moment or two, glanced away, and then turned back to the R.E.8. It was no longer there.

He stared—and stared harder. Then he saw it, three thousand feet below, plunging earthwards in flames. Screwing his head round a little farther he made out three German Albatros streaking for home. They must have made their attack on the two-seater under the

* British two-seater biplane designed for reconnaissance and artillery observation purposes.

177

very noses of the Pups, and, well satisfied with the result of their work, were removing themselves from the vicinity without loss of time. But they were well below the Pups, and Mahoney, who was leading, tore down after them in a screaming dive, closely followed by the rest of the formation.

As they went down, something—he could not say what—made Biggles, who was an outside flank man, look back over his shoulder. There was really no reason why he should but the fact that he did so provided another example of the uncanny instinct he was developing for detecting the presence of Huns.

The sight that met his gaze put all thought of the escaping Albatroses clean out of his head. A German High Patrol of not fewer than twenty Triplanes were coming down like the proverbial ton of bricks.

Biggles' first idea was to warn Mahoney of the impending onslaught, but, try as he would, he could not overtake his leader. Yet he knew that if the Huns were allowed to come on in a solid formation on their tails, most of them would be wiped out before they knew what had hit them. He could think of only one thing to do, and he did it, although it did not occur to him that he was making something very much like a deliberate sacrifice of his own life. That he was not killed was due no doubt to the very unexpectedness of his move, which temporarily disorganized the Hun circus*. He swung the Pup round on its axis, cocked up his nose to face the oncoming Huns, and let drive at the whole formation.

The leader swerved just in time to avoid head-on

---

* Formations of German fighter aircraft usually named after their leader e.g. Richthofen circus.

collision. His wing tip missed Biggles by inches. The lightning turn threw the others out of their places, and they, too, had to swerve wildly to avoid collision with their leader.

Biggles held his breath as the cloud of gaudy-coloured enemy machines roared past him, so close that he could see the faces of the pilots staring at him. Yet not a bullet touched his machine. Nor did he hit one of them—at least, as far as he could see.

The Huns pulled up, hesitating, to see if their leader was going on after the other Pups or staying to slay the impudent one. At that moment, Mahoney, missing one of his men, looked back. In that quick flash it must have seemed to him that Biggles was taking on the entire German Air Force single-handed, and he hung his Pup on its prop as he headed back towards the mêlée.

He knew what Biggles himself did not know; that the German formation was the formidable Richthofen circus, led by the famous Baron himself, his conspicuous all-red Fokker triplane even then pouring lead at the lone Pup.

Biggles could never afterwards describe the sensation of finding himself in the middle of Germany's most noted air fighters. He was, as he put it, completely flummoxed. He merely shot at every machine that swam across his sights, wondering all the while why his Pup did not fall to pieces.

The reason why it did not was probably that put forward by Captain Albert Ball, V.C., in defence of his method of plunging headlong into the middle of an enemy 'circus'. Such tactics temporarily disorganized the enemy formation, and the pilots dared not shoot as freely as they would normally for fear of hitting or colliding with their own men. Be that as it may, in the opening stage of the uproar Biggles' Pup was hit less than a dozen times, and in no place was it seriously damaged.

By the time the Huns sorted themselves out Mahoney and the other three Pups were on the scene. Even so, the gallant action of the leader in taking on such overwhelming odds would not have availed had it not been for the opportune arrival of a second formation of Pups and a squadron of Bristols—Biggles' old squadron, although he did not know it. That turned the tide.

The huge dog-fight lost height quickly, as such affairs nearly always did, and was soon down to five thousand feet. It was impossible for any pilot to know exactly what was happening; each man picked an opponent and stuck to him as long as he could. If he lost him he turned to find another.

That was precisely what Biggles did, and it was utterly out of the question for him to see if he shot anyone down. If a machine at which he was shooting fell out of the fight, someone else was shooting at him before he could determine whether his Hun was really hit or merely shamming.

He saw more than one machine spinning, and two or three smoke-trails where others had gone down in flames. He also saw a Bristol and a triplane that had collided whirling down together in a last ghastly embrace.

At four thousand feet he pulled out, slightly dizzy, and tried to make out what was happening. He picked out Mahoney by his streamers, not far away, and noted that the fight seemed to be breaking up by mutual consent. Odd machines were still circling round each other, but each leader was trying to rally his men.

Mahoney, in particular, was trying frantically to attract the attention of the surviving members of his patrol, for the fight had drifted over German territory and it was high time to see about getting nearer the Lines.

Biggles took up position on Mahoney's flank, and presently another Pup joined them. Of the other two there was no sign.

The Bristols were already streaming back towards home in open formation and Mahoney followed them. They passed the charred remains of the R.E.8 that had been the cause of all the trouble, gaunt and black in the middle of No Man's Land. They reached the Lines and turned to fly parallel with them.

Their patrol was not yet finished, but all the machines had been more or less damaged, so after waiting a few minutes to give the other two Pups a chance of joining them if they were still in the air, they turned towards the aerodrome. It was as well they did, for Biggles' engine began to give trouble, although by nursing it he managed to reach home.

They discovered that the squadron had already been informed of the dog-fight, artillery observers along the Line reporting that five British and seven German machines had been seen to fall. There seemed little chance of the two missing Pups turning up. The surviving members of the patrol hung about the tarmac for some time, but they did not return. That evening they were reported 'missing'.

Chapter 15
Caught Napping

'How often do you run into shows as big as that?' Biggles asked Mahoney, at lunch.

'Oh, once in a while! Not every day, thank goodness!' replied Mahoney. 'Why?'

'I was just wondering.' Biggles ruminated a minute or two. 'You know, laddie, we do a lot of sneering at the Huns, and say they've no imagination.'

'What about it?'

'Well, I'm not so sure about it, that's all.'

'What! You turning pro-Hun, or something?'

'But it seems to me they're using their brains more than we are.'

'How?'

'We just fly and fight, and that's all we think about.'

'What do you mean?'

'Well, in the first place, the Huns mostly stay over their own side of the Lines, knowing that we'll go over to them. How often do you see a big formation of Hun scouts over this side? Mighty seldom. That isn't just luck. That's a clever policy laid down by the German higher authority.

'Then there's this grouping of their hot-stuff pilots into "circuses". And the way that bunch arrived this morning wasn't a fluke—you can bet your life on that. It was all very neatly arranged. Can't you see the idea? The old R.E.8 was the meat; three Huns go down after it just when they knew we were about due back, and that we were certain to follow them—go down after them. It pans out just as they expected, and off they go, taking us slap under the big mob who were sitting up topsides waiting for us. Although I say it as shouldn't, it was a bit of luck I happened to look back. As it turned out, the Hun plan went off at half-cock, but it might not have done. That's why I say these tripe-hound merchants are flying with their heads.'

'Well, I can't stop 'em, if that's what you mean.'

'I never suggested you could, did I? But there's nothing to prevent us exercising our grey matter a bit, is there?'

'You're right, kid,' joined in Maclaren, another flight-commander, who had overheard the conversation. 'You're absolutely dead right!'

'I think I am,' replied Biggles frankly. 'War-flying is too new for strategy to be laid down in the text-books; we've got to work it out for ourselves.'

'What's all this?' asked Major Mullen, who had entered the room and caught the last part of the conversation.

Briefly, Maclaren gave him the gist of the conversation. The C.O. nodded as he listened, then he looked at Biggles.

'What do you suggest?' he asked.

'Well, sir, it seems to me we might have a word with the other scout squadrons about it, and work out a scheme. At present we all do our shows independently, so to speak, but if we could work out a plot together— an ambush, if you like, like the Huns did this morning—we might give the tripe merchants over the way something to think about. If we did happen to catch them properly it would have the effect of making them chary about tackling odd machines for a bit. They'd always be worried for fear they were heading into a trap.'

'That sounds like common-sense to me,' agreed the C.O. 'All right, Bigglesworth, you work out the plot and submit it to me, and I'll see what can be done about it. But we shall have to keep it to ourselves. If Wing heard about it they'd probably knock it on the head, on the ground that such methods were irregular, although perhaps I shouldn't say that.'

'We all know it, sir, without you saying it, anyway!' grinned Biggles.

After dinner he sat down with a pencil and paper to work out his 'plot', and before he went to bed he had the scheme cut and dried. It was fairly simple, as he explained to the others in the morning, and based upon the methodical habits of the enemy, and the assumption that the other scout squadrons would co-operate.

'From my own personal observation,' he explained, 'the Huns—by which I mean the big circuses, particularly the Richthofen crowd which is stationed at Douai—do two big shows a day. Sometimes, when things are lively, they do three. They always do a big evening show, one that finishes about sunset, just before they pack up for the night. Very well. It gets dark now about half past six. That means that the Huns must leave the ground on their last show between four and four-thirty. Now, if they have a dog-fight they don't all go home together, but do the same as we do—trickle home independently, in twos and threes. They did that this morning. I saw them. Now, I reckon that the last place they'd expect big trouble would be on the way home, near their own aerodrome, and that's where I propose to spring the surprise packet.

'To carry out my idea with maximum safety, it would

need three squadrons—four would be even better. This is the way of it: at four o'clock one squadron pushes along to some prearranged sector of the Line, and makes itself a nuisance—shooting up the Hun trenches, or anything to make itself conspicuous. The Hun artillery observers will see this, of course, and are almost certain to ring up the Richthofen headquarters to say there is a lot of aerial activity on their bit of Front. It stands to reason that the circus will at once make for that spot; give them their due they don't shirk a roughhouse. Right-ho. The squadron that is kicking up the fuss keeps its eyes peeled for the Huns. It'll pretend not to see them until they're fairly close. Then they scatter, making towards home. The Huns are almost bound to split up to chase them, and our fellows can please themselves whether or not they stay and fight. But they must remember that their job is to split up the Huns.

'As soon as this business is well under way, the other two—or three—squadrons will take off, climb to the limit of their height, and head over the Lines on a course that'll bring them round by Douai. Get the idea? The Huns will think the show's over and come drifting home in small parties, without keeping very careful watch. We shall be there to meet them, and we shall have height of them. Huns on the ground may see us, but they won't be able to warn the fellows in the air. In that way, if the scheme works out as I've planned it, we shall catch these pretty birds bending when they're least expecting it. That's all. If the worst comes to the worst we should be no worse off than we are on an ordinary show, when we always seem to be outnumbered. At the best, we shall give the Huns a shock they'll remember for some time. What do you think about it, sir?'

'I certainly think there is a good deal to be said for it,' agreed the major. 'I'll speak to the other squadrons. Perhaps your old squadron would oblige by kicking up the fuss with their Bristols. Then, if 287, with their S.E.s, and 231, and ourselves, get behind the Huns we shall at least be sure of meeting them on even terms, even if they do happen to keep in one formation. All right; leave it to me. I'll see what I can do.'

It took nearly a week of conferences to bring the scheme to a stage where it was ready to be tried out, but at last, burning with impatience and excitement, Biggles made his way to the sheds with the others for the big show.

Watches had been carefully synchronized on the instrument boards of all pilots taking part, and every possible precaution taken to prevent a miscarriage of plans. Major Paynter, of Biggles' old squadron, had agreed to send every Bristol he could raise into the air, to make itself as obnoxious as possible at a given spot, at the arranged time.

The others were to rendezvous over Maranique in 'layer' formation (machines flying in tiers) at four-thirty—No. 266 Squadron at ten thousand feet, 231 Squadron at thirteen thousand feet, and 287 Squadron at sixteen thousand feet. Major Mullen was leading the whole show on a roundabout course that would bring them behind the enemy, assuming, of course, that the enemy circus would concentrate in the area where the Bristols were to lure them.

Three-quarters of an hour later, Major Mullen swung round in a wide circle that brought them actually within sight of Douai, the headquarters of the most

186

famous fighting scouts in the German Imperial Air Service. Biggles never forgot the scene. The sun was low in the west, sinking in a crimson glow. A slight mist was rising, softening the hard outlines of roads, woods, hedges, and fields below, as though seen through a piece of lilac-tinted gauze. To the east, the earth was already bathed in deep purple and indigo shadows.

No enemy aircraft were in sight, not even on the ground, as they turned slowly over the peaceful scene to seek the enemy in the glowing mists of the west. They had not long to wait.

Biggles saw two Triplanes, flying close together, slowly materialize in the mist, like goldfish swimming in a pale milky liquid. The enemy pilots were gliding down, probably with their eyes on the aerodrome, and it is doubtful if they even saw the full force of British machines that had assembled to overwhelm them. Biggles felt almost sorry for them as Major Mullen shook his wings, as a signal, and the nine Pups roared down on the unsuspecting Triplanes.

It was impossible to say which machine actually scored most hits. One Triplane broke up instantly. The other jerked upwards as if the pilot had been mortally wounded, turned slowly over on to its back, plunged downwards in a vicious spin with its engine full on and bored into the ground two miles below.

The Pups resumed formation and returned to their original height and course. Another Triplane emerged from the mist, but something evidently caught the pilot's eye—perhaps the sun flashing on a wing—and he looked upwards. He acted with the speed of light and flung his machine into a spin to seek safety on the ground. The Pups did not follow, for the Triplane was far below them and they would not risk getting too low so far over the Line.

A few minutes later a straggling party of seven machines appeared, followed at a distance by five more. It was obvious from the loose formation in which they were flying that they considered themselves quite secure so near their nest. They, too, must have been looking at the ground, and Biggles was amazed at the casual manner in which they continued flying straight on with death literally raining on them from the sky.

He picked out his man and poured in a long burst of bullets before the pilot had time to realize his peril. A cloud of smoke, quickly followed by flame, burst from the Triplane's engine. Biggles zoomed upwards and looked back. The seven machines had disappeared. Two long pillars of smoke marked the going of at least two of them.

How many had actually fallen he was unable to tell. Away to the left the other five Triplanes were milling around in a circle, hotly pursued by the second squadron of Pups, whilst the S.E.s were sitting slightly above, waiting to pounce on any enemy machine that tried to leave the combat.

It was the last real surprise of the day, not counting a lonely straggler that they picked up near the Lines and which they had sent down under a tornado of lead. Biggles quite definitely felt sorry for that pilot. Two or three more machines had appeared while the main combat was in progress, but the dog-fight had lost height, and they saw it at once, so were able to escape by spinning down.

The engagement really resolved itself into the sort of show that Biggles had anticipated. The enemy had been caught napping, and many of them had paid the penalty. The three squadrons of British machines reached the Line at dusk, without a single casualty and almost unscathed. One machine only, an S.E.5 of 287b Squadron, had to break formation near the Lines with a piece of archie shrapnel in its engine. Except for that, the Pups and S.E.s returned home in a formation as perfect as when they started.

Congratulations flew fast and furious when Major Mullen's squadron landed, for it had unquestionably been one of the most successful 'shows' ever undertaken by the squadron. A quick comparison of notes revealed that seven Triplanes had been destroyed for certain, either having been seen to crash or fall in flames. How many others had been damaged, or enemy pilots wounded, they had, of course, no means of knowing.

But the most successful part of the issue was that not a single British machine had been lost. Major Mullen thanked Biggles personally and congratulated him on his initiative, in the Squadron Office, in front of the other pilots.

'Well, I'm glad it has turned out as I hoped it would, sir. We've given the Huns something to talk about in mess tonight. Maybe they won't be quite so chirpy in future!' observed Biggles modestly.

The party was about to break up when Watt Tyler, the Recording Officer, hurried into the room waving a strip of paper above his head; his eyes were shining as he laid it on the C.O.'s desk.

Major Mullen read the signal, and a grim smile spread over his face. 'Gentlemen,' he said, 'I am glad to be able to tell you that we shall be able to give the Huns something else to think about before long; the squadron is to be equipped with the long-secret super-scout at last. Our Pups are to be replaced by Sopwith Camels*.'

A moment's silence greeted this important announcement.

It was broken by Biggles. 'Fine!' he said. 'Now we'll show the Huns what's what!'

* Single seater fighter aircraft, with two fixed machine guns firing through the propeller. A more powerful development of the Pup but tricky to fly.

Chapter 16
The Yellow Hun

No. 266 Squadron, R.F.C., at Maranique, had been
equipped with Sopwith Camels for nearly a month,
and with the improved equipment the pilots were showing the enemy—as Biggles had put it—what was what.
Except for two pilots who had been killed whilst learning to fly the very tricky Camels, things had gone along
quite smoothly, and Biggles had long ago settled down
as a regular member of the squadron. Indeed, he was
beginning to regard himself as something of a veteran.

It was a warm spring afternoon, and as he sat sun-
ning himself on the veranda after an uneventful morning patrol he felt on good terms with himself and the
world in general. 'Where's the Old Man?' he suddenly
asked Mahoney, who had just returned from the sheds,
where he had been supervising the timing of his guns.

'Dunno,' was the reply. 'I think he's gone off to
Amiens, or somewhere, for a conference. Oh, here he
comes now. He looks pretty grim. I'll bet something's
in the wind!'

The C.O. joined them on the veranda. He looked at
Biggles as if he were about to speak, but he changed
his mind and looked through the open window into the
ante-room, where several other officers were sitting. He
called to them to come outside.

'I've a bit of news—or perhaps I should say a story,'
he began, when everyone had assembled. 'It will be of
particular interest to you, Bigglesworth.'

Biggles stared. 'To me, sir?' he cried in surprise.

'Yes. You haven't been over to your old squadron lately, have you?'

Biggles shook his head. 'No, sir, I haven't!' he said wonderingly.

'Then you haven't heard about Way?'

'Mark Way!' Biggles felt his face going white. Mark had been his gunner and great friend when they were together in 169 Squadron. 'Why, he isn't—?' He could not bring himself to say the fatal word.

'No, he isn't dead, but he'll never fly again,' said the C.O. quitely.

Biggles' lips turned dry. 'But how—what?' he stammered.

'I've just seen him,' went on the C.O. 'I had to attend a conference in Amiens, and I ran into Major Paynter, who was going to the hospital to see Way. He told me about it. Way is now en route for England. He'll never come back.'

'But I don't understand!' exclaimed Biggles. 'He was due to go home when I came here; he was going to get his pilot's wings. In fact I thought he'd actually gone.'

'That's right,'said the C.O. 'He packed up his kit and set off, but apparently he was kept hanging about the port of embarkation for some time. Then the Huns made their big show, and he with everyone else who was waiting to go home was recalled to his squadron.'

'But why didn't he let me know?' cried Biggles.

'He hadn't time. He arrived back just in time to be sent on a show with Captain Mapleton. They didn't return, and were posted missing the same day. Way arrived back yesterday, having crawled into our front line trench, minus his right hand and an eye.'

'Good heavens!'

'He asked to be remembered to you, and said he would write to you as soon as he was able, from home.'

'But what happened, sir?'

'I'm coming to that. In point of fact, what I'm about to say was intended for you alone—his last message— but I think it is a matter that concerns everyone, so I shall make no secret of it.' The C.O.'s face hardened. 'This is what he told me,' he continued. 'As I said, he was flying with Mapleton—'

'Where's Mapleton now?' broke in Biggles.

'Mapleton was killed. But let me continue.'

Biggles gripped the rail of the veranda, but said nothing.

'He was, I say, acting as gunner for Mapleton,' went on the C.O. 'They were attacked by a big bunch of enemy machines, near Lille. By a bit of bad luck they got their engine shot up in the early stages of the fight, and had to go down, and the Hun who had hit them followed them down, shooting at them all the time. Their prop had stopped, and they waved to him to show that they were going to land, but he continued shooting at them while they were, so to speak helpless.'

A stir ran through the listeners.

'It was at this juncture that Way was struck in the eye by a piece of glass; but he didn't lose consciousness. Mapleton made a perfect landing in spite of the damage the machine had suffered and it looked as if they would both escape with their lives—as indeed they should have done. But the Hun thought differently. Thank Heaven they are not all like him. He deliberately shot them up after they had landed—emptied his guns at them.'

'The unspeakable hog!' Biggles ground the words out through clenched teeth.

'Mapleton fell dead with a bullet through his head. Way's wrist was splintered by an explosive bullet, and his hand was subsequently amputated in a German field hospital. Three days ago, on the eve of being transferred to a prison camp, he escaped, and managed to work his way through the Lines. He arrived in a state of collapse, and Major Paynter thinks that it was only the burning desire to report the flagrant breach of the accepted rules of air fighting, and the passion for revenge, which he knew would follow, that kept him on his feet. The Hun seems to have been a Hun in every sense of the word; he actually went and gloated over Way in hospital.'

'Mark didn't learn his name, by any chance?' muttered Biggles harshly.

'Yes. It's Von Kraudil, of Jagdstaffel Seventeen.'

'What colour was his kite?' asked Biggles, his hands twitching curiously.

'Yes, that's more important, for by this we shall be able to recognize him.' The C.O. spoke softly, but very distinctly. 'He flies a sulphur-yellow Albatros with a black nose, and a black diamond painted on each side of the fuselage.'

'I've seen that skunk!' snarled McLaren, starting up. 'Yellow is a good colour for him. I'll—'

The C.O. held up his hands as a babble of voices broke out. 'Yes, I know,' he said quickly. 'Most of us have seen this machine; it's been working on this part of the Front for some time, so I hope it is still about.'

'I'll nail his yellow hide up in the ante-room!' declared Mahoney.

'Such methods would have been in order a few hundred years ago, but we can hardly do that sort of thing to-day,' smiled the C.O. 'All the same, a piece of yellow fuselage might look well—'

'Leave that to me, sir!' interrupted Biggles. 'Mark Way was my—'

'Not likely! No fear!' a chorus of protests from the other pilots overwhelmed him, and the C.O. was again compelled to call for silence. 'It's up to everyone to get him,' he went on. 'And the officer who gets him may have a week's leave!'

'I'll get that leave—to go and see Mark!' declared Biggles.

'All right, gentlemen, that's all,' concluded the C.O.

'He says that's all!' muttered Biggles to Mahoney. 'It isn't, not by a long shot!'

Under the influence of his cold fury his first idea was to rush off into the air and stay there until he had found the yellow Hun. Instead, he controlled himself, and made his way to his room to think the matter over. He was in a curious state of nerves, for the news had stirred him as nothing had ever done before. He was depressed by the tragic end of the man whom he still regarded as he best friend, and with whom he had had so many thrilling adventures. And tears actually came into his eyes when he thought of his old flight-commander, Mapleton, whom they all called Mabs, one of the most brilliant and fearless fighters in France.

He was suffering from a mild form of shock, although he did not know it, and behind it all was the burning desire for vengeance. That by his cold-blooded action the yellow Hun had signed his own death warrant Biggles did not doubt, for not a single member of either his old squadron or his present one would rest until Mabs had been avenged. But Biggles wanted to shoot the man down himself. He wanted to see his tracer bullets boring into that yellow cockpit. The mere fact that the Hun had fallen under the guns of someone else would not give him the same satisfaction. In fact, as he pondered the matter, he began to feel afraid that someone else might shoot the Hun down before he could come to grips with him.

The matter was chiefly his concern, after all, he reasoned. Mark had been his friend, and Mabs his flight-commander. No doubt machines were already scouring the sky for the murderer—for that was almost what the action of shooting at a machine on the ground amounted to.

'Well,' he muttered at last, 'if I'm going to get this hound I'd better see about it!'

He rose, washed, picked up his flying kit, and made his way to the sheds. 'Where's everybody?' he asked Smyth, the flight-sergeant.

'In the air, sir.'

'Ah, I might have known it,' breathed Biggles. He was so accustomed to the sound of aero engines that he had hardly noticed the others taking off. But he knew only too well why the aerodrome was deserted, and he hastened to his own machine.

Within five minutes he was in his Camel, heading for the Lines. He hardly expected to find Von Kraudil cruising about the sky alone; that would be asking too much. He would certainly be flying with a formation of single-seaters. If that were so, he, Biggles, would stand a better chance of finding his man by flying alone, as the Huns would certainly attack the lone British machine if they saw him, whereas they might refuse to engage the others if they were flying together.

In any case, a wide area would have to be combed, for the enemy machines operated far to the east and west of their base. So in order to expedite matters, Biggles deliberately asked for trouble by thrusting deep into the enemy country. Ground observers could hardly fail to see him, and would, he hoped, report his presence to the nearest squadrons, in accordance with their usual practice.

Far and wide he searched, but curiously enough the sky appeared to be deserted. Once he saw a formation of three Camels, and a little later three more, but he did not join them. Never had he seen the sky so empty.

At the end of two hours he was forced to return to the aerodrome without having seen an enemy aircraft of any sort, and consequently without firing a shot. On the ground he learned that the other machines had already returned, refuelled, and taken off again.

Then he had a stroke of luck—or so he regarded it. His tanks had been filled, and he was about to take off again, when Watt Tyler rushed out of the Squadron Office and hailed him. 'You're looking for that yellow devil, I suppose?' he inquired shortly.

'Who else do you suppose I'd be looking for?' replied Biggles coldly.

'All right, keep your hair on! I was only going to tell you that forward gunner observers have just reported that a large enemy formation has just crossed our Lines in pursuit of two Camels.'

'Where?'

'Up by Passchendaele.'

Biggles did not stop to thank Watt for the information. He thrust the throttle open, and his wheels left the ground he soared upwards in a steep climbing turn in the direction of the well-known town.

He saw the dog-fight afar off. At least, he saw the archie bursts that clustered thickly about the isolated machines, and he roared towards the spot on full throttle, peering ahead round his windscreen to try to identify the combatants. Presently he was able to make out what had happened, for the two Camels that had been pursued had turned, and were now hard at it, assisted by half a dozen Bristols. There seemed to be about twelve or fourteen Huns, all Albatroses. He guessed that they had chased the Camels over the Line, and, on turning, found their retreat cut off by the Bristols. That, in fact, was exactly what had happened.

The enemy machines were still too far away for their colours to be distinguished, but as he drew nearer he saw one, dark blue in colour, break out of the fight some distance below him and streak for the Line.

'Not so fast!' growled Biggles, as he altered his course slightly and tore down after the escaping Hun. The enemy pilot, who did not even see him, was leaning out of his cockpit on the opposite side of the fuselage, looking back at the dogfight as if he expected the other machines to follow, and wondered why they did not. For a few seconds he omitted to watch the sky around him and paid the penalty for that neglect—as so many pilots did, sooner or later.

Biggles fired exactly five rounds at point-blank range, and the Hun's petrol tank burst into flames. Biggles zoomed clear, amazed at the effectiveness of his fire, for hitherto he had fired many rounds before such a thing had happened. His first shot must have gone straight through the tank. He glanced down, to see the Hun still falling, the doomed pilot leaning back in his cockpit with his arms over his face. It crashed in a sheet of flame near a British rest camp, and Biggles turned again to the dog-fight, which had now become more scattered over a fairly wide area.

Several Huns had broken out of the fight and were racing towards the Lines. But, as far as Biggles could see, there was not a yellow one amongst them, although he wasted some precious time chasing first one and then another in the hope of recognizing the particular one he sought. He turned back towards the spot where several machines were still circling, and as he drew nearer he saw something that would normally have given him satisfaction, but on this occasion brought a quick frown to his forehead. With a quick movement of his left hand he pushed up his goggles to make quite certain that he was not mistaken. But there was no mistake about it.

A bright yellow Hun had broken clear of the fight, but was being furiously attacked by a Camel—which Biggles instantly recognized by its markings as the one belonging to Mahoney. He had never seen a Camel handled like it before, and he sensed the hatred that possessed the pilot and inspired such brilliant flying.

The Hun hadn't a ghost of a chance; it was out-manœuvred at every turn. Once, as if to make suspicion a certainty, it turned broadside on towards Biggles, who saw a large black diamond painted on its yellow wooden side. That the Hun would fall was certain. It was only a matter of time, for the Camel was glued to its tail, guns spouting tracer bullets in long, vicious bursts. The pilot of the yellow machine seemed to be making no effort to retaliate but concentrated his efforts in attempting to escape, twisting and turning like a fish with an otter behind it.

Biggles had no excuse for butting-in, and he knew it. Mahoney was quite capable of handling the affair himself, and his presence might do more harm than good. If he got in the way of the whirling machines,

199

the two Camel pilots would certainly have to watch each other to avoid collision, and in the confusion the Hun might escape.

That was a contingency Biggles dared not risk, much as he would have liked to take a hand. So he kept clear, and, circling, watched the end of a very one-sided duel. Suddenly in a last frantic effort to escape, the Hun spun, came out, and spun again; but the Camel had spun down behind it and was ready to administer the knock-out. Mahoney let drive again, but the Hun did not wait for any more. Once again he spun, only to pull out at the last minute, then drop in a steep sideslip to a rather bad landing in a handy field.

Biggles, who had followed the fight down, beat the side of his cockpit with his clenched fist in impotent rage. 'The yellow skunk!' he grated. 'He's got away with it. Never mind, this is where Mahoney treats him to a spot of his own medicine.'

But Mahoney did nothing of the sort, as Biggles, in his heart, knew he would not. The Flight-Commander simply could not bring himself to shoot at a man who was virtually unarmed.

The knowledge that he, Biggles, could not either, made him still more angry, and with hate smouldering in his eyes, he dropped down and landed near Mahoney who had already put his machine on the ground not far from the Hun.

As they jumped from their cockpits and raced towards the yellow machine Biggles was afraid that Von Kraudil would set fire to his Albatros before they could reach him; but the Boche had no such intention, either because he forgot to do so, or because he was too scared.

'I got him!' roared Mahoney as they ran.

200

'All right, I know you did. I'm not arguing about it, am I?' answered Biggles shortly. The fact that his flight-commander had shot down the yellow machine, the pilot of which, had after all escaped just retribution, was rather a bitter pill for him to swallow. He slowed down while still some yards away, for the German pilot certainly did not look the sort of man Biggles imagined he would be. He had taken off his cap and goggles and was leaning against the fuselage flaxen-haired and blue-eyed—eyes now wide open with apprehension. A trickle of blood was running down his ashen cheek, and he endeavoured to stem it with a handkerchief while he looked from the two pilots to a crowd of Tommies who, with an officer at their head, were coming at the double across the field.

Mahoney eyed his prisoner coldly, but said nothing.

'What's your name?' snapped Biggles, eyes bright with hostility.

The German shook his head, making it clear that he did not understand.

Biggles pointed at the man. 'Von Kraudil?' he asked.

'*Nein, nein!*' was the reply.

Biggles looked at Mahoney, and Mahoney looked at Biggles.

'I don't believe it's him after all!' declared Biggles. 'This kid doesn't look like a murderer to me. I say,' he went to the infantry officer, who now joined them, 'do you, or any of your fellows, happen to speak German?'

'I know a bit,' admitted the youthful, mud-splashed subaltern.

'Then would you mind asking him his name?' requested Biggles.

The officer put the question to the Boche, and turned back to Biggles.

'He says his name is Schultz.'

'Ask him for his identification disc; I have special reasons for not wanting to make any mistake about this.'

Again the infantry officer addressed the German, who groped under his tunic and produced a small, round piece of metal.

'He's telling the truth,' went on the subaltern, after a quick glance at it. 'Here's his name right enough—Wilhelm Schultz.'

'Then ask him if he's flying Von Kraudil's machine.'

'No!' came the prompt reply from the subaltern, who had continued the interrogation. 'He says this used to be Von Kraudil's machine, but it was handed over to him the other day; Von Kraudil has a new one—a blue one.'

Biggles stared.

'Blue, did you say?'

The Hun stared from one to another as the question was put to him, evidently unable to make out what the questions were leading up to.

'Yes. He says Von Kraudil's machine is blue, with a white diagonal bar behind the cross on the fuselage.'

'So that was Von Kraudil, eh?' mused Biggles softly.

'Why do you say "was"?' asked Mahoney.

'Because I got him after all!' cried Biggles exultantly. 'I got a machine answering to that description ten minutes ago! Come on, let's go and confirm it!'

'How did you manage to get mixed up in this affair?' asked Mahoney, as Biggles led the way to where the blue machine had crashed in flames. 'You were missing when the rest of us took off—asleep in your room or something.'

'Asleep, my foot!' snorted Biggles. 'I was doing a

spot of thinking—wondering what was the best way to get at that yellow Hun. It was sheer luck I heard about your dog-fight. I was making for my machine when Watt Tyler gave me the news that a formation of Huns was chasing two Camels. He gave me the direction so I beetled along. I saw the blue machine break away from the fight as I came up, went after it, and sent it down a flamer.'

'How about the pilot?' asked Mahoney. 'Did he manage to jump clear of his machine? If he didn't, we're going to have a job proving that Von Kraudil was flying it. We've only that other pilot's word for it that it was Von Kraudil's machine, you know.'

'H'm!' grunted Biggles. 'I hadn't thought of that. I certainly didn't see him jump, but he may have been flung clear when his machine crashed. Anyway,' he added, as the still smoking remains of the blue machine came into view, 'we'll soon know.'

A crowd of officers and men from the near-by rest camp were clustered around the remains. Forcing their way through the crowd, Mahoney and Biggles approached as near as they could to the hot debris of the machine. It was a terrible jumble of fused and twisted wires, utterly unrecognizable as an aeroplane.

'Gosh! What a mess!' muttered Biggles.

It was impossible to search the hot debris for the body of the pilot, and from the distance it was impossible to distinguish any sign of human remains. Mahoney turned to one of the officers. 'Can you tell me what happened to the pilot of this machine?' he asked.

'Why, yes,' replied the other. 'We found his body lying some distance away. He must have been killed when he was thrown out, but he had been badly burned beforehand. We took the body to the camp.'

'We want to find out his name,' said Mahoney. 'So we'll go along to the camp.'

'No need to do that,' said the officer. 'His name was Von Kraudil. I examined the identity disc.'

'Then it was our man, after all!' exclaimed Biggles. 'Come on; let's get back and report. I think I'll take that week's leave the Old Man spoke about—and go and see Mark.'

BIGGLES
FLIES EAST

Foreword

The careers of most of those who served in the Great War* for any length of time resolve themselves, in retrospect, into a number of distinct phases, or episodes, rather than one continuous period of service in the same environment. For example, an artillery officer serving in France might find himself, a month later, acting as an aerial gunner on the Italian Front, and after seeing service in that capacity for a while would be sent home to England to get his pilot's wings. Later, when he qualified, he might be rushed off to fill a vacancy in another theatre of war—possibly Salonika or East Africa.

Each of these periods was quite unlike the others; it represented a different climate, a different set of faces, and an entirely different atmosphere.

The career of Captain James Bigglesworth, M.C., D.F.C. (known to his friends as 'Biggles'), was no exception, as those who have read his already published war experiences will agree. But there was one period that has not so far been mentioned, and the reasons have been twofold.

In the first place Biggles, far from taking any credit for the part he played in this particular affair, regards the whole tour of duty with such distaste that even his

* The First World War 1914–18. Principal contenders, the Allies: Britain, France, Russia, Italy, Serbia, Belgium, Japan (1915), Romania (1916), USA (1917). Against the Central Powers: Germany, Austria-Hungary, Turkey and Bulgaria (1915).

friend, the Honourable Algernon Lacey (who, it will be remembered, served with him in No. 266 Squadron when it was stationed at Maranique, in France), seldom if ever referred to it. Just why Biggles should feel this way about what were undoubtedly vital affairs of national importance is hard to see, but the fact remains. Like many other successful air fighters, he was a law unto himself, and intolerant of any attempt to alter his point of view—which may have been one of the reasons why he was successful.

Secondly, the Official Secrets Act* has been tightened up, and as one of the principal actors in the drama that is about to be disclosed was alive until recently— not only alive, but holding an important position in the German Government—it was thought prudent to remain silent on a subject that might have led to embarrassing correspondence and possibly international recriminations. This man, who at the time of the events about to be narrated was a trusted officer of the German Secret Service, in the end met the same fate as those of his enemies who fell in his hands—blindfold, with his back to a wall, facing a firing party in the cold grey light of dawn. Whether or not he deserved his fate is not for us to question.

There is little more to add except that Biggles, at the time, was a war-hardened veteran of twelve months' active service. He had learnt to face the Spandaus** of the German Fokkers without flinching, and the *whoof, whoof, whoof* of 'archie'*** bursting around his machine

* Official Secrets Act. An agreement which, when a British subject signs, forbids him or her to disclose confidential information prejudicial to the State.
** German machine-guns were often referred to as Spandaus, due to the fact that many were manufactured at Spandau, Germany.
*** Anti-aircraft gunfire, a Royal Flying Corps expression.

left him unmoved. He afterwards confessed to Algy
that it was not until his feet had trodden the age-old
sands of the Promised Land that he learnt to know the
real meaning of the word Fear.

When he went there he was, like many another air
warrior, still a boy; when he came back he was still a
boy, but old beyond his years. Into his deep-set hazel
eyes, which less than eighteen months before had pondered arithmetic with doubt and algebra with despair,
had come a new light; and into his hands, small and
delicate—hands that at school had launched paper
darts with unerring accuracy—had come a new grip as
they closed over joystick and firing lever. When you
have read the story perhaps you will understand the
reason.

1935   W.E.J.

The word 'Hun' as used in this book, was the common generic term for anything belonging to the enemy. It was used in a familiar sense, rather than derogatory. Witness the fact that in the R.F.C. a hun was also a pupil at a flying training school.

W.E.J

Chapter 1
How it Began

I

Captain James Bigglesworth, R.F.C.*, home from France on ten days' leave, stopped at the corner of Lower Regent Street and glanced at his watch. 'Ten to one; I thought it felt like lunch-time,' he mused, as he turned and strolled in the direction of the Caprice Restaurant, the famous war-time rendezvous of R.F.C. officers in London. At the door he hesitated as a thought occurred to him, and he contemplated dubiously the clothes he was wearing, for he was what would be described in service parlance as 'improperly dressed', in that he was not in uniform but civilian attire. The reason for this was quite a natural one.

His uniform, while passable in Flanders, where mud and oil were accepted as a matter of course, looked distinctly shabby in London's bright spring sunshine, and his first act on arrival had been to visit his tailor's with a view to getting it cleaned and pressed. This, he was informed, would take some hours, so rather than remain indoors he had purchased a ready-made suit of civilian clothes—to wear while his uniform was being reconditioned, as he put it. It was an obvious and pardonable excuse from his point of view, but whether or not it would be accepted by the Assistant Provost

* Royal Flying Corps 1914–1918. An army corps responsible for military aeronautics, renamed the Royal Air Force (RAF) when amalgamated with the Royal Naval Air Service on 1 April 1918.

Marshal or the Military Police, if he happened to run into them, was quite another matter. So he hesitated when he reached the fashionable meeting-place, torn between a desire to find someone he knew with whom he could talk 'shop', and a disinclination to risk collision with the A.P.M. and his minions who, as he was well aware, kept a vigilant eye on the Caprice.

'What does it matter, anyway? At the worst they can only cancel my leave, which won't worry me an awful lot,' he decided, and pushed open the swing doors. There were several officers and one or two civilians lounging round the buffet, but a swift scrutiny revealed that they were all strangers, so he selected a small table in a secluded corner and picked up a menu card.

He was still engrossed in the not unpleasant task of choosing his lunch when, out of the corner of his eye, he saw some one appear at his side, and thinking it was only a waiter he paid no immediate attention; but when he became conscious of the fact that some one was in the act of settling in the opposite chair he looked up with surprise and disapproval, for there were plenty of vacant tables.

'Good morning, Captain Brunow,' said the newcomer, easily, and without hesitation.

'Sorry, but you're making a mistake,' replied Biggles curtly, resuming his occupation.

'I think not,' went on the other coolly. 'Have a drink.'

Biggles eyed the speaker coldly. 'No, thanks,' he answered, shortly. 'I have already told you that you are making a mistake. My name isn't Brunow,' he added, in a tone that was calculated to end the conversation forthwith.

'No! Ha, ha, of course not. I quite understand. In the circumstances the sooner a name like that is forgotten the better, eh?'

Biggles folded the menu and laid it on the table with deliberation before raising his eyes to meet those of his *vis-à-vis*. 'Are you suggesting that I don't know my own name?' he inquired icily.

The other shrugged his shoulders with an air of bored impatience. 'Don't let us waste time arguing about a matter so trivial,' he protested. 'My purpose is to help you. *My* name, by the way, is Broglace—Ernest Broglace. I—'

'Just a minute, Mr Broglace,' interrupted Biggles. 'You seem to be a very difficult person to convince. I've told you plainly enough that my name is not Brunow. You say yours is Broglace, and, frankly, I believe you, but I see nothing in that to get excited about. As far as I am concerned it can be Dogface, Hogface, or even Frogface. And if, as I suspect, your persistent efforts to force your company upon me are prompted by the fond hope of ultimately inducing me to buy a foolproof watch, a bullet-proof vest, or some other useless commodity, I may as well tell you right away that you are wasting your time. And what is more important, you are wasting mine. I require nothing today, and if I did I shouldn't buy it from you. I trust I have now made myself quite clear. Thank you. Good morning.'

Broglace threw back his head and laughed heartily, while Biggles watched him stonily.

'For sheer crust, your hide would make elephant-skin look like tissue paper,' went on Biggles, dispassionately, as the other showed no sign of moving. 'Are you going to find another table—or must I?'

Broglace suddenly leaned forward, and his manner changed abruptly. 'Listen, Brunow,' he said quietly but tersely. 'I know who you are and why you're in

mufti*. I know the whole story. Now, I'm serious. The
service has outed you, and there is nothing left for you
but to be called up as a conscript, be sent to France,
and be shot. What about earning some easy money—
by working for people who *will* appreciate what you
do?'

Biggles was about to make a heated denial when
something in the face opposite seemed to strike a chill
note of warning, of danger, of something deeper than
he could understand, and the words he was about to
utter remained unsaid. Instead, he looked at the man
for a moment or two in silence, and what he saw only
strengthened his suspicions that something serious,
even sinister, lay behind the man's uninvited atten-
tions.

There was nothing very unusual in the stranger's
general appearance. Of average height and built, he
might have been a prosperous City man, just over
military age, possibly a war profiteer. His hair was fair,
close cut, and began high up on a bulging forehead.
His neck was thick, and his face broad and flat, but
with a powerful jaw that promised considerable
strength of will. But it was his eyes that held Biggles,
and sent a curious prickling sensation down his spine.
They were pale blue, and although partly hidden
behind large tortoiseshell glasses, they held a glint, a
piercing quality of perception and grim determination,
that boded ill for any one who stood in his path. Biggles
felt an unusual twinge of apprehension as they bored
into his own and he looked away suddenly. 'I see—I
see,' he said slowly.

There was a sound of laughter from the door, and a
party of R.F.C. officers poured into the room, full of

* Civilian clothes worn by someone who usually wears a uniform.

214

the joy of life and good spirits; some made for the buffet and others moved towards the luncheon-tables. Biggles knew one or two of them well, and they gave him the excuse he needed, although he acted more upon intuition than definite thought.

'Look here,' he said quickly, 'I know some of these fellows; perhaps it would be as well—'

'Exactly. I agree,' replied the other, rising swiftly to his feet. 'I shall be here between tea and dinner—say about 6.30. The place will be empty then.' With a parting nod, he walked away quickly and was lost in the crowd now surging through the entrance.

Biggles sat quite still for some minutes after he had gone, turning the matter over in his mind. Then he made a quick, light meal and joined the crowd at the buffet. He exchanged greetings with Ludgate of 287 Squadron, whom he knew well, and drew him aside. 'Listen, Lud,' he said. 'I want to ask you something. Did you ever hear of a chap named Brunow?'

'Good gracious! yes; he's just been slung out of the service on his ear, and about time too. He was an awful stiff.'

'What was it about?'

'I don't know exactly, but I heard some fellows talking about it in the Alhambra last night. I believe he was hauled up on a charge of "conduct unbecoming an officer and gentleman", but I fancy there was more to it than that. Anyway, he was pushed out, and that's the main thing.'

'Did you know him personally?'

'Too true I did. I was at the same Training School with him.'

'Was he anything like me—in appearance, I mean?'

Ludgate started. 'Well, now you come to mention it,

he is, a bit; not so much, though, that any one knowing you would make a mistake.'

'I see. Thanks, laddie—see you later.'

'Where are you going?'

'Oh, just for a look round,' replied Biggles airily. Which was not strictly true, for he looked neither right nor left as he strode briskly along Coventry Street and down St Martin's Lane into the Strand, where he turned sharply into the Hotel Cecil, the Headquarters of the Air Board.

After the usual wait and interminable inquiries, he at length found himself outside a door, bearing a card on which was neatly printed:

AIR STAFF INTELLIGENCE

Major L. Bryndale

He tapped on the door, and in reply to the invitation to enter, walked in and found himself facing a worried-looking officer who was working at a ponderous desk littered with buff correspondence-jackets and memo-sheets.

'I'm Captain Bigglesworth of 266 Squadron, home on leave, sir,' began Biggles.

'Why are you not in uniform?'

'That is one of the things I shall have to explain, sir, but I have something else to tell you that I think you should know.' Briefly, but omitting nothing of import-ance, he described his recent encounter in the res-taurant.

The Intelligence Officer looked at him long and earn-estly when he had finished, and then, with a curt, 'Take a seat, don't go away', left the room, to return a few

216

minutes later with a grey-haired officer whose red tabs bespoke a senior Staff appointment.

Biggles rose to his feet and stood at attention.

'All right, sit down,' said the Staff Officer crisply. 'Have you seen this fellow who accosted you before to-day?'

'Never, sir.'

'Describe him.'

Biggles obeyed to the best of his ability.

'You know about the Brunow affair, I suppose?' asked the other when he had finished.

'Vaguely, sir. I ascertained, subsequent to my conversation with Broglace, that he had been dismissed from service recently.'

'Quite.' The General drummed on the table with his fingers. 'Well,' he went on, 'this may lead to something or it may not, but I think we should follow it up. Your leave is cancelled with effect from to-day and you will be posted to this department for special duty forthwith. I'll see that your leave is made up later on. In the meantime, I want you to try to get inside this fellow's confidence; find out just what he is up to, and report back here tomorrow. Meet him to-night as he suggests.'

'Very good, sir.'

'And I think it would be a wise precaution if you employed the next few hours making yourself thoroughly acquainted with Brunow's history, so that you can assume his identity if necessary. Major Bryndale will give you his dossier.' Then, turning to Major Bryndale, 'I'll leave Bigglesworth with you,' he said, and left the room.

II

At ten-thirty the following morning Biggles was ushered by Major Bryndale into the more spacious office of Brigadier-General Sir Malcolm Pendersby; his face wore a worried expression, for although he was not exactly nervous, he was by no means pleased at the turn events were taking.

The General glanced up as he entered. 'Well, Bigglesworth—sit down—what happened yesterday after you left us? Did the fellow turn up?'

'He did, sir,' answered Biggles, 'and it certainly looks as if—well—'

'Tell me precisely what happened.'

Biggles wrinkled his forehead. 'To tell the truth, sir, it isn't easy. You see, nothing definite was said, and no actual proposition made. It seemed to me that Broglace had something to put forward, but was being very careful.'

'As indeed he was bound to be if he is engaged in espionage,' put in the General dryly.

'Quite so, sir. As I was saying, it was all very indefinite; his conversation consisted chiefly of hints and suggestions, but if I may judge, the position at the moment is this. Broglace thinks I am Brunow; he knows Brunow has been cashiered*, and somehow or other knows quite a lot about his history. For example, he knew quite well what I only learnt yesterday from Brunow's dossier—that he is of Austrian extraction and was in the Argentine when war broke out. He knows, too, that although his financial interests are—or were—British, his sympathies, by reason of his parentage, may be with Germany and the Central Powers. He is

* Dismissed from the Armed Forces with dishonour and disqualified from entering public service.

218

working on the assumption that Brunow's disgrace has embittered him against the British—an assumption that I took care not to dispel—and that he might be induced to turn traitor.'

'But you say he made no definite offer.'

'That is quite true, sir, but it struck me that he was trying to convey his idea by suggestion rather than by actual words, in the hope that I would make the next move. He dare not risk going too far, in case he was making a mistake.'

'How did you leave matters?'

'I told him in a half-hearted sort of way that there was nothing doing, but at the same time tried to create the impression that I might be persuaded if it was made worth my while.'

'Excellent! Go on.'

'That's all, sir. Naturally, I didn't want to lose touch with him, in case you decided to arrest him, so I have made a provisional appointment—'

'Arrest!' The General opened his eyes in mock astonishment.

'Why, yes, sir,' faltered Biggles, puzzled. 'I thought that if there was a chance of him being a spy, you would arrest him on—'

'The General waved his hand. 'Good gracious, Bigglesworth,' he cried, 'we don't work like that. If the man is indeed a spy he will be far more useful to us at large than in the Tower of London*. Once we know his game we can use him to our advantage.'

'I am afraid that's rather beyond me, sir,' confessed Biggles, 'but I've done what I could, and that is the

---

* During the First World War, the Tower of London was used to house spies, prior to their trial. Some were later executed at the Tower.

end of it as far as I am concerned. May I now continue my leave?'

'Not so fast—not so fast,' replied the General quickly. 'Who said you had finished? This may be only the beginning. Pure chance seems to have placed a card in our hands that we may not be able to use without you, and I should like to give the matter a little consideration before reaching a final decision. Help yourself to cigarettes; I shan't keep you long.' He gathered up some papers on which he had been making notes and left the room.

Nearly an hour elapsed, however, before he returned, a period that left Biggles plenty of time to ruminate on the position—an unlucky one from his point of view— in which he found himself.

The General's face was grave when he returned and sat down at his desk, and he eyed Biggles speculatively. 'Now, Bigglesworth,' he commenced, 'I am going to have a very serious talk with you, and I want you to listen carefully. While I have been away I have examined the situation from every possible angle. I believe that Broglace's next move will be to make a definite offer to you, provided you do not give him cause for alarm. If our assumption is correct, he will suggest tentatively that you work for him, which means, of course, for Germany; I would like you to accept that offer.'

'Accept it?' cried Biggles incredulously.

The General nodded slowly. 'In that way we could take full advantage of an opportunity that seldom presents itself.'

Biggles thought swiftly. 'What you mean, sir, is that you would like me to become a German spy, working for the British,' he said bluntly.

The General looked rather uncomfortable. 'Without

mincing matters, that is precisely what I do mean,' he said gravely. 'Obviously, I cannot detail you for such work, but it is hardly necessary for me to remind you that it is the duty of every Englishman to do his best for his side whatever sacrifice it may involve. That is why I am asking you to volunteer for what may prove a very difficult and dangerous task. I have looked up your record, and you appear to be unusually well qualified for it, otherwise I would not contemplate the project seriously for one moment. Major Raymond, the Intelligence Officer attached to your Wing in France, speaks highly of your ability in this particular class of work; you have helped him on more than one occasion. Frankly, to handle an affair of this sort with any hope of success would be beyond the ability of the average officer. Still, the final decision must be left to you, and I should fail both in my duty and in fairness to you if I tried to minimize the risks. One blunder, one slip, one moment's carelessness—but there, I think you appreciate that, so there is no need for me to dwell on it. Well, how do you feel about it?'

Biggles thought for a moment or two. 'To pretend that I view the thing with favour would be sheer hypocrisy,' he said rather bitterly, 'but as you have been good enough to point out my obvious path of duty, I cannot very well refuse, sir.'

The General flushed slightly. 'I quite understand how you feel,' he said in a kindly tone, 'but I knew you would not refuse. Now let us examine the contingencies that are likely to arise, so that we shall know how to act when they do . . .'

Chapter 2

Algy gets a Shock

I

Lieutenant Algernon Lacy, of 266 Squadron, stationed at Maranique, in France, acting flight-commander in the absence of Biggles, his friend and flying partner, landed his Sopwith Camel* more carefully than usual, and taxied slowly towards the sheds, keeping a watchful eye on a shattered centre section strut as he did so. On reaching the tarmac he switched off his engine, climbed stiffly to the ground, and walked towards the Squadron Office to make out his combat report. He was feeling particularly pleased with himself, for he had just scored his third victory since Biggles had departed on leave.

He pushed open the door of the flimsy weatherboard building, but seeing Major Mullen, his C.O.** in earnest conversation with 'Wat' Tyler, the Recording Officer, would have withdrawn had not the C.O. called him back.

'All right, Lacey, come in,' he said. 'I was waiting to have a word with you, although I am afraid it is bad news.'

Algy paused in the act of pulling off his gauntlets and looked at the Major with a puzzled frown. 'Bad news?' he repeated, and then, as a ghastly thought

---

* A single seat biplane fighter with twin machine-guns synchronised to fire through the propeller. See cover illustration.
** Commanding Officer

struck him, 'Don't tell me Biggles has crashed,' he added quickly.

'Oh, no; nothing like that. You've been posted away.'

'Posted!'

'To Headquarters Middle East—in Cairo.'

Algy stared uncomprehendingly. 'Posted to Middle East,' he repeated again, foolishly. 'But what have I done?'

'Nothing, as far as I am aware. I can only tell you that this posting has not come from Wing Headquarters, or even General Headquarters in France. It has come direct from the Air Board.'

'But why?'

'I am sorry, Lacey, particularly as I hate losing a good officer, but it is time you knew that the Air Board is not in the habit of explaining or making excuses for its actions. You are posted with effect from to-day, and you are to catch the 7.10 train to Paris to-night. You will have to take a taxi across Paris in order to catch the 11.10 from the Gare de Lyon to Marseilles, where you will report to the Embarkation Officer at Quay 17. Your movement Order is ready. That's all. I'll see you again before you go.'

Algy sat down suddenly, and, as a man in a dream, watched the C.O. leave the office. Then, as the grim truth slowly penetrated his stunned brain, he turned to Wat in a cold fury. 'So that's all the thanks—' he began, but the Recording Officer cut him short.

'It's no use storming,' he said crisply.

'Wait till Biggles gets back; he'll have something to say about it.'

'Biggles isn't coming back.'

Algy blinked. 'Not coming back! Suffering rattle-snakes! What's happened? Has the Air Board gone balmy?'

223

'Possibly. I can only tell you that Biggles is posted to H.E.'

'Home Establishment,' sneered Algy. 'My gosh! that proves it. Fancy posting a man like Biggles to H.E. He'll set 'em alight, I'll warrant, and serve them right, too. Does the Air Board imagine that fighters like Biggles grow on gooseberry bushes? Well,' he rose despondently and turned towards the door, 'that's the end of this blinking war as far as I am concerned. I've no further interest.'

Wat eyed him sympathetically. 'It's no use going on like that, laddie,' he said quietly. 'That sort of talk won't get you anywhere. You do your job and put up a good show, and maybe you'll be able to wangle a posting back to 266. We shall miss you, and Biggles— I need hardly tell you that. Oh! by the way, I'll tell you something else, although you're not supposed to know.'

'Go ahead; you can't shock me any more.'

'You'll have a travelling companion, some one you know.'

'Who is it?'

'Major Raymond of Wing Headquarters. He's also been posted to Headquarters Middle East.'

'Good! I shall be able to tell him what I think of the Air Board.'

'And finish under close arrest. Don't be a fool, Algy. We're at war, and no doubt the Air Board knows what it's doing.'

'Maybe you're right,' agreed Algy sarcastically, as he picked up his gauntlets and left the office.

II

Ten days later, tired and travel-stained, he stepped out of a service tender at Kantara, Palestine, the aerodrome to which he had been sent on arrival in Egypt. No explanation for this further move had been asked or given; he had accepted his instructions moodily, and without interest. Kantara, Almaza, Heliopolis, Ismailia, Khartoum, or Aden, it was all the same as far as he was concerned—at least, so he had told Major Raymond when they had parted company outside Middle East Headquarters in Cairo. Where Raymond had gone Algy did not know, for he had not seen him since.

'Take my kit to the Mess Secretary's office until I fix up my quarters,' he told the driver, and then swung round on his heel as he heard his name called. Major Raymond, in khaki drill uniform, was walking briskly towards him.

'Hello, Lacey,' he cried cheerily, 'so we meet again.'

'Hello, sir,' replied Algy in surprise. 'I didn't know you were coming to Palestine, too. I'm feeling very homesick, so it's a treat to see some one I know. Why couldn't they have sent us along together, I wonder?'

'Never wonder at anything in the service, Lacey,' smiled the Major. 'Remember that there's usually a method in its madness. I had to attend an important conference after I left you in Cairo, but I got here first because I flew up—or rather, was flown up. Are you very tired?'

'Not particularly, sir. Why?'

'Because I want a word with you in private. I also want you to meet somebody; it is rather urgent, so I would like to get it over right away.'

'Good enough, sir,' returned Algy shortly.

The Major led the way to a large square tent that stood a little apart from the rest. 'This is my head-quarters,' he explained, with a curious expression on his face, as he swung aside the canvas flap that served as a door.

The tent was furnished as an office, with a large desk, telephone, and filing cabinets, but Algy noticed none of these things. He was staring at a man dressed in flying overalls who rose from a long cane chair and walked quickly towards him, laughing at his thunder-struck expression.

'I don't think an introduction is necessary,' observed Major Raymond, with a chuckle.

Algy's jaw had sagged foolishly and his lips moved as if he was trying to speak, but no words came. 'Biggles,' he managed to blurt out at last. 'Why the—what the dickens—oh, Great Scott, this has got me beaten to a frazzle.'

'Let's sit down; it's too hot to stand,' suggested the Major. 'And now let us try to work out what has happened, and why we are here,' he went on, when they were all comfortably settled. 'I'm by no means clear about it, so the sooner we all know the real pos-ition the better. You probably know more than any-body, Bigglesworth, so you had better do the talking.'

Biggles smiled rather wanly as he leaned back in his chair and unfastened his overalls, exposing the R.F.C. tunic he wore underneath. 'If you'll listen I'll tell you all I know,' he said quietly.

Briefly, he told them of his encounter with Broglace, and his subsequent conferences at the Air Board. 'You see,' he explained, 'I realized that the General was quite right when he said that it was up to every one to do his best. I hated and loathed the idea, but what could I do? In the end I told him that I would go on

226

with the business on the understanding that no one knew except himself and two persons I should name, the idea being that those two persons should act as liaison officers with me. I have only one life to lose, and I want to hang on to it as long as I can, so I didn't feel inclined to make my reports through strangers, even though they were officers of the British Intelligence Service. Sooner or later a counter-spy would get hold of the tale, and then the balloon would go up as far as I was concerned.

'Mind you, the question of going to Egypt or Palestine hadn't been raised then; that came later. Anyway, I agreed to go on with the thing if I could work with two people I knew I could trust absolutely. The General agreed, and when I named you he was quite pleased, because, as he said, apart from the question of trust, you, Algy, would be valuable because you could fly, and you, sir, because you were already on the Intelligence Staff. Now you know why you were posted.

'The next move came when I saw Broglace that evening. When he realized that I was ready to talk business he put his cards on the table and made me an offer of high wages if I would join the German Secret Service, and that showed me just where I stood. I said I'd think it over, went back to the General, and asked him what I was to do about it. He told me to accept, but if possible get to this part of the world, where the war was going to pieces as far as we were concerned, because the place was rotten with German spies—due chiefly to the activities of a Hun named El Shereef. Our people only know him by his Arab name; they very badly want to get a slant on him, and that was to be my job. They suggested that when I got here—if I did—I should get in touch with our leading Intelligence

Agent, Major Sterne. He's a free-lance, and as far as I can make out tears about the desert on a camel, or on horseback, pulling the wires through Arab chiefs and tribesmen. El Shereef and Sterne are the two big noises out here, apparently, and each has been trying to get at the other's throat for months.

'I said I'd try to get out here but would prefer to play a lone hand; I didn't like the idea of working under anybody, not even Major Sterne, although they say he's brilliant. Well, to make a long story short, I saw Broglace and told him I was prepared to fall in line with him. He wanted me to go to Belgium, but I shot him a line about being well known, and sooner or later was bound to bump into somebody who knew me. He quite saw the wisdom of my protest, and asked me to which other theatre of war I would prefer to go. I told him Palestine, and that was that.'

'But how on earth did you get out here?' asked Algy curiously.

'Ah, that would make a story in itself,' replied Biggles mysteriously. 'Broglace gave me a ring, a signet ring with a hinged flap that covered a peculiar device, and told me it would work like an oracle. And he was right. It did. I'd flown home on leave, as you know, so I went and got my machine, and instead of flying to France, went straight to Brussels. Broglace thought I'd stolen it—but that's by the way. It was a sticky trip, believe me, with Huns trying to shoot me down all the way, but I got there. As soon as I landed I was taken prisoner, but I flashed my ring and it acted like a charm. You should have seen the Huns bowing and scraping round me. I was pushed into a train for Berlin, where I had to go through a very dickens of a cross-examination from a kind of tribunal. It put the wind up me properly, and I don't mind admitting it. Then I was sent on to Jerusalem, where I reported to the Intelligence people, who posted me to Zabala under Count von Faubourg, who is O.C.* of the German Secret Service on this particular sector of the front.

'I got there two days ago, and was sent out on a reconnaisance this morning to get my general bearings.'

'But how on earth did you manage to land on our side of the lines in a Hun machine?' asked Algy in amazement.

'I didn't say anything about a Hun machine. I'm flying a British machine, a Bristol Fighter**. The Huns have two of our machines, a two-seater—the Bristol— and a Sopwith 'Pup'. They must have forced-landed over the wrong side of the lines at some time or other, and been repaired. Anyway, I slipped over right away to try to get in touch with you in order that we could make some sort of plan, and fix a rendezvous where we could meet when I have anything to report. I fancy the Boche*** idea is that I shall land over here and take back any information I pick up. That's why I'm still wearing a British uniform, although I have a German one as well.

'I daren't stay very long, or they may wonder what I'm up to. While I've been waiting I've jotted down some suggestions on a sheet of paper; I'd like you both to read them, memorize them, and then destroy it. Algy, I imagine you will be exempt from ordinary duty; the Major will be able to arrange all that. As a temporary measure I have decided on the oasis of Abba Sud as an emergency meeting-place. It's well out in the

* Officer Commanding.
** Two seated biplane fighter with remarkable manoeuvrability, in service 1917 onward. It had one fixed Vickers gun for the pilot and one or two mobile Lewis guns for the observer/gunner.
*** A derogatory slang term for the Germans.

229

desert, a good way from either British or German forces, so it should be safe. Here it is.'

He crossed over to a large wall-map that hung on the side of the tent, and laid his finger on a small circle that bore the name Abba Sud. 'I want you to hang round there as often as you can, and watch for me,' he went on. 'I may be flying a British machine, or a German, and in either case I will try to fire a red Very* light to let you know it's me. Then we'll land, talk things over, and you can report to Major Raymond. Now I must go. We're in touch, and that's a load off my mind. We shall have to settle details later to suit any conditions that may arise; it's all been such a rush that I haven't been able to sort the thing out properly yet.'

He rose to his feet, fastened his overalls, and held out his hand. 'Good-bye for the present, sir. Cheerio, Algy.'

Algy sprang up in a mild panic. 'But you're not going back—to land behind the Hun Lines?' he cried aghast.

'Of course I am.'

Algy turned a trifle pale and shook his head. 'For God's sake be careful,' he whispered tersely. 'They'll shoot you like a dog if they spot what you're doing.'

'I know it,' returned Biggles calmly, 'so the thing is not to get caught. You keep your end up and it will pan out all right. Remember one thing above everything. Trust nobody. The spy system on this front is the best in the world, and if one whisper gets out about me, even in the Officers' Mess here, I'm sunk. Cheerio!' With a final wave of his hand he left them.

As he walked swiftly towards the aerodrome where

* A coloured flare fired as a signal from a special short-barrelled pistol.

he had left his machine he paused in his stride to admire a beautifully mounted Arab who swept past him, galloping towards the camp. The Arab did not even glance in his direction, and Biggles thought he had never seen a finer example of wild humanity.

'Who's that?' he asked a flight-sergeant, who was going in the direction of the hangars.

The N.C.O.* glanced up. 'Looks like Major Sterne, sir, coming in from one of his raids,' he replied casually. 'He's always poppin' up when he's least expected.'

'Thanks, flight-sergeant,' replied Biggles, and looked round with renewed interest. But the horseman had disappeared.

Deep in thought, he made his way to his machine and climbed into the cockpit. The engine roared. For a hundred yards he raced like an arrow over the sand and then swept upwards into the blue sky, turning in a wide circle towards the German lines.

---

* Non-commissioned officer, e.g. a corporal or sergeant.

Chapter 3
Biggles gets a Shock

During the short journey to Zabala, which besides being the headquarters of the German Intelligence Staff was the station of two German squadrons, one of single-seater Pfalz Scouts and the other of two seater Halberstadts, he pondered on the amazing chain of circumstances that had resulted in the present situation. That the work to which he had pledged himself would not be to his liking he had been fully aware before he started, yet curiously enough he found himself playing his part far more naturally than he had imagined possible. At first, the natural apprehension which the field-grey uniforms around him inspired, combined with the dreadful feeling of loneliness that assailed him when he found himself in the midsts of his enemies, almost caused him to decide to escape at the first opportunity; but when the dangers which he sensed at every turn did not materialize the feeling rapidly wore off, confidence grew, and he resolved to pursue his task to the bitter end.

But for Hauptmann* von Stalhein he would have been almost at ease. Of all the Germans he had met during his journey across Europe, and in Zabala, none filled him with the same indefinable dread as von Stalhein, who was Count von Faubourg's chief of staff. The Count himself was simply a rather coarse old man of the military type, brutal by nature and a bully to those

* Captain.

who were not in a position to retaliate. He had achieved his rank and position more by unscrupulous cunning, and the efforts of those who served under him, than by any great mental qualifications.

The other German flying officers he had met were quite normal and had much in common with British flying officers, with the possible exception of Karl Leffens, to whom he had taken a dislike on account of his overbearing manner—a dislike that had obviously been mutual.

Erich von Stalhein was in a very different category. In appearance he was tall, slim, and good-looking in a rather foppish way, but he had been a soldier for many years, and there was a grim relentlessness about his manner that quickly told Biggles that he was a man to be feared. He had been wounded early in the war, and walked with a permanent limp with the aid of two sticks, and this physical defect added something to his sinister bearing. Unlike most of his countrymen, he was dark, with cold brooding eyes that were hard to meet and held a steel-like quality that the monocle he habitually wore could not dispel. Such was Hauptmann Erich von Stalhein, the officer to whom Biggles had reported in Zabala and who had conducted him into Count von Faubourg's office for interview.

Biggles sensed a latent hostility from the first moment that they met, and felt it throughout the interview. It was almost as if the man suspected him of being an imposter but did not dare to question the actions of those who had been responsible for his employment. Whether or not von Stalhein was aware that he, as Lieutenant Brunow, had previously served in the British R.F.C. he did not know, nor did he think it wise to inquire. Of one thing he was quite certain, however, and that was that the German would watch him like a cat watching a mouse, and pounce at the first slip he made.

Another thing he noticed was that all the Germans engaged in Intelligence work wore a signet ring like the one that had been given to him by Broglace; it appeared to be a kind of distinguishing mark or identification symbol. The Count wore one, as did von Stalhein and Leffens; he had also seen one or two other officers wearing them. His own, when opened, displayed a tiny dagger suspended over a double-headed eagle, with a small number 117 engraved below. Just how big a part it played in the German espionage system he had yet to learn.

If he had been sent to Zabala for any special reason he had not yet been informed of it. The Count, his Chief had merely said that he would be employed in the most useful capacity at the earliest opportunity, but in the meantime he was to make himself acquainted with the positions of the battle fronts. Nevertheless he suspected that his chief duty would be to land behind the British lines, for the purpose of either gathering information or verifying information that had already been acquired through other channels. In this he was not mistaken.

Of El Shereef he had seen no sign—not that he expected to. The name was almost a legend, hinted at rather than spoken in actual words. Still, there was no doubt that the man existed: General Pendersby had assured him of that. He could only keep his ears and eyes open and wait for some clue that might lead to the identification of the German super-spy.

At this period of the war the German Secret Service in Palestine was the most efficient in the world, and of its deadly thoroughness he was soon to have a graphic example. Quite unaware of this, he reached Zabala without incident, and after making a neat landing, taxied into the hangar that had been reserved for the British machines. He did not report to the office at once, but went to his quarters, where he changed into his German uniform. Naturally the British uniform was not popular, and for this reason he invariably wore overalls when he was compelled to wear it. Having changed, he made his way slowly to the Officers' Mess* with a view to finding a quiet corner in order to study a German grammar he had bought, for his weak knowledge of the language was one of the most serious difficulties with which he was faced, and for this reason he had worked hard at it since his arrival in German territory.

He had not been seated many minutes when an orderly entered and handed him a note from the Count requesting his presence at the Headquarters office immediately. With no suspicion of anything unusual in his mind, he put the book in his pocket, picked up his cap, and walked down the tarmac to the old Turkish fort that served both as his Chief's headquarters and as sleeping quarters for the senior officers, while the courtyard and stables had been converted, by means of barbed wire, into a detention barracks for prisoners of war.

He knocked at the door and entered. The Count was leaning back in his chair with the collar of his tunic unfastened, in conversation with von Stalhein, who half sat and half leaned against the side of the desk. A fine coil of blue smoke arose lazily from the cigarette he was smoking in a long amber holder, and this, with the rimless monocle in his eye, only served to accentuate his effeminate appearance; but as he took in these

* The place where officers eat their meals and relax together.

details with a swift glance, Biggles thought he detected a sardonic gleam in the piercing eyes and experienced a twinge of uneasiness. He felt rather than saw the mocking expression that flitted across von Stalhein's face as he stood to attention and waited for the Count to speak.

'So! Here you are, Brunow,' observed von Faubourg easily. 'You went out flying this morning—yes?' He asked the question almost casually, but there was a grim directness of purpose about the way he crouched forward over his desk.

Biggles sensed danger in the atmosphere, but not by a quiver of an eyelid did he betray it. 'I did, sir, acting under your instructions,' he admitted calmly.

'Why did you land behind the British lines?' The easiness had gone from the Count's manner; he hurled the question like a spear.

Biggles turned stone-cold; he could feel the two pairs of eyes boring into him, and knew that if he hesitated he was lost. 'Because I thought it would be a good thing to ascertain immediately if such landings could be made with impunity,' he replied coolly. 'The occasion to land in enemy country might arise at any time, and it seemed to me that a preliminary survey of the ground for possible danger was a sensible precaution.'

The Count nodded slowly. 'And is that why you visited the Headquarters tent of the British Intelligence Service?'

Biggles felt the muscles of his face grow stiff, but he played his next card with a steadiness that inwardly amazed him. His lips parted in a smile as he answered carelessly and without hesitation, 'No, sir. I had no choice in that matter. I was sent for—it was all very amusing.'

236

'How?'

'The idea of being invited into the very place which I imagined would be most difficult to enter. I am afraid I have not been engaged in this work long enough to lose my sense of humour.'

'So it would seem. Why were you sent for?'

'Because I had said in the Officers' Mess that I was a delivery pilot*, and he—that is, the officer who sent for me—was merely interested to know if I was going to Heliopolis as he had a personal message for some one stationed there.'

'What did you say?'

'I told him I was sorry, but I was not going near Heliopolis.'

'Anything else?'

'Nothing, sir. The matter ended there and I came back.'

'Who was the other officer with Major Raymond?'

The words reacted on Biggles's tense nerves like an electric shock; there seemed to be no limit to German knowledge of British movements. 'No wonder we are getting the worst of it,' was the thought that flashed through his mind, as he answered with all the nonchalance he could muster, 'I've no idea, sir. I saw another officer there, a young fellow, but I did not pay any particular attention to him. If I thought anything at all I imagined him to be an assistant of some sort.'

'You knew the other was Major Raymond, who has just arrived here from France?'

'I know now, sir. I was told to report to Major Raymond: that's how I knew his name. I knew nothing

* The pilot who delivers aeroplanes to service squadrons from the manufacturers or repair depots.

about his just having arrived until you told me a moment ago.'

'Have you ever seen him before?'

'Not to my knowledge.'

'He didn't recognize you?'

'Oh, no, sir—at least, I have no reason to suppose he did. He was quite friendly.'

The answer apparently satisfied the Count, for he looked up at von Stalhein with a look which said as plainly as words, 'There you are: I told you so. Quite a natural sequence of events.' But von Stalhein was still watching Biggles with a puzzled smile, and continued to do so until the Count told him that he might return to his quarters, although he must remain at hand in case he was needed.

Biggles drew a deep breath as he stepped out into the blazing sunshine. His knees seemed to sag suddenly, and his hands turned ice-cold although they did not tremble. 'My word! I've got to watch my step and no mistake; these people have eyes everywhere,' he reflected bitterly, and not without alarm, as he walked slowly towards his quarters.

Chapter 4
A Meeting and a Duel

He had just finished dressing the following morning when his presence was again demanded by Count von Faubourg. His mind ran swiftly over his actions since the last interview, and although he could think of nothing he had done that could be regarded as a suspicious action, it was with a feeling of trepidation that he approached the fort. 'It's this beastly ever-present possibility of the unknown, the unexpected, turning up, that makes this business so confoundedly trying,' he thought, as he knocked on the door.

As he entered the office he instinctively looked round for von Stalhein, but to his infinite relief he was not there. Moreover, the Count seemed to be quite affable.

'Good morning, Brunow,' he called cheerfully. 'I have a real job for you at last.'

'Thank you, sir,' replied Biggles, with an enthusiasm he certainly did not feel. 'I shall be glad to get down to something definite.'

'I thought perhaps you would,' answered the Count. 'Now this is the position. We have received word that a large body of British troops, chiefly Australian cavalry, has recently left Egypt. There is a remote chance that they may have gone to Salonika, but we do not think so. It is far more likely that they have been disembarked and concealed somewhere behind this particular front in readiness for the big push which we know is in course of preparation. You may find it hard to believe that twenty thousand men can be moved,

and hidden, without our being aware of their destination, but such unfortunately is the case. The British
have learnt a bitter lesson, and they are acting with
circumspection. I want you to try to find those troops.
If they are in Palestine, then it is most likely that they
are somewhere in the hills — here.'

He indicated an area on his large-scale wall-map.
'Search there first, anyway,' he continued. 'The fact
that our reconnaissance machines have been driven off
every time they have attempted to approach that zone
suggests that our deductions are correct; if you will take
one of the British machines you will not be molested. If
you cannot find the camp from the air it may be necessary for you to land and make discreet inquiries.'

'Very good, sir.' Biggles saluted, returned to his
quarters, put on his British uniform and his overalls,
and then made his way to the hangar where the British
machines were housed. He ordered the mechanics to
get out the Sopwith Pup,* and then glanced along the
tarmac as an aero-engine came to life farther down. A
silver and blue Pfalz Scout** was taxi-ing out into
position to take off, and he watched it with interest as
its tail lifted and it climbed swiftly into the shimmering
haze that hung over the sandy aerodrome.

'That's Leffen's machine; I wonder what job he's
on,' he mused, as he climbed into his cockpit, started
the engine, and waited for it to warm up. But his
interest in the other machine waned quickly as he
remembered the difficult work that lay before him, for
the task was one of the sort he had been dreading.

* Single seater biplane fighter with a single machine gun synchronised
to fire through the propeller. Superseded by the Sopwith Camel.
** Very successful German single-seater biplane fighter, fitted with two
or three machine guns synchronised to fire through the propeller. See
cover illustration.

To report the position of the Australian troops to the Germans, even if he discovered it, was obviously out of the question; yet to admit failure, or, worse still, name an incorrect position that the enemy would speedily prove to be false, was equally impossible.

'I'd better try to get word to Raymond and ask him how I am to act in cases of this sort; maybe he'll be able to suggest something,' he thought, as he pushed open the throttle and sped away in the direction of the British lines. For some time, while he was in sight of the aerodrome, he held steadily on a course that would take him over the area indicated by von Faubourg, but as the aerodrome slipped away over the horizon behind him he turned north in the direction of Abba Sud.

A few desultory bursts of German archie blossomed out in front of him, but he fired a green Very light, the 'friendly' signal that had been arranged for him by headquarters and the German anti-aircraft batteries, and they died away to trouble him no more.

He kept a watchful eye open for prowling German scouts, who would, of course, shoot him down if they failed to notice the white bar that had been painted across his top plane for identification purposes, but he saw nothing, although it was impossible to study the sky in the direction of the blazing tropical sun. 'I hope to goodness Algy is about,' he thought anxiously, twenty minutes later, as he peered through his centre section in the direction of the oasis.

He searched the sky in all directions, but not a sign of a British machine could he see, and he was about to turn away when something on the ground caught his eye. It was a Very light that curved upwards in a wide arc, and staring downward he made out an aeroplane bearing the familiar red, white, and blue marking standing in the shade of the palms that formed the oasis.

'By jingo, he's down there,' he muttered in a tone of relief, as he throttled back and began to drop down towards the stationary aeroplane. A doubt crossed his mind about the suitability of the sand as a landing surface, but realizing that the R.E.8*—for as such he recognized the waiting machine—must have made a safe landing, he glided in and touched his wheels as near to the trees as possible.

Somewhat to his surprise, he saw two figures detach themselves from the shadows and walk quickly towards him, but when he identified them as Algy and Major Raymond he smiled with satisfaction and relief. 'This is better luck than I could have hoped for,' he called, as he switched off, and hurried to meet them.

'I had an idea you'd be over to-day, so I got Lacey to bring me along,' returned the Major as he shook hands. 'Well, how are things going?'

'They're not going at all, as far as I can see,' answered Biggles doubtfully. 'I'm supposed to be looking for this fellow El Shereef, but I haven't started yet, for the simple reason that I haven't the remotest idea of where to begin; I might as well start looking for a pebble in the desert. I'm scared stiff of making a boob, and that's a fact. Do you know that by the time I got back yesterday the Huns knew I had been to see you?'

'Impossible,' cried the Major aghast.

'That's what I should have said if it had been any one else, but you wouldn't have thought so if it had been you standing on the mat in front of the Count, and that swine von Stalhein,' declared Biggles, with a

* British two-seater biplane designed for reconnaissance and artillery observation.

242

marked lack of respect. 'I don't mind telling you that I could almost hear the tramp of the firing party when the Old Man pushed the accusation at me point blank. I went all groggy, but I lied like a trooper and got away with it. That's what I hate about this spy game: it's all lies; in fact, as far as I can see, nobody tells the truth.'

'I'm sorry, but it's part of the game, Bigglesworth,' put in the Major quickly. 'What excuse have you made for getting away this morning?'

'No excuse was necessary; I've been sent out on a job, and that's why I'm so glad to see you.' In a few words he explained his quest.

The Major looked grave. 'It's very difficult, and how the Huns knew about these reinforcements is more than I can imagine,' he observed, with a worried frown. 'No, by Jove! There is a way,' he added quickly.

'I'm glad to hear that,' murmured Biggles thankfully.

'The Australian troops are hidden in the palm-groves around Sidi Arish, but they are leaving there to-night to take their places in the support trenches. You can report their position at Sidi Arish when you get back, and it will be quite safe; von Faubourg will get a photographic machine through by hook or by crook, and he will see that you are correct. The chances are that he will launch a bomb raid to-night, after midnight, by which time the Australians will have gone. In that way we can kill two birds with one stone. You'll put your reputation up with von Faubourg, and consolidate your position, and the Huns will waste a few tons of bombs.'

'Fine! We couldn't have planned a better situation,' declared Biggles delightedly. 'And look here, Algy, while I think of it. I have been wondering how you could get a message through to me in case of emergency. There's only one way that I can think of and

243

it's this, although it mustn't be done too often. Behind our aerodrome at Zabala there's a large olive-grove. You could fly over low at night and drop a non-committal message, cutting your engine twice in quick succession as a signal to let me know that you've done it.'

'It sounds desperate,' observed Algy doubtfully.

'It is, but it would only be done to meet desperate circumstances.'

'Quite, and I think it's a good idea,' broke in the Major. 'I've only one more thing to say. I'm afraid you won't like it, but an idea has been put up to me by H.Q., although they have no idea, of course, of the means I might employ to carry it out. As you are probably aware, the German troops along a wide sector of this front get their water by a pipe-line that is fed from the reservoir just north of your aerodrome.'

'I've noticed the reservoir from the air, but I didn't know it watered the troops. What about it, sir?'

'Can you imagine what a tremendous help it would be to us in making preparations for the next big attack if that water-supply failed?'

'I hope you are not going to ask me to empty the water out of the reservoir,' smiled Biggles.

'No, I was going to ask you to blow it up.'

The smile disappeared from Biggles' face like magic, and he staggered. 'Great goodness!' he gasped; 'you're not serious, sir?'

'Would I be likely to joke at such a juncture?'

'But you can't make troops die of thirst.'

The Major's brow darkened. 'My dear Bigglesworth,' he said firmly, 'how many times am I to remind you that we are at war? Either we go under, or Germany. The Germans wouldn't die of thirst anyway; they would merely be seriously inconvenienced.'

'But am I not taking enough risks already, without

going about blowing things up?' complained Biggles bitterly. 'It sounds a tall order to me.'

'On consideration you may find that it is not so difficult as you imagine. I can supply you with the instrument, a small but powerful bomb—in fact, I brought it with me on the off-chance. You could conceal it in your machine, and hide it when you got back; put it in a safe place until you are ready to use it. Then all you would have to do would be to touch off the time-fuse, set, say, for half an hour, and return to your quarters. That's all.'

'All! By Gosh! and enough, too,' cried Biggles. 'All right, sir,' he added quickly, in a resigned tone. 'Get me the gadget and I'll put it in my machine; I'll see what I can do.'

A small but heavy square box was quickly transferred from the back seat of the R.E. 8 to the underseat pocket of the Pup, and Biggles prepared to take his departure. 'It's going to be jolly awkward if the Huns want me to collect information, as I expect they will,' he observed thoughtfully. 'I wish you could arrange for some dummy camps, or aerodromes, to be put up so that I can report—' He broke off abruptly and stared upwards.

The others, following the direction of his eyes, saw a tiny aeroplane, looking like a silver and blue humming bird, flash in the sun as it turned, and then race nose down towards them.

Biggles recognized the machine instantly, and understood exactly what had happened. 'It's Leffens,' he yelled, 'the cunning devil's followed me. He's spotted me talking to you. Swing my prop, Algy—quick.'

He leapt into the cockpit of the Pup as the silver and blue Pfalz roared overhead, with the pilot hanging over the side staring at them.

In answer to Biggles' shrill cry of alarm Algy darted to the propeller of the Pup, and at the word 'contact', swung it with the ability of long practice. The engine was still hot, and almost before he could jump clear the machine was racing over the sand, leaving a swirling cloud of dust in its wake.

Biggles, crouching low in the cockpit, was actuated by one overwhelming impulse as he tore into the air, which was to prevent the Pfalz pilot from reaching Zabala and there denouncing him. That Leffens was flying at such an out-of-the-way spot by pure chance he did not for one moment believe; he knew instinctively that he had been followed, possibly at von Stalhein's instructions—but that was immaterial. The only thing that really mattered was that Leffens had seen him at what could only be a pre-arranged rendezvous with British R.F.C. officers, and he had no delusions about how the man would act or what the result would be. He knew that if he was to continue his work—and possibly the whole success of the British campaign in Palestine hung on his efforts—Leffens must not be allowed to return to Zabala.

Nevertheless, it looked as if he would succeed in getting back, and indeed he had every opportunity of doing so, for his flying start had given him a clear lead of at least two miles. But suddenly he did a curious thing: he turned in a wide circle and headed back towards the oasis. It may have been that he felt safe from pursuit; it may have been that he did not give Biggles credit for acting as promptly as he did; or it may have been that he wished to confirm some detail on the ground. Be that as it may, the fact remains that he turned, and had actually started a second dive towards the oasis when he saw the Pup zooming towards him like an avenging angel. He turned back

246

sharply on his original course and sought to escape, but he had left it too late, for the Pup was slightly faster than the Pfalz.

Biggles pulled up the oil pressure handle of his Constantinesco* synchronizing gear and fired a short burst to warm his guns. His lips were set in a thin straight line, and with eyes fixed on the other machine he watched the gap close between them. He had no compunction about forcing a combat with Leffens. Quite apart from the fact that the German disliked him, or possibly suspected him, and was therefore a permanent source of danger, he now knew too much. Yet he was by no means a foeman to be despised, for six victories had already been recorded against his name in the squadron game-book**.

Biggles' hand closed over his firing lever, and he sent a stream of bullets down the wake of the fleeing scout. The range was, he knew, far too long for effective shooting, but the burst had the desired effect, and his lips parted slightly in a mirthless smile as he saw the Pfalz begin to sideslip.

'He's nervous,' was his unspoken thought, as he began to climb into position for attack.

But Leffens was looking back over his shoulder and started off on an erratic course to throw his pursuer off his mark. But it availed him little; in fact, in the end such tactics proved to be a disadvantage, for the manoeuvre caused him to lose speed, and with the Pup roaring down on his tail he was compelled to turn and fight.

With the cold deliberation of long experience, Biggles

* The synchronizing gear for machine-guns which interrupts the firing mechanism ensuring that the bullets do not hit the propeller blades but pass safely between them.
** Record of all enemy aircraft shot down by squadron members.

waited until he saw the stabbing tongues of flame leaping from the Pfalz's Spandau guns, and then he shoved the joystick forward with both hands. Straight down across the nose of the black-crossed machine he roared like a meteor, and then pulled up in a vertical Immelmann turn*. It was a brilliant move, beautifully executed, and before Leffens could grasp just what had happened the Pup was on his tail, raking the beautifully streamlined fuselage with lead.

But the Pfalz pilot was by no means beaten. He whirled round in a lightning turn and sent a stream of tracer bullets in the direction of the Pup. Biggles felt them hitting his machine, and flinched as he remembered the bomb under his seat, but he did not turn.

The German, unable to face the hail of lead that he knew was shooting his machine to pieces about him, acted with the speed of despair and took the only course left open to him: he flung joystick and rudder-bar over and spun earthward. But if he hoped by this means to throw Biggles off his tail he was doomed to disappointment: not for nothing had his opponent fought half a hundred such combats. The spin was the obvious course, and for a pilot to take the obvious course when fighting a superior foeman is suicidal, for the other man is prepared for the move and acts accordingly.

Leffens, grasping the side of his fuselage with his left hand, and still holding the machine in a spin, looked back, and saw the Pup spinning down behind him. He knew he could not spin for ever. Sooner or later he would have to pull out or crash into the sun-baked surface of the wilderness.

* The manoeuvre consists of a half roll off the top of a loop thereby quickly reversing the direction of flight. Named after Max Immelman, successful German fighter pilot 1914–1916 with seventeen victories, who was the first to use this turn in combat.

Biggles knew it, too, and waited with the calculating patience of the experienced air fighter. He saw the earth, a whirling band of brown and yellow, floating up to meet him, and saw the first movement of the Pfalz's tail as the German pilot kicked on top rudder to pull out of the spin. With his right hand gripping the firing lever he levelled out, took the silver and blue machine in his sights, and as its nose came up, fired. The range was too close to miss. The stricken Pfalz reared high into the air like a rocketing pheasant as the pilot convulsively jerked the joystick into his stomach; it whipped over and down in a vicious engine stall, and plunged nose first into the earth. Biggles could hear the crash above the noise of his engine, and caught his breath as a cloud of dust rose high into the air.

He passed his hand over his face, feeling suddenly limp, and circled round the wreck at stalling speed. In all directions stretched the wilderness, flat, monotonous, and forbidding, broken here and there by straggling camel-thorn bushes. The thought occurred to him that the German pilot might not have been killed outright, and the idea of leaving a wounded man in the waterless desert filled him with horror.

'I shall have to go down,' he muttered savagely. 'I don't want to, but I shall have to; I can't just leave him.'

He chose an open space as near as possible to the crash, landed safely, and hurried towards the shattered remains of the German machine. One glance told him all he needed to know. Karl Leffens was stone dead, shot through the head. He was lying in the wreckage with his right hand outflung. His glove had been thrown off, and Biggles caught the gleam of yellow metal. Stepping nearer, he saw that it was the signet ring, shining in the sunlight. Automatically, he stooped and picked it up and dropped it in his pocket with a muttered, 'Might be useful—one never knows.'

Then he saluted his fallen opponent. 'Sorry, Leffens,' he said in a low voice, 'but it was either you or me for it. Your people threw the hammer into the works, so you can't blame anyone but yourself for the consequences.' Then, making a mental note to ask Algy to send out a burying party, he took off and returned to the oasis. But of the R.E.8 there was no sign, so he turned again and headed back towards Zabala.

On the way he unfolded his map and looked up the position of Sidi Arish, and smiled grimly when he saw that it was on the fringe of the area pointed out to him by von Faubourg. 'I hope the Old Man* will think I have done a good morning's work,' he murmured, as he opened his throttle wide and put his nose down for more speed.

* Slang: person in authority, the Commanding Officer.

Chapter 5
The New Bullet

It may have been fortunate for Biggles that by the time he reached Zabala a slight wind had got up and was sweeping low clouds of dust across the sandy expanse that served as the aerodrome, and that its direction made it necessary for him to swing round over the sheds in order to land. But it was not luck that made him look carefully below, and to left and right, as he skimmed in over the tarmac in order to see who was about. Thus it was that his eyes fell on von Stalhein standing alone on the lee side of the special hangar. There was nothing unusual about that, but with Biggles the circumstances were definitely unusual, for on the floor of his cockpit reposed an object that could hardly fail to excite the German's curiosity if he saw it. It was the explosive charge provided by Major Raymond.

It was not very large; indeed, it would have gone into the side pocket of his tunic; but the bulge would have been conspicuous, and it was not customary for airmen to fly with bulging pockets while canvas slots and cavities were provided in aeroplanes for the reception of such trifles as Very pistols, maps, and notebooks.

Consequently Biggles deliberately overshot and finished his run on the far side of the aerodrome in a slight dip that would conceal the lower part of his machine from watchers on the tarmac. He reached far over the side of the cockpit and dropped the bomb lightly on the sand with confidence, for as far as he

251

knew that part of the aerodrome was seldom visited by any one, and the small object would hardly be likely to attract attention if a pilot did happen to see it.

It was as well that he took this precaution, for von Stalhein was waiting for him outside the hangar when he taxied in. Biggles nodded casually as he switched off, and without waiting to remove his flying kit set off in the direction of Headquarters 'Just a minute; where have you been?' von Stalhein called after him.

'I have been making a reconnaissance over the Jebel-Tel country—why?' replied Biggles carelessly.

'Did you see anything of Leffens? I believe he was going somewhere in that direction.'

'I saw a blue and silver machine—those are his colours, aren't they?'

The German's eyes never left Biggles' face. 'So! you saw him?' he exclaimed.

'I've said so, haven't I?' answered Biggles shortly. 'Is there anything particularly funny about that, if he was working in the same area? The heat made visibility bad, but I think it was his machine. I wish he'd keep away from me in the air; if the British see him hanging about without him attacking they may wonder why.'

'Did you have any trouble?'

'Nothing to speak of. But I've got an important report to make, so I can't stay talking now.' So saying, Biggles turned on his heel and walked quickly in the direction of the fort.

There was an odd expression on the Count's face as he looked up from his desk and saw who his visitor was. 'Well, what is it?' he asked irritably.

'The Australian troops are hidden among the palms around Sidi Arish, sir,' stated Biggles, without pre-amble.

A look of astonishment spread over the Count's face,

but it was quickly replaced by another in which grim humour, not unmixed with suspicion, was evident. 'So!' he said, nodding his head slowly. 'So! Where is Hauptmann von Stalhein?'

'On the tarmac, sir—or he was a moment ago.'

'Ask him to come here at once. That's all.'

Biggles left the room with the feeling that something had gone wrong, although he could not imagine what it was. Had the Count been pleased with his report, or had he not? He did not know, and the more he thought about it the less was he able to decide. He hurried around the corner of the sheds in search of von Stalhein, and then stepped back quickly as he saw him. For a moment he watched, wondering what he was doing, for he appeared to be working on the Pup's engine.

Biggles heard footsteps approaching, and rather than be found in the act of spying on his superior officer, he stepped out into the open and walked towards von Stalhein, who was now examining something that he held in the palm of his hand, something that he dropped quickly into his pocket when he heard some one coming.

'Will you please report to the Count immediately,' Biggles told him with an assurance he was far from feeling.

'Certainly,' replied the other. 'I shall be glad to see him,' he added, with a suspicion of a sneer, and limped off towards the fort without another word.

Biggles watched him go with mixed feelings.

'What the dickens was he up to?' he muttered in a mystified tone, as the German disappeared through the entrance to the fort. He took a swift pace or two to where von Stalhein had been standing. One glance, and he knew what had happened, for there, plain to see in the cowling, was a small round hole that could only have been made by one thing—a bullet. His heart gave an unpleasant lurch as he realised just what it implied, and his teeth came together with a click. 'That cunning devil misses nothing,' he growled savagely. 'He knows now that I've been under fire.' Then, seized by a sudden alarm, he lifted the cowling, and looking underneath, saw what he had feared. In a direct line with the puncture in the cowling there was another jagged hole in the wooden pattern that divided the engine from the cockpit. But the hole did not go right through. The bullet must have been stopped by it, in which case it should still be sticking in the stout ash board; but it was not.

'He found it, and he's dug it out with his pen-knife,' thought Biggles, moistening his lips. 'He'll know it's a German bullet,' he went on, thinking swiftly, with his brain trying to grasp the full purport of the new peril. then he gave a sigh of relief as an avenue of escape presented itself. 'It might have been fired some time ago; if he says anything about it I can say that it's always been there—was probably one of he shots fired by the Hun who brought the machine down,' he decided, turning towards the aerodrome buildings, for he did not want von Stalhein to return and see him examining the machine.

For a moment or two he was tempted to turn and jump into the machine and escape to the British lines while he still had an opportunity of doing so, but he fought back the desire, and then started as his eyes fell on two soldiers who had appeared round the corner of the hangars. He noticed that they carried rifles. They stopped when they saw him and leaned carelessly against the side of the hangar. 'Watching me, eh? You'd have shot me too, I expect, if I'd tried to get back into that machine,' he thought banefully. 'Well, now we know where we are, so I might as well go and get some lunch; it looks as if it might be my last.'

He walked unhurriedly to his room, changed, and then strolled into the ante-room of the Mess, where a number of officers were lounging prior to going in to lunch. A word or two of conversation that was going on between a small group at the bar reached his ears, and a cold shiver ran down his spine as he deliberately paused to listen. 'Leffens . . . late . . . new bullets . . .' were some of the words he heard.

In the ordinary way most of the regular flying officers ignored him, no doubt on account of his assumed traitorous character—not that this worried him in the least—but one of them, whose name he knew to be Otto Brandt, now detached himself from the group and came towards him.

'Haff you seen Leffens?' he asked, anxiously, in fair English.

Biggles felt all eyes on him as he replied, 'Yes, I saw him this morning, or I thought I did, near Jebel-Tel, but I was not absolutely certain. Why?'

'He hass not come back. It is tragic—very bad,' replied the German heavily.

'Very bad?' queried Biggles, raising his eyebrows.

'*Ja*, very bad—if he has fell. He was making test of the new bullets that came only yesterday. If he has fell in the British trench they will know of our new bullets at once, which is very bad for us.'

'Yes,' said Biggles, vaguely, in a strangled voice, wondering how he managed to speak at all, for his heart seemed to have stopped beating. He walked over to the window and stared out across the dusty aerodrome. 'So Leffens was carrying a new type of bullet,' he breathed, 'and von Stalhein has found one of them in my machine. 'That'll take a bit of explaining. Well, if they'll only give me until to-night I'll blow up their confounded reservoir, and then they can shoot me if they like.'

With these disturbing thoughts running through his head he walked through to the dining-room, had lunch, and then repaired to the aerodrome, observing that the two soldiers still followed him discreetly at a respectful distance. He was just in time to see a two-seater Halberstadt* take off and head towards the lines. Half a dozen Pfalz scouts followed it at once and took station just above and behind it.

'There goes the photographic machine with an escort,' he thought dispassionately, as they disappeared into the haze. He wondered vaguely what von Stalhein was doing, and how long it would be before he was confronted with Leffen's bullet and accused of double dealing; but then, deciding that it was no use meeting trouble half-way, he turned leisurely towards the pilot's map-room, where he studied the position of the reservoir, which was a well-known landmark. Satisfied that he could find the place in the dark, he returned to his quarters, to plan the recovery of the bomb which he had left on at the aerodrome, and await whatever might befall.

He had not long to wait, Heavy footsteps, accompanied by the unmistakable dragging stride of von Stalhein, sounded in the passage. They halted outside the door, which was thrown open. The Count and von Stalhein stood on the threshold.

'May we come in?' inquired von Stalhein, rather unnecessarily, tapping the end of his cigarette with his

* German two-seater fighter and ground attack biplane with two machine guns, one synchronised to fire through the propeller for the pilots use.

forefinger to knock off the ash, a curious habit that Biggles had often noticed.

'Of course,' he replied quickly. 'There isn't much room, but—'

'That's all right,' went on von Stalhein easily. 'The Chief would like to ask you a question or two.'

'I will do my best to answer it, you may be sure,' replied Biggles. Through the window, out of the corner of his eye, he saw the Halberstadt and its escort glide in, but his interest in them was short-lived, for the Count was speaking.

'Brunow, this morning you reported to me that you had located a division of Australian cavalry at Sidi Arish.' It was both a statement and a question.

'I did, sir.'

'Why?'

Biggles was genuinely astonished. 'I'm afraid I don't quite understand what you mean,' he answered frankly, with a puzzled look from one to the other.

'Then I will make the position clear,' went on the Count, evenly. 'The story I told you of the movement of Australian troops from Egypt was purely imaginary. I merely wished to test your—er—zeal, to find out how you would act in such circumstances. Now! What was your object in rendering a report which you knew quite well was incorrect?'

'Do you doubt my word, sir?' cried Biggles indignantly. 'I don't understand why you should consider such a course necessary. May I respectfully request, sir, that if you doubt my veracity you might post me to another command where my services would be more welcome than they are here?' He glared at von Stalhein in a manner that left no doubt as to whom he held responsible for the suspicion with which he was regarded.

The Count was obviously taken aback by the outburst. 'Do you still persist, then, that your report is authentic? Surely it would be a remarkable coincidence—'

There was a sharp tap on the door, and Mayer, the Staffel leader of the Halberstadt squadron, entered quickly. 'I'm sorry to interrupt you, sir,' he said briskly, 'but I was told you were here, and I thought you'd better see this without loss of time.' He handed the Count a photograph, still dripping from its fixing bath.

The Count held it on his open hand, and von Stalhein looked down at it over his shoulder.

'*Himmel*!*' Von Faubourg's mouth opened in comical surprise, while von Stalhein threw a most extraordinary look in Biggles' direction.

'Brunow, see here,' cried the Count. 'But of course, you have seen it before, in reality.'

Biggles moved nearer and looked down at the photograph. It was one of the vertical type, and showed a cluster of white, flat-topped houses upon which several tracks converged. At intervals around the houses were three small lakes, or water-holes, beyond which were extensive groves of palm-trees. But it was not these things that held the attention of those who now studied the picture with practised eyes. Between the palms were long rows of horse-lines and clusters of tiny figures, foreshortened to ant-like dimensions, that could only be men.

The Count sprang to his feet. 'Splendid, Brunow,' he exclaimed, 'and you, too, have done well, Mayer. Come on, von Stalhein, we must attend to this.'

'But—' began von Stalhein, but the Count cut him short.

* Heavens!

258

'Come along, man,' he snapped. 'We've no time for anything else now.' With a parting nod to Biggles, he left the room, followed by the others. At the door von Stalhein turned, and leaning upon his sticks, threw another look at Biggles that might have meant anything. For a moment Biggles thought he was going to say something, but he did not, and as the footsteps retreated down the passage Biggles sank back in his chair and shook his head slowly.

'This business gives me the heebie-jeebies,' he muttered weakly; 'there's too much head-work in it for me. Well, the sooner I blow up the water-works the better, before my nerve peters out.'

Chapter 6
More Shocks

He remained in his quarters until the sun sank in a blaze of crimson and gold, and the soft purple twilight of the desert enfolded the aerodrome in its mysterious embrace. Quietly and without haste he donned his German uniform and surveyed himself quizzically for a moment in the mirror, well aware that he was about to attempt a deed that might easily involve him in the general destruction; then he crossed to the open window and looked out.

All was quiet. A faint subdued murmur came from the direction of the twinkling lights that marked the position of the village of Zabala; nearer at hand a gramophone was playing a popular waltz tune. There were no other sounds. He went across to the door and opened it, but not a soul was in sight. Wondering if the guard that had been set over him had been withdrawn, he closed the door quietly and returned to the window. For some minutes he stood still, watching the light fade to darkness, and then, feeling that the hush was getting on his nerves, he threw a leg across the window-sill and dropped silently on to the sand.

His first move he knew must be to retrieve the bomb before the moon rose; fortunately it would only be a slim crescent, but even so it would flood the aerodrome with a radiance that would make a person walking on it plainly visible to any one who happened to be looking in that direction. The light of the stars would be, he

260

hoped, sufficient to enable him to find the small box that contained the explosive.

Resolutely, but without undue haste, he reached the tarmac and sauntered to its extremity to make sure no one was watching him before turning off at right angles into the darkness of the open aerodrome. He increased his pace now, although once he stopped to look back and listen; but only a few normal sounds reached him from the sparse lights of the aerodrome buildings, and he set about his search in earnest.

In spite of the fact that he had marked the place down very carefully, it took him a quarter of an hour to find the bomb, and he had just picked it up when a slight sound reached him that set his heart racing and caused him to spread-eagle himself flat on the sandy earth. It was the faint chink of one pebble striking against another.

That pebbles, even in the desert, do not strike against each other without some agency, human or animal, he was well aware, and as far as he knew there were no animals on the aerodrome. So, hardly daring to breathe, he lay as still as death, and waited. Presently the sound came again, nearer this time and then the soft pad of footsteps. He looked round desperately for a hiding-place. A few yards away there was a small wind-scorched camel-thorn bush, one of several that still waged a losing battle for existence on the far side of the aerodrome. As cover it was poor enough and in daylight it would have been useless, but in the dim starlight it was better than nothing, and he slithered towards it like a serpent. As he settled himself behind it facing the direction of the approaching footsteps, a figure loomed up in the darkness on the lip of the depression in which he lay. It was little more than a silhouette, but as such it stood out clearly, and he breathed a sigh of relief when he saw that it was an Arab in flowing burnous and turban. But what was an Arab doing on the aerodrome, which had been placed out of bounds for them? The man, whoever he was, was obviously moving with a fixed purpose, for he strode along with a swinging stride; he looked to neither right nor left and soon disappeared into the darkness.

Biggles lay quite still for a good five minutes wondering at the unusual circumstance. Had it been his imagination, or had there been something familiar about that lithe figure? Had it stirred some half-forgotten chord in his memory, or were his taut nerves playing him tricks? But he could not wait to ponder over the strange occurrence indefinitely, so with the bomb in his pocket, he set off swiftly but stealthily towards the distant lights.

He had almost reached them when, with an ear splitting bellow, an aero-engine opened up on the far side of the aerodrome, almost at the very spot where he had just been; it increased quickly in volume as the machine moved towards him, obviously in the act of taking off. In something like a mild panic lest he should be knocked down, he ran the last few yards to the end of the tarmac, and glancing upwards, could just manage to make out the broad wings of an aeroplane disappearing into the starlit sky. For a second or two he watched it, not a little mystified, for it almost looked as if the Arab he had seen had taken off; but deciding that it would be better to leave the matter for further consideration in more comfortable surroundings, he looked about him. No one was about, so holding the bomb close to his side, he hurried back to his quarters. 'I'd better see how this thing works before tinkering about with it in the dark, otherwise I shall go up instead of the waterworks,' he thought grimly.

262

He reached his room without incident, and, as far as he could ascertain, without being seen. Placing the bomb in the only easy chair the room possessed, he was brushing the sand from his uniform when a soft footfall made him turn. Count von Faubourg, in pyjamas and canvas shoes, was standing in the doorway.

Biggles' expression did not change, and he did not so much as glance in the direction of the box lying in the chair. 'Hello, sir,' he said easily. 'Can I do something for you?'

'No, thanks,' replied the Count, stepping into the room. 'I saw your light, so I thought I'd walk across to say that you did a good show this morning. I wasn't able to say much about it this afternoon because von Stalhein—well, he's a good fellow but inclined to be a bit difficult sometimes.'

'That's all right, sir, I quite understand,' smiled Biggles, picking up a cushion from one of the two upright chairs and throwing it carelessly over the box. He pushed the upright chair a little nearer to his Chief. 'Won't you sit down, sir?' he said.

'Thanks,' replied the Count. But to Biggles horror he ignored the chair he had offered and sat down heavily in the armchair. 'Hello, what the dickens is this?' he went on quickly, as he felt the lump below the cushion.

'Sorry, sir, I must have left my cigarettes there,' apologized Biggles, picking up the box and throwing it lightly on to the chest of drawers. In spite of his self-control he flinched as it struck heavily against the wood.

'What's the matter?' went on the Count, who was watching him. 'You look a bit pale.'

'I find the heat rather trying at first,' confessed Biggles. 'Can I get you a drink, sir?'

'No, thanks; I must get back to dress. But I thought

I'd just let you know that your work of this morning will not be forgotten; you keep on like that and I'll see that you get the credit for it.'

'Thank you very much, sir,' said Biggles respectfully, but inwardly he was thinking, 'Yes, I'll bet you will, you old liar,' knowing the man's reputation for taking all the credit he could get regardless of whom it really concerned. He was tempted to ask about the machine that had just taken off, but decided on second thoughts that perhaps it would be better not to appear inquisitive.

'Yes, I must be getting along,' repeated the Count, rising. 'By the way, I'll have one of your cigarettes.' He reached for the box.

'Try one of these, sir: they're better,' invited Biggles, whipping out his case and opening it. To his infinite relief the Count selected one, lit it, and moved towards the door.

'See you at dinner,' he said with a parting wave.

Biggles bowed and saluted in the true German fashion as his Chief departed, but as the door closed behind him he sat down limply and wiped the perspiration from his forehead. 'These shocks will be the death of me if nothing else is,' he muttered weakly, and glanced at his watch. He sprang to his feet and moved swiftly, as he saw that he had exactly one hour and ten minutes to complete his task and get back to the Mess before the gong sounded for dinner, when he would have to be present or his absence would be remarked upon.

He picked up the box, opened it, took out the metal cylinder it contained and examined it with interest. Down one side was a graduated gauge, marked in minutes, and operated by a small, milled screw. On the top was a small red plunger which carried a warning to the effect that the bomb would commence to operate from the moment it was depressed.

Not without some nervousness he screwed the gauge to its limit, which was thirty minutes, replaced the bomb in its box, and slipped it into his pocket. Then, picking up his cap and leaving the light still burning, he set off on his desperate mission.

The distance to the hill on which the reservoir was situated was not more than half a mile in a straight line, but he deliberately made a detour in order to avoid meeting any soldiers of the camp who might be returning from the village. He had become so accustomed to unexpected difficulties and dangers that he was both relieved and surprised when he reached the foot of the hill without any unforeseen occurrence; he found a narrow track that wound upwards towards the summit, and followed it with confidence until he reached the reservoir.

It was an elevated structure built up of several thicknesses of granite blocks to a height of perhaps five feet above the actual hill-top, and seemed to be about three-quarters full of water, a fact that he ascertained by the simple expedient of looking over the wall. Searching along the base, he found a place where the outside granite blocks were roughly put together, leaving a cavity wide enough to admit the bomb. The moon was just showing above the horizon, but a cloud was rapidly approaching it, so without any more ado he took the bomb from its case, forced the plunger home, and thrust it into the side of the reservoir. For a moment he hesitated, wondering as to the best means of disposing of the box; finally, he pushed it in behind the bomb, where its destruction would be assured. Then he set off down the hill just as the cloud drifted over the face of the moon.

He had taken perhaps a dozen paces when he was pulled up short by what seemed to be a barbed-wire fence; at first he could not make out what it was, but on looking closer he could just make out a stoutly built wire entanglement. An icy hand seemed to clutch his heart as he realized that it was unscalable, and that he was trapped within a few yards of a bomb which might, if there was any fault in its construction, explode at any moment.

Anxiously he looked to right and left, hoping to see the gap through which the path had led, but in the dim light and on the rocky hill-side he perceived with a shock that, having lost it, it might be difficult to find again.

The next five minutes were the longest he could ever remember. Stumbling along, he found the gap at last, as he was bound to by following the fence, but his nerves were badly shaken, and he ran down the path in a kind of horrible nightmare of fear that the bomb would explode before he reached camp.

'No more of this for me,' he panted, as, tripping over cactus and camel-thorn in his haste, he made his way by a roundabout course to the aerodrome. He struck it at the end of the tarmac, and was hurrying towards his quarters when he heard a sound that made him look upwards in amazement. It was the wind singing in the wires of a gliding aeroplane that was coming in to land.

It taxied in just as he reached the point where he had to turn to reach his room, and in spite of his haste, with the memory of the Arab still fresh in his mind, he paused to see who was flying in such strange conditions. He was half disappointed therefore when he saw Mayer climb out of the front seat of the machine, a Halberstadt, and stroll round to the tail unit to examine the rudder as if it was not working properly. There appeared to be no passenger, so without further loss of time Biggles went to his room, washed, brushed his clothes, and then went along to the dining-room. As he entered his eyes went instinctively to the clock. It was five minutes to eight. Dinner would be served in five minutes, and one minute later, if the bomb was timed accurately, the reservoir would blow up.

Several of the pilots nodded to him, from which he assumed that the success of his morning's reconnaissance had been made public property. Some were in semi-flying kit, and from snatches of conversation that he overheard he gathered that they had been detailed for a bombing raid which was to leave the ground shortly before midnight.

'Going to bomb the palm-trees at Sidi Arish,' he thought. 'Well, I—' His pleasant soliloquy ceased abruptly, and he stiffened instinctively as a sound floated in through the open windows. It was the low, musical cadence of an aero-engine rapidly approaching. Aeroplanes were common enough at Zabala, but not those carrying Rolls-Royce engines. Biggles recognized the deep, mellow drone, and knew that a British machine was coming towards the camp, probably an F.E. 2D.* So did some of the German pilots, and there was a general stampede towards the door.

'Put those lights out,' yelled von Faubourg, who appeared from nowhere, so to speak, without his tunic.

'Now we see der fun,' said Brandt, who stood at Biggles' elbow. 'Watch for der fireworks.'

Biggles started, for he, too, was expecting some fireworks—on a big scale, from the direction of the reser-

---

* Two-seater 'pusher' biplane with the engine behind the pilot and the gunner in the forward cockpit.

voir—but he did not understand Brandt's meaning. 'Fireworks?' he queried, as they stared up into the darkness.

'Der new battery on der hill is of der grandest—so! straight from der Western front, where it makes much practice. Watch der Engländer in der fireworks—ha!'

The exclamation was induced by a searchlight that suddenly stabbed in to the night sky from somewhere behind the hangars; it was followed immediately by another that flung its blinding shaft upward from a point of vantage near the top of the hill.

The pilot of the British machine, as if aware of his peril, pushed his nose down for more speed—a move that was made apparent to the listeners on the ground by the sudden increase of noise. Still visible, but with the searchlights sweeping across the sky to pick it up, it seemed to race low across the back of the fort and then zoom upwards. A hush fell on the watchers as its engine cut out, picked up, cut again, and again picked up.

Biggles felt the blood drain from his face as he recognized the signal. 'Dear goodness, it's Algy,' he thought, and itched to tell him to clear off before the searchlights found him; but he could only stand and watch helplessly.

A babel of excited voices arose from the German pilots as the nearest searchlight flashed for a fleeting instant on the machine, lost it, swept back again, found and held it. An F.E. 2D stood out in lines of white fire in the centre of the beam. The other lights swung across and intensified the picture. Instantly the air was alive with darting flecks of flame and hurtling metal from the archie battery on the hill which, with the cunning of long experience, had held its fire for this moment.

Bang—whoof . . . bang—whoof . . . bang—whoof . . .

thundered the guns as the British pilot, now fully alive to the danger, twisted and turned like a snipe to get out of the silent white arms that clung to him like the tentacles of an octopus.

A shell burst almost under the nose of the F.E., and a yell of delight rose from the Germans. 'I told you to watch der fireworks,' smiled Brandt knowingly, with a friendly nudge at Biggles, and then clutched at him wildly to prevent himself from falling as the earth rocked under their feet. It was as if the hill had turned into a raging volcano. A sheet of blinding flame leapt upwards, and a deep throated roar, like a thunderclap, almost shattered their ear-drums.

Simultaneously both searchlights went out, and a ghastly silence fell, a stillness that was only broken by the sullen plop—plop—plop of falling objects. Then a medley of sounds occurred together: yells, shrill words of command, and the rumble of falling masonry; but above these arose another noise, one that caused the Germans to stare at each other in alarm. It was the roar of rushing waters.

Biggles, who had completely forgotten his bomb in the excitement of watching the shelling of the F.E., was nearly as shaken as the others, but he was, of course, the only one who knew exactly what had happened.

Some of the officers darted off to see the damage, while others, discussing the explosion, drifted in to dinner, and Biggles, saying nothing but doing his best to hear the conversation, followed them. Some were inclined to the view that the explosion had been caused by a bomb dropped from the aeroplane, while others scouted the idea, pointing out that the machine had not flown over the hill while it had been under observation, or if it *had* flown over it before they were aware of its presence, then the delay between then and the time of the explosion was too long to be acceptable. Of von Stalhein there was no sign, and Biggles was wondering what had happened to him when the officers who had gone to the hill began to trickle back in ones or twos.

They had a simple but vivid story to tell. One wall of the reservoir had been blown clean out, and the vast weight of the pent-up water, suddenly released, had swept down the hill-side carrying all before it. It had descended on the archie battery even before the gunners were aware of it and had hurled them into the village, where houses had been swept away and stores destroyed. The earth had been torn from under the guns, which had rolled down the hill and were now buried under tons of rock, sand, and debris. The Count was on the spot with every man he could muster, trying to sort things out and collect a provisional store of water in empty petrol-cans, goat-skins, or any other receptacle he could lay hands on.

Biggles heard the story unmoved. That he had succeeded beyond his wildest hopes was apparent, and he only hoped that Algy had seen and would therefore report the incident to Major Raymond, who would in turn notify General Headquarters and enable them to take advantage of it. Thinking of Algy reminded him of the signal and what it portended, but to look for the message in the darkness was obviously out of the question. That was a matter that would have to be attended to in the morning.

He sat in the mess reading his German grammar until the noise of engines being warmed up told him that the night bombers were getting ready to start, so he went out on to the tarmac to watch the preparations.

A strange sense of unreality came over him as he watched the bustle and activity inseparable from such an event. How many times had he watched such a scene, in France, from his right and proper side of the lines. The queer feeling of loneliness came back with renewed force, and in his heart he knew that he loathed the work he was doing more than ever; he would have much preferred to be sitting in the cockpit of a bomber, waiting for the engine to warm up; in fact he would not have been unwilling to have taken his place in one of the Halberstadts, either as pilot or observer, and risk being shot down by his own people. 'It's all wrong,' he muttered morosely, as one by one the bombers took off, and the drone of the engines faded away into the distance. Lights were put out and silence fell upon the aerodrome; the only sounds came from the direction of the hill, where the work of salvage and repair was still proceeding. Feeling suddenly very sick of it all, he made his way, deep in thought, to his room, and without switching on the light threw himself upon the bed.

He suspected that he had dozed when some time later he sprang up with a start and stood tense, listening. Had he heard an aeroplane, or had he been dreaming? Yes! he could hear the whistling hum of an aeroplane gliding in distinctly now, and he crossed to the window in a swift stride, with a puzzled frown wrinkling his forehead. 'What the dickens is going on,' he muttered. 'I never heard so much flying in my life as there is in this place.' The thought occurred to him that it might be one of the bombers returning with engine trouble and he waited for it to taxi in, but when it did not come his rather vague interest increased to wonderment.

As near as he could judge, the machine must have landed somewhere over the other side of the aerodrome, near the depression in which he had dropped the bomb and from which the mysterious machine had taken off

271

earlier in the evening. 'That's the same kite come back home, I'll warrant,' he thought with increasing curiosity, and settling his elbows on the window-sill he stared out across the silent moon-lit wilderness. But he could see nothing like an aeroplane, and he was about to turn away when a figure came into view, walking rapidly. At first it was little more than a dim shadow, but as it drew nearer he saw that it was an Arab in burnous and turban. Was it the same man . . . ?

Breathlessly he watched him approach. He wanted to dash outside in order to obtain a clearer view of him in case he disappeared, so he continued watching from the window with a kind of intense fascination while his fingers tingled with an excitement he found difficult to control. It was a weird picture. The silent moonlit desert and the Arab striding along as his forebears had done in Biblical days.

It soon became clear that he was making for the fort. Biggles watched him disappear through the entrance, and a few seconds later a light appeared in one of the end windows. He knew that there was no point in watching any longer. 'I've got to see inside that window,' he muttered, as he kicked off his shoes and stole out into the corridor.

With the stealth of an Indian, he crept along the back of the hangars until the black bulk of the old building loomed up in front of him. The light was still shining in the window, which was some six feet above ground-level, just too high for him to reach without something to stand on. He hunted round with desperate speed, afraid that the light would go out while he was thus engaged, and in his anxiety almost fell upon an old oil drum that lay half buried in the sand. He dragged it out by brute strength, and holding it under his arm, crept back to the wall of the fort, below the window from which streamed the shaft of yellow light. A cautious glance round and he stood the drum in place.

His heart was beating violently; he began to raise himself, inch by inch, to the level of the window. Slowly and with infinite care, he drew his eyes level and peeped over the ledge.

He was down again in an instant, struggling to comprehend what he had seen, almost afraid that the man within would hear the thumping of his heart, so tense had been the moment. At a large desk in the centre of the room von Stalhein was sitting in his shirt sleeves, writing. The inevitable cigarette smouldered between his lips and his monocle was in place. His sticks rested against the side of the desk.

Biggles' first reaction was of shock, followed swiftly by bitter disappointment, for it seemed that he had merely discovered von Stalhein's private office, and it was in this spirit that he picked up the drum, smoothed out the mark of its rim in the sand, and replaced it where he had found it. Then he hurried back towards his room. On reaching it he crossed to the window and looked out. The light had disappeared.

Slowly, and lost in a whirl of conflicting thoughts, he took off his uniform and prepared for bed. 'I wonder,' he said softly—'I wonder.'

What he was wondering as he sank into sleep was if a slim dandy with a game leg could change his identity to that of the brilliant, athletic, hard-riding Arab who was known mythically on both sides of the lines as El Shereef, the cleverest spy in the German Secret Service.

Chapter 7
Still More Shocks

Tired out, he was still in bed the following morning when he was startled by a peremptory knock on the door, which, without invitation, was pushed open, and the Count closely followed by von Stalhein strode into the room. If any further indication were needed that something serious was afoot, a file of soldiers with fixed bayonets who halted in the corridor supplied the deficiency.

Biggles sprang out of bed with more haste than dignity, and regarded the intruders with astonishment that was not entirely feigned.

'All right, remain standing where you are,' ordered the Count curtly. 'Where were you last night?'

'In my room, sir, where you yourself saw me,' replied Biggles instantly. 'After dinner—'

'Never mind that. Where were you between the time I left you and dinner time?'

'I stayed here for a little while after you had gone, and then as the heat was oppressive—as you will remember I complained to you—I went out and sat on the tarmac.'

'Were you with anybody?'

'No, sir, by myself.'

'In which case you have no proof that you were where you *say* you were.'

'On the contrary, I think I can prove it to you, sir.'

'How?'

'Because while I was sitting there I saw Mayer land

274

in a Halberstadt. You can verify that he did so. If I had not been there I could not have seen him.'

'That's no proof. Every one in the Mess knew that Mayer was flying,' put in von Stalhein harshly.

Biggles met his eyes squarely. 'I can tell you exactly how he behaved when he landed,' he said quietly. 'I couldn't learn that in the Mess.'

'Send for Mayer,' said the Count crisply.

There was silence for two or three minutes until he came.

'Can you remember exactly what was the first thing you did when you landed last night?' asked the Count tersely.

Mayer looked puzzled.

'May I prompt his memory, sir?' asked Biggles. And then, looking straight at Mayer, he went on, 'You jumped out as soon as you reached the tarmac and walked back to the empennage* of the machine. You then tried the rudder as if it was heavy on controls.'

Mayer nodded. 'That's perfectly true; I did,' he agreed.

'All right, you may go,' barked the Count, and then turning to Biggles. 'Very well, then, we'll say you were on the tarmac,' he said grimly, 'in which case you may find it hard to explain how *that* found its way to the hill-side, near the reservoir.' He tossed a small gold object on to the table.

Biggles recognized it at once; it was his signet ring. It did not fit very well, and must have fallen from his finger while he was hunting for the gap in the wire. The most amazing thing was he had not missed it. To say that he was shaken as he stared at it, gleaming

---

* General term referring to the tail unit of any aircraft—the tail plane, elevators, fin and rudders.

dully on the table, would be an understatement of fact. He was momentarily stunned by such a damning piece of evidence. For a period of time during which a man might count five he stared at it dumbfounded, inwardly horror-stricken.

In the deathly hush that had fallen on the room the match that von Stalhein struck to light his cigarette sounded like a thunderclap.

Biggles' brain, which for once seemed to have failed, like an aero engine when the spark is cut off, suddenly went on again at full revs. He dragged his eyes away from the unmistakable evidence of his guilt and looked at the Count with a strange expression on his face, aware that von Stalhein's eyes were boring into him, watching his every move.

'I think I can explain that, sir, although you may find it hard to believe.'

'Go on, we are listening.'

'Leffens must have dropped it there.'

'*Leffens!*'

'Yes, sir, he had my ring.'

'*Had your ring!*' The Count's brain was working slowly, and even von Stalhein dared not interrupt.

'Yes, sir; I lent it to him yesterday morning. I met him on the tarmac, just as he was getting into his machine. He told me he had forgotten his ring, and that it would mean bad luck to go back for it. So as he was in a hurry I lent him mine.'

'But I saw you wearing yours only yesterday evening,' snapped von Stalhein, unable to contain himself.

'Not mine, Leffen's,' answered Biggles suavely. 'He suggested I had better borrow his during his absence, and told me that it was lying on his dressing-table. I fetched it and have worn it ever since. I've been meaning to report the matter.'

276

'Then why aren't you wearing it now?'

'I always take it off to wash, prior to going to bed,' returned Biggles easily.

He took Leffens' ring from the drawer of his dressing-table where he had placed it when he returned from the flight in which he had shot down the rightful owner of the ring. He tossed the tiny circle of gold on to the table with the other.

Another ghastly silence fell in which he could distinctly hear the ticking of his wrist-watch. In spite of the tension his brain was running easily and smoothly, with a deadly precision born of dire peril, and he looked at his interrogators, whose turn it was to stare at the table, with an expression of injured dignity on his face.

Strangely enough, it was the Count who recovered himself first, and he looked back at Biggles half apologetically and half in alarm. 'But your ring was found on the hill-side,' he said in a half whisper. 'Surely you are not suggesting that Leffens had any hand in the blowing up of the reservoir?'

Biggles shrugged his shoulders. He saw von Stalhein feeling in his pocket and knew he was searching for the incriminating bullet, so he went on quickly. 'I am not suggesting anything, sir, nor can I imagine how it got there. I only know that for some reason Leffens disliked me; in fact, he tried to kill me.'

'*Tried to kill you?*' The Count literally staggered.

'Yes, sir; he dived down at me out of the sun and tried to shoot me down. It was a clever attack, and unexpected; some of his bullets actually hit the machine. He zoomed back up into the sun and disappeared, but not before I had seen who it was. There is just a chance, of course, that he mistook my machine for an authentic enemy aircraft.' Biggles could see that even von Stalhein was impressed.

'But why in the name of heaven didn't you report it?' cried the Count aghast.

'I most certainly should have done so, sir, had Leffens returned. After I made my report to you I went back to the tarmac to hear his explanation first. But he did not come, and assuming that he had been shot down, I decided, rightly or wrongly, to let the matter drop rather than make such an unpleasant charge in his absence. Do you mind if I smoke, sir?'

'Certainly, Brunow, smoke by all means,' answered the Count in a change of voice.

Biggles lit a cigarette. Out of the corner of his eye he saw von Stalhein drop the bullet back into his pocket and knew that he had spoken just in time. 'Have I your permission to dress now, sir?' he asked calmly. 'And I should like a few minutes' conversation with you when you have a moment to spare.'

'Certainly, certainly. But why not speak now? I shall be very busy to-day; this confounded reservoir business is the very devil.'

'Very well, sir.' Biggles swung round and his jaws set grimly. 'I have a request to make, but before doing so, would respectfully remind you that I came here under open colours, not at my own instigation or by my own wish, but at the invitation—under the orders if you like—of the German Government. But it seems that for some reason or other I have been regarded with suspicion from the moment I arrived by certain members of your staff. I therefore humbly beg your indulgence in what is to me a very unhappy position, and would ask you to post me to another station, or give me leave to go my own way.'

It was a bold stroke of bluff, and for one ghastly moment Biggles thought he had gone too far, for the last thing he wanted at that juncture was to be posted away.

But the Count reacted just as he hoped he would. 'Nothing of the sort, Brunow,' he said in a fatherly tone. 'I'm sorry if there has been a misunderstanding in the past, but I think we all understand each other now.' He glanced at von Stalhein meaningly. 'You get dressed now and hurry along for your coffee,' he went on. 'As far as I know I shan't be needing you this morning, but don't go far away in case I do. Come on Erich.'

They went out and closed the door behind them.

Biggles poured himself out a glass of water with a hand that trembled slightly, for the ordeal he had just been through had left him feeling suddenly weak. Then he slumped down into a chair and buried his face in his hands. 'Gosh!' he breathed, 'that was closeish—too close for my liking.'

Chapter 8
Forced Down

'Well, I must say that was a good start for a day's work,' he went on as he pulled himself together, dressed, and walked over to the Mess for morning coffee. 'I got away with it that time, but I shan't do it every time; one more boob like that and it'll be the last.'

With these morbid thoughts, he made his way to the olive grove where, after ascertaining as far as it was possible that he was not watched, he began a systematic search for the message he knew Algy must have dropped. It took him a long time, but he found it at last caught up in the branches of one of the grey, gnarled trees that must have been old when the Crusaders were marching on Jerusalem. It was merely a small piece of khaki cloth, weighted with two cartridges, to which was attached a strip of white rag about a yard long. A thousand people might have seen it and taken it for a piece of wind-blown litter without suspecting what it contained.

After a cautious glance around he secured it, opened the khaki rag, and removed the slip of paper he guessed he would find in it; the improvised rag streamer and cartridges he dropped into a convenient hole in the tree. One glance was sufficient for him to memorize the brief message. In neat Roman capitals had been printed:

IMPORTANT NEWS. SPEAK AT RENDEZVOUS AS SOON AS
POSSIBLE.

That was all. He rolled the paper into a ball, slipped
it into his mouth, chewed it to a pulp, and then threw
it away.

'What's wrong now?' he wondered, as he made his
way back to the tarmac. 'Why didn't he write the
message down while he was about it? No, of course, he
daren't do that: it would have been too risky; and he
would have had no means of knowing if I'd got it,
anyway.'

Still turning the matter over in his mind, and trying
to think of a reasonable excuse to go for a flight, he
reached the aerodrome. There were a few mechanics
about, most of them at work on machines, but nearly
all the serviceable aeroplanes were in the air. Of the
Count there was no sign; nor could he see von Stalhein.
Thinking of von Stalhein reminded him of his nocturnal
adventure and the mysterious Arab; he had little time
to think, but he felt instinctively that he was now on
the track of something important. That von Stalhein
might be El Shereef had not previously occurred to
him, and even now he only regarded it as a remote
possibility, for the two characters were so utterly different from the physical aspect alone that the more he
thought about it the more fantastic a dual personality
appeared to be. Nevertheless, he had already decided
to watch von Stalhein, and keep an eye open after
dark for the Arab who appeared to have access to
the Headquarters' offices; but at the moment his chief
concern was to get to Abba Sud as quickly as possible.

To fly without permission after having been warned
by the Count to keep close at hand would have been
asking for trouble, so he made his way boldly to the

281

fort and asked the Count if he could do a reconnaissance, making the excuse that it was boring doing nothing. To his great relief the Count made no objection, and he hurried back to the hangars in high spirits. He half regretted that he was wearing his German uniform, for it meant taking a German machine, but in the event of a forced landing on either side of the lines a German officer in a British machine would certainly be looked at askance. So more with the idea of making himself acquainted with its controls than for any other reason, he ordered out a Halberstadt in preference to a Pfalz, and was soon in the air.

He set off on a direct course for the lines, but as soon as he was out of sight of the aerodrome he swung away to the east in the direction of the oasis. Twice he was sighted and pursued by British machines, and rather than risk being attacked by pilots whose fire, for obvious reasons, he would be unable to return, he climbed the Halberstadt nearly to its ceiling, keeping a sharp look-out all the time.

He had been flying on his new course about ten minutes, and was just congratulating himself that he was now outside the zone of air operations, when his roving eyes picked out, and instantly focused on, a tiny moving speck far to the south-east. At first glance he thought it was an eagle, for mistakes of this sort often occurred in eastern theatres of war, but when he saw that it was almost at his own height he knew that it must be an aeroplane. He edged away at once a few points to the south, in order to place himself between the sun and the other machine, and putting his nose down for more speed, rapidly overhauled the stranger. While he was still a good two miles away he saw that it was a Halberstadt like his own, and his forehead wrinkled into a puzzled frown when he perceived that it was heading out over the open desert. 'Where the dickens does that fellow think he's going?' he mused, for as far as he could remember there was nothing in that direction but wilderness for a hundred miles, when the flat desolation gave way to barren hills. There were certainly no troops or military targets to account for its presence.

'I'll keep an eye on you, my chicken,' he thought suspiciously. 'It will be interesting to see what your game is.' It struck him that it might be a pilot who had lost his way, but the direct course on which the machine was flying quickly discountenanced such a theory; a pilot who was lost would be almost certain to turn from side to side as he looked for possible landmarks.

'My word! it's hot, even up here,' he went on, with a questioning glance at the sun, which had suddenly assumed an unusual reddish hue. Later he was to recognize that significant sign, but at the time he had not been in the East long enough to learn much about the meteorological conditions. But he dismissed the phenomenon from his mind as the other machine started losing height, and throttling back to half power, he followed it, still taking care not to lose his strategical position in the sun. And then a remarkable thing occurred; it was so odd that he pushed up his goggles with a quick movement of his hand and stared round the side of the windscreen with an expression of comical amazement on his face. The machine in front had disappeared. In all his flying experience he had never seen anything like it. He had seen machines disappear into clouds, or into ground mist, but here there were no clouds; nor was there a ground mist. Wait a minute, though! He was not so sure. The earth seemed to have become curiously blurred, distorted. 'Must be heat haze,' he thought, and then clutched at a centre-section

283

strut as the Halberstadt reeled and reared up on its tail. Before he could bring it to even keel it seemed to drop right out of his hands, and he clenched his teeth as his stomach turned over in the most terrific bump* he had ever struck. The machine hit solid air again with a crash that he knew must have strained every wire and strut; it was almost like hitting water.

For a moment he was too shaken and startled to wonder what had happened; if he thought anything at all in the first sickening second, it was that his machine had shed its wings, for it had fallen like a stone for nearly two thousand feet, as his altimeter revealed; but as the first spatter of grit struck his face and the horizon was blotted out, he knew that he had run into a sandstorm, a gale of wind that was tearing the surface from the desert and hurling it high into the air.

He wasted no time in idle contemplation of the calamity. He had never before seen a sandstorm, but he had heard them described by pilots who had been caught in them and had been lucky enough to survive. With the choking dust filling his nostrils and stinging his cheeks, he forgot all about the machine he had been following and sought only to evade the sand demon. He shoved the throttle wide open, turned at right angles, and with the joystick held forward by both hands, he raced across the path of the storm. At first the visibility grew rapidly worse as he encountered the full force of it, and the Halberstadt was tossed about like a dead leaf in an autumn gale, but presently the bumps grew less severe and the ground again came into view, mistily, as though seen through a piece of brown, semi-opaque glass. As far as he could see

---

* A local disturbance of air currents causing rough or uneven flying. Due either to clouds, wind or changes in the air temperature.

stretched the wind-swept desert, with the sand dunes rolling like a sea swell and a spindrift of fine grit whipping from their crests. But in one place a long narrow belt of palms rose up like an island in a stormy ocean, and towards it he steered his course. From the vicious lashing of the trees he knew that the wind must be blowing with the force of a tornado, and to land in it might be a difficult matter, but with the certain knowledge that the dust which was now blinding him would soon work its way into the engine and cut it to pieces, he decided that his only course was to get down as quickly as possible, whatever risks it involved; so he pushed his nose down at a steep angle towards the trees, aiming to touch the ground on the leeward side of them.

The landing proved to be more simple than he thought it would be; he could not see the actual surface of the ground as he flattened out on account of the thick stream of air-borne sand that raced over it like quicksilver, but he knew to a few inches where it was. He felt his wheels touch, bump, bump again, and he kicked his rudder bar to avoid a clump of trees that straggled out in the desert a little way from the main group. The landing was well judged, and there was no need to open the throttle again, for his run had carried him amongst the outlying palms of the oasis. He was out in a flash, carrying two of the sandbags with which all desert-flying machines are equipped against such an emergency. Dropping to his knees, he dragged the sand into the bags with both arms and then tied them, by the cords provided for the purpose, to the wing-skids.* He was only just in time, for even with these

* Semicircular hoops attached below the wings, towards the tips, to prevent damage to the wings when taxi-ing the aircraft.

anchors the machine began to drag as the wind increased in violence, so he fetched the two remaining sandbags, filled them, and tied them to the tail-skid.

'If you blow over now, well, you'll have to blow over; I can't do any more,' he thought, as, choking and half blinded by the stinging sand, he ran into the oasis and flung himself down in the first dip he reached. The sand still stung his face unmercifully, so he took off his tunic, wrapped it about his head, and then lay down to wait for the storm to blow itself out.

He was never sure how long he lay there. It might have been an hour; it might have been two hours; it seemed like eternity. The heat inside the jacket was suffocating, and in spite of all he could do to prevent it, the sand got inside and found its way into his nose, mouth, and ears. It was with heartfelt thankfulness that he heard the wind abating and knew that the worst of the storm was over; at the end it died away quite suddenly, so removing the coat, he sat up and looked about with interest. His first thought was for the machine, and he was relieved to find that it had suffered no damage, so he turned his attention to the immediate surroundings.

The oasis was exactly as he expected it to be; in fact oases in general were precisely as he had always imagined. Some things are not in the least like what artists and writers would lead us to expect; many are definitely disappointing; very few reach the glamorous perfection of our dreams, but the oasis of the desert is certainly one of them.

He found himself standing on a frond-littered sandy carpet from which the tall, straight columns of the date palms rose to burst in feathery fan-like foliage far overhead. Nearer to the heart of the oasis tussocks of coarse grass sprouted through the sand and gave promise of more sylvan verdure within, possibly water. 'In any case the water can't be far below the surface,' he thought as he hurried forward in the hope of being able to quench his thirst. He topped a rise and saw another one beyond. Almost unthinkingly he strode across the intervening dell and ran up the far side. As his eyes grew level with the top, he stopped, not quickly, but slowly, as if his muscles lagged behind his will to act. Then he sank down silently and wormed his way into a growth of leathery bushes that clustered around the palm-boles at that spot. For several seconds he lay quite still, while his face worked under the shock which for a moment seemed to have paralysed his brain. 'I'm dreaming. I'm seeing things. It must be a mirage,' he breathed, as he recovered somewhat and crawled to where he could see the scene beyond. But the sound of voices reached him and he knew it was no illusion.

In front of him the ground fell away for a distance of perhaps fifty yards into a saucer-like depression, in the bottom of which was obviously a well. Around the well, in attitude of alert repose, were about a score of Arabs, some sitting, some lying down, and others leaning against the parapet of the well from which they had evidently been drinking. But they were all looking one way; and they were all listening—listening to a man who stood on the far side of the well with his hands resting on the parapet, talking to them earnestly. It was Hauptmann Erich von Stalhein.

To Biggles the whole thing was so unexpected and at the same time so utterly preposterous that he could only lie and watch in a kind of fascinated wonder. And the more he watched and thought about it the more incomprehensible the whole thing became. How on earth had von Stalhein got there when only two hours before he had interrogated him in his room at Zabala,

287

which could not be less than sixty miles away? What was he doing there, with the Arabs? Why was he addressing them so fervently?

His astonishment gave way to curiosity and then to intense interest as he watched the scene. It seemed to him that von Stalhein, from his actions, was exhorting the Arabs to do something, something they were either disinclined to do, or about which they were divided in their opinions. But after a time it became apparent that the powerful personality of the man was making itself felt, and in the end there was a general murmur of assent. Then, as if the debate was over, the party began to break up, some of the Arabs going towards a line of wiry-looking ponies that were tethered between the trees, and others, with von Stalhein, going into a small square building that stood a short distance behind the well. It was little more than a primitive hut, constructed of sun-dried mud bricks and thatched with dead palm fronds.

The Arabs who went to their horses mounted and rode away through the trees, and presently those who had gone into the building reappeared, and they, too, rode away. Silence fell, the blazing sun-drenched silence of the desert.

Biggles lay quite still, never taking his eyes off the hut for an instant, waiting for von Stalhein to reappear. An hour passed and he did not come out. Another hour ticked slowly by. The sun passed its zenith and began to fall towards the west, and still he did not come. Biggles' thirst became unbearable. 'I've got to drink or die,' he declared quietly to himself, as he rose to his feet and walked towards the well. 'If he sees me I can only tell the truth and say I was forced down by the storm, which he can't deny,' he added thoughtfully.

He reached the well, and dragging up a bucket of

the life-saving liquid, drank deeply; that which he could not drink he splashed over his smarting face and hands. 'And now, Erich, let us see how you behave when you get a shock,' he thought humorously, for the drink had refreshed him, as he walked boldly up to the door of the hut, which stood ajar. He pushed it open and entered. A glance showed him that the entire building comprised a single room, but it was not that which made him stagger back and then stand rooted to the ground with parted lips. The room was empty. At first his brain refused to accept this astounding fact, and he looked from floor to ceiling as if expecting to see them open up and deliver the missing German in the manner of a jack-in-the-box. He also looked round the walls for a door that might lead to another room, but there was none.

'Well, I've had some shocks in my time, but this beats anything I've ever run up against before,' he muttered. Beyond doubt or question von Stalhein had gone into the hut; only Arabs had come out. Where was von Stalhein? He left the hut, and hurrying to where the horse lines had been, saw a wide trail of trampled sand leading to the edge of the oasis. A long way out in the desert to the south-west a straggling line of horsemen was making its way towards the misty horizon; farther south a solitary white Bisherin racing camel, with a rider on its back, was eating distance in a long rolling stride that in time could wear down the finest horse ever bred. 'So you've changed the colour of your skin again, have you, Mr. von Stalhein?' thought Biggles, as the only possible solution of the problem flashed into his mind. 'Good; now we know where we are. I fancy I'm beginning to rumble your little game — El Shereef.'

As he turned away a wave of admiration for the

German surged through him. 'He's a clever devil and no mistake,' he thought. 'But how the dickens did he get here? He must have flown; there was no other way he could have done it in the time. That's it. He was in the machine I saw. Some one flew him over, dropped him at the oasis, and then went back. They didn't hear me arrive because of the noise of the wind and I was on the lee-side of them. The Arabs were waiting here for him, and now he has gone off on some job. I wonder if this place is a regular rendezvous.'

The word rendezvous reminded him of Algy and his belated appointment. 'He'll think I'm not coming,' he muttered as he broke into a run that carried him over the brow of the hill behind which he had left the Halberstadt. As it came into view he gave a gasp and twisted suddenly; but it was too late. A sea of scowling faces surged around him. He lashed out viciously, but it was no use. Blows rained on him and he was flung heavily to the ground, where, half choked with sand, he was held down until his hands were tied behind his back.

Cursing himself for the folly of charging up to the machine in the way he had, and for leaving his revolver in the cockpit, he sat up and surveyed his captors sullenly. There were about fifteen of them, typical Bedouins* of the desert, armed with antiquated muskets. A medley of guttural voices had broken out, but he could not get the hang of the conversation; he rather suspected from the way some of them fingered their wicked-looking knives that they were in favour of dispatching him forthwith, and were only prevented from doing so by others who pointed excitedly towards the

* A tent-dwelling nomadic Arab. Different groups supported both sides in the First World War.

290

west. Eventually these seemed to get the best of the argument, for he was pulled to his feet and invited by actions and grimaces to mount a horse, which was led forward from a row that stood near the machine. The Arabs all mounted, and without further parley set off at a gallop across the desert in a straggling bunch with Biggles in the centre.

Chapter 9
A Fight and an Escape

That ride will live in Biggles' memory for many a day. The heat, the dust, thirst, the flies that followed them in a cloud, all combined to make life almost unbearable, and as the sun began to fall more quickly towards the western horizon he prayed for the end of the journey wherever or whatever it might be.

It came at last, but not in the manner he expected; nor, indeed, in the manner the Bedouins expected. The sand had gradually given way to the hard, pebbly clay, with occasional clumps of camel-thorn, which in Palestine usually forms the surface of the wilderness proper, and low rocky hills began to appear. They were approaching the first of these when without warning a line of mounted horsemen, riding at full gallop and shooting as they came, tore round the base of the hill and swept down towards them.

Their appearance was the signal for a general panic amongst the Bedouins. Without halting, they swerved in their course and sought safety in flight; in this way one or two of the better mounted ones did eventually succeed in escaping, but the others, overhauled by their pursuers, could only turn and fight stubbornly. Their prisoner they ignored, and Biggles was left sitting alone on his horse until, stung by a ricochetting bullet, it reared up and threw him. With his hands still tied he fell heavily, and the breath was knocked out of him, so he lay where he had fallen, wondering how long it would be before one of the flying bullets found him.

He had no interest in the result of the battle, which appeared to be purely a tribal affair between locals; if his captors won, then matters would no doubt remain as they were; if the newcomers won, his fate could not be much worse, for at that moment it seemed to him that death was better than the intolerable misery of being dragged about the wilderness.

Presently the firing died away and the sound of horses' hooves made him sit up. Of his original captors none remained; those who had been compelled to fight lay dead or dying, a gruesome fact that caused him little concern. The newcomers, nearly fifty of them, were riding in, obviously in high spirits at their success.

To his astonishment they lifted him to his feet, cut his bonds, and made signals that he had nothing more to fear. They tried hard to tell him something, but he could not follow their meaning, so after a brief rest he was again invited to mount a horse and the whole party set off at a swinging gallop towards the hills. Dusk fell and they were compelled to steady the pace, but still they rode on.

Biggles was sagging in the saddle, conscious only of a deadly tiredness, when he was startled by the ringing challenge of a British sentry.

'Halt! who goes there?'

Several voices answered in what he assumed was Arabic, and there followed a general commotion, in which he was made to dismount and walk towards a barbed-wire fence which he could see dimly in the fast failing light. Behind its protective screen were a number of canvas bell tents, camouflaged in light and dark splashes of colour. Nearer at hand was a larger tent, rectangular in shape, and a number of British Tommies in khaki drill jackets, shorts, and pith helmets. A young officer, tanned to the colour of mahogany by the sun,

stepped forward towards the Arabs, and another conversation ensued in which Biggles could only understand a single word, one that appeared often—*bak-
sheesh**. Eventually the officer went back to the larger
tent, and presently returned with a corporal and two
men who carried rifles with fixed bayonets; in his hand
was a slip of paper which he handed to the man who
appeared to be the leader of the Arabs, and who, without another word, turned his horse and rode away into
the night followed by the others.

Biggles was left facing the officer, with a soldier on
each side of him. At a word of command they moved
forward to a gate in the wire, and halted again a few
yards from the large tent, in which a light was now
burning.

Then Biggles saw a curious thing. A distorted
shadow of a man, who was evidently standing inside
the tent between the canvas and the light, leaned forward; a hand was lifted with a perfectly natural movement of the arm, and tapped the ash off the cigarette
it held between its fingers. Biggles had seen the same
action made in reality too many times to have any
doubt as to who it was; of all the men he knew only
one had that peculiar trick of tapping the ash off his
cigarette with his forefinger. It was von Stalhein. As
he watched the shadow dumbfounded, wondering if his
tired eyes were deceiving him, it disappeared, and the
officer addressed him.

'Do you speak English?' he asked curtly.

'A little—yes,' replied Biggles, in the best German
accent he could muster.

'Will you give me your parole?'

'Parole?'

* Money, payment.

'Will you give your word that you will not attempt to escape?'

Biggles shook his head. '*Nein**,' he said harshly.

'As you wish. It would have made things easier for you if you had. Don't give me more trouble than you can help, though; I may as well tell you that I have just had to pay out good British money to save your useless hide.'

'Money?'

'Yes; those Arabs demanded fifty pounds for you or threatened to slit your throat there and then. I couldn't watch them do that even though you are a German, so I gave them a chit for fifty pounds which they will be able to cash at any British pay-office. I mention it in the hope that you will be grateful and not give me more trouble than you can help before I can get rid of you; I've quite enough as it is. What is your name?'

'Leopold Brunow.'

'I see you're a flying officer.'

Biggles nodded.

'Where is your machine?'

'It is somewhere in the desert.'

'What is the number of your squadron?'

'I regret I cannot answer that question.'

'Perhaps you're right,' observed the officer casually. 'No matter; they'll ask you plenty of questions at head-quarters so I needn't bother about it now. I will make you as comfortable as I can for the night, and will send you down the lines in the morning. I need hardly warn you that if you attempt to escape you are likely to be shot. Good-night.' He turned to the N.C.O. 'All right, Corporal, take charge.'

Biggles bowed stiffly, and escorted by the two

---

* German: No.

Tommies, followed the corporal to a tent that stood a little apart from the others.

'There you are, Jerry.* No 'arf larks and you'll be as right as ninepence, but don't come any funny stuff—see, or else—' The corporal made a gesture more eloquent than words.

Biggles nodded and threw himself wearily on the camp bed with which the tent was furnished. He was tired out, physically and mentally, yet he could not repress a smile as he thought of his position. To be taken prisoner by his own side was an adventure not without humour, but it was likely to be a serious setback to his work if he was recognized by any one who knew him. Moreover, the delay might prove serious, both on account of his non-arrival at Abba Sud, where Algy would be waiting for him, and in the light of what he had recently discovered. To declare his true identity to the officer in charge of the outpost was out of the question—not that he would be believed if he did—yet to attempt to escape might have serious consequences, for not only would he have to run the risk of being shot, but he would have to face the perils of the wilderness.

He remembered the incident of the shadow on the tent, and it left him both perplexed and perturbed. He could not seriously entertain the thought that it had been von Stalhein, yet quite apart from his unique trick of tapping his cigarette, every other circumstance pointed to it. The German was certainly somewhere in the neighbourhood, there was no doubt about that. Still, it was one thing to be prowling about disguised as an Arab, and quite another matter to be sitting inside the headquarters tent of a British post, he reflected.

* Slang: German.

With these conflicting thoughts running through his head he dropped off into a troubled sleep, from which he was aroused by the corporal, who told him in no uncertain terms that it was time to be moving, as he would shortly have to be on his way, although he did not say where. It was still dark, but sounds outside the tent indicated that the camp was already astir and suggested that it must be nearly dawn. He had nothing to do to get ready beyond drink the tea and eat the bully beef and biscuits which the corporal had unceremoniously pushed inside, so he applied his eye to the crack of the tent flap in the hope of seeing something interesting. In this he was disappointed, however, for the only signs of life were a few Tommies and Arab levies moving about on various camp tasks. So he sat down on the bed again, racking his brain for a line of action to adopt when he found himself, as he had no doubt he shortly would be, penned behind a stout wire fence with other prisoners of war.

From the contemplation of this dismal and rather difficult problem he was aroused by the sound of horses' hooves, and hurried to the flap, but before he reached it, it was thrown back, and the youthful officer who had spoken to him the night before stood at the entrance; behind him were six mounted Arabs armed with modern service rifles; one of them was leading a spare horse.

'Can you ride, Brunow?' asked the subaltern.

'Yes.' replied Biggles sombrely.

'Then get mounted; these men are taking you down the lines, and the sooner you get there the better, because you'll find it thundering hot presently. And I must warn you again that the men have orders to shoot if you try to get away.'

Biggles was in no position to argue, so with a nod of

farewell he mounted the spare horse, and was soon trotting over the twilit wilderness in the centre of his escort.

For a few miles they held on a straight westerly course, but as the sun rose in a blaze of scarlet glory they began to veer towards the south, and then east, until they were travelling in a direction almost opposite to the one in which they had started. Biggles noted this subconsciously with an airman's instinct for watching his course, but it did not particularly surprise him. 'Perhaps there is some obstacle to be avoided,' he thought casually, but as they continued on the same course he suddenly experienced a pang of real alarm, for either his idea of locality had failed him, or else his mental picture of the position of the post was at fault, for wherever they were going, it was certainly not towards the British lines. He spoke to his guards, but either they did not understand, or else they did not wish to understand, for they paid no attention to his remarks.

The sun was well up when at last they reached a wadi* that cut down into a flat plain, where the guards dismounted and signalled to him to do the same. For a few minutes they rested, drinking a little water and eating a few dates; then one who appeared to be in charge of the party handed him a small package, and indicating that he was to remain where he was, led the others round the nearby bend in the rock wall. This struck Biggles as being very odd, but he did not dwell on it. His first thought was of escape, and had his horse been left with him he would certainly have made a dash for it; but the Arabs had taken it with them, and he knew that on foot he would be recaptured before he

* The dry bed of a river.

298

had gone a hundred yards. The idea of wandering about the waterless desert without a mount, looking for a human habitation, was out of the question, so he sat back in the shade of the rock and awaited the return of his escort, who he assumed had no doubt taken his predicament into consideration before leaving him.

'Those fellows are a long time,' he thought, some time later, and moved by sheer curiosity, he walked down to the place where they had disappeared. To his infinite amazement they were nowhere in sight; nor was there, as far as he could see, a place where they could hide. He ran up the side of the wadi, and standing on the edge of the desert, looked quickly towards all points of the compass, but the only sign of life he could see was a jackal slinking among the rocks. He even called out, but there was no reply.

Wrestling with this new problem, he returned to the wadi, when it occurred to him that possibly the package that had been given to him might supply a clue, and he tore it open eagerly. He was quite right; it did. The package contained an 'iron' ration consisting of biscuits and a slab of chocolate, and a flask of water. Attached to the flask by a rubber band was a sheet of notepaper on which had been written, in block letters, three words. The message consisted of the single word, 'Wait'. It was signed, 'A Friend'.

He held up the paper to the light, and a low whistle escaped his lips as his eyes fell on the familiar 'crown' watermark. 'So I, a German officer, have a friend in a British post, eh?' he thought. 'How very interesting.'

He folded the paper carefully, put it in his pocket, and was in the act of munching the chocolate when he was not a little surprised to hear an aeroplane approaching. But his surprise became wonderment when he saw it was a Halberstadt, which was, moreover, gliding towards the plain at the head of the wadi with the obvious intention of landing. With growing curiosity he watched it approach. 'If this sort of thing goes on much longer I shan't know who's fighting who,' he muttered helplessly. 'I thought I knew something about this war, but I'm getting out of my depth,' he opined. 'I wonder who's flying it? Shouldn't be surprised if it's the Kaiser*.'

It was not the Kaiser but Mayer who touched his wheels on the hard, unsympathetic surface of the wilderness, and then taxied tail up towards the place where Biggles was standing watching him. He ran to a standstill and raised his arm in a beckoning gesture.

Biggles walked across. 'Hello, Mayer,' he said. 'Where the dickens have you come from?'

Mayer gave him a nod of greeting. 'Get in,' he said shortly, indicating the rear cockpit.

'Where are we going?' shouted Biggles above the noise of the engine, as he climbed into the seat.

'Home: where the devil do you think?' snapped Mayer as he pulled** the throttle open and sped across the desolate waste.

* The ruler of Germany.
** The controls of German aeroplanes worked in the opposite direction to the British. Thus, he pulled the throttle towards him instead of pushing it away, as would normally have been the case.

Chapter 10
Shot Down

Biggles sat in the cockpit and watched the wadi fall away behind as Mayer lifted the machine from the ground and began climbing for height. He had no flying cap or goggles, for he had been carrying them in his hand when he was attacked by the Arabs on the oasis, and had dropped them in the struggle; not that he really needed them, for the air was sultry.

So he stood up with his arms resting on the edge of the cockpit, and surveyed the landscape in the hope of picking out a landmark that he knew, at the same time turning over in his mind the strange manner of his rescue. Who was the friend in the British post? He could think of no one but von Stalhein, although he would never have guessed but for the shadow on the tent. By what means had he arranged for the Arab levies to connive at his escape? It looked as if the Arabs, while openly serving with the British forces, were actually under the leadership of the Germans. 'The more I see of this business the easier it is to perceive why the British plans have so often failed. It looks as if the whole area is rotten with the canker of espionage,' he mused. Even assuming that von Stalhein had been responsible for his escape, how could Mayer have known where he was? That he had not turned up at such a remote spot by mere chance was quite certain.

Dimly the situation began to take form. Von Stalhein, disguised as an Arab, was operating behind the British lines. That was the most outstanding and important feature, for upon it everything else rested. He may have been responsible for the sheikhs turning against the British, in spite of the brilliant and fearless efforts of Major Sterne to prevent it, although Sterne had sometimes been able to win back their allegiance with gold, rifles, and ammunition, the only commodities for which the Arabs had any respect or consideration. The Halberstadt Squadron at Zabala, while carrying out regular routine duties, was also working with von Stalhein, flying him over the lines and picking him up at pre-arranged meeting-places—not a difficult matter considering the size and nature of the country. The previous day provided a good example, when von Stalhein had been flown over to try to influence the Arabs at the oasis. Later, he must have learned that Brunow was a prisoner in British hands, and in some way had been able to arrange for him to be sent down the lines in charge of Arabs who were in his pay, in order to effect his rescue, not for personal reasons but because he would rather see Brunow behind the German lines than behind the British.

The more he thought about this hypothesis the more Biggles was convinced that he was right, and that at last he was on the track of the inside causes of the British failures in the Middle East. Thinking of the oasis reminded him that they must be passing somewhere close to it; as near as he could judge by visualizing the map, both Abba Sud and the oasis where he had seen von Stalhein must both be somewhere between ten and twenty miles to the east or south-east. He turned, and pushing his Parabellum gun* aside out of the way, looked out over the opposite side of the cockpit.

* A mobile gun for the rear gunner, usually mounted on a U-shaped rail to allow rapid movement with a wide arc of fire.

Far away on the horizon he could just make out a dull shadow that might have been an oasis, but he was too uncertain of his actual position to know which of the two it was, if indeed it was either of them. Perhaps Mayer had a map; if so, he would borrow it. He reached forward and tapped the German on the shoulder, and then sprang back in affright as the shrill chatter of a machine-gun split the air from somewhere near at hand. A shower of lead struck the Halberstadt like a flail. There was a shrill *whang* of metal striking against metal, and a ghastly tearing sound of splintering wood-work. The stricken machine lurched drunkenly as the engine cut out dead and a long feather of oily black smoke swirled away aft.

Instinctively Biggles grabbed his gun, and squinted through his slightly open fingers in the direction of the sun whence the attack had come. The blinding white orb seared his eyeballs, but he caught a fleeting glimpse of a grey shadow that banked round in a steep stalling turn to renew the attack. He turned to warn Mayer, and a cry of horror broke from his lips as he saw him sagging insensible in his safety belt; a trickle of blood was oozing from under the ear flaps of his leather helmet.

As in a ghastly nightmare, Biggles heard the staccato clatter of the guns again, and felt the machine shudder like a sailing ship taken aback, as the controls flapped uselessly. Its nose lurched downwards; the port wing drooped, and the next instant the machine was spinning wildly earthward.

Biggles, cold with fear, acted with the deliberation of long experience, moved with a calmness that would have seemed impossible on the ground. He knew that the machine was fitted with dual controls, but the rear joystick was not left in its socket for fear of the observer being hit and falling on it in a combat, thus jamming the controls. It was kept in a canvas slot in the side of the cockpit. Swiftly he pulled it out, inserted the end in the metal junction and screwed it in. Without waiting to look out of the cockpit, he pushed the stick forward and kicked on full top rudder. The machine began to respond instantly; would it come out of the spin in time? He dropped back into his seat, and snatching a swift glance at the ground, now perilously near, knew that it was going to be touch and go. Slowly the nose of the machine came up as it came out of the spin.

With another five feet of height the Halberstadt would just have managed it; she did in fact struggle to even keel, but still lost height from the speed of her spin, as she was bound to for a few seconds. Biggles pulled the stick back and held his breath; he had no engine to help him, and the best he could hope for was some sort of pancake* landing. But luck was against him, for the ground at that point was strewn with boulders, some large and some small, and it must have been one of the large ones that caught the axle of his undercarriage. The lower part of the machine seemed to stop dead while the upper part, carried on by its momentum, tried to go forward; then several things happened at once. Biggles was flung violently against the instrument board; the propeller boss bored into the ground, hurling splinters of wood and rock in all directions; the tail swung up and over in a complete semicircle as the machine somersaulted in a final tearing, rending, splintering crash. Then silence.

Biggles, half blinded by petrol which had poured over him when the tank sheered off its bearers and

---

* Instead of the aircraft gliding down to land, it flops down from a height of a few feet, after losing flying speed.

burst asunder, fought his way out of the wreck like a madman, regardless of mere bruises and cuts. The horror of fire was on him, as it is on every airman in similar circumstances, but his first thought was for his companion. 'Mayer' he croaked, 'where are you?' There was no answer, so he tore the debris aside until he found the German, still strapped in his seat, buried under the tangled remains of the plane. Somehow—he had no clear recollection of how it was done—he got him clear of the cockpit, and dragged him through the tangle of wires and struts to a spot some distance away, clear of fire should it break out. Then he sank down and buried his face in his hands while he fought back an hysterical desire to burst into tears. He had seen stronger men than himself do it, and knew that it was simply the sudden relaxation of nerves that had been screwed up to breaking-point.

Then he rose unsteadily to his feet, wiped a smear of blood from a cut in his lip, and turned to his partner-in-misfortune, for the cause of the trouble was already a tiny speck in the far distance. So swift and perfectly timed had been the attack that he hadn't even time to identify the type of machine that had shot them down.

He took off Mayer's helmet, and a long red weal across the side of his head told its own story. As far as he could see the bullet had not actually penetrated the skull, but had struck him a glancing blow that had knocked him unconscious, and might, or might not, prove fatal. He could find no other bullet wounds, although his clothes were badly torn about and his face bruised, so he made him as comfortable as possible in the shade of the rock and then went to see if he could get a little water from the leaking radiator. It was hot and oily, but it was better than nothing, so he soaked his handkerchief and returned to Mayer. Had it been possible, he would have tried to save some of the precious liquid that was fast disappearing into the thirsty ground, but he had no receptacle to catch it, so he went back to the unfortunate German and cleaned the wound as well as he could. His efforts were rewarded, for after a few minutes Mayer opened his eyes and stared about him wonderingly. Wonderment gave way to understanding as complete consciousness returned, and he smiled weakly.

'What happened?' he whispered through his bruised lips.

'An Engländer dropped on us out of the sun and hit us with his first burst,' replied Biggles. 'A bullet hit you on the side of the head and the box* spun before I could get my gun going. I managed to get her out of the spin with the spare joystick before she hit the ground, but the engine had gone, so I had to get down as well as I could—which wasn't very well, as you can see,' he added dryly. 'There are too many rocks about for nice landings; but there, we were lucky she didn't catch fire.'

Mayer tried to move, but a low groan broke from his lips.

'I should lie still for a bit if I were you,' Biggles advised him. 'You'll be better presently.'

'You'd better go on,' the German told him stolidly.

'Go on? And leave you here? No, I'll wait for you.'

'Do you know where we are?' inquired Mayer, bitterly.

'Not exactly.'

'We're fifty miles from our lines, and it's fifty miles of waterless desert, so you'd better be starting.'

'No hurry, I'll wait for you.'

* German slang for an aeroplane.

306

'It'll be no use waiting for me.'

'Why not?'

'Because I shan't be coming.'

'Who says so?'

'I do. My leg is broken.'

Biggles felt the blood drain from his face as he realized just what Mayer's grim statement meant. 'Good heavens,' he breathed.

The German smiled curiously. 'The fortune of war,' he observed calmly. 'Before you go I would like you to do something for me.'

'What is it?'

'Go and look in my cockpit and see if you can find my pistol. I shall need it.'

'No, you won't,' Biggles told him tersely, for he knew well enough what was in the other's mind.

'You wouldn't leave me here to die of thirst—and the hyenas,' protested Mayer weakly.

'Who's talking about leaving you, anyway,' growled Biggles. 'Just you lie still while I think it over.'

'If you've any sense you'll go on. There's no need for us both to die,' said Mayer, with a courage that Biggles could not help but admire.

'I'm not talking about dying, either,' he declared. 'We'll find a way out; let me think a minute.' Then he laughed. The idea of an Englishman and a German each trying to save the other's life struck him as funny.

'What's the joke?' asked Mayer suspiciously.

'No joke—but it's no use bursting into tears,' returned Biggles brightly. He walked across and examined the machine. There were still a few drops of water in the radiator, but it was poisonous-looking fluid and he watched it drip away into the sand without regret. He dug about in the wreckage until he found Mayer's map, when he sat down and plotted their position as nearly as he could judge it. As Mayer had said, they were a good fifty miles from the German lines, and farther still from the British lines, but to the south and east there were two or three oases, unnamed, from which he guessed they were very small, not less than fifteen and not more than twenty miles away. Fifteen miles! Could he do it in the heat of the day? Alone, perhaps, but with a wounded companion, definitely no. Suppose he left Mayer, and tried to find the oasis where he had seen von Stalhein; could he fly back in the Halberstadt, assuming that it was as he had left it? No, he decided, for the German would certainly have died of thirst in the meantime.

The idea of leaving Mayer to perish did not occur to him. In the desperate straits in which they found themselves, he no longer regarded him as an enemy, but as a brother pilot who must be supported while a vestige of hope remained. He regarded the crashed machine with a speculative eye, and half smiled as a possibility occurred to him. Near at hand was one of the undercarriage wheels, with the bent axle still attached; the tyre had burst, but otherwise it was undamaged. The other wheel lay some distance away in the desert where it had bounced after the crash. He retrieved it and then set to work, while Mayer watched him dispassionately.

At the end of an hour he had constructed a fairly serviceable two-wheeled trailer from the undercarriage and remains of the wing spars. He had found plenty of material to work with; in fact, more than he needed. Finally he hunted about in the wreckage for the seat cushions, smiling as he caught sight of his unshaven, blood-stained face in the pilot's reflector. He found them, threw them on the crazy vehicle, and picking up some pieces of interplane struts and canvas, approached the German.

Mayer regarded him dubiously. 'You've wasted a lot of time,' he said irritably.

'Maybe,' replied Biggles imperturbably. 'Help me as much as you can while I get this leg of yours fixed up.'

'Do what?' ejaculated Mayer. 'What are you going to do?'

'Tie your leg up in these splints, so that it won't hurt more than can be helped while I get you on the perambulator.'

'Don't be a fool—'

'If you don't lie still, I'll fetch you a crack on the other side of your skull,' snarled Biggles. 'Do you think I want to hang about here all day? Come on—that's better.'

Not without difficulty he bound up Mayer's leg in the improvised splints, and then lifted him bodily on to the trailer. He handed him a piece of fabric to use as a sunshade, and without another word set off in the direction in which he judged the oasis to be.

Fortunately the ground was flat and fairly open, but the punctured wheel dragged heavily through the patches of loose sand that became more frequent as he went on. The sun climbed to its zenith and its white bars of heat struck down with relentless force.

Nowhere could he find rest for his eyes; in all directions stretched the wilderness, colourless and without outline, a vast undulating expanse of brown and grey that merged into the shimmering horizon. The land had no definite configuration, but was an eternal monotony of sand and rock, spotted here and there with the everlasting camel-thorn. There was no wild life—or if there was he did not see it. Once he straightened his back and looked round the scene, but its overwhelming solitude made him shudder and he went on with his task doing his best to fight off the dreadful feeling of depression that was creeping over him.

The demon thirst began to torture him. Another hour passed, and another, and still he struggled on. His lips were black and dry, with a little ring of congealed dust round them. He no longer perspired, for the sun drank up every drop of moisture as soon as it appeared. Mayer was more fortunate, for he had lapsed into unconsciousness. At first Biggles had tried to keep the fabric over his face, but he soon got tired of picking it up and struggled on without it. A feeling crept over him that he had been pulling the trailer all his life; everything else that had ever happened was a dim memory; only the rocks and the sand were real.

Presently he began to mutter to himself, and eyed the sun malevolently. 'I'd give you something, you skunk, if I had my guns,' he grated through his clenched teeth. It did not occur to him to leave his companion; the fixedness of purpose that had won him fame in France kept the helpless German ever before his mind. 'Poor old Mayer,' he crooned. 'Tough luck, getting a cracked leg. Why the dickens isn't Algy here; I'll twist the young scallywag's ear for him for leaving the patrol like this.'

Mayer began to mutter in German, long meaningless sentences in which the word Rhine occurred frequently.

'When we wind up the watch on the Rhine,' cackled Biggles. 'Your watch is about wound up, old cock,' and he laughed again. He stumbled on a rock, and swinging round in a blaze of fury, kicked it viciously and uselessly. He reached the top of a fold in the ground and stared ahead with eyes that seemed to be two balls of fire searing his brain. A line of cool green palm trees stood up clearly on the skyline. 'Ha, ha, you can't catch me like that,' he chuckled. 'Mirage; I've heard about you. Thinks it can catch me. Ha, ha!'

A big bird flopped down heavily not far away and regarded him with cold beady eyes. He dropped the handle of the trailer, snatched up a stone, and hurled it with all his strength. The bird flapped a few yards further away and settled again. 'You Hun,' he croaked. 'You dirty thieving Hun. I can see you sitting there; I'll knock the bottom out of your fuselage before I've finished with you.' He picked up the handle of the trailer and struggled on.

He began to sway as he walked. Once he fell, and lay where he had fallen for a full minute before he remembered his burden, whereupon he scrambled to his feet and set off with a fresh burst of energy. He topped another rise and saw a long group of green palm fronds against the blue sky above the next dip. At first he regarded them with a sort of detached interest, but slowly it penetrated his bemused mind that they were very real, very close, and very desirable. He broke into a drunken run, still dragging the trailer, and breathing in deep wheezing gasps; the palm trees seemed to float towards him, and presently he was amongst them, patting the rough boles with his hands. The place was vaguely familiar and he seemed to know exactly where to go, so he dropped the handle of the trailer and reeled towards the centre of the oasis, croaking as he saw that he was not mistaken. In front of him was the well and the hut where, the afternoon before, he had seen von Stalhein. He had returned to his starting point. He staggered to the well, seized the hide rope in his shaking hands, dragged up the receptacle attached to it and drank as he had never drunk before. Then he refilled the makeshift bucket and ran back to where he had left Mayer. He rolled him off the trailer and with difficulty got some of the water between his parched lips, at the same time dabbing his face and neck with it. He continued giving him a little water for some time, occasionally drinking deep draughts himself; but when he felt that he could do no more for the sick man, he returned to the well and buried his face and arms in the cool liquid.

He still had the remains of the chocolate ration in his pocket, so he munched a little and felt better for it. Then he walked up to the hut, but it was empty, so he returned to Mayer with the idea of making him as comfortable as possible before going to the spot where he had left the Halberstadt, to make sure it was still there and undamaged. But suddenly he felt dreadfully tired and sat down near the trailer to rest. The shade, after the heat of the sun which was now sinking fast, was pleasant, and he closed his eyes in ecstasy. His head nodded once or twice, and he slipped slowly sideways on to the cool sand, sound asleep.

Chapter 11
A Night Flight

I

He awoke, and sitting up with a start, looked around in bewilderment, for it was night, and for a moment or two he could not recall what had happened. The moon was up; it hung low over the desert like a sickle and cast a pale blue radiance over a scene of unutterable loneliness. Then, in the hard, black lattice-like shadows of the palms, he saw Mayer, and remembered everything. The German's face was ghastly in the weird light, and he thought he was dead, but dropping on his hands and knees beside him, was relieved to hear faint but regular breathing.

Then he sprang to his feet as a strange sound reached his ears, and he knew instinctively that it was the same noise that had awakened him; it reminded him of the harsh confused murmur of waves upon a pebbly beach, afar off, rising and falling on the still night air. For a little while he sat listening, trying to identify the sound, but he could not; it seemed to come from the other side of the oasis, so he made his way cautiously through the palms to a slight rise from which he could see the desert beyond. As he reached it and looked out he caught his breath sharply and sank down swiftly in the shadow of a stunted palm, staring with wide-open eyes.

He did not know what he had expected to see, but it was certainly not the sight that met his incredulous eyes. Mustering in serried ranks was an army of Arabs;

at a rough computation he made out the number to be nearly four thousand, and fresh bands were still riding in from the desert, gathering together for what could only be one of the biggest Arab raids ever organized— for he had no delusions as to their purpose. What was their objective? Were they being mustered by von Stalhein to harass the British flank, or by Major Sterne to launch a crippling blow at the German lines of communication? Those were questions he could not answer, but he hoped that by watching he might discover. He was glad that whoever was in charge had not decided to use the oasis itself as a meeting-place, or he would have been found, but a moment's consideration revealed the impracticability of such a course; a body of men of that size could only parade in the open.

For half an hour he lay and watched them, and at the end of that time they began to move off, not in any regular order, but winding like a long sinuous snake out into the desert; and he had no need to watch them for very long to guess their objective, for the direction they took would bring them within a few hours to the eastern outposts of the British army.

'If that bunch hits the right wing of our lines of communication without warning it'll go right through them like a knife through butter, and our fellows in the front-line trenches will be cut off from supplies and everything else,' he muttered anxiously. 'I shall have to let our people know somehow.' As the tail-end of the column disappeared into the mysterious blue haze of the middle distance he glanced at the moon and made a swift calculation. 'It must be somewhere about eleven o'clock—not later,' he thought. 'At an average speed of six miles an hour, and they can easily manage that, seven hours will see them ready to strike at our flank at just about dawn, which is probably the time they have fixed for the attack.'

He got up and ran back swiftly to where he had left Mayer. He was still unconscious, so he hurried round the edge of the oasis to where he had left the Halbertstadt the previous day. 'If it's gone, I'm sunk,' he murmured, and then uttered a low cry of delight as his eyes fell on it, standing just as he had left it. 'Now! what's my best plan of action?' he thought swiftly. 'Shall I leave Mayer here and dash down to Kantara in the hope of getting in touch with Algy? If I do, I daren't land, for if I did every officer on the station would know that a German machine had landed on the aerodrome, which would mean that the Germans would know it too. That's no use. The only thing I can do is to write a message, drop it, and then signal to Algy and Major Raymond as we arranged. That's the safest way; they would be bound to find it on the aerodrome. But what about Mayer? I can't leave him here and risk a night landing in order to pick him up afterwards; I might run short of petrol anyway, and I don't want to get stuck in the desert again. I shall have to take him with me. But I had better have a look at the machine.'

He found it exactly as he had left it, and thanked the lucky chance that ordained that not only should he have landed at what seemed to be the little-used end of the oasis, but amongst the trees, where the machine could not be seen from the desert. After removing the sandbag anchors he lifted up the tailskid and dragged the Halberstadt into the open, a task that presented no difficulty as the slope was slightly downhill. He climbed into the cockpit, turned on the petrol tap, and then returned to the front of the machine, where he turned the propeller round several times in order to suck the

315

petrol gas into the cylinders. The machine was not fitted with a self-starter, so he switched on the ignition and then returned to the propellor in order to swing it. Before he did so, however, he took a leaf from his notebook, wrote a message on it, and addressed it to Algy. This done, he took off his tunic, ripped a length of material from his shirt to form a streamer, and tying the message in it with a pebble to give it weight, put it in his pocket and returned to the engine.

In the warm air it started at once, and in the stillness of the desert night the din that it made was so appalling that he started back in alarm. 'Great Scott! what a row,' he muttered as he climbed quickly into his seat and began to taxi carefully to the place where he had left the German. Mayer was still unconscious and lying in the same position, so he set to work on the formidable task of getting him into the rear cockpit. This he finally managed to do with no small exertion by picking him up in the 'fireman's grip' and dropping him bodily over the side; the unfortunate man fell in a heap, but there was no help for it, and as Biggles observed to himself as he got him into a sitting position, in the seat, with the safety belt round his waist, 'He's unconscious, so it isn't hurting him, anyway.'

Before climbing back into his cockpit he looked long and critically down the track over which he would have to take off. 'If I hit a brick, there's going to be a nasty mess,' was his unspoken thought as he eased the throttle open and held the stick slightly forward. But any fears he may have had on the matter of buckling a wheel—with calamitous results—against a rock were set at rest as the machine rose gracefully into the air, and he settled down to his task with a sigh of relief and satisfaction.

It was a weird experience, flying over the moonlit

desert that in the early days of history had been the scene of wars of extermination, and the pictures of many famous Biblical characters floated up in his imagination. Below him, more than twenty centuries before, Joseph had wandered in his coat of many colours, and the Prodigal Son had wasted his money in riotous living. 'There wouldn't be much for him to spend his money on to-day, I'm afraid,' thought Biggles whimsically, as he surveyed the barren land that once, before the great rivers had dried up, had flowed with milk and honey. 'Still, maybe it will regain some of its prosperity again one day when human beings come to their senses and stop fighting each other,' he mused, as he turned his nose a little more to the north, in order to avoid being heard by the raiders, and von Stalhein in particular, who he suspected was leading them, and who would certainly recognize the drone of his Mercedes engine.

A white wavering finger suddenly probed the sky some distance ahead, and he knew he was approaching the British lines. Soon afterwards a blood-red streak of flame flashed across his vision, and he knew that the anti-aircraft gunners were at work. He was not very perturbed, for he had climbed fairly high and knew that the chances of being hit were very remote; but as the archie barrage grew more intense, he throttled back and began a long glide towards the aerodrome at Kantara. Several searchlight beams were combing the sky for him, but he avoided them easily and smiled grimly as the lights of the aerodrome came into view. 'If I was carrying a load of bombs instead of a sick German, those fellows would soon be getting what they are asking for,' he growled, and shut off his engine as he dived steeply towards his objective. White lines of tracer bullets were streaking upwards, but in the darkness the shooting was chiefly guesswork and none of them came near him, although he realized that this state of affairs was likely to change when he opened his engine and by so doing disclosed his whereabouts.

With one hand on the throttle and the message lying on his lap, he raced low over the aerodrome; when he reached the middle he tossed the message overboard, and opened and closed the throttle twice in quick succession. Then he pulled it wide open and zigzagged out of the vicinity, like a startled bird, as the searchlights swung round and every gun within range redoubled its efforts to hit him. But he was soon outside their field of fire and racing nose down towards the German lines. Once he glanced back to satisfy himself that Mayer was still unconscious. 'If he'd come round just now he might well have wondered what the dickens was going on,' he thought, 'and he might have asked some awkward questions when we got back—or caused the Count to ask some. As it is, he'll wonder how on earth he got home when he wakes up and finds himself in Zabala.'

The rest of the flight was simply a fight against the lassitude that overtakes all pilots after a period of flying, when they have nothing to do but fly on a straight course, for the comfortable warmth that fills the cockpit, due to the proximity of the engine, induces sleep, and the regular drone of the wind in the wires becomes a lullaby hard to resist. He found himself nodding more than once, and each time he started up and beat his hands on the side of the cockpit, and held his face outside the shield of the windscreen to allow the cool slipstream to play on his weary eyes.

The scattered lights of Zabala came into sight at last, and he glided down without waiting for landing lights to be put out. There was no wind, so he was able to land directly towards the sheds, and finished his run within a few yards of them. He switched off the engine and sat quite still, for now that his task was finished, and the need for mental and physical energy no longer required, he let himself go, and his aching nerves collapsed like a piece of taut elastic when it is cut in the middle.

As in a queer sort of dream he heard voices calling, and brisk words of command; but they seemed to be far away and barely penetrated his rapidly failing consciousness, and he paid no attention to them. He blinked owlishly as a flashlight was turned on his face, and felt arms lifting him to the ground. 'Mayer . . . get Mayer . . . mind his leg,' he muttered weakly. Then darkness surged up and around him as he fell into a sleep of utter exhaustion.

II

When he awoke the sun was throwing oblique shafts of yellow light through the gaps in the half-drawn curtains of his room. For a little while he saw them without understanding what they were, but as wakefulness cast out the last vestiges of sleep, he sat up with a yawn and stretched.

'So here we are again,' he thought, glancing round and noting that nothing appeared to have been touched. His hand came in contact with his chin and he started, but then smiled as he rubbed the stubble ruefully. He jumped out of bed, threw back the blinds, and surveyed himself in the mirror. 'Very pretty,' he muttered. 'A comely youth withal. Gosh! what a scallywag I look. I'm no oil painting at any time, but goodness me! I didn't think I could look quite such a scarecrow.'

319

That may have been taking rather a hard view, but his appearance was certainly anything but prepossessing. Two days' growth of sparse bristles on his chin formed a fitting background for a nasty cut in his lower lip, which was badly swollen, while his right eye was surrounded by a pale greenish-blue halo that did nothing to improve matters. A scratch across the forehead on which the blood had dried completed the melancholy picture. 'I'd better start work on myself,' he thought, reaching for his razor.

An orderly appeared while he was in the bath, and finding he was up, speedily returned with breakfast on a tray, and a broad smile which suggested to Biggles that he was in the Squadron's good books.

The Count arrived, beaming, while he was dressing, and after congratulating him on his rescue of Mayer, startled him by announcing in a grandiose voice that he had recommended him for the Iron Cross.

'It was not worth such an honour,' protested Biggles uncomfortably, for the idea of being decorated by the enemy did not fill him with enthusiasm. 'How is Mayer, by the way?'

'As well as one might expect, considering everything. The wound in his head is nothing, but his leg will take some time to get right. He has been awake a long time, and I have been with him; he had to wait for the ambulance to take him to the hospital in Jerusalem. While we waited he told me the story of what happened, or as much as he knows of it. How did you come to be taken prisoner in the first place?'

'I ran into a sandstorm and was forced down,' replied Biggles truthfully. 'I waited for the storm to pass, and was just getting back into my machine when a party of Arabs turned up and carted me off to the nearest

British post, where they held me to ransom, or sold me—or something of the sort.'

The Count frowned. 'They're unreliable these Arabs,' he said. 'I wouldn't trust them an inch. They betray either side for a handful of piastres and would cut the throat of every white man in the country if they could, or if they dared. Von Stalhein thinks a lot of them though, perhaps because he was out here before the war and knows their habits and language. That's why he's here now. Between ourselves, he's got a big show on at this very moment which—which—' He broke off abruptly as if he realized suddenly that he was saying too much. 'Come along down to the Mess as soon as you're ready,' he continued, changing the subject, as he moved towards the door. 'I want you to meet Kurt Hess.'

'Kurt Hess? I seem to have heard the name. Who is he?'

'He's our crack pilot in the East. He has scored twenty-six victories and is very proud of it, which is pardonable. He arrived this morning; he's only here for a few days, and between ourselves—' the Count dropped his voice to a confidential whisper—'he's not very pleased because every one is talking about you, and your exploit with Mayer. Perhaps he thinks, not unnaturally, that they should be talking about him.'

'I see,' answered Biggles as he brushed his tunic, and made a mental note that if he knew anything about German character he would find a ready-made enemy in the German Ace. 'I shall be proud to meet him,' he went on slowly, wondering what the Count would say if he knew that his own bag of enemy machines exceeded that of the German's.

'See you presently, then,' concluded the Count, as he went out and closed the door.

321

'So von Stalhein *is* leading the Arabs,' thought Biggles, 'and he isn't back yet. Well, I hope he gets it in the neck; it would save me a lot of trouble.' But even as the thought crossed his mind there was a roar overhead and a Halberstadt side-slipped steeply to a clever landing; it swung round and raced tail up towards the sheds. Before it had stopped, von Stalhein, in German uniform, had climbed out of the back seat and was limping quickly towards headqarters.

'It looks to me as if we might soon be hearing some interesting news,' mused Biggles, with a thrill of anticipation, as he went out and strolled towards the Mess.

322

Chapter 12
A New Pilot—And a Mission

I

There was no need to wonder which of the assembled officers was Hess. Holding the floor in the centre of an admiring group was a tall, slim, middle-aged man from whose throat hung the coveted Pour le Mérite, the highest award for valour in the German Imperial Forces. His manner and tone of voice were at once so haughty—one might say imperious—and supercilious, that Biggles, although he was half prepared for something of the sort, instinctively recoiled. 'What amazing people the Huns are,' he thought, as he watched the swaggering gestures of the Ace. 'Fancy any one of our fellows behaving like that and getting away with it. Why, he'd be slung out on his ear into the nearest pig-trough, and quite right, too. What an impossible sort of skunk he must be; yet here are all these fellows kow-towing to him as if he were an object for reverence just because he has had the luck to shoot down a few British machines. I doubt if he has ever run up against any one really hot; he'd soon get the dust knocked out of his pants if he was sent to France, I'll warrant.'

He walked across and stood on the outskirts of the group, listening respectfully, but the conversation was, of course, in German, so he could not follow it very well. He picked up a word or two here and there, however, sufficient for him to judge that the German was enlarging upon the simplicity of killing Englishmen when once one had the knack, for they had neither courage nor ability.

In spite of himself Biggles was amused at the man's overweening conceit, and his thoughts must have found expression on his face, for the German suddenly broke off in the middle of a sentence and scowled in a manner so puerile and affected that it was all Biggles could do to prevent himself from laughing out loud.

With the air of a king accepting homage from minions, the Ace moved slowly through the group until he stood face to face with the object of his disapproval; then with his lip curled in a sneer he said something quickly in German that Biggles did not understand. That it was something unpleasant he could feel from the embarrassed manner of the other Germans present.

Biggles glanced around the group calmly. 'Will some gentleman kindly tell him that I do not understand?' he said quietly in English.

But an interpreter was unnecessary. 'So!' said the Ace, in the same language, with affected surprise. 'What have we here—an Engländer?'

'He is of the Intelligence Staff,' put in Schmidt, who was Mayer's usual observer, and may have been prompted by a feeling of gratitude for what Biggles had done for his pilot. 'He's the officer who brought Mayer back last night.'

'So!' sneered Hess, with a gesture so insolent that Biggles itched to strike him. 'We know what to do with Engländers, we of the Hess *Jagdstaffel** Perhaps you

---

* A hunting group of German fighters, consisting of approximately twelve aeroplanes. Also just called a 'staffel'. The equivalent of a British squadron.

would like to hear how I make them sizzle in their seats,' he continued, addressing Biggles directly. 'I myself have shot down twenty-six—twenty-six—' he repeated the number, presumably to make sure that there could be no mistake—'like this.' He went through what was intended to be a graphic demonstration of the art of air fighting, but to Biggles it was merely comical. 'Twenty-six,' said Hess yet again, 'and by to-night it will be twenty-seven,' he added, 'for to-day is my birthday, and I have sworn not to sleep until I have sent another down like roast beef in his own oven.'

Biggles was finding it hard to keep his temper, for he knew that to fall out with the German idol would mean serious trouble. 'Excellent, *mein Hauptmann*,' he said, 'but take care you don't meet one that turns your own "box" into a coffin instead, for what would the Fatherland do without you?' The sarcasm which he could not veil was quite lost on the German, but it was not overlooked by one or two of the others, who stirred uncomfortably.

The Ace drew himself up to his full height and struck a pose. 'Do you suggest that an Engländer might shoot *me* down?' he inquired haughtily.

'There's just a chance, you know,' replied Biggles easily, clenching and unclenching his hands in his pockets. 'The English have some good fighters in France, and one may come out here one day. After all, were not Immelmann and Boelcke—'

'Zut! they were foolish,' broke in the Ace, with a movement of his arm that was probably intended to convey regret, but at the same time a suggestion of contempt, as if they were not in the same category as Kurt Hess.

Just where the matter would have ended it is impossible to say, but fortunately at that moment the Count, accompanied by von Stalhein, came into the room. One glance at their faces told Biggles all that he wanted to know about the Arab attack. That it had failed was certain, for the Count looked worried, while von Stalhein was pale under his tan and wore a bandage on his left hand.

The Count turned to speak to Hess while von Stalhein beckoned to Biggles, who walked over quickly to where the German was waiting for him.

'Count von Faubourg has just told me about the business of Mayer,' began von Stalhein abruptly. 'From what I gather, you put up a remarkably fine performance. Can you remember exactly where Mayer's machine crashed?'

'I think I can mark the position to within a mile or two, but Mayer was flying, not me, so I couldn't guarantee to be absolutely correct,' replied Biggles, wondering what was coming.

'Do you think you could find the crash?'

'Oh yes, there should be no difficulty about that.'

'Good! Then I want you to fly over and drop an incendiary bomb on the wreck. You must set it on fire with a direct hit, otherwise there is no point in going. The machine must be utterly destroyed. Do you think you could manage it?'

'I'm quite sure of it,' returned Biggles quickly, looking out of the window so that the other could not see the satisfaction in his eyes for the mission presented an opportunity for which he was anxiously waiting.

'Very well. Then get off at once; and will you please take a camera with you? To satisfy myself I should like to see a photograph—'

'Do you doubt my word, sir?' asked Biggles with an air of injured innocence.

'No, but important matters are at stake, and the only

way to be quite sure of a thing is to see it with one's own eyes.'

'I understand,' replied Biggles. 'I'll take a Pfalz and go over immediately.' He bowed and left the room and, collecting his overalls and flying kit from his room, made his way to the tarmac. As he walked along to the hangars of the Pfalz Squadron he stopped for a moment to look at a new scarlet and white Pfalz D. III Scout, around which a number of mechanics were standing, lost in admiration, for it was the latest product of the famous Pfalz works and far and away the best thing they had ever turned out. There was no aircraft in the Middle East to touch it for speed and climb, and to Biggles, who knew something of the value of these qualities in a fighting aeroplane, the chief reason for the successes of the German Ace was made clear—for he had no doubt to whom the Pfalz belonged.

There was a strange, ruminating look in his eyes as he walked on to the Pfalz Squadron, and asked if he could have a machine for a special mission. On being answered in the affirmative, he requested that four twenty-pound incendiary bombs be fitted to the bomb racks, and in a few minutes, with these in place, he taxied out and took off in the direction of his previous day's adventure.

II

He found plenty to occupy his mind as he cruised watchfully towards the place where the remains of the unfortunate Halberstadt were piled up, but the two chief matters that exercised his thoughts were von Stalhein's anxiety to secure the destruction of the machine, and the possibility of having a word with Algy.

As far as the crashed machine was concerned, it seemed certain that it contained something of importance, something that von Stalhein did not want to leave lying about, possibly a document of some sort. 'Obviously, I shall have to try to find out what it is before I start the bonfire,' he decided. 'I'd better attend to that first, and then go on to Abba Sud afterwards to see if Algy is still hanging about.'

He found the crash without difficulty, and after circling round for a few minutes looking for the best landing place, finally selected a patch free from rocks and camel-thorn, about half a mile away; it was the nearest place where he could get down without taking risks that he preferred to avoid. Leaving the propeller ticking over, he hastened to the well-remembered scene, and began a systematic search of the wreckage. At first he concentrated on the battered pilot's cockpit, going through all the pockets in turn; but they yielded nothing. For half an hour he hunted, and then, just as he was about to abandon the quest, thinking that perhaps after all von Stalhein was simply concerned with the destruction of the machine, he came upon an article so incongruous that he regarded it in stupefied amazement. He found it in what had evidently been a secret stowage place between the two cockpits, but the cavity had been burst open by the crash, revealing what lay within. It was a British officer's field service cap. There was nothing to show to whom it belonged, but the maker's name was that of a well-known London outfitter.

'Well, I don't know what I expected to find, but if I'd been given a thousand guesses I should never have guessed *that*,' thought Biggles, as he turned the cap over and over in his hands. 'But all the same, that must be the thing that friend Erich was scared about; or is it simply a souvenir? It's no use burning a good hat, so I'll take it with me. And I might as well make sure of setting the crash alight, in case I miss it with my bombs,' he went on, as he took out a box of matches, struck one and held it to the sun-dried fabric. When it was well alight he ran back to his machine, took off, and dropped his bombs on the conflagration. Then he took two or three photographs of the fire with the oblique camera that he had brought for the purpose; still not entirely satisfied, he waited for a few minutes until the destruction of the machine was clearly revealed, when he took another photograph, and then raced off in the direction of the oasis of Abba Sud.

He saw Algy afar off long before he reached the oasis, a tiny speck in the sky that circled round and round the dark belt of trees, and presently resolved itself into an aeroplane of unorthodox design. The straight top plane, and lower ones set at a pronounced angle, could not belong to any other machine than a Sopwith Camel. At first Biggles could hardly believe his eyes as it came towards him, and he stared at it wonderingly. He fired a red Very light, the prearranged signal, to ensure that there should be no mistake, and his first words, as he jumped from his cockpit and ran towards the other machine that had landed near him, were, 'Algy! where did you get that kite?'

'Never mind about that; where the dickens have you been all this time?' growled Algy. 'I've been frizzling here like a herring in a pan for the last two blinking days. I was just beginning to think that the Huns must have shot you.'

'I've been busy,' retorted Biggles. 'Do you think I've nothing to do but chase to and fro between Zabala and here? I repeat, where did you get that Camel?'

'It's a special one that's been sent up for headquarters use. Fellows were beginning to grouse because a Hun—Hess, we hear his name is—is playing Old Harry up and down the lines with one of the Pfalz D. III's, and we've nothing to get near him in.'

'So I believe. I was talking to Hess this morning. The Huns think he's a prize piece of furniture, but, as a matter of fact, he's the prince of all swine.'

'Well, we got a Camel up from Heliopolis, and it's been handed over to me *pro tem.*,' went on Algy. 'I shot down a Halberstadt yesterday.'

Biggles started and his eyes narrowed. 'Where?' he asked coldly.

'About twenty miles to the north-east of where we are now. It hit the floor a dickens of a crack and went to pieces.'

'You needn't tell me: I was in it,' Biggles told him, grimly.

'You were—Oh, great Scott! Well, I wasn't to know that, was I? Why didn't you fire a red light?'

'A fat lot of chance you gave me. I didn't even see you until you started pumping out lead.'

'Of course; I didn't think of that. My word! I might have killed you.'

'Might! You thundering nearly did.'

'Well, I wasn't to know. I saw a Hun and I went for him. It didn't occur to me that you might be in it, because I thought you were wandering about behind the British lines.'

Biggles looked perplexed. 'How the deuce did you know that?' he demanded.

'Because sometime about midnight young Fraser, the lad who is in charge of Number Five post, rang up headquarters to say that he had collected a Hun prisoner named Brunow from a bunch of Arabs and wanted to know what he was to do with him. Headquarters told him to hang on to him until the morning and then send him along. Then they sent out the usual chit to Intelligence people asking if they wanted to interrogate him. Poor old Raymond nearly threw a fit when he heard it was you. He sent for me in a hurry, and at the first crack of dawn I went up with special instructions to fly you down to Kantara, but when I got there I found you'd already left in charge of a party of Major Sterne's Arabs who—'

'*Whose* Arabs?' Biggles fired the question like a pistol shot.

'Sterne's—why, what's wrong?'

Biggles looked at him oddly. 'Was Sterne up there when you got there?' he asked quietly.

'No, he'd just gone; pushed off out into the desert on one of his trips.'

Biggles stared and said nothing for a moment. 'Go on,' he murmured at last.

'Well, I went back to report what had happened, and in the afternoon the Arabs rolled up with a tale of how you'd escaped,' continued Algy.

'How had I escaped?'

'By jumping on the best horse while you were all resting, and leaping a terrific chasm over which it was impossible to follow you. They fired at you but missed, and then you disappeared behind some rocks and were never found again.'

'So, that's what they told you, is it?' mused Biggles. 'My gosh! what a tale. Makes those yarns about the Arabian Nights sound tame. I expect you got quite a kick out of it.'

'Why, didn't you bolt?'

'Bolt, my foot. But I haven't time to tell you the whole story now. Mayer, one of our Huns at Zabala, picked me up, and we were on our way back when you butted in and shot us down. Mayer got a crack on the side of the nut from one of your bullets, but he wasn't dead, so I dragged him to an oasis where I saw a big bunch of Arabs collecting. I'd got a machine there—don't ask me how or why—so I flew down to Kantara to let you know what was going on. Did you get my message?'

'We certainly did. The telephone wires were red hot for a bit, I can tell you, and a whole lot of troops, mostly Australian cavalry, lost their beauty sleep. When the Sheikhs rolled up they were waiting for them, and they gave them such a plastering that they're not likely to forget in a hurry. Some got killed and some got away, but a lot were taken prisoners, and they're bleating for the blood of the man who led them into the trap, for that's what they swear happened. When—'

'I see. That clears things up a bit,' interrupted Biggles. 'I begin to see daylight. By the way, did you see the waterworks blow up when you were over Zabala the other night?'

Algy laughed. 'Too true I did,' he cried. 'What a wizard it was! I hooted like a coot in spite of the archie.'

'You reported it when you got back?'

'Of course. Our people were tickled to death, although they still don't know who did it, or how it was done. Raymond is as dumb as a church mouse.'

'I'm glad he is,' declared Biggles. 'And what about that news you had for me—the news you mentioned in the message you dropped?'

'Oh yes! I've been waiting to tell you about that. Raymond got a direct dispatch, in code, from London,. The Air Board told him that if possible he was to warn you to beware of Broglace.'

'Broglace! What the dickens has he got to do with it? He's in London.'

'No, he isn't. Something must have happened in London, and although our people were watching him like a cat watching a mouse, he disappeared suddenly as if he'd got the wind up, and they fancy it was something to do with you. They traced him as far as Hull, and then lost track of him, but they think he departed for Germany hot foot, via Holland. They thought you ought to be warned, in case he turned up here.'

'Why should he?'

'Don't ask me; I don't know.'

'I see.'

'Look! There's one last thing,' went on Algy. 'We've laid out a dummy aerodrome, twelve miles south-east of Kantara. It looks fine from the air. If you want to please the Huns and at the same time would like to see them waste some bombs, you can tell them where it is. It's all ready, fairly aching to be bombed,' he concluded with a broad grin.

'That's fine,' Biggles walked over and took the officer's cap that he had found in Mayer's cockpit from the back seat of his machine and handed it to Algy. 'Hang on to that,' he said. 'Take it back to Raymond when you go and tell him to hide it—bury it if he likes. He can do what he likes with it, but on no account must any one see it. Got that?'

'Yes. That's quite clear.'

'Good! Now lend me that Camel for half an hour. You can wait here for me; I'll bring it back.'

Algy's jaw dropped. 'Lend you the Camel?' he gasped.

'That's what I said,' returned Biggles. 'What are you gaping at; is it an unnatural request?'

'Er—no. But what do you want it for?'

'Because I've a strong urge to be myself for a few minutes.'

'Be yourself? What are you talking about? Have you got a touch of sun or something?'

'My goodness! You are dense this morning. I just have a feeling that I'd like to forget that I'm Brunow for a little while and be what I am—a junior officer in the R.F.C.'

'But what for?'

Biggles looked exasperated. 'All right, if you *must* know,' he said slowly and deliberately. 'There's a fellow floating about the atmosphere in a red and white Pfalz D. III who thinks he's cock of the roost. He's promised to fry his twenty-seventh Englishman to-day—the conceited ass—and when I saw your Camel it struck me that it wouldn't be a bad scheme if I took a hand in this frying business.'

'You mean Hess.'

'Yes rhymes with Hess, and so does mess, which is as it should be,' observed Biggles, 'because I'm going to do my best to get Mr. Hess in the biggest mess he was ever in. Are these guns O.K.?'

'Perfectly O.K.'

'Then give me a swing.'

Algy ran to the propeller. The engine sprang into life, and the Camel sped across the desert like a blunt-nosed bullet with the slipstream hurling a cloud of sand high into the air behind it.

Chapter 13
Vickers Versus Spandaus

In his heart Biggles knew that from the first moment he saw the swaggering German Ace the greatest ambition of his life was to see him given the lesson he so richly deserved, the lesson which would inevitably be administered sooner or later by somebody; and he had resolved to set about the task that morning in the Pup he assumed Algy would be flying. That his partner was, in fact, flying a Sopwith Camel was better luck than he could have imagined, for it evened things up.

Previously, in a Pfalz D.III, Hess could choose his own battle-field and select his opponent, for in the event of his catching a foeman who turned out to be a tartar, he could break off the combat and escape by virtue of his superior speed. This advantage of superior equipment was the dominating factor that enabled many German Aces to pile up big scores during certain periods of 1916 and 1917, a lamentable state of affairs that came to a sudden end with the arrival at the front of the Camel and the S.E.5, as the appalling death roll of German Aces towards the end of 1917 reveals.

Sopwith Camels had been in France, where the fighting was most intense, for some time, but none had reached the outlying theatres of war; consequently, a German pilot arriving in one of the distant battle-fields with the latest German fighting machine, finding himself opposed to aeroplanes of obsolete type, had every opportunity of acquiring a reputation that was often proved to be false when he encountered opponents on level terms.

But with these matters Biggles was not concerned as he sped towards the German side of the battlefield, which he knew would be the most likely place to find the German Ace lying in wait for a British two-seater; and he was jubilant at once more finding himself in the cockpit of a Camel for two reasons. In the first place he was thoroughly at home, and secondly he would be able to force the German to fight, provided he found him, for the simple reason that he would not be able to run away, as the two machines were about equal in performance.

He might, of course, have shot the German down from his own Pfalz, but the thought did not occur to him, for it would have been little short of murder; he felt that in a regular British aircraft he was perfectly justified in fighting Hess. He would forget for the moment that he had ever existed as Brunow, and behave precisely as if he had been posted to the Middle East as an ordinary pilot of a fighter squadron. In those circumstances the combat, if it occurred, would be perfectly fair.

He reached the lines but could see no signs of aerial activity, so climbing steadily for height, he began a systematic search of the whole sector. Once he saw a Halberstadt in the distance but he ignored it, for it was not the object of his quest, and he continued on his way, eyes probing the skies above and below for the red and white fuselage of the Pfalz. A little later he passed close to an antiquated B.E.2 C* and exchanged

* Designed in 1912 for observation and artillery co-operation this two-seater biplane whose top speed of 72 mph was just half that of the fastest fighters, was clearly obsolete by 1918.

greetings with its crew, at the same time admiring their courage for taking the air in a conveyance so hopelessly out of date. 'That's the sort of kite Hess is hoping to meet, I'll bet; and if he could poke in a burst of fire without being seen he'd be tickled to death; probably go back to Zabala and tell the boys how easy it is to shoot down Englishmen,' he mused. 'Pah! Well, we'll see.'

He had flown on for some little distance and was scanning the sky ahead when something—possibly the instinct which experienced air fighters seemed to develop—made him look back long and searchingly at the B.E., now a speck in the eastern sky. Was it his imagination, or was there a tiny speck moving far above it? He closed his eyes for a moment and then looked again, forcing them to focus in spite of the glare; then he caught his breath sharply and swung the Camel round in the lightning right-hand turn that was one of its most famous characteristics. He had not been mistaken. Far above the plodding B.E. a minute spark of light had flashed for a brief instant. No one but an old hand would have seen it or known what it portended; but Biggles knew that it was the sun's rays catching the wings of a banking aeroplane.

A minute or two later he could see it clearly as it stalked its quarry from the cover of the sun's blinding glare; he could see from its shape that it was a Pfalz, but it was still too far off for him to make out its colours. 'No matter,' he thought; 'I shall have to give those two boys in the B.E. the tip, whether it's Hess or not, or else it looks like being their unlucky day.'

He was flying rather higher than the German scout, which in turn was some distance above the slow two-seater, and his advantage of height gave him the extra speed necessary to come up with them. While he was

337

still half a mile away his lips parted in the grim smile he always wore when he was fighting as he picked out the colours of the Pfalz. They were red and white. It had placed itself in an ideal position for attack, and its nose was already going down to deliver the thrust that would send the British two-seater to its doom.

Biggles shoved his joystick forward savagely, and the needle of his air speed indicator swung upwards to the one hundred and eighty miles an hour mark; but he did not see it, for his eyes were glued on the now diving scout. He snatched a glance downwards and saw the gunner of the B.E. leaning over the side of his cockpit, looking down at the ground and making notes in a writing-pad, unconscious of the hand of death that was falling on him from the skies.

Biggles was afraid he was going to be too late, so he took the only course open to him; his hand closed over the firing lever of his guns and he fired a long deflexion* shot in the direction of the Hun, more with the object of calling attention to himself than in any real hope of hitting it. Hess apparently did not hear the shots, for he continued his swoop, but the British pilot did, and acted with admirable presence of mind. He glanced up, not at the Pfalz but in the direction from which the rattle of guns had come, and saw the Camel. Whether he suspected that the British pilot had mistaken him for a Hun, or whether he felt the presence of some unseen danger, Biggles never knew, but he turned sharply, so sharply that his gunner fell back into his seat with alarm as he reached for his gun.

The action was quite enough to disconcert the Pfalz pilot, who may have suspected a trap, for he swerved

* The amount a gunner or pilot must aim ahead of a fast moving aircraft, passing at right angles, in order to hit it.

wildly and careered round in a wide circle, looking over his shoulder for the cause of the B.E. pilot's manœuvre. It was a foolish move, and at once betrayed the man's lack of real ability, for Biggles swept down on him and could have fired a burst which might well have ended the combat there and had he been so inclined. But this was not his intention. Moved by some impulse altogether foreign to his nature and his usual methods of fighting, he roared down alongside Pfalz, passing it so closely that their wing tips almost touched. As he passed he tore off his helmet and goggles, flung them on the floor of the cockpit, and stared with smouldering eyes into the face of the German. There was no smile on his own face now, but a burning hatred of the man who shot down machines of inferior performance and then boasted of his prowess. He saw the look of recognition spring into the German's eyes, and the fear that followed it. 'Not so sure of yourself now, are you?' snarled Biggles. 'Come on, you skunk—fight!'

With a savage exaltation that he had never known before, he whirled round, and nearly collided with the B.E. which, with the best intentions, had decided to take a hand. For a moment he saw red. 'Get out of my way, you fool,' he raged, uselessly as he tilted his wing, and missing the B.E. by inches, gave its pilot the shock of his life.

The moves had lost him two seconds of time, and before he was on even keel again the Pfalz had got a lead of a quarter of a mile, and was racing, nose down, for home. 'Not so fast, my cock,' growled Biggles, as he stood on the rudder and shoved the stick forward. What happened to the B.E. after that he did not know, for he never saw it again. He sent a stream of tracer down the slipstream of the red and white machine, and sneered as the pilot swerved away from it, regardless of the fact that at such a range the odds were a thousand to one against a hit.

'You cold-footed rabbit; what about the frying you were so anxious about this morning?' muttered Biggles, as he closed the gap that separated them and sewed a line of leaden stitches down the red and white fuselage. The German swung round with the desperate courage born of despair and sprayed a triple* line of bullets at his relentless pursuer; but Biggles touched his rudder-bar lightly and side-slipped away, whereupon Hess, acknowledging his master, cut his engine and began to slip towards the ground.

'You're not getting away with that, you rat,' grated Biggles, blazing up with fury at such a craven display. 'If you want to go down, then go, and I'll help you on your way,' he snarled, as he roared down on the tail of the falling Ace. He held his fire until his propeller was a few feet from the blackcrossed rudder, and then pressed the gun lever. A double line of orange flame leapt from his engine cowling. To Biggles' atonishment, the German made no effort to defend himself. For a fraction of a second he looked back over his shoulder and read his fate in the spouting muzzles of the twin Vickers guns; then he slumped forward in his cockpit. A tiny tongue of flame curled aft from the scarlet petrol tank; it grew larger and larger until it was a devouring furnace that dropped through the air like a stone.

Biggles pulled out of his dive and turned away feeling suddenly sick, as he often did when he sent down an enemy machine in flames; when he looked back a great cloud of black smoke, towards which tiny figures were running, marked the funeral pyre of the man who had

---

* Some models of the Pfalz DIII were fitted with three Spandau machine guns, synchronised to fire through the propeller.

sworn to fry an Englishman as his own birthday present.

'I might as well get back,' he thought, glancing round the sky. The B.E. had disappeared, and there were no other machines in sight, so he set a course for the oasis, feeling tired and irritable now that his anger had burned itself out.

He found Algy examining the Halberstadt with professional interest when he got back to Abba Sud.

'Any luck?' queried Algy, expectantly, as he walked towards him.

'You can call it luck if you like,' replied Biggles, simply, 'but Hess won't worry our fellows any more. Make out a combat report when you get back and put in a claim for a red and white Pfalz that fell in flames three miles north of Jebel Tire at 10.51 a.m. Our forward observation posts must have seen the show and will confirm it.

'I shall do nothing of the sort,' cried Algy indignantly; 'he was your meat.'

'I don't want the Huns to know that, do I, you ass?' snapped Biggles. 'You do what you're told. And remember, you don't know it's Hess. Our people will get that information from the other side in due course. That's all, laddie,' he went on with a change of tone. 'I must be getting back now.' He looked suddenly old and tired.

'O.K., Skipper,' replied Algy, looking at him under his lashes, and noting the symptoms of frayed nerves. 'When am I going to see you again?'

'I don't know,' muttered Biggles, 'but pretty soon, I hope. Tell Raymond that I'm running on a hot scent,' he went on wistfully, 'and I hope to be back in 266 Squadron again before the end of the month—or else—'

341

'Or else?' questioned Algy.

'Nothing.' Biggles looked Algy squarely in the eyes. 'Thank God it will soon be over one way or the other,' he said quietly. 'I wasn't made for this game, and I've had about enough. But I've got to go on—to the end—you see that, don't you, old lad?'

'Of course,' replied Algy, swallowing something in his throat.

'I thought you would. Well, cheerio, old boy.'

'Cheerio, old son.'

Their hands met in a firm grip, the only time during the whole war that either of them allowed their real feelings to get uppermost.

Algy stood beside the Camel and watched the Halberstadt until it disappeared from sight. 'Those soulless hounds at the Air Board need boiling in oil for sending a fellow like Biggles on a job like this,' he muttered huskily. 'Still, I suppose it's what they call war,' he added, as he climbed slowly into his cockpit.

Chapter 14
Biggles Flies a Bomber

Biggles arrived back at Zabala just as the station was closing down work for lunch. He handed his camera to the photographic sergeant with instructions to be particularly careful with the negatives, and to bring him a print of each as quickly as possible, and he was walking down to the headquarters offices when he saw von Stalhein and the Count, who had evidently heard him land, waiting for him.

'Did you manage it all right?' inquired von Stalhein, with his eyes on Biggles' face.

'I burnt the machine and took the photographs, but naturally I can't say what they're like until I've seen them.'

'Did you land?' Von Stalhein asked the question sharply, almost as if his intention was to catch Biggles off his guard.

'Land!' replied Biggles with a puzzled frown. 'Why should I risk a landing in the desert when I had incendiary bombs with me?'

'Oh, I merely wondered if you had—just as a matter of interest,' retorted von Stalhein. 'You've been a long time, haven't you?'

'As a matter of fact, I have,' admitted Biggles. 'I intended going straight there and back, but I saw something that intrigued me and I thought it was worth while following it up.'

'Indeed! and what was it?' asked the Count, interestedly.

'A new type of British machine, sir,' answered Biggles. 'I didn't think they had any of them on this front; maybe they have only just arrived.'

'What sort of machine was it?'

'A very fast machine with no dihedral on the top plane; they call it the Camel, I think, and it's made at the Sopwith works.'

The Count grimaced. 'I've heard of them in France,' he said quickly. 'What did you do?'

'I took up a position in the sun and watched it, thinking it might possibly lead to the aerodrome of a new squadron.'

'Splendid! What then?'

'The machine crossed the British lines and began to glide down, so I climbed as high as my machine would take me and saw it land at what looks like a new aerodrome about twelve miles south-east of Kantara. I'm not sure about it being a new aerodrome because I haven't had time to verify it in the map-room; it may have been there a long time, but I've never noticed it before.'

'I've never heard of an aerodrome there,' declared the Count, while von Stalhein looked puzzled.

'It wasn't there a few days ago,' he said slowly.

Biggles wondered how he knew that, but said nothing.

'Very well, go in and get some lunch,' went on the Count. 'Our Brunow is becoming quite useful, eh, Erich?'

Von Stalhein smiled a curious smile that always gave Biggles a tingling feeling down the spine, but whatever his thoughts were he did not disclose them, so Biggles saluted and departed in the direction of the Mess.

He had just finished lunch when an orderly arrived with a message that he was wanted at headquarters, so he tossed his napkin on the table, swallowed the last drop of coffee in his cup, and with an easy mind made his way to the Count's office.

'Ah, Brunow, there you are,' began von Faubourg, who was sitting at his desk while von Stalhein leaned in his usual position against the side, blowing clouds of cigarette smoke into the air. 'We've been talking about this report of yours concerning the new aerodrome,' continued the Count, 'and we have decided that there is a strong probability that the British have brought out a new squadron, in which case it would be a good plan to let it know what to expect. If we can put some of the machines out of action so much the better, otherwise we're likely to have some casualties. I suppose you've heard that Hess hasn't come back from his morning patrol? We don't take the matter seriously, but I've rung up the other squadrons who say that they have seen nothing of him, so it rather looks as if he had forced landed somewhere.'

Biggles nodded. 'That must be the case, sir. One can hardly imagine him coming to any harm,' he said seriously.

'No, the thought is preposterous. But about this projected bomb raid. You marked down the exact position of the aerodrome, did you not?'

'I did, sir.'

'I thought I understood you to say that. I've detailed six machines to go over this afternoon and strike while the iron is hot, so to speak, and in order that there should be no mistake I want you to fly the leading one.'

Biggles started. 'You want me to lead the bombers, sir?' he ejaculated.

'Why not? It is a trifle irregular, I know, and Oberleutnant* Kranz, who is commanding the *Staffel* in Mayer's absence, may feel hurt about it, but as you know where the place is you will be able to go straight to it. Kranz can still be in command, but you could show the way and take charge of the operation just while you were over the British lines. Is that quite clear?'

'Quite, sir,' replied Biggles, whose head was in a whirl at this fresh complication. The idea that he might have to accompany a raid, much less lead one, had not occurred to him.

'Each machine will carry two heavy bombs,' continued the Count, 'and one machine will, of course, take a camera so that we can study the layout of the aerodrome at our leisure as well as see if the bombs do any damage.'

'I'll take the camera if you like, sir,' volunteered Biggles, who thought he might as well be hung for a sheep as a lamb.

'That would be excellent. Then I'll leave it to you to fix up the details with Kranz. Good luck!'

Biggles saluted and withdrew with mixed feelings, for the fact that the dummy aerodrome lure had worked out well was rather overshadowed by the part that he had been detailed to play, and he realized that during the next two hours there was a strong possibility that he would be shot down by his own countrymen; and he did not overlook the fact that in the event of his formation being attacked, he might find it difficult not to put up some sort of fight, or pretence of fighting, yet he had no desire to be responsible for the death of a British pilot.

'I shall have to hope for the best, that's all there is

* Flying Officer in the German Air Force

346

to it,' he thought as he walked along to the hangars where the bustle indicated that preparations for the raid were going forward.

Half an hour later the six machines left the ground in V-formation with Biggles flying at the spear-head, and climbed steeply for altitude. For nearly an hour they roared upwards on a broad zigzag course before heading straight for the lines. They crossed over through a thin and futile archie barrage, and then raced on full throttle towards the now visible aerodrome.

Biggles, who, of course, had not seen it before, was completely amused at the realism of the bait. It was complete in every detail, even to some machines standing on the tarmac. There was no wind so it was unneccesary to turn in order to deliver the attack, and the first six bombs sailed down. But to Biggles' disgust they nearly all went wide; one only fell on the aerodrome and none touched any of the buildings. He had hoped to take a really thrilling photograph back to the Count, showing at least one hangar in flames.

The six machines turned slowly in a wide circle in order not to lose formation, and then returning from the opposite direction, laid their remaining eggs, that is, all except Biggles, who was determined to score a hit, for now that he was actually engaged in the task, the idea of bombing a British aerodrome amused him.

This time the aim was better. Two bombs fell on the aerodrome, and one in the end hangar, but still he was not satisfied, so he dived out of formation, losing height as quickly as possible, and turning again towards the aerodrome, took the centre buildings in his bomb-sight and pulled the toggle. For a few seconds the bomb diminished in size in a remarkable manner as it plunged earthwards, and then a pillar of smoke and flame leapt high into the air. It was a direct hit. He had his

347

camera over the side in an instant, but the movement might almost have been a signal, for he had only taken two photographs when such a tornado of archie burst around him that he dropped the instrument quickly on to the floor of the cockpit and pulled up his nose to rejoin the formation.

The other five machines were in no better case, and it seemed to him as he raced through a sea of smoke and flame that every anti-aircraft gun on the British front had been concentrated on the spot.

'Of course they have: what a fool I am,' he swore. 'Raymond would know that I'd give the Huns the position of the aerodrome, in which case it would be certain that sooner or later a formation of Boche bombers would come over. He could easily get the guns together without disclosing anything about my part of the business. My gosh! I ought to have thought of that.' He flinched as a piece of metal tore through his wing and made the machine vibrate from nose to rudder. A shell burst under his tail, and his observer, a youth named Bronveld, made desperate signals to him to get out of the vicinity as soon as possible.

He needed no urging. His one idea at that moment was to remove himself with the utmost possible speed from the hornets' nest he had stirred up, and all the time he was wondering what the other pilots would say, and more important still, what the Count would say when they got back—if they did—for the whole exploit bore a suspicious likeness to a well-laid trap. 'No,' he reasoned, as he side-slipped away from a well-placed bracket* that blossomed out in front of him, 'they can't blame me very well, for after all, I'm in the show myself, and no one is fool enough to step into a

* Bursting shells on both sides of a target

348

trap they have themselves set. In fact, it begins to look almost as if it were a good thing that I came on the show, otherwise—'

His high speed soliloquy was cut short by an explosion under his wing tip that nearly turned him upside down. He tried the controls with frantic haste, and breathed a prayer of thankfulness when he found that they were still functioning, but a long strip of fabric that trailed aft from his lower starboard plane made him feel uneasy. One of the other machines suddenly dipped its nose and began gliding down; he noted that its propeller had stopped, but thought it might just manage to reach the German lines that now loomed up ahead of them.

The formation, which had become badly scattered in the barrage, now began to re-form, and he had just taken his place in the lead when, glancing forward through the centre-section, he saw something that set his finger-tips tingling. Cutting across their front on a course that would effectually cut them off from the German lines were two squadrons of aeroplanes that needed no second look to identify them. One squadron, approaching from the west, was composed of eight Sopwith Pups with a solitary Camel hanging on its flank; the other, which was coming up from the east, comprised six Bristol Fighters.

Biggles eyed the Camel with a strange expression on his face, for the circumstances were so—well, he didn't know quite what to call them, for never before had he seen comedy and imminent tragedy so hopelessly intermingled. 'I'd bet a month's pay to a piastre that Algy has a smack at me first; he always does like taking on the leader,' he muttered. 'And I'd have won,' he went on bitterly, as the Camel pulled up in a steep zoom, half-rolled, and then whirled round for the attack with its nose pointing down at Biggles' Halberstadt.

For once Biggles was nonplussed and a thousand ideas flashed through his brain, only to be abandoned instantly as he realized their uselessness. He glanced back over his shoulder and saw Bronveld crouching over his gun, waiting for the Camel to come within range. The lad's face was grim and set, but his hands were steady, and Biggles felt a thrill of apprehension. 'That kid's going to put up a good fight,' he thought anxiously. 'And from the way Algy is handling that Camel it looks to me as if the young fool stands a good chance of stopping a packet of Spandau bullets. He must be crazy to come down on top of us like that, straight over our rear gun.'

Then something like panic seized him as he visualized the unthinkable picture of his gunner killing Algy, or conversely, Algy's feelings when he found he had shot down his best friend. Whatever else happened, that must be avoided at all costs. Better to betray himself and be shot by the Huns than that should happen. 'At least I can let him know it's me,' he thought as, white-faced, he reached for his signal pistol, slipped in a red cartridge, and sent a streak of scarlet fire blazing across the nose of the diving Camel. But to his horror the pilot paid no attention to it, although, as if actuated by a common motive, the four remaining Halberstadts banked hard to the right and closed in on him. More with the object of avoiding a collision, he swung round in a fairly steep bank, and the other machines fell in line behind him.

The movement disconcerted the British pilots, who now found themselves facing an ever-circling ring from which guns spat every time they tried to approach, and while they were still milling round them in indecision,

Biggles darted out of the circle at a tangent and raced, nose down, for home. By the time the Pups and Bristols realized what had happened the other Halberstadts had followed on his tail and had established a clear lead, which they were able to keep until they were well inside their own territory. The danger was averted.

Biggles brushed his hand across his forehead. 'Phew! that was quite enough of that,' he muttered, as he looked back over his shoulder, and then stiffened with horror at the sight that met his eyes. The British machines, with the exception of one, had turned back, but the Camel, by reason of its superior speed, had continued the chase and had caught them. What was worse, its pilot was evidently still determined to strike at the leader of the Hun formation, and was roaring down in a final effort. As it came within range jets of orange flame darted from the muzzles of the guns on its engine cowling, and at the same moment, Bronveld, who was alive to the danger and crouching low behind his Parabellum gun, pulled the trigger. His aim was true. Biggles saw the tracer leap across the intervening space in a straight line that ended at the whirling engine of the British machine. Something stung his shoulder but he hardly felt it, for his eyes were fixed on the Camel in a kind of fascinated horror. Its nose had jerked up in a vertical zoom; for a moment it hung in space with its propeller threshing the air uselessly; then it turned slowly over on to its back and plunged earthward.

In a state of mental paralysis Biggles watched it hurtling through space. He couldn't think. He couldn't act. He could only stare ashen-faced at the spinning machine. He saw a wing break off, and the fuselage with its human cargo drop like a cannon-ball; then he turned away. He shifted his gaze to Bronveld, who was clapping his hands jubilantly. As their eyes met the German showed his teeth in a victorious smile and turned his thumbs upwards, a signal that means the same thing the world over. Biggles could not find it in his heart to blame him, for it was the boy's first victory, and once, long ago, he had behaved in exactly the same way; only that time the spinning machine had black crosses on its wings, not red, white, and blue circles.

He turned back to his own cockpit feeling as if he had turned into a block of stone. Something seemed to have died inside him, leaving in its place only a bitter hatred of the war and everything connected with it. He ground his teeth under the emotion that shook him like a leaf, while in his mind hammered a single thought, 'Algy has gone west . . . Algy has gone west.' The wind seemed to howl it in the wires, and the deep-throated Mercedes engine purred it in a monotonous vibrating drone.

Through a shimmering atmosphere of unreality he saw the aerodrome at Zabala loom up, and automatically throttled back to land. His actions were purely instinctive as he flattened out and taxied slowly up to the hangars. The Count, von Stalhein, and several other officers were standing on the tarmac waiting, but none of them meant anything to him now. He no longer feared von Stalhein. He no longer cared a fig if he was suspected, arrested, or even shot.

He switched off, climbed stiffly to the ground, and walked slowly towards the spot upon which the others were converging. He could hear a babel of voices around him, German voices, and a wave of hatred swept over him. What was happening? He hardly knew. He became aware that Bronveld was tapping him on the back while he spoke rapidly to Faubourg. They were all laughing, talking over the battle, and a strange feeling swept over Biggles that he had seen it all before. Where had he seen the same thing? Suddenly he knew. The scene was precisely that which occurred on any British aerodrome after a raid; only the uniforms and the machines with the sinister Maltese crosses were different. As in a dream he heard the Count speaking.

'Splendid,' he was saying, 'splendid. Kranz is full of praise for the way you handled a nasty situation. Your firing of the red signal to form circle when you did, he says, saved the whole formation. And that last bomb of yours, and the way you left the formation to make sure of a hit, was brilliant. Your recommendation for the Iron Cross shall go off to-day. And Bronveld has shot down a Camel. We knew that before you got home; it fell in our lines and the artillery rang up to say they are sending the body here for burial. We will see that it is done properly, as we always do, because we know the British do the same for us. But what's this? Why! you're wounded, man.' He pointed to Biggles' shoulder, where a nasty-looking red stain was slowly spreading round a jagged tear in his overalls.

'Oh, that.' Biggles laughed, a hard, unpleasant sound. 'That's nothing. I hardly noticed it. The Camel fired the shot,' he added, wishing that it had gone through his head instead of his shoulder.

'While you were holding your machine steady so that Bronveld could shoot,' observed the Count. 'That is the sort of courage that will serve the *Vaterland*.* But go and get your shoulder attended to and make out your reports, all of you. I am looking forward to seeing the photographs.'

Biggles removed his flying cap and goggles and walked towards the Medical Officer's tent. He was

---

* The Fatherland: Germany

conscious that von Stalhein was watching him with the same puzzled expression that he had worn after the Mayer exploit. 'He doesn't know what to make of me,' he thought. 'Well, a fat lot I care what he thinks. I'll fly over to Raymond to-morrow, and throw my hand in; in future I'm flying in my own uniform, in France, or not at all. I've had enough of this dirty game and I never want to see a palm tree again.'

The wound, which was little more than a graze, was washed and bandaged by the elderly, good-natured German doctor, after which he went to his room and threw himself on his bed. The sun was sinking like a fiery orange ball in a crimson sky that merged into purple overhead, and threw a lurid glow on the hangars and the sentinel-like palms. It flooded into his room and bathed his bed, his uniform, and his tired face in a blood-red sheen.

For a long time he lay quite still, trying to think, trying to adjust himself to the new state of things, but in vain. His most poignant thought, the thing that worried him most, was the fact that he had been responsible for Algy's death in the first place by causing him to be posted from France to the land of the Israelites. That Algy might have been killed if he had remained in France did not occur to him. 'But there, what does it matter? What does anything matter? The lad's gone topsides, and that's the end of it,' he thought, as he rose wearily. He washed, and was drying his face, when an unusual sound took him to the window. A tender had stopped and half a dozen grey-coated soldiers in the uniform of the German Field Artillery, under the supervision of a Flying Corps officer, were unloading something. It was a long slim object shrouded in a dark blanket.

He watched with an expressionless face, for he was

past feeling anything. It was all a part of the scheme, the moving of the relentless finger of Fate that had lain over Palestine like a blight for nearly two thousand years and left a trail of death in its wake. He watched the soldiers carry the body into the tent that had been set aside as a temporary mortuary. He saw them come out, close the flap behind them, salute, and return to the tender, which, with a grinding of gears, moved slowly across the sand and disappeared from sight. It was like watching a scene in a play.

Then, moved by some impulse, he picked up his cap, left the room, and strode firmly towards the tent. 'I might as well say good-bye to the lad,' he thought, with his nostrils quivering. He threw aside the flap, entered, and stood in dumb misery at the end of the camp bed on which the pitiful object rested. Slowly and with a hand that shook, he lifted the end of the blanket—and looked.

How long he stood there he never knew. Time seemed to stand still. The deathly hush that falls over the desert at the approach of twilight had fallen; some-where in the desert a sand-cricket was chirping. That was all. And still he stared—and stared.

At last, with a movement that was almost convulsive, he replaced the blanket, stepped back, and leaned against the tent-pole while he fought back an hysterical desire to laugh aloud—for the face was not Algy's. It was that of a middle-aged man in the uniform of an infantry regiment, with pilot's wings sewn on his tunic above the white and violet ribbon of the Military Cross. It was quite peaceful. A tiny blue hole above the left eyebrow showed where life had fled, leaving a faint smile of surprise on the countenance, so suddenly had the end come.

Biggles pulled himself together with a stupendous

effort and walked reverently from the presence of Death. With his teeth clenched, he hurried back to his room and flung himself face downwards on his bed, laughing and sobbing in turn. He did not hear the door open quietly to admit an orderly with tea on a tray, who, when his startled eyes fell on his superior officer, withdrew quickly and returned to the camp kitchen.

'Karl,' he called to the cook, 'Brunow's finished— nerve's gone to bits. Funny how all these flyers go the same in the end. Well, I don't care as long as they'll let me keep *my* feet on the ground.'

Chapter 15
Ordeal by Night

The German orderly, although he had good reason for thinking that 'Brunow's nerves had gone to bits', was far from right. Biggles' nerves were unimpaired, although it must be admitted that he had been badly shaken by the belief that Algy had been killed, but after the first reaction had spent itself the knowledge that the whole thing had been nothing more than a bad dream was such a relief that he prepared to resume his work with a greater determination than before. Lying propped up on his pillow, he reviewed the events of the day which, taking things all round, might have panned out a good deal worse. Hess had gone west, and he had no regrets on that score. 'Yes, taking it all round I've been pretty lucky to-day,' he mused, which was not strictly true, for such successes as he had achieved had been due more to clear thinking and ability than to good fortune. His only stroke of what could be regarded as luck was the firing of the red signal light which had saved the formation, thereby putting up his reputation with the *Staffel*, for when he had fired it he had not the remotest idea that it was the German signal to 'form circle', a fact that he could only assume was the case from what followed.

By dinner-time he was normal again but eager to see the end of his masquerade in order that he might return to normal duties. So deep-rooted was this longing that he was prepared to take almost any chance, regardless of risks, in order to expedite the conclusion of the affair.

Certain vital facts he had already grasped; of others, a shrewd suspicion was rapidly forming in his mind, and he only needed confirmation of them to send him to British headquarters and place his knowledge at the disposal of those who would know best how to act upon it.

It was with a determination born of these thoughts that he decided during dinner to pursue his quest in a manner which inwardly appalled him, but which, he thought, if successful could hardly fail to produce results. The idea came to him on the spur of the moment when he heard a machine taxi out across the aerodrome. Subconsciously he waited, expecting to hear it take off, but when it did not he knew—guessed would perhaps be a better word—that it was standing on the far side of the aerodrome waiting for a passenger about whose identity there was no doubt in his mind. And when a few minutes later von Stalhein left his chair, and after a whispered conversation with the Count, went out of the room, he fancied that he knew what was about to take place.

He would have liked to follow at once in order to watch von Stanhein, but that was out of the question, for it was a matter of etiquette that until the Count rose and led the way to the ante-room, no one could leave his place without asking his permission, and then a very good excuse would be demanded.

So he sat where he was, sipping his coffee, but listening for the sound that would denote von Stalhein's departure for the British lines; and he had not long to wait. Within a few minutes there came the distant roar of an aero engine; it swelled to a deep crescendo and then died away in the distance. 'There he goes,' he thought. 'If I could only be at the other end when he lands I might learn something.'

358

Now that his mind was made up on a course of action he fidgeted with impatience for the meal to end, and when at length the Count got up, the signal for a general move, he followed the others through to the ante-room with a light-heartedness which sprang, not from anticipation of the self-imposed undertaking before him, but from relief of knowing that the time had come to begin. He hung about conspicuously for a little while, turning over the pages of a magazine, and then satisfied that everyone was settling down for a quiet evening, he left the room and walked unhurriedly to his quarters, where he changed his regulation boots for a pair of the canvas shoes that most of the officers wore when off duty, and slipped an electric torch into his pocket. This done, he strolled towards the tarmac. He did not go as far as the front of the hangars, but turned to the left behind them and moved along in the direction of the fort. The building was in darkness, but knowing that a sentry would be on door duty, he kept to the rear, and then worked his way down the side until he stood under the window where, a few nights before, he had seen von Stalhein writing.

With his heart thumping in spite of his outward calm, he took a swift glance around to make sure that he was not being watched, and then, reaching for the window-sill, drew himself up until he could throw a leg across the wooden frame. The other followed, and he slipped quietly inside.

After the bright starlight outside he could see nothing at first, but by waiting a minute or two for his eyes to become accustomed to the darkness, he could just make out the general outlines of the furniture. He crossed swiftly to the door, and tried it, but as he expected, it was locked, so he went over to the writing-desk upon which a number of documents were lying, but they were, of course, written in German, so he did not touch them. In any case he was not particularly concerned with them. Working swiftly but quietly, he made a complete inspection of the room, and then turned to the tall wardrobe which stood against the far wall. He opened it, and shielding the torch with his cupped hands, he flashed it on the interior, when he heard a sound that brought him round with a start although not particularly alarmed, for it came from the direction of the window. It seemed to be a soft scraping noise, a rustling, as if a large bird had settled on the ledge.

Bending forward, he could just make out two dark objects that moved along the window-sill with a kind of groping movement. For a moment he could not make out what they were, and then he understood. They were hands. Some one was coming in through the window.

Now even in the flash of time that remained for him to think, he knew there were only two courses open to him. One was to step forward and confront the marauder, who, by his clandestine method of entry, obviously had no more right in the room than he had, and the other was to hide. Of the two the latter found more favour, for the very last thing he wanted was the hullabaloo that might conceivably take place if he allowed himself to be seen. So he stepped back, squeezed himself into the wardrobe, and pulled the door nearly shut behind him just as a man's head appeared in the square of star-spangled deep blue that marked the position of the window. Even in the uncertain light a single glance was sufficient to show that it was not a European, for the dark-bearded face was surmounted by a turban. As silent as a shadow, the Arab swung his legs and body over the sill with the feline grace of a panther, and stood in a tense attitude, listening, precisely as Biggles had done a few minutes before. Then, still without making a sound, he glided forward into the room.

For one ghastly moment Biggles thought he was coming straight to the wardrobe, and he had already braced himself for the shock of meeting when the man stepped aside and disappeared from his limited line of vision. For a moment he wondered if he had gone to the electric light switch with the object of turning it on, but the half-expected click did not come. Nor did the man reappear. Nothing happened. All was as silent as the grave. A minute passed, and another, and still nothing happened.

Then began a period of time which to Biggles' keyed-up nerves seemed like eternity; but still nothing happened. Where was the man? What was he doing? Was he still in the room? Could it be possible that he had slipped out of the window again without being noticed? No, that was quite impossible. Had he in some way opened the door and gone out into the corridor? Definitely no; in such an aching silence, for any one to attempt to turn the handle, much less the lock, without being heard, was manifestly absurd. What, then, was happening?

Such were Biggles' thoughts as he stood in his stuffy hiding-place fighting to steady his palpitating heart. Another ten minutes passed slowly and he began to wonder if there had been a man at all. Could the whole thing have been a vision conjured up by his already overtaxed nerves? The tension became electric in its intensity, and he knew he could not stand the strain much longer. Could he rush to the window, throw himself through, and bolt before the man in the room had recovered from the shock of discovering that he was not alone? He thought he could, but it was a desperate expedient that he preferred not to undertake until it became vitally necessary.

Then at last the silence was broken, broken by a sound which, as it reached his ears, seemed to turn his blood to ice. He had heard it many times before, and it never failed to fill him with a vague dread, but in his present position it literally paralysed him. It was the slow dragging gait of a lame man, and it was coming down the corridor. Then it stopped and there was a faint tap, tap, and Biggles knew that von Stalhein was propping his stick against the wall while he felt for his keys. In his agitated imagination he could see him, follow his every action, and the grinding of the key in the lock sounded like the first laborious move of a piece of badly oiled machinery. Slowly the door creaked open on its hinges. There was a sharp click, a blaze of blinding light, and von Stalhein stepped into the room.

At that moment the Arab sprang. Biggles saw him streak across the room with a brown arm upraised, and caught the flash of steel. But if the Arab hoped to catch the German unaware, he was doomed to disappointment.

Never in his life before had Biggles seen anything quite so swift as that which followed. With a lithe movement that would have been miraculous even for an athlete, von Stalhein dived forward with a galvanic jerk; the top part of his body twisted, and the curved blade that was aimed at his throat missed his shoulder by what must have been literally a hair's breadth. His sticks crashed to the floor. All the force of the Arab's arm must have been behind the blow, for his lunge carried him beyond the German, who was round in a flash. His hand darted to his hip pocket, but before he could draw the weapon he obviously kept there the

Arab was on him again, and he was compelled to use both hands to fight off his attack.

Again the Arab sprang, and as his right arm flashed down von Stalhein caught it with his left, while his right groped through the folds of his flowing burnous for the brown throat. In that position they remained while Biggles could have counted ten, looking for all the world like a piece of magnificent statuary. Neither of them spoke; only the swift intake of breath revealed the quivering energy that was being expended by each of them to hold the other off. Then the tableau snapped into lightning-like activity.

Biggles couldn't see just what happened. All he knew was that the knife crashed to the floor; at the same moment the Arab tore himself free and flung himself at the window. He went through it like a greyhound, but, even so, the German was faster. His right hand flashed down and came up gripping a squat automatic, and at the precise moment that the Arab disappeared from sight a spurt of yellow flame streaked across the room. Von Stalhein was at the window before the crash of the report had died away; with the agility of an eel he threw his legs across the sill and sprang downward out of sight.

Biggles seized his opportunity; he stepped out of the wardrobe, closed it behind him, darted to the door and sped down the corridor. He hesitated as he reached the main entrance, eyes seeking the sentry, but no one was in sight, so he ran out and took refuge behind the nearest hangar. At that stage he would have asked nothing more than to be allowed to return to his room, but he saw figures hurrying towards the fort from the Mess, so he turned about and ran back as if he had heard the report of the shot and was anxious to know the cause. Doors were banging inside and voices were

363

calling; he paid no attention to them but ran round the side of the building, and then pulled up with a jerk as he almost collided with von Stalhein and the door sentry, who were bending over a recumbent figure on the ground. He saw that it was the Arab.

'Good gracious, von Stalhein,' he exclaimed, 'what's happened? What was that shot?'

'Nothing very much,' replied the German coolly. 'Fellow tried to knife me, that's all. One of the sheikhs who was on the raid the other night; the poor fools are blaming me because the thing went wrong. By the way, where have you just sprung from?'

It was on the tip of Biggles' tongue to say 'from my room', but something warned him to be careful. Instead, 'I was admiring the night from the tarmac,' he smiled; 'I can't sit indoors this weather. Why?'

'Because I looked into your room just now to have a word with you, and you weren't there,' was the casual reply.

Biggles caught his breath as he realized how nearly he had made a blunder. 'What did you want me for?' he inquired.

'Oh, merely a job the Count had in mind, but don't worry about it now; I'll see you in the morning. I shall have to stay and see this mess cleared up, confound it.' Von Stalhein touched the Arab with the toe of his patent leather shoe.

'All right. Then I think I'll get to bed,' returned Biggles, as several officers and mechanics joined the party.

Safely out of sight round the corner of a hangar he mopped his face with a handkerchief. 'My gosh,' he muttered, 'this business is nothing but one shock after another. "Where have you just sprung from?" he asked. I felt like saying, "And where the dickens have *you*

364

come from?" He couldn't have been in that machine that took off, after all; I'm beginning to take too much for granted, which doesn't pay, evidently, at this game. And so he's got a job for me in the morning, eh? Well, with any luck I shan't be taking on many more jobs in this part of the world, I hope.'

Chapter 16
Checked

The next morning he was awakened by his batman* bringing early morning tea. He got out of bed, lit a cigarette, and sat by the open window while he considered the results of his investigations. How far had he progressed? How much had he learned about El Shereef, the German super-spy? Had he arrived at a stage when, figuratively speaking, he could lay his cards on Major Raymond's desk and ask to be posted back to his old squadron, leaving the Intelligence people to do the rest? No, he decided regretfully, he had not. He had learned something, enough perhaps to end von Stalhein's activities, but that was not enough, for while the British Intelligence Staff might agree that he had concluded his task, something inside told him that it was still incomplete; that something more, the unmasking of a deeper plot than either he or British headquarters at first suspected, remained to be done. Just what that was he did not know, but he had a vague suspicion, and at the moment he felt he was standing on the threshold of discoveries that might alter the whole course of the war in that part of the world. Moreover, it was unlikely that another British agent would ever again be in such a sound position to bring about the exposure; so it was up to him to hang on whatever the cost to himself.

---

* An attendant serving an officer. A position discontinued in today's Royal Air Force.

That von Stalhein was the super-spy, El Shereef, he no longer doubted, for it was hardly possible that there could be two German spies masquerading as Arabs behind the British lines, and that von Stalhein did adopt Arab disguise was certain; the incident at the oasis was sufficient proof of that. If further proof were needed there was the business of the feigned limp, which he felt was all part of a clever pose to throw possible investigators off the scent. The limp was so pronounced, and he played the part of a lame man to such perfection, that the very act of abandoning it would have been a disguise in itself. No one could even think of von Stalhein without the infirmity. For what purpose other than espionage, or disguise, should he pretend to be incapacitated when he was not?

He knew now that von Stalhein was as active as any normal man. The way he had behaved when attacked by the Arab in his room revealed that, for he had dropped his sticks and dashed to the window with a speed that would have done credit to a professional runner. If he were not El Shereef, why the pose? As Erich von Stalhein he made his headquarters at Zabala; at night he changed, and under the pseudonym of El Shereef, worked behind the British lines, coming and going by means of a special detailed aeroplane. And the more Biggles thought about it the more he was convinced that he was right.

'The pilot flies him over, lands him well behind the lines—at the oasis for instance—and then comes home. Later, at a pre-arranged time and place, he goes over and picks him up,' he mused. 'That's what Mayer was doing the day he picked me up. Mayer landed for von Stalhein, but when he found me there instead he knew he had to bring me back. If only I could catch von Stalhein in the act of landing, there would be an end to it, but I'll bet he never again uses the place where *I* was picked up; he'd be too cunning for that; he doesn't trust me a yard, in spite of the fact that he has no foundation for his suspicions. He must have an instinct for danger like a cat. The only other way to nab him would be to find out the Arab name he adopts when he is over there, hanging about our troops picking up information. The thing I can't get over is that shadow on the tent, and but for the fact that he must have been somewhere around in order to learn that I was a prisoner, and then effect my rescue, I should feel inclined to think that I'd been mistaken. It's rather funny he has never mentioned a thing to me, taken credit for getting me out of the mess. No, perhaps it isn't funny. Oh, dash it, I don't know . . . unless . . .'

He stared thoughtfully at the desert for some time, drumming on the window-sill with his fingers. 'Well, I'd better go and see what the Count wants, I suppose,' he concluded, as he finished his toilet and went down to the Mess to breakfast, after which he walked along to the fort. He found von Stalhein in the headquarters office, but the Count had not yet arrived.

'Good morning, Brunow,' greeted the German affably. 'Quite a good photo—look.' He passed the last photograph Biggles had taken of Mayer's burning Halberstadt.

'Good morning, von Stalhein,' replied Biggles, taking it and looking at it closely, aware that that the German's eyes were on him. He finished his scrutiny and passed it back, wondering if von Stalhein had overlooked something in the photograph which he had spotted instantly. The photograph had been taken from a very low altitude and from an oblique angle, which showed not only the charred, smoking wreck but the desert beyond. Across the soft sand where he had landed ran a line of wheel tracks; they began some distance from the crash and ran off the top right-hand corner of the photograph. He looked up to see von Stalhein looking at him; his eyes were smiling mockingly, but there was no smile about his thin lips.

'I may be mistaken, but I understood you to say that you didn't land,' observed the German, in a low careless voice that nevertheless held a hard, steely quality.

Biggles raised his eyebrows. 'No, you were not mistaken,' he replied; 'why did you say that?'

'I was wondering how the wheel marks got there, that's all.'

Biggles laughed. 'Oh, those,' he said. 'Those were the marks made by my home-made trailer, I expect— have a cigarette?'

He offered his case as if his explanation of such a trivial point was sufficient—as indeed it was.

'Of course,' said von Stalhein, slowly—very slowly. 'Funny, I didn't think of that.'

'One cannot always expect to think of everything,' rejoined Biggles simply. 'What does the Count want— do you know?'

'Here he is, so he'll tell you himself,' answered von Stalhein shortly.

Biggles sprang to attention. 'Good morning, sir,' he said.

'Good morning, Brunow— morning, Erich. Going to be hot again,' observed the Count, dropping into his chair behind the desk. And then, glancing up at Biggles, he asked, 'Has Hauptmann von Stalhein told you what we were discussing last night?'

'No, sir.'

'I see.' The Count unfastened his stiff upright collar. 'Well, the position is this,' he went on. 'As you are no doubt aware, the chief reason why you were sent here was because of your knowledge of the English and their language. It was thought that you might be able to undertake duties that would be impossible for a—one of our own people. You have a British R.F.C. uniform, and we have British aeroplanes, yet neither have been fully exploited. In fact, you are rapidly becoming an ordinary flying officer engaged on routine duties, and in that capacity you have done remarkably well; in fact, if it goes on one of the *Staffels* will be putting in a request for you to be posted to them. I think it's time we did something about it, don't you?'

'As you wish, sir. I have thought about it myself, but I didn't mention it because I thought you'd give me orders for special duty when you were ready.'

'Quite so.' The Count turned to von Stalhein. 'We shall make a good German officer of him yet, Erich,' he observed dryly, in German.

'Thank you, sir,' put in Biggles absent-mindedly, in the same language.

'Ah-ha, so you are progressing with your German, too,' asserted the Count, raising his eyebrows.

Biggles flushed slightly, for the words had slipped out unthinkingly. 'I'm doing my best, and what with my book and conversations in the Mess, I am picking it up slowly,' he explained.

'Capital. But let us come to this business we are here for,' continued the Count. He lit a long black cigar and studied the glowing end closely before he went on. 'Last night I was merely concerned with the idea of sending you over to the British lines for a day or two to pick up any odd scraps of information that might be useful, paying particular regard to the preparations the British are making for the attack we know is soon to be launched near Gaza—at least, everything points to the battle being fought there. Since then, however, a blow

370

has fallen the importance of which cannot be exaggerated. It is, in fact, the most serious set-back we have had for a long time. Fortunately it does not affect us personally, but I hear that General Headquarters in Jerusalem is in a fever about it; if we could recover what we have lost, it would be a feather in our caps.'

'In your cap, you mean,' thought Biggles, but he said nothing.

'Tell me, Brunow'—the Count dropped his voice to little more than a whisper—'have you ever heard of one who is called El Shereef?'

Had he pulled out a revolver and fired point blank he could hardly have given Biggles a bigger shock. How he kept his face immobile he never knew, for the words set every nerve in his body jangling. He pretended to think for a moment before he replied. 'I seem to recall it, sir, but in what connexion I cannot think— yes, I have it. You remember the first day I came here I landed at Kantara. I heard some of the officers in the Mess using the name quite a lot, but I didn't pay much attention to it.'

'Then I will tell you. El Shereef was a—an agent, a German agent. Not only was he the cleverest agent in Palestine, but in the world.'

'Was . . . ?'

'He has been caught at last.'

Biggles felt the room rocking about him, but he continued staring straight at the Count, struggling to prevent his face from betraying what he was thinking. 'What a pity,' he said at last. For the life of him he couldn't think of anything else to say.

'Pity! it's a tragedy—an overwhelming misfortune. He was taken yesterday in a cunningly set trap by Major Sterne, who as you may know is one of the cleverest men on the British side.'

'By Major Sterne,' repeated Biggles foolishly.

The Count nodded. 'So we understand. The British have made no announcement about it—nor do we expect them to—yet. But General Headquarters, by means known only to themselves, got the news through late last night.'

Von Stalhein was lighting a fresh cigarette as if the matter hardly interested him.

Biggles tried to think, but could not. His mind seemed to have collapsed in complete chaos as all his so-called facts, conjectures, and suppositions crashed to the ground. He could hardly follow what the Count was saying when he continued.

'Well, there it is. The British will give him a trial— of sorts—of course, but we shall know only one thing more for certain—and that soon—and that is that El Shereef has faced a firing party. If you are to do anything it will have to be done at once.'

'Do anything, sir,' ejaculated Biggles. 'Me! What can I do?'

'You can get into the British lines. I was hoping that you might try to effect a rescue.'

Biggles nearly laughed aloud, for he felt that he was going insane. Was the Count seriously asking him to rescue El Shereef, when . . . ? The thing was too utterly ridiculous. He saw the Count was waiting for his answer. 'I'll do anything I can, sir,' he offered. 'If you could give me any further information that might be useful I should be grateful.'

The Count shook his head. 'All I can tell you is that El Shereef will probably be sent under special escort to British General Headquarters for interrogation.'

'Then I'd better go over and do what I can,' said Biggles thoughtfully; and then added in a flash of inspiration, 'Can you give me any idea of what he looks like, so that I shall be able to recognize him when I see him?'

'Yes, I can do that,' agreed the Count. 'He is, as you no doubt imagine, really a German, although he will of course be dressed as an Arab. He has lived with the Arabs for so long that he is nearly one of them—looks Arab—thinks Arab—speaks Arabic. Tall, brown—really brown, not merely grease paint—drooping black moustache. Dark eyes, and rather a big nose, like the beak of a hawk. Not much of a description, but it's the best I can give you. If you can get near him, show your ring and he'll understand. He will still have his hidden about him if the British didn't take it away when they searched him.'

'Very good, sir; I'll get off right away.' Biggles did not so much as glance at von Stalhein as he saluted, turned on his heel and departed to his room.

When he reached it he slumped down wearily on his bed and gave expression to his disappointment and mortification, for his feelings at that moment were not unlike those of a very tired man who, in the act of sitting down, realizes that some one has pulled the chair away from under him. After a period of deadly risk and anxiety he thought he had the situation well summed up, and all he needed to do to win was to play his trump cards carefully. The knowledge that his cards were useless was a disappointment not easily overcome, and it was followed by an almost overwhelming sense of depression, for if what the Count had told him was true, he had been running on a false scent all along. The only redeeming thing about the new development was that, if the British had really caught El Shereef, then this work was finished, and there was no longer any reason why he should stay at Zabala. Officially, his retirement from the scene would now be permissible, even though he had failed, but he knew he could not conscientiously do so while in his heart he was still certain that von Stalhein was engaged in some sinister scheme about which the British authorities knew nothing. Suppose the story were not true? Suppose the whole thing was pure fabrication, a story invented by the Count and von Stalhein to draw a red herring across the trail of British agents whom they suspected— or knew—to be engaged in counter-espionage behind their lines. Conversely, might it not be a gigantic piece of bluff devised by the British Intelligence Staff to mislead the Germans, or cause them to make a move which might betray the very man whom they claimed to have caught? Both theories were possible.

Thinking the new situation over, Biggles felt like a man who, faced with the task of unravelling a tangled ball of string, sees a dozen ends sticking out, but does not know which is the right one. 'I've had a few boneshakers since I started this job, but this one certainly is a bazouka,' he mused. 'Well, I suppose I'd better do something about it, and the best thing I can do is to push off through the atmosphere to Kantara to find out how much truth there is in it.'

He changed into his R.F.C. uniform, pulled his overalls on over it, went down to the tarmac, ordered out the Bristol Fighter, and landed at Kantara exactly thirty-five minutes later. He taxied up to the hangars, and telling the duty N.C.O. to leave his machine where it was in case he needed it urgently, went straight to Major Raymond's tent.

He found the Major working at his desk.

'Good morning, Bigglesworth—'

But Biggles was too impatient to indulge in conventional greetings. 'Is this tale true about your catching El Shereef, sir,' he asked abruptly.

'Quite true.'

Biggles stared. 'Well, I'll be shot for the son of a gun,' he muttered. 'You're quite sure—I mean, you're not just spinning a yarn?'

'Good gracious, no. But how did you know about it?'

'Von Faubourg told me this morning.'

'He wasn't long getting the news then.'

'So it seems. How did you work it?'

'Sterne did it. He's been on the trail for some time, working in his own way. He managed to pick up a clue and laid a pretty trap, and El Shereef, cunning as he is, walked straight into it.'

'That's what the Huns told me,' nodded Biggles. 'It begins to look as if it's true.'

'Of course it's true—we've got him here.'

'What! at Kantara?'

'Well, at Jebel Zaloud, the village just behind. General Headquarters are there. They've had El Shereef there trying to get some information out of him, but it's no use. He won't speak. He won't do anything else if it comes to that—won't eat or drink. He's an Arab, you know.'

'Arab? You mean he's disguised as an Arab?'

'If it's a disguise, then it's a thundering good one.'

'It would be. He's lived amongst the Arabs half his life, until he is one, or as near as makes no difference. The Count told me so himself.'

'I don't know about that, but it's no wonder things went wrong over here. He is—or rather, was—one of our most trusted Sheikhs. He's a fellow with a big following, too.'

'How do you know it's El Shereef?'

'Sterne was sure of it before he collared him. When we took him he was wearing one of those same rings

375

that you've got—the German Secret Service ring. I've got it here: here it is. He had also got some very interesting documents on him—plans of British positions, and so on.'

Biggles picked up the ring that the Major had tossed on to the table and looked at it with interest. 'I should like to see this cove,' he said quietly.

'I think it could be arranged, although I can't see much point in it. You'll have to make haste, though.'

'Why?'

'He was tried by a specially convened Field General Court Martial this morning and sentenced to death.'

'Good God! When is sentence to be carried out?'

'To-day, some time. He's too tricky a customer to keep hanging about. He'll certainly be shot before sundown.'

Biggles jaw set grimly. 'That's awkward,' he said.

'Why?'

'Because I've been sent over here to rescue him.'

It was the Major's turn to look startled. 'Are you serious?' he asked incredulously.

'Too true I am.'

'What are you going to do about it?'

'Nothing—now. I'm through. If you've got the fellow, then that's the end of the story as far as I'm concerned.'

'That's what I thought; in fact, that's why I sent Lacey over to let you know.'

'You did what?'

'Sent Lacey over. I couldn't do less. There was no point in your going on risking your neck at Zabala.'

'Where's Algy now?'

'He's gone. He took off just before you landed. He's going to do the message-dropping stunt in the olive grove. It's a pity he went, but naturally I didn't expect the Huns would tell you about our catching El Shereef.'

Biggles nodded sagely. 'Which, to my mind, is a perfectly good reason why you might have guessed they'd do it,' he declared. 'In my experience, it's the very last thing that you'd expect that always happens at this game. My word! dog-fighting* is child's play to it.'

'Well, what are you going to do? I'm busy over this affair, as you may imagine.'

'Just as a matter of curiosity I'd like to have a dekko at this nimble chap who is called El Shereef.'

'Very well; after what you've done we can hardly refuse such a natural request. I'll see if it can be arranged.' The Major reached for his telephone.

---

* An aerial battle rather than a hit and run attack.

Chapter 17

Hare and Hounds

Two hours later Biggles again sat in Major Raymond's tent with his face buried in his hands; the Major was busy writing on a pad. 'How's this?' he said, passing two sheets of paper. 'The first is an official notification of the execution that will appear in to-night's confidential orders; the other is the notice that will be issued to the press. Naturally, we make as much of a thing like this as we can; it's good propaganda, and it bucks up the public at home to know that we are as quick-witted as the Huns.'

Biggles read the notices. 'They seem to be O.K., sir,' he said, passing them back. 'I'll be going now,' he added, rising and picking up his cap.

'You still insist in going back to Zabala?'

'I don't want to go, sir, don't think that, but I think it's up to me to try to get the truth about von Stalhein's game while I can come and go. I know I said I wouldn't go back, but I've been thinking it over. I shan't be long, anyway. If I find things are getting too hot I'll pack up and report here.'

'As you wish,' agreed the Major.

Biggles walked towards the door. 'Cheerio for the present, then, sir,' he said. 'You might remember me to Algy when he comes back.'

'He's probably back by now; can't you stay and have a word with him?'

'No, I haven't time now; besides, I've nothing particular to talk about,' decided Biggles. Lost in thought, he walked slowly back to where he had left his Bristol, climbed into the cockpit, and took off. Still in a brown study, he hardly bothered to watch the sky, for while he was over the British side of the lines he had nothing to fear, and over the German side the white bar on his wings made him safe from attack from German aeroplanes.

Once he caught sight of a large formation of Pfalz Scouts, but he paid no attention to them; he did not even watch them but continued on a straight course for Zabala, still turning over in his mind the knotty problems that beset him.

It was, therefore, with a start of surprise and annoyance that he was aroused from his reverie by the distant clatter of a machine-gun, and while he was in the act of looking back for the source of the noise he was galvanized into activity by a staccato burst which he knew from experience was well inside effective range. Cursing himself for his carelessness, he half-rolled desperately, but not before he had felt the vicious thud of bullets ripping through his machine. 'What the dickens do the fools think they're playing at?' he snarled, as he levelled out and saw that he was in the middle of a swarm of Pfalz. 'They must be blind,' he went on furiously, as he threw the Bristol into a steep bank in order to display the white bar on his top plane. But either the Germans did not see it or they deliberately ignored it, for two or three of them darted in, guns going, obviously with the intention of shooting him down.

Biggles knew that something had gone wrong, but the present was no time to wonder what it was. He must act quickly if he was to escape the fate that he had often meted out to others, but he was at once faced with a difficult problem. At the back of his mind still lingered the conviction that the Pfalz pilots had forgotten all about his distinguishing mark, and would presently see and remember it, but whether that was so or not, the only thing that really counted at the moment was that they were doing their best to kill him. And by reason of their numbers they were likely to succeed. In the ordinary way, had he been flying a real British machine, the matter would not have worried him unduly; he would simply have fought the best fight he could as long as his machine held together and remained in the air. He had, in fact, fought against even greater odds and escaped, but then he had been able to give as good as he got. 'If I shoot any of these fellows down it puts the tin hat on my ever going back to Zabala, even if I do get away with it,' he thought desperately, as he turned round and round, kicking on right and left rudder alternately to avoid the streams of lead that were being poured at him from all directions.

He knew that the only thing he could do was to attempt to escape, either by trying to get back to the British lines, or by making a dash for Zabala, which was nearer. He would have spun down and landed had it been possible to land, but it was not, for the country below was a vast tract of broken rock and camel-thorn bushes. Nevertheless, he threw the Bristol into a spin with the object of getting as near to the ground as possible, and 'hedge-hopping'—or rather, rock-hopping—home. Looking back over his shoulder he saw the Pfalz spinning down behind him. He pulled out at a hundred feet above the ground, but still eased the stick forward until his wheels were literally skimming the rocks; and swerving from side to side to throw the gunners off their mark, raced for Zabala. Behind him screamed the Pfalz, like a pack of hounds after the hare.

Occasionally the sound of guns reached his ears, and once in a while a bullet bit into the machine, but the chance of being hit by a stray shot was the risk he had to take. By flying low he had made shooting difficult for the Boche pilots, who dare not dive as steeply as they would have liked to have done, and could have done higher up. Their difficulty was that of a diver who knows that the water into which he is about to plunge is shallow; to dive deep would mean hitting the bottom. In the case of the Pfalz, they dare not risk over shooting* their target for fear of crashing into the ground. So, unable to dive, they could only hang behind and take long shots. Their task was not made any easier by the fact that the Bristol did not fly on the same course for more than two or three seconds at a time; it turned and twisted from side to side like a snipe when it hears the sportsmen's guns.

This sort of flying needs a cool head and steady nerves, and Biggles possessed both; his many battles in France had given him those desirable qualities. He had to have eyes in the back of his head, as the saying goes, for it was necessary to keep a sharp look-out in front for possible obstacles, and at the same time keep watch behind for the more daring pilots who sometimes took a chance and came in close, whereupon he would turn at right angles and dash off on a new course, thereby upsetting their aim.

In spite of his precarious position, he smiled as the chase roared over the heads of a squadron of cavalry, sending the horses stampeding in all directions. On another occasion a German Staff car that was racing along the road down which he was then roaring in the opposite direction, pulled up so quickly that he was

* To fly past another aeroplane when following through an attack.

given the never-to-be-forgotten spectacle of a German general in full uniform, with his head through the wind-screen.

As he approached Zabala the German scouts doubled their efforts to stop him, evidently under the impression that the British two-seater intended to bomb their aerodrome, and the consequence was that Biggles, who by this time was not in the least particular as to how or where he got down, made a landing that was as spectacular as it was unusual. He throttled back, side-slipped off his last few feet of height, flattened out and hurtled down-wind across the sun-baked sandy aerodrome. His wheels touched, but he did not stop. The hangars seemed to rush towards him, and he braced himself for the collision that seemed inevitable.

Leaning over the side of his cockpit to get a clear view round his windscreen, he saw German mechanics hauling a Halberstadt out of his path with frantic haste; others were unashamedly sprinting for cover. But the machine was beginning to lose speed, and fifty yards from the tarmac Biggles risked applying a little rudder and aileron, although he clenched his teeth as he did so, fully expecting to hear the undercarriage collapse under the strain. A grinding jar proclaimed the Bristol's protest, but the wheels stood up to the terrific strain, and slowly the machine swung round until it was tearing straight along the tarmac in a cloud of dust.

The Count himself, and von Stalhein, who had heard the shouting and had dashed out to see what was happening, just had time to throw themselves aside as the Bristol ran to a standstill in front of the fort, leaving a line of staring mechanics and swirling sand to mark it tempestuous course.

'What the devil do you think you're doing?' roared the Count, white with anger.

Biggles climbed out and pushed up his goggles before he replied. 'With all respect to you, sir,' he said bitterly, 'I think that is a question that might well be put to the pilots of the Pfalz *Staffel.*'

'What do you mean?' asked the Count, glancing up at the scouts, some of which were already landing, while others circled round awaiting their turn.

Biggles glared at von Stalhein as a new suspicion flashed into his mind. 'They've done their best to shoot me down, sir,' he told the Count. 'Look at my machine,' he added, nearly choking with rage as he thought he saw the solution of the whole thing. Von Stalhein still mistrusted him, and had deliberately set the Pfalz on to him as the easiest way to removing him without awkward questions or the formality of a court martial.

The Count looked in surprise at the bullet holes in the wings and tail of the Bristol. 'I don't understand this,' he said with a puzzled expression. 'Do you, Erich?' He turned to von Stalhein, who shook his head.

'I suppose there must be an explanation,' he said calmly. 'Here come the Pfalz pilots: perhaps they can tell us what it is.'

The scout pilots who now arrived on the scene pulled up short when they saw the pilot of the Bristol Fighter; they seemed to have difficulty in finding words. For a few moments nobody spoke. The Count looked from one to the other. Von Stalhein waited, with a faint inscrutable smile on his face. Biggles glared at all of them in turn. 'Well, he said at last, 'what about it?'

One of the German pilots said something quickly and half apologetically to the Count; Biggles caught the words, 'mark and wings'.

Von Faubourg started and turned to Biggles. 'He says you've no markings on your wings,' he cried.

'No markings,' exclaimed Biggles incredulously.

'Impossible!' He swung up and stood on the side of the fuselage from where he could see the whole of the top plane. From end to end it was painted the standard dull biscuit colour; there was not a speck of white on it anywhere. He stared as if it were some strange new creature that he had never seen before, while his brain struggled to absorb this miracle, for it seemed no less. He jumped down, eyes seeking the maker's number on the tail; and then he understood. It was not the number of his original machine. For some reason as incomprehensible as it was unbelievable, the machine he had flown over to Kantara that morning had been removed while it was standing on the tarmac, and another substituted in its place. It must have been done during the three hours he was with Major Raymond or away from the aerodrome.

He pulled himself together with an effort and turned to the Count. 'He's quite right, sir,' he said, 'there is no white mark. But do not ask me to explain it, because I cannot. The only suggestion that I can offer is that a change of machines took place while I was at Kantara.'

The Count was obviously unconvinced, but as he could offer no better explanation he dismissed the matter with a wave of his hand. 'Come along to my office, Brunow, I want you,' he said, and with von Stalhein at his side, disappeared into the porch of the fort.

Biggles turned to follow, but before he went in he turned to one of the Pfalz pilots who he knew spoke a little English and said, 'How was it you happened to be where you were—when I came along?'

'Well, we are usually somewhere about there,' replied the German, 'but as we were taking off von Stalhein told us that we should probably find some British machines there this morning.'

'I see,' said Biggles, 'thanks.' Then he followed the Count into his office.

'What happened over the other side?' was the curt question that greeted him as he stepped into the room.

'I'm sorry, sir, but I was too late to do anything,' answered Biggles simply.

'Too late?'

'Sheikh Haroun Ibn Said, better known as El Shereef, of the German Intelligence Staff, was tried by Field General Court Martial this morning and sentenced to death for espionage,' said Biggles in a low voice. 'The sentence was carried out within an hour on the grounds of the undesirability of keeping such a dangerous man in captivity. I'm not sure, but I believe the British are making an official announcement about it to-night.'

The Count sat down slowly in his chair and looked at von Stalhein. Biggles also looked at him, and thought he detected a faint gleam of triumph in the unflinching eyes. There was silence for a few minutes broken only by the Count tapping on his teeth with a lead pencil. 'Ah, well,' he said at last with a shrug of his massive shoulders, 'we have failed, but we did our best. Did you learn anything else while you were over there?'

'Only that there seems to be a good deal of activity going on, sir.'

'We are already aware of that. Anything else?'

'No, sir.'

'What excuse did you give to account for your presence at Kantara?'

'The same as before. I said I was a delivery pilot; they are always coming and going and nobody questioned it.'

'I see. That's all for the present.'

Biggles saluted and marched out of the room into

the blazing sunshine, but he did not go straight to his room, which, as events showed, was a fortunate thing. Instead, he walked along to the hangar where the two British machines were kept, with the object of testing a theory he had formed during his interview with the Count. Several mechanics were at work on the damaged Bristol, covering the bullet holes with small slips of fabric, but he went past them to where the Pup was standing in a corner and put his hand on the engine. One touch told him all he needed to know. The engine was still warm.

'I'm right,' he thought. 'That's how it was done.'

Chapter 18
An Unwelcome Visitor

'Yes, that's how he did it, the cunning beggar,' he mused again, as he walked back slowly to his room and changed into his German uniform. 'One false move now, and he'll be on me like a ton of—hello! what's going on over there, I wonder?' He broke off his soliloquy to watch with casual interest a little scene that was being enacted at the entrance gate of the camp, which was quite close to his quarters, and which he could just see by leaning out of the window. The sound of what seemed to be an argument reached him, and looking out to see what it was all about, he noticed that a service tender had drawn up to discharge a single passenger who was now engaged in a heated discussion with the N.C.O. in charge of the guard.

From his actions it was clear that he was trying to obtain admission to the station, but he was in civilian clothes, and the attitude of the N.C.O. suggested that he was not satisfied with his credentials. The man's suitcase had been stood on the ground, and as Biggles automatically read the name that was painted on its side in black letters he drew in his breath sharply, while his fingers gripped the window-sill until his knuckles showed white through the tan. The name on the suitcase was L. Brunow.

For a moment he came near to panic, and it was all he could do to prevent himself from dashing down to the tarmac, jumping into the first aeroplane he came to, and placing himself behind the British lines in the shortest possible space of time. He knew that he was in the tightest corner of his life, but he did not lose his head. He slipped his German Mauser revolver into his pocket and hurried round to the gate.

'What is the matter?' he asked the N.C.O. in German—one of the phrases he had learnt by heart.

The N.C.O. saluted and said something too quickly for him to catch, so Biggles resorted to the friend that had so often before helped him in difficult situations— bluff. He waved the N.C.O. aside, and indicated by his manner that the newcomer was known to him, and that he would accept responsibility for him. At the same time he picked up the suitcase and held it close to his side so that the name could not be read.

The real Brunow—for Biggles was in no doubt whatever as to the identity of the new arrival—wiped the perspiration from his face with a handkerchief. 'Can you speak English by any chance?' he said apologetically; 'I'm afraid my German isn't very good.'

'A leedle,' replied Biggles awkwardly. 'I understand better than I speak perhaps—yes?'

'Thank goodness. Then will you show me Count von Faubourg's office; I have an important message for him.'

'Yes, I will show you,' replied Biggles, but the thought that flashed through his mind was, 'Yes, I'll bet you have'. 'Der Count has just gone away,' he went on aloud. 'You must have the thirst, after your journey in der sun. I go to my room for a drink now—perhaps you come—no?'

'Thanks, I will,' replied Brunow with alacrity. 'I can't stand this heat.'

'It vas derrible,' agreed Biggles, as he led the way to his room, wondering what he was going to do with the man when he got there.

Brunow threw himself into a chair while Biggles took from the cupboard two glasses, a siphon of soda-water, and a bottle of brandy that he kept for visitors. The amount of brandy that he poured into Brunow's glass nearly made him blush, but Brunow did not seem to notice it, so he added a little soda-water and passed it over. His own glass he filled from the siphon, at the same time regretfully observing that he had had a touch of dysentery, and was forbidden alcohol by doctor's orders. He half smiled as Brunow drank deeply like a thirsty man—as he probably was—and decided in his mind that whatever happened Brunow must not be allowed to leave the room, for if ever he reached the Count's office his own hours were numbered.

'How long is the Count going to be, do you think?' inquired Brunow, setting down his empty glass, which Biggles casually refilled.

'He may be gone some time,' he answered in his best pseudo-German accent. 'Why, is it something impor-tant—yes?'

Brunow took another drink. 'I should say it is,' he retorted, settling himself down more comfortably in the chair. 'Too important to be put in a dispatch,' he added, rather boastfully, as an afterthought.

Biggles whistled softly, and made up his mind that his best chance of getting into the man's confidence was through his vanity. 'So! and they send you,' he exclaimed.

'That's right,' declared Brunow. 'They've sent me all the way from Berlin rather than trust the telegraph or the post-bag.' He leaned forward confidentially and looked up into Biggles' face. 'Perhaps I shouldn't tell you—keep this to yourself—but there's going to be a fine old row when I see the Count.'

Biggles laughed and refilled the glasses. 'That will

be not new,' he said. 'We of the staff have plenty of those.'

'But this one will be something to remember,' Brunow told him with a leer.

Biggles looked sceptical, which seemed to annoy Brunow.

'What would you say if I told you there was a spy here—here—here at Zabala?' he asked bellicosely.

Biggles shrugged his shoulders. 'It would be a funny place where there were no rumours about spies,' he said inconsequentially.

The combined effects of the heat and the brandy were becoming apparent in Brunow's manner. He put his feet up on the table and frowned at Biggles through half-closed eyes. 'Are you suggesting that I don't know what I'm talking about?' he inquired coldly. 'You'll be telling me next that I'm drunk,' he added with the aggressive indignation of a man who is well on his way to intoxication.

'I should hope not,' replied Biggles, in well simulated surprise. 'We are all two-bottle men here. Have another drink?' Without waiting for a reply, he filled the glasses again, inwardly disgusted that a man on special duty could behave in a manner so utterly foolish and irresponsible. 'Well,' he thought, 'it's either him or me for it, so it's no time to be squeamish.'

'Funny thing, you know,' went on Brunow confidingly; 'I'm not really German, but I went to Germany to offer my services. When I got there and told them my name, what do you think they did?'

'I'm no good at riddles,' admitted Biggles.

'They threw me in clink,' declared the other, picking up his glass.

'Clink?'

'In quod—you know, prison.

'*Donner blitz**,' muttered Biggles, looking shocked.

'They did,' went on Brunow reflectively, sinking a little lower in his chair. 'Had the brass face to tell me that I was already serving in the Secret Service. What would you say if any one told you that, eh?'

'Biggles shook his head. 'Impossible!' he exclaimed, for want of something better to say.

'That's what I told them,' swore Brunow, waxing eloquent. 'The funny thing is, though, they were right. Can you beat that, eh?'

'It vas not possible.'

'Wasn't it! Ha! that's all that you know about it. I kicked up a proper stink and showed them my papers; when they saw those they smelt a rat and got busy. Quick wasn't the word. To make a long story short, they found that some skunk had got in under the canvas and was pretending to be me—*me*! What do you know about that?'

Biggles knew quite a lot about it but he did not say so. 'Too bad,' he murmured sympathetically.

'Too bad!' exploded Brunow, starting up. 'Is that all you've got to say about it? Don't you realize that this other fellow is a *spy*? Well, I've got it in for him,' he declared venomously, as he sank back. 'They believe it's a fellow named Bigglesworth, who's disappeared from France, though it beats me how they found that out. But whoever he is, he's here at Zabala.'

Biggles poured out more brandy with a hand that shook slightly, for Brunow had raised his voice. Twilight was falling over the desert, and in the hush the sound of voices carried far.

'So you've come here to put an end to his little game,

* By thunder!

391

eh?' he said quietly. 'Good! Still, there's no need to get excited about it.'

'Who are you, telling me not to get excited about it?' fumed Brunow. 'These cursed British chucked—' He pulled up as if he realized that he was saying too much. 'I want to see them shoot this skunk Bigglesworth, and I want to see him twitch when he gets a neck full of lead. That's what I want to see,' he snarled.

'Well, maybe you will,' Biggles told him.

'That's what I've come here for. The people in Berlin were going to send a telegram; then they thought they'd send a dispatch, but in the end they decided to send a special messenger. They chose me, and here I am,' stated Brunow. 'Pretty good, eh?'

'How about another drink?' smiled Biggles, and the instant he said it he knew he had gone too far. A look of suspicion darted into Brunow's bloodshot eyes, and the corners of his mouth came down ominously. 'Say! what's the big idea?' he growled. 'Are you trying to get me tanked?'

'Tanked?' Biggles tried to look as if he did not understand.

'Yes—blotto . . . sewn up. You sit there swilling that gut-rot, lacing me with brandy, and letting me do the talking. Do you know this skate Bigglesworth? You must have met him if you're stationed here. That's it. Is he a pal of yours, or—'

Biggles could almost see Brunow's bemused brain wrestling with the problem. The half-drunken man knew he had said too much, and was trying to recall just how much he had said. Then into his eyes came suddenly a new look; it was as if a dreadful possibility had struck him. Quickly, as he stared into Biggles face, doubt changed to certainty, and with certainty came hate and fear. He sprang to his feet, and grabbing the brandy bottle by the neck, swung it upwards; the table went over with a crash. 'Curse you,' he screamed. 'You're—'

Biggles dodged the bottle that would have brained him if it had reached its mark, and grabbed him by the throat. So sudden had been the attack that he was nearly caught off his guard, but once he realized that Brunow, in a flash of drunken inspiration, had recognized him, he acted with the speed of light, knowing that at all costs he must prevent him from shouting. One call for help and he was lost.

As his right hand found Brunow's throat and choked off the cry that rose to his lips, his left hand gripped the wrist that still held the bottle and a wave of fighting fury swept over him. It was the first time in his life that he had actually made physical contact with one of the enemy, and his reaction to it was shattering in its intensity; it aroused a latent instinct to destroy that he had never suspected was in him, and the knowledge that the man was not only an enemy but a traitor fanned the red-heat of his rage to a searing white-hot flame. 'Yes,' he ground out through his clenched teeth, 'I'm Bigglesworth—you dirty traitorous rat.'

But Brunow was no weakling. He was a trifle older than Biggles, and more heavily built, but what he gained from this advantage was lost by being out of condition, although he fought with the fear of death on him.

Locked in an unyielding embrace, they lost their balance and toppled over on to the bed. For a moment they lay on it panting, and then with a sudden wrench, Brunow tore himself free; but Biggles clung to his wrist and they both crashed to the floor. The shock broke his hold and they both sprang up simultaneously.

Brunow had lost too much breath to shout; he aimed

a murderous blow with the bottle, but he was a fraction of a second too slow. Biggles sprang sideways like a cat and then darted in behind the other arm, while as he moved his right hand flashed down and up, bringing the Mauser with it. The force Brunow had put behind his blow almost over-balanced him, and before he could recover Biggles brought the butt of his gun down on the back of his head.

Brunow swayed for a moment with a look of startled surprise on his face, and then pitched forward over the table.

Biggles stood rigid, listening, wondering fearfully if the noise of the struggle had been heard, and his lips closed in a thin straight line as his worst fears were realized. Slowly dragging footsteps were coming down the corridor, accompanied by the tap, tap, of walking-sticks.

He literally flung Brunow under the bed and kicked his suitcase after him. He set the table on its legs, replaced the siphon and the bottle which had fallen from Brunow's hand, and put one of the tumblers beside it. The other had been broken and there was no time to pick up the pieces. Then he pushed the Mauser under his pillow, and flung himself down on the disarranged bed in an attitude of sleep.

With every nerve tingling, he heard the footsteps stop outside; the door was opened quietly and he knew that von Stalhein was standing looking into the room.

How long the German stood there he did not know. He did not hear him go, and for some time he dare not risk opening his eyes; but when at length he risked a peep through his lashes the door was closed again. Still, he took no chances. He got up like a man rising from a deep sleep, but seeing that the room was really empty he glided to the window and looked out. In the twilight he could just see von Stalhein limping towards the fort. 'Thought I'd been drinking, I suppose,' mused Biggles, as he began to act on the plan he had formed while lying on the bed.

Brunow must be disposed of, that was vital. How long it would be before the people in Berlin became aware of his non-arrival he did not know; nor did he care particularly. The first thing must be to put Brunow where he could do no harm. But how—where? To murder a man in cold blood was unthinkable; to keep him hidden in his room for any length of time was impossible; yet every moment he remained would be alive with deadly danger. 'Somehow or other I've got to get him into that Bristol and fly him over the lines; that's the only possible solution,' he thought swiftly, although he was by no means clear as to how he was going to get him from his room to the aeroplane. 'If I can get the machine out I'll manage it somehow or other, but I shall have to leave him here while I go down to see about it,' were the thoughts that raced through his mind.

His first action was to retrieve the revolver and slip it into his pocket. Next, he pulled the still unconscious man from under the bed, tied his hands and feet securely with a strip of towel and gagged him with a piece of the same material. Then he pushed him back far under the bed and hurried down to the tarmac, feeling that time was everything. It was nearly dark, and it could only be under cover of darkness that he could hope to get Brunow to the machine. What the mechanics would think about getting the Bristol out at such an hour he hardly knew, but there was no help for it. They could think what they liked providing they raised no objection. He found them just knocking off work, and the sergeant in charge looked at him in surprise when he asked that the two-seater be stood out on the tarmac in readiness for a flight. 'I understand I am to do some night flying soon,' Biggles told him carelessly, 'and I want some practice. Just stand her outside; there is no need for you to wait, and it may be some time before I take off. I shall be able to manage by myself.' He spoke of course in German and hoped that the N.C.O. understood what he said, but he was no means sure of it.

He breathed a sigh of relief as the mechanics obeyed his orders unquestioningly, and then disappeared in the direction of their quarters. 'All I've got to do now is to get the body there and think of a good excuse to account for my flip when I get back—if I decide to come back. Confound the fellow; what the dickens did he want to roll up here for just at this time,' he thought angrily.

He started off back towards his room, but before he reached it he saw von Stalhein hurrying along the tarmac to intercept him. 'Now what the dickens does he want, I wonder?' he muttered savagely, as the German hailed him.

'Ah, there you are,' cried von Stalhein as he came up. 'I've been looking for you. I came up to your room, but you seemed to be—well, I thought it best not to disturb you,' he smiled.

Biggles nodded. 'I had a drink or two and I must have dropped off to sleep,' he admitted.

'That's all right, but I've got a little job I want you to do for me if you will.'

'Certainly,' replied Biggles, outwardly calm but inwardly raging. 'What is it?'

'We've just had a prisoner brought in and he's as close as an oyster,' answered von Stalhein. 'He won't say a word—just sulks. We want to try the old trick on him to see if he knows anything worth knowing. Will you slip on your British uniform and we'll march you in as if you were another prisoner—you know the idea? He'll probably unloosen a bit if you start talking to him.'

'All right,' agreed Biggles, wishing that the unfortunate prisoner had chosen some other time to fall into the hands of the enemy. The trick referred to by von Stalhein was common enough. When a prisoner refused to speak, as duty demanded, and his captors thought he might be in possession of information of importance, it was customary to turn another so-called prisoner in with him, dressed in the same uniform, in the hope that confidences would be exchanged.

To Biggles this interruption of his plans at such a crucial moment was unnerving, but he could not demur, so he went to his room, and after ascertaining that Brunow was still in the position in which he had left him, he changed quickly and went along to the fort, where he found von Stalhein waiting for him with an escort of two soldiers armed with rifles and fixed bayonets.

'Where is he?' he asked.

'In the pen,' replied von Stalhein, nodding to the barbed-wire cage beside the fort in which a number of wooden huts had been erected to provide sleeping quarters.

Biggles took his place between the escort, who marched him ceremoniously to the gate of the detention camp, where another sentry was on duty. At a word of command the gate was thrown open and Biggles was marched inside. He was escorted to a room in which a light was burning. The door was unlocked; he was pushed roughly inside and the door closed behind him. But he remained standing staring unbelievably at a

British officer who sat dejectedly on a wooden stool near the far side of the room. It was Algy.

Chapter 19
Biggles Gets Busy

I

It would be hard to say who of the two was more shaken, Biggles or Algy. For a good ten seconds they simply stared at each other in utter amazement, and then they both moved together. Algy sprang up and opened his mouth to speak, but Biggles laid a warning finger on his lips, at the same time shaking his head violently. He covered the intervening distance in a stride. 'Be careful—there may be dictaphones*,' he hissed. Then aloud he exclaimed in a normal voice for the benefit of possible listeners. 'Hello, it looks as if we were both in the same boat. How long have you been here?'

'They got me this afternoon,' said Algy aloud in a disgruntled voice, but he nodded to indicate that he grasped the reason of Biggles' warning.

'Well, it looks as if the war's over as far as we're concerned,' continued Biggles.

'Looks like it,' agreed Algy.

Then began an amazing double-sided conversation, one carried on in a natural way, and consisting of such condolences and explanations as one would expect between two British officers who found they were brothers in misfortune. The other consisted of a whis-

---

*During the war both sides used hidden microphones, in prisoner of war camps, to overhear the prisoners' conversation. These conversations would be recorded on a dictaphone.

pered dialogue of why's and wherefore's, in which Biggles learnt that Algy's engine had failed and let him down in enemy country while he was flying over to Zabala with the message about the capture of El Shereef.

This went on for about half an hour, during which time Biggles racked his brains for a means of overcoming the difficulties and dangers that seemed to be closing in on him. All his original plans went by the board in the face of this new complication; first and foremost now was the pressing obsession that whatever else he did, or did not do, he must free Algy from the ghastly ordeal of spending the rest of the war in a German prison camp. What with Algy being a prisoner, Brunow tied up in his room, and von Stalhein already suspicious and waiting to spring, it can hardly be wondered at that he was appalled by the immediate prospect. One thing was certain; he must make the most of his time with Algy if ways and means of escape were to be discussed.

'I can't tell you all about it now,' he breathed, 'but things are fairly buzzing here. I don't know what's going to happen next, but I'm going to try to get you out before I do anything else; I can't tell you how exactly because I don't know myself, but I shall think of something presently. When the time comes you'll have to take your cue from me and do what you think is the right thing. For heaven's sake don't make a slip and say anything—or do anything—that will lead them to think that we know each other. I expect they'll come back in a minute to fetch me in order that I can make my report on what you've been saying, unless, of course, they've got the conversation taken down in shorthand from a dictaphone. After I've gone, stand by for anything. You come first now; I've got to get you away, and I can't worry any more about von Stalhein and his rotten schemes until that's done. In fact, this looks to me like the end of the whole business, and believe me, I shan't burst into tears if it is. I've had about enough of it. Be careful, here they come,' he went on quickly as heavy footsteps and a word of command were heard outside. 'Don't worry; I shan't be far away.'

Taking up the role he was playing, he looked over his shoulder as the door opened and the escort entered.

'Come—you,' said the N.C.O. in the harsh German military manner. He beckoned to Biggles.

Biggles rose obediently. 'Cheerio, old fellow, I may see you later perhaps,' he said casually to Algy as he left the room.

As soon as he was outside all pretence was abandoned, as of course the guards knew him, and knew quite well what was going on. The N.C.O. saluted, as did the sentry on gate duty as he left the *gefangenenlager** and walked briskly towards the fort, thinking with the speed and clarity that is so often the result of continual flying.

Just before he reached the porch he heard an aeroengine start up and a machine begin to taxi from the Halberstadt sheds towards the far side of the aerodrome. He had a nasty moment, for at first he thought that it might be some one moving the Bristol, but he breathed again as he recognized the unmistakable purr of a Mercedes engine. He paused in his stride and a queer look came into his eyes as he peered through the darkness in the direction of the sound. 'That's the same Halberstadt going out to wait on the far side of the aerodrome, which means that friend Erich is going off

* German: prison camp.

401

on one of his jaunts,' he thought swiftly. For another moment or two he lingered, still thinking hard, and then he turned and walked boldly through the main porch of the fort. A light showed under the Count's door, and another under von Stalhein's, but he passed them both and went on to the far end of the corridor to what had originally been the back door of the building. He tried it and found that it was unlocked, so he went through and closed the door quietly behind him. For a moment he stood listening, and then made his way swiftly to his room where, after satisfying himself that Brunow was still unconscious, he changed into his German uniform and then hurried back to the fort. He went in by the way he had come out and emerged again through the front porch for the benefit of the sentry on duty. He did not stop but went on straight to the prison camp. 'Well, it's neck or nothing now,' he mused as he beckoned to the N.C.O. in charge of the guard. 'Bring the officer-prisoner,' he said curtly; 'Hauptmann von Stalhein wishes to speak with him.'

The N.C.O. obeyed with the blind obedience of the German soldier; he called the escort to attention, marched them to Algy's door and called him out. Biggles did not so much as glance at him as he walked back towards the main entrance of the fort with the prisoner and his escort following.

'Wait,' he told the guards shortly, and signalling to Algy to follow, he led the way into the corridor. But he did not stop at von Stalhein's door, nor at the Count's, but went straight on to the back of the building. Little beads of perspiration were on his forehead as he opened the door and they both went outside, for he knew that if either the Count or von Stalhein had come out during the few moments they were walking through the corridor all would have been lost.

As they stepped quietly outside he looked swiftly to left and right, but no one was in sight as far as he could see, which was not very far for the moon had not yet risen. 'Come on,' he said tersely, and set off at a quick trot towards his room with Algy following close behind.

Their footfalls made no sound on the soft sand as they sprinted along the back of the hangars to the side of the building in which Biggles' room was situated. 'I daren't risk taking you in through the door in case we meet some one coming out,' he said softly, leading the way to the window. 'I had to take you through the fort to get rid of the guards,' he explained, 'but if either von Stalhein or the Count go out and see them standing there they may smell a rat, so we've no time to lose. Here we are; give me a leg up.' A jump and a heave and he was on the window-sill, reaching down for Algy, and a second later they were both standing inside the room breathing heavily from their exertion.

'Now listen,' said Biggles quietly. 'I've got a Bristol standing on the tarmac. You're going to fly it back; but you've got to take a passenger.'

'You mean—you?'

'No.'

'Who?'

'Brunow, the real Brunow. He turned up to-day.'

Algy's eyes opened wide. 'My gosh!' he breathed, 'where is he now?'

'Here.' Biggles stooped down and dragged the still unconscious man from under the bed. 'I'm afraid I socked him on the head rather hard,' he observed, 'but he asked for it. Get him to the M.O.* as soon as you can when you get back; don't for goodness' sake let him escape. Now do exactly what I tell you to,' he

* Medical Officer.

403

went on as he ripped off his German tunic. 'Slip this on—make haste, never mind your own tunic. If we meet any one look as much like a Hun as you can. Don't speak. I'm going to put on my overalls, but I shall be recognized so it doesn't matter much about me. Got that clear?'

'Absolutely.'

'Come on then, bear a hand; we've got to get Brunow down to the Bristol. If we are spotted I'll try to bluff that there has been an accident, but if there is an alarm follow me. I shall leave Brunow and make a dash for the machine. I'll take the pilot's seat; you get to the prop and swing it. When she starts get in as fast as you can; it would be our only chance. Are you ready?'

'Quite.'

'Then off we go. Steady—don't drop the blighter through the window, we don't want to break his neck.' Biggles looked outside, but all was silent, so between them they got the limp figure to the ground and set off at a clumsy trot towards the hangar where the British machines were housed. They reached it without seeing a soul, and to Biggles' infinite relief he saw that the Bristol was still standing as he had left it. 'We're going to have a job to get him into the cockpit,' he muttered. 'Just a minute—let me get up first.' He climbed up into the back seat, and reaching down, took Brunow by the shoulders. 'It's a good thing you got shot down to-day after all,' he panted. 'I should never have managed this job alone. He's heavier than I thought—go on—push.

Between them they got the unconscious man into the back seat and fastened the safety-belt tightly round him. 'That's fine,' muttered Biggles with satisfaction. 'If he happens to come round while you're in the air,

404

he'll think he's dead and on the way to the place where he ought to be,' he grinned. 'Go on—in you get.'

Algy climbed into the pilot's seat while Biggles ran round to the propeller.

'Hold hard, what are you going to do?' cried Algy in sudden alarm.

'That's all right, off you go.'

'And leave you here? Not on your life.'

'Don't sit there arguing, you fool; some one will come along presently. Do as you're told.'

'Not me—not until you tell me how you're going to get back.'

'I shall probably follow you in the Pup.'

'Where is it?'

'In the hangar.'

'Can you start it alone?'

'Yes, I shall probably take straight off out of the hangar.'

'Why not get it started while I'm here?'

'I'll give you a thick ear if you don't push off,' snarled Biggles. 'I shall be all right, I tell you.'

Algy looked doubtful. 'I don't like leaving you; why not dump Brunow and let's fly back together?' he suggested.

'Because when I start on a job I like to finish it,' snapped Biggles.

'What do you mean?'

'Von Stalhein—now will you go?'

'But why—?'

'I'll shoot you if you don't start that blooming engine,' grated Biggles.

Algy saw that Biggles was in no mood to be trifled with. 'All right,' he said shortly. 'Switches off!'

'Switch off!'

'Suck in!'

'Suck in.'

Biggles pulled the big propeller round several times and then balanced it on contact. 'Contact!' he called.

'Contact!' Biggles balanced himself on the ball of his right foot and swung the blade of the propeller down. With a roar that sounded like the end of the world, the Rolls Royce engine came to life and shattered the silence with its powerful bellow.

For a minute or two Algy sat waiting for it to warm up and then looked round to wave good-bye; but Biggles had disappeared. Slowly he pushed the throttle open and the Bristol began to move over the darkened aerodrome, slowly at first but with ever increasing speed. Its tail lifted and it roared upwards into the night sky.

II

Biggles watched the Bristol take off from the inside of the hangar into which he had run for cover when the engine started. He knew that by allowing Algy to take the Bristol he had burnt his boats behind him as far as staying at Zabala was concerned, for when the prisoner was missed, and the N.C.O. in charge of the guard explained—as he was bound to—how the Engländer had been taken by Leutnant 'Brunow' to Hauptmann von Stalhein for interview, the fat would be in the fire with a vengeance. No, Zabala was finished for ever, and he knew it; all that remained for him to do was to follow the Bristol as quickly as possible into the security of the British lines.

Two methods of achieving this presented themselves, and the first was—or appeared to be—comparatively simple. It was merely to pull out the Pup, now standing in the hangar, start it up, and take off. The other made

406

a far greater appeal to him, but it was audacious in its conception and would require nerve to bring off. Curiously enough, it was while he was still weighing up the pros and cons that his mind was made up for him in no uncertain manner. It began when he walked to the back of the hangar and struck a match to see if the Pup was still in its usual position. It was, but he was staggered to see that its engine had been taken out, presumably for overhaul, and while he had not made up his mind to use the machine except in case of emergency, it gave him a shock to discover that his only safe method of escape from Zabala was effectually barred. He could have kicked himself for not finding it out earlier, for he might have based his plans on the understanding that the Pup would be airworthy. 'My word! I should have been in a bonny mess if I'd wanted it in a hurry,' he thought, and then dodged behind the wide canvas door-flap as he heard soft footsteps on the sand near at hand.

Peeping out, he saw the station *Vize-feldwebel**, who acted in the capacity of Adjutant**, standing on the tarmac looking about with a puzzled air. From his manner it was clear that he had heard the British machine take off and had hurried down to see what was going on, and Biggles blamed himself for leaving things so late, for the arrival of the *Feldwebel* was something that he had not bargained for; and he had still greater cause to regret the delay when a minute or two later the Adjutant was joined by von Stalhein. He was in a state of undress with a dressing-gown thrown over his shoulders; he, too, had evidently heard the Bristol take off and had hurried along to ascertain the cause.

---

* German: Sergeant Major.
** An officer specially appointed to assist the commanding officer.

He said something that Biggles did not catch to the *Feldwebel*, who went off at the double and presently returned with the Sergeant of the Flight responsible for the upkeep of the British machines — the same man to whom Biggles had given instructions regarding the preparation of the Bristol. A crisp conversation ensued, but it was carried on too quickly for Biggles to follow it, although by the mention of his name more than once, and the sergeant's actions, he guessed that the N.C.O. was explaining the reason why Leutnant Brunow was flying.

To Biggles' horror they all came into the hangar. The light was switched on, but they did not stay very long, for after von Stalhein had satisfied himself that the Bristol had actually gone, he went off and the others followed soon afterwards.

Biggles lingered no longer; the discovery of the dismantled Pup left him no choice of action, and he knew that he was faced with one of the most desperate adventures of his career, one that would either see him successful in his quest, or — but he preferred not to think of the alternative.

He was curiously calm as he stepped out of his hiding-place and set off in long swinging strides towards the far side of the aerodrome. As he walked he hummed the tune *Deutschland Über Alles* which he had often heard sung in the Mess, for the desert was forbidding in its deathly silence, and the very atmosphere seemed to be peopled by the spirits of a long-forgotten past. 'Gosh! This place gives me the creeps,' he muttered once as he stopped to get his bearings from the distant lights of Zabala, to make sure he was keeping in the right direction. 'Give me France every time.' He was far too much of a realist to be impressed by the historical associations of the ground over which he walked, land which had once been trodden by Xenophon, at the head of his gallant ten thousand, Alexander the Great, Roman generals, and Crusaders at the head of their armed hosts, but he was conscious of the vague depression that is so often the result of contact with remote antiquity. 'I don't wonder that people who get lost in the desert go dotty,' he said quietly to himself, as he quickened his pace.

He passed the bush behind which he had lain hidden on the night when he had first seen von Stalhein disguised as an Arab, and gave a little muttered exclamation of satisfaction when he saw a Halberstadt standing just where he expected to find it. Its pilot had not seen him, for he had his back towards him as he turned the propeller in the act of starting the engine. Biggles waited till the engine was ticking over and the pilot had taken his place in the front seat; then he walked up quickly, put his foot in the fuselage stirrup, swung himself up beside the pilot and tapped him on the shoulder. 'The Count wants you urgently,' he said in his best German.

'What?' exclaimed the startled pilot.

'The Count wants you,' repeated Biggles. 'There is a change of plans. I have been sent out to relieve you. Hurry up.'

'But I have been—'

'I know,' interrupted Biggles desperately, for he was afraid that von Stalhein might turn up at any moment. 'You are to go back at once. I am to fly to-night.'

To his unutterable relief the man, a rather surly fellow named Greichbach, whom he had spoken to once or twice in the Mess, made no further demur, but climbed out of his seat and stood beside the self-appointed pilot.

'What is the course to-night?' asked Biggles carelessly. 'They told me, but I had no time to write it down; I think I remember but I'd like to confirm it.'

'Jebel Hind—Galada—Wadi Baroud—Pauta,' replied the other without hesitation.

'Where do you usually land?'

'You may not have to land, but you will know in the air about that.'

'Thanks. You'd better get back now. Don't go straight across the aerodrome, though, in case I run into you taking off; go round by the boundary,' Biggles told him, and a grim smile played about the corners of his mouth as he watched the German set off in the desired direction. At the same time he released his grip on the butt of his Mauser, for the moment had been an anxious one. If was fortunate for Greichbach that he had not questioned the instructions, for Biggles had determined to have the Halberstadt even if he had to take it by force. He saw the figure of the German disappear into the darkness, still taking the course he had suggested, for the last thing he wanted to happen was for Greichbach to meet von Stalhein on the way out.

He buckled on his flying cap, pulled his goggles low over his face, removed the spare joystick from the back seat, took his place in the front cockpit, and waited. The seconds ticked by. Minutes passed and he began to feel uncomfortable, worried by the fear that Greichbach might get back to the station before von Stalhein left; but his muscles tightened with a jerk as a tall figure in Arab costume suddenly loomed up in the darkness close at hand, and without saying a word swung up into the rear cockpit.

Biggles felt a light tap on the shoulder; the word 'Go' came faintly to his ears above the noise of the engine. With a curious smile on his set face he eased the throttle

410

open and held the stick forward. The Mercedes engine roared; the Halberstadt skimmed lightly over the sand and then soared upwards in a steep climbing turn.

Biggles saw the lights of the camp below him, and knew that whatever happened he was looking at them for the last time. Then he turned in a wide circle and, climbing slowly for height, headed for the lines.

Chapter 20
The Night Riders

I

For twenty minutes he flew on a straight course for Jebel Hind, the first landmark mentioned by Greichbach, crouching well forward in the cockpit and taking care not to turn his head to left or right, which might give von Stalhein a view of his profile. At first he could not dismiss from his mind the fear that the German would speak to him or make some move that would require an explanation, in which case exposure would be inevitable, and he wondered vaguely what von Stalhein would do about it.

As usual in two-seater aeroplanes, the pilot occupied the front seat and the observer the back one, and in this case the two cockpits were not more than a couple of feet apart. Biggles would have felt happier if the German had been in the front seat, for then he could have watched him; it was unnerving to know that an enemy whom he could not see was sitting within a couple of feet of him; but, on the other hand, he realized that if von Stalhein had been in the front seat and had happened to turn round, he would have seen him at once and discovered that a change of pilots had taken place.

'Suppose he does discover who I am, what can he do about it?' thought Biggles. 'Nothing, as far as I can see. If he hits me over the back of the head, the machine will fall and we shall both go west together, for he couldn't possibly get into my seat and take over the controls without first throwing me out; and he wouldn't have time to do that before we crashed. He'd be crazy to start a free fight in an aeroplane, anyway. The next thing is, what am *I* going to do? If he tells me to go down and land I should be able to handle the situation all right provided there isn't a party of Huns or Hun-minded Arabs waiting for him. But suppose he says nothing about landing? He'll want to know what's up if I try to land on my own account. It's no use pretending that the engine has failed, because as soon as I throttle back he'll know it by the movement of his own throttle lever. If I cut the switch and lose the engine altogether, we should probably crash trying to land, in which case I stand a better chance than he does of getting hurt. Well, we shall see.'

The lifeless rocky country around Jebel Hind loomed up ahead, and the machine bumped once or twice as the change in the terrain affected the atmosphere. The mountains of rock, heated nearly to furnace heat by the sun during the day, were not yet cool, and were throwing up columns of hot air. Cooler air from the desert was rushing in to fill the partial vacuum thus caused, and the result was vertical currents of considerable velocity.

Overcoming an almost irresistible desire to look back and see what von Stalhein was doing, he concentrated on correcting the bumps, which now became more frequent as the country below grew more rugged. A solitary searchlight stabbed a tapering finger of white light into the starry sky some little distance ahead, and he knew he was approaching the British lines. Jagged flashes of orange and crimson flame began to appear around him, showing that the anti-aircraft batteries were aware of his presence; but the searchlight had failed to pick him up and the shooting was poor, so he roared on through the night until he reached the village of Galada, when he turned sharply to the right and continued on a course that would bring him to the Wadi Baroud, which, according to Greichbach, was the next landmark.

They were flying over desert country again now, a flat expanse of wilderness surrounded on all sides by hills on which twinkled the many camp fires of troops who were being concentrated in preparation for the coming battle. 'A sort of place he might ask me to land,' thought Biggles, correcting an unusually bad bump, but the expected tap on the shoulder did not come and he roared on through the star-lit sky.

He seemed to have been flying for a long time; the cockpit was warm and cosy and his fear of the man in the back seat began to give way to lassitude. 'It's about time he was doing something,' he thought drowsily, wondering what the outcome of the whole thing would be. Strange thoughts began to drift into his mind. 'Winged chariots! Some one on the ground down there had said something about winged chariots three thousand years ago. Or was it later?' He couldn't remember, so he dismissed the matter as of no consequence, and then pulled himself up with a jerk, for he realized with a shock that he had been on the point of dozing.

The edge of the moon crept up above the rim of the desert; from his elevated position he could see it, but he knew that it was still invisible to people on the ground, which remained a vast well of mysterious darkness, broken only by vague, still darker shadows which marked the position of hills and valleys. Still he flew on, heading towards Pauta, his next landmark, which still lay some distance to the west.

Then, far ahead over his port wing appeared a little

414

cluster of yellow lights that he knew was the British aerodrome of Kantara; he thought for a moment, and then eased the nose of the machine a trifle towards it. Would von Stalhein notice the move and call attention to it? No, apparently not, for nothing happened. Again he touched the rudder-bar lightly and brought his nose in a straight line with the aerodrome, and almost started as a new thought flashed into his mind. 'What could he do if I decided to land there,' he mused, quivering at the idea. 'Nothing. I don't see that he could do a thing; at least, not until we were actually on the ground. Then he'd probably try to pull a gun on me, jump into the pilot's seat and escape. Well, I can act as quickly as he can,' he thought. The more he toyed with the plan the more it appealed to him. It would end the whole business one way or the other right away. To march the German up to Major Raymond's tent would be a fitting end to his adventures. Von Stalhein's plans, whatever they were, would not — could not — materialize then. But whatever he did would have to be done quickly. 'The moment I start to glide down he'll know something's wrong, and he'll be on his feet in a jiffy,' he thought. 'And then anything can happen. No! When I go down I'll go so fast that he won't be able to speak, move, or do anything else except hang on. Maybe he'll think that something has broken and we're falling out of control; so much the better if he does.'

Tingling with excitement, he held on to his course, watching the aerodrome lights creeping slowly nearer. They were nearly under the leading edge of his port wing now — still nearer they crept — nearer. Suddenly they disappeared from sight and he knew he was over the middle of the aerodrome. A glance at the luminous altimeter showed the needle resting on the five-thousand-feet mark. It was now or never. 'Well, come on,' he muttered aloud, and did several things simultaneously. With his left hand he cut the throttle; his left foot kicked the rudder-bar, while with his right hand he flung the joystick over to the left and then dragged it back into his right thigh.

To any one in the back seat, experienced or otherwise, the result would have been terrifying—as indeed he intended it to be. The machine lurched drunkenly as it quivered in a stall; its nose flopped over heavily, swung down, and then plunged earthward in a vicious spin. With his eyes glued on the whirling cluster of lights below, Biggles counted the revolutions dispassionately. When he reached number five he shoved the stick forward, kicked on top rudder, and then spun in the opposite direction. At what he judged to be trifle less than a thousand feet he pulled out of the spin, and then pushed his left wing down in a vertical side-slip. A blast of air struck him on the side of the face, while struts and wires howled in protest—but still the machine dropped like a stone.

Only at the last moment did he level out, make a swift S turn and glide in to a fast wheel landing. As his wheels touched the ground he flicked off the ignition switch with a sharp movement of his left hand while with his right he felt for the Mauser. The tail-skid dropped, dragged a few yards, and the machine stopped. Biggles made a flying leap at the ground, revolver in hand.

'Stick up your hands, von Stalhein,' he snapped.

There was no reply.

'Come on, stick 'em up; I've got you covered. One false move and it's your last—I mean it.'

Still no reply.

Biggles stooped low so that he could see the silhouette of the cockpit against the sky, but he could not see the German. 'Come on, look lively,' he snarled. 'It's no use crouching down there on the floor. In five seconds I shall start shooting.'

Still no reply.

Biggles felt a thrill of doubt run through him. Had von Stalhein jumped out, too? He dodged round to the far side of the machine and looked around; he could see a hundred yards in all directions, but there was no one in sight. With his revolver ready, he put his foot in the fuselage stirrup and stood up so that he could see inside the back cockpit. One glance was enough. It was empty.

He put the gun back into his pocket and leaned weakly against the trailing edge of the lower wing. 'I'm mad,' he muttered, 'daft—dreaming. I've got sun-stroke—that's what it is.' He closed his eyes, shook his head violently, and then opened them again. 'No, it isn't a dream,' he went on, as he saw mechanics racing towards the spot. The reaction after the terrific strain of the last few minutes, when every nerve had been keyed up to breaking-point, was almost overwhelming. The unexpected anti-climax nearly upset his mental balance. He threw back his head and laughed aloud.

'Hands up, there, Jerry!' yelled the leading mechanic as he ran up.

'What are you getting excited about?' snarled Biggles.

The shock to the unfortunate ack emma* when he heard a normal English voice was nearly as great as Biggles' had been a few moments before. He stared at the pilot, then at the machine, and then back at Biggles.

A flight-sergeant pushed his way to the front of the

* Slang: Aircraft Mechanic.

417

rapidly forming group of spectators. 'What's all this?' he growled.

'It's all right; I've brought you a souvenir, flight-sergeant,' grinned Biggles, indicating the machine with a nod. 'You can take it, you can keep it, and you can jolly well stick it up your tunic as far as I'm concerned. And I hope it bites you,' he added bitterly, as he realized that his well-laid plans, carried out at frightful risk, had come to naught.

, 'Any one else in that machine?' asked the flight-sergeant suspiciously.

'Take a look and see,' invited Biggles. 'As a matter of fact there is, but I can't find him. Just see if you can do any better.'

The flight-sergeant made a swift examination of the Halberstadt. 'No, sir, there's nobody here,' he said.

'That's what I thought,' murmured Biggles slowly.

The flight-sergeant eyed him oddly, and then looked relieved when a number of officers, who had heard the machine land, ran up and relieved him of any further responsibility in the matter. Major Raymond was amongst them, and Biggles took him gently by the arm. 'Better get the machine in a hangar out of the way, sir,' he said. 'If people start asking questions I shall tell them that I'm a delivery pilot taking a captured machine down to the repair depot, but I lost my way and had to make a night landing. I'll wait for you in your tent. Is Algy back?'

'Yes; he was in the Mess having his dinner when I came out. He said something about not letting stray Huns interfere with his meals.'

'He wouldn't,' replied Biggles bitterly. 'Has he told you—'

'Yes, he's told me all about it.'

'And Brunow?'

418

The Major nodded. 'Yes, we've got him where he can do no harm. You'd better trot along to the Mess and get something to eat, and then come and see me in my tent.'

'Right you are, sir.' Biggles started off in the direction of the distant Officers' Mess.

II

An hour later he reclined in a long cane chair in Major Raymond's tent. The Major sat at his desk with his chin resting in the palms of his hands; Algy sat on the other side of him, listening.

'Well, there it is,' Biggles was saying. 'I think it was, without exception, the biggest shock I have ever had in my life—and I've had some, as you know. It was also the biggest disappointment. I'll tell you straight, sir. I could have burst into tears when I landed and found he wasn't there. I couldn't believe it, and that's a fact. When I think of all the trouble I went to, and risks I took—but there, what's the use of moaning about it? I only hope he broke his blinking neck on a perishing boulder when he hit the floor.'

'How do you mean?'

'Well, there's no doubt about what he did. When he was over the place where he wanted to get to he just stepped over the side with a parachute; there's no other solution that I can think of—unless, of course, he suddenly got tired of life and took a running jump into space. Or he may have decided to go for a stroll, forgetting where he was, but knowing von Stalhein pretty well I should say that's hardly likely. No! the cunning blighter stepped over with a brolley, and I can guess where it happened. I remember an extra bad bump. And for all I know he's been getting into our lines like

419

that all the time. After all, it's no more risky than landing in an aeroplane in a rough country like this. The point is he's still alive and kicking, and from my point of view, the sooner he makes his last kick the better. He's not a man; he's a rattlesnake. He's somewhere over this side of the lines floating about in his Ali Baba outfit. How are we going to find him?—that's what I want to know. By the way, Algy, how did you get on with Brunow?'

'Right as rain, no trouble at all. I flew straight back and landed here. I dumped him in my room with a sentry on guard, slipped an overcoat over my Hun uniform, and reported to the Major. Brunow came round just as I got back and took off my coat. He started bleating a prayer of thanksgiving when he saw my uniform, and then told me in no uncertain terms just what sort of swine the British were and what he thought of you in particular. He asked me if you'd been arrested yet, and if so, when were you to be shot.'

'Go on,' put in Biggles interestedly. 'What did you tell him?'

'I just broke the news gently, and told him he'd got things all wrong. He wouldn't believe it at first, and I had to explain that since the last time he was awake he'd been on a long, long journey, and was now nicely settled in the hands of the British swines.'

'What did he say to that?'

'He didn't say anything; he just went all to pieces. Now he's trying to pretend that he didn't mean it.'

'Where is he now?'

'In the Kantara prison camp, in solitary confinement,' put in the Major.

'What are you going to do with him, sir?'

'He'll be tried by General Court Martial, of course.

But what about this fellow von Stalhein? That's far more important.'

'I was coming to that,' answered Biggles slowly. 'I think we can lay him by the heels, but I shall want some help.'

'What sort of help?'

'Personal assistance from somebody who knows the country well—and the Arabs; Major Sterne for instance.'

Major Raymond looked serious. 'He's a difficult fellow to get hold of,' he said. 'He's all over the place, and we seldom know just where he is. Won't any one else do?'

'I'd prefer Sterne. It's only right that as he caught El Shereef, he should have a hand in the affair. Surely if you sent out an SOS amongst the Arabs it would reach his ears and he'd come in.'

'He might. He doesn't like being interfered with when he's on a job, but if the matter was exceptionally serious he might take it the right way. Just what do you suggest?'

'I suggest that a message be sent out that his presence is urgently required at General Headquarters in connexion with plans for the British advance, so will he please report as quickly as possible. That should bring him in.'

'But good gracious, man, the General would never consent to that.'

'Why not? He more than any one else should be glad to lay a dangerous fellow like von Stalhein by the heels.'

'And suppose I can arrange it: where would you like to see Sterne?'

'At General Headquarters, if possible; it would save him coming here. If you'll get the message out I'll go

to headquarters with Lacey and wait until he comes.
Perhaps you'd like to come along too?'

'The General isn't going to be pleased if you waste
his time.'

'I shan't be pleased if I waste my own, if it comes
to that,' observed Biggles coolly. 'I've been risking my
neck, so he can hardly object to giving up a few minutes
of his time. All right, sir, let's start moving.'

Chapter 21
Sterne Takes a Hand

The pearly glow of a new day spread slowly over the eastern sky; it threw a cold grey light over the inhospitable wilderness, and intensified the whiteness of a house that stood on the outskirts of the village of Jebel Zaloud, a house that once had been the residence of the merchant Ali Ben Sadoum, but was now the air Headquarters of the British Expeditionary Force in Palestine.

A wan beam crept through the unglazed window of a room on the ground floor, and awoke two officers who were sleeping uncomfortably in deck chairs. Biggles started, blinked, and then sprang to his feet as he observed the daylight. 'Looks as if he isn't coming, Algy,' he said crisply. 'It's getting light.'

Algy rubbed his eyes, yawned, and stood up, stretching. 'You're right,' he said. 'In which case we shall have to try to find the wily Erich ourselves, I suppose.'

'Yes; it's a pity though,' muttered Biggles thoughtfully, rubbing his chin. 'I hoped we should save ourselves a lot of trouble.' He yawned. 'We must have dropped off to sleep soon after midnight. Well, well, it can't be helped, but I expect the General will be peeved if he's been waiting about all night.'

'He wasn't going to bed anyway,' Algy told him. 'I heard the Brigade-Major say that the General would be up most of the night working on important dispatches. Where is Raymond do you suppose?'

'Up in the General's room, I imagine—he was last night.'

'Gosh! he'll be sick if we let the General down.'

'I expect he will; as I said before, it's a pity, but it can't be helped. I've acted as I thought best.'

There was a tap on the door and an orderly appeared. 'The General wishes to see you in his room immediately,' he said.

Biggles grimaced. 'This is where we get our ears twisted,' he muttered ruefully, as he followed the orderly to a large apartment on the first floor.

The General looked up wearily from his desk as they entered. Several Staff officers and Major Raymond were there, and they regarded the two airmen with disapproval plainly written on their faces.

'Which of you is Bigglesworth?' began the General.

Biggles stepped forward. 'I am, sir,' he said.

'Will you have the goodness to explain what all this means? Major Raymond has told me of the excellent work you have done since you have been in Palestine, and in view of that I am prepared to take a broad view, but I am very tired, and this business all seems very pointless.'

Biggles looked uncomfortable. 'I agree, sir, it does,' he admitted; 'but I had hoped to prove that my unusual request was justified.'

'I believe it was on your intervention that stay of execution was granted in the death sentence promulgated in connexion with Sheikh Haroun Ibn Said, otherwise the spy, El Shereef. Frankly, Bigglesworth, we are prepared to give officers sent out here on special detached duty from the Air Board a lot of rope, but there is a limit as to how far we can allow them to interfere with ordinary service routine.'

424

'Quite, sir. I hope to repay you for your consideration.'

'How?'

'By saving you from the mental discomfort you would surely have suffered when you discovered that you had shot an innocent man, sir.'

'Innocent man! What are you talking about?'

'The Sheikh Haroun Ibn Said is not El Shereef, sir.' Biggles spoke quietly but firmly.

'Good heavens, man, what do you mean?'

'What I say, sir. The whole thing was a frame-up— if I may use an American expression. Sheikh Haroun is what he has always claimed to be—a good friend of the British. By causing him to be arrested and—as they hoped—shot as a spy, the German agent who handled the job hoped to achieve two ends. To remove a powerful Sheikh who was sincerely loyal to British arms, and at the same time lull you into a sense of false security by leading you to believe that you had at last put an end to the notorious activities of the spy, El Shereef. Sheikh Haroun Ibn Said, in his ignorance of western matters, was easily induced to wear a German Secret Service ring, and carry on his person incriminating documents without having the slightest idea of what they meant. In short, he was induced to adopt the personality of El Shereef.'

The General's face was grim. 'By whom?' he snapped.

'By El Shereef, sir,' said Biggles simply.

The General started and a look of understanding dawned in his eyes. Silence fell on the room. What Biggles had just told him might not have occurred to him, but its dreadful possibilities were now only too apparent. 'Good God!' he breathed. 'Are you sure of this?'

'I am, sir.'

'So El Shereef is still at large.'

'He is, sir.'

'Who is the man whom you flew into the British lines last night—Major Raymond has told me about it—this Hauptmann Erich von Stalhein. Has he any connexion with El Shereef?'

'He has, sir.'

'What is it?'

'He's the same man, sir—El Shereef.'

Another silence fell. The General sat staring like a man hypnotized, and so did his staff for that matter, although one or two of them looked incredulous.

'Why did you not tell me this before?' asked the General harshly. There was reproach and anger in his voice.

'Because there was a thing that I valued above all others at stake, sir,' replied Biggles firmly. 'For that reason I told nobody what I had discovered.'

'And what was that?'

'My life, sir. I do not mean to be disrespectful, but German agents have ears in the very highest places— even in your headquarters, sir.'

The General frowned. 'I find it hard to believe that,' he said. 'Still, this story of yours puts a very different complexion on things. Von Stalhein, alias El Shereef, is still at large, and you want Sterne to help you run him to earth—is that it?'

'That is correct, sir.'

'I see. I sent out a general call for him last night, but it begins to look as if he isn't coming. If he does come, I'll let you know.'

There was a sharp rap on the door, and the duty Staff sergeant entered. 'Major Sterne is here, sir,' he said.

426

'Ask him to come up here at once,' ordered the General. 'I'll speak to him first and tell him what is proposed,' he added quickly, turning to Biggles.

'Thank you, sir.' Biggles, after a nod to Algy, stepped back against the far wall.

The next moment he was watching with a kind of fascinated interest a man who had swept into the room, for he knew he was looking at one of the most talked-of men in the Middle East, a man whose knowledge of native law was proverbial and who could disguise himself to deceive even the Arabs themselves. Even now he was dressed in flowing Arab robes, but he clicked his heels and raised his hand in the military salute.

'Hello, Sterne, here you are then,' began the General, as he reached over his desk and shook hands. 'You got my message?'

'Yes, sir,' replied the other briskly. 'I was anxious to know what it was about.'

'It's about this confounded fellow, El Shereef,' continued the General. 'It seems that there has been some mistake; the fellow you brought in was not El Shereef at all.'

Biggles stepped forward quietly.

'Not El Shereef!' cried Sterne. 'What nonsense! If *he* isn't El Shereef, then who is?'

'You are, I think,' said Biggles quietly. 'Don't move—von Stalhein.'

The man who had been known as Major Sterne spun round on his heel and looked into the muzzle of Biggles' revolver. He lifted eyes that were glittering with hate to Biggles' face. 'Ah,' he said softly, and then again, 'Ah. So I was right.'

'You were,' said Biggles shortly, 'and so was I.'

Von Stalhein slowly raised his hands. As they drew level with the top of his burnous, he tore the garment off with a swift movement and hurled it straight into Biggles' face. At the same time he leapt for the door. Algy barred his way, but he turned like a hare and sprang at the window with Algy at his heels. For a second pandemonium reigned.

Biggles dared not risk shooting for fear of hitting Algy or the Staff officers who tried to intercept the German; but they were too late. Biggles saw a flash of white as von Stalhein went through the window like a bird. He did not attempt to follow, but dashed through the door, shouting for the headquarter's guard. 'Outside, outside,' he shouted furiously, as they came running up the stairs. He dashed past them, raced to the door, and looked out. An Arab, bent double over a magnificent horse, was streaking through the village street. Before Biggles could raise his weapon horse and rider had disappeared round the corner of the road that led to Kantara.

'Get my car, get my car,' roared the General. 'Baines! Baines! Where the devil are you? Confound the man, he's never here when he's wanted.'

'Here, sir.' The chauffeur, very red about the ears, for he had been snatching a surreptitious cup of tea with the cook, started the big Crossley tourer and took his place at the wheel.

The General jumped in beside him, and the others squeezed into the back seats. There was not room for Algy, but determined not to be left behind, he flung himself on the running board.

'Faster, man, faster,' cried the General, as they tore through the village with Arabs, mangy dogs, scraggy fowls, and stray donkeys missing death by inches. The car, swaying under its heavy load, dry-skidded round the corner where von Stalhein had last been seen, and the open road lay before them.

A mile away the tents of Kantara gleamed pink and gold in the rays of the rising sun; two hundred yards this side of them von Stalhein was flogging his horse unmercifully, as, crouching low in the saddle, he sped like an arrow towards the hangars.

'He'll beat us,' fumed the General. 'He'll take one of those machines just starting up.'

It was apparent that such was von Stalhein's intention. Several machines of different types were standing on the tarmac; the propeller of one of them, a Bristol Fighter, was flashing in the sunlight, warming up the engine while its pilot and observer finished their cigarettes outside the Mess some thirty or forty yards away.

Von Stalhein swerved like a greyhound towards the machine. The pilot and observer watched his unusual actions in astonishment; they made no attempt to stop him.

At a distance of ten yards von Stalhein pulled up with a jerk that threw the horse on to its haunches; in a twinkling of an eye he had pulled away the chocks from under the wheels and had taken a flying leap into the cockpit. The engine roared and the Bristol began to move over the ground.

'We've lost him,' cried the General. Then, as an afterthought, he added, 'Stop at the archie battery, Baines.'

The usual protective anti-aircraft battery was only a hundred yards down the road, the muzzles of its four guns pointing into the air like chimneys set awry as the crews sleepily sipped their early morning tea. But the arrival of the General's car brought them to their feet with a rush. A startled subaltern ran forward and saluted.

'Get that machine,' snapped the General, pointing at the Bristol that was now a thousand feet in the air and climbing swiftly towards the German lines. 'Get it and I'll promote you to Captain in to-night's orders.'

The lieutenant asked no questions; he shouted an order and dashed to the range-finder. Mess tins were flung aside as the gunners leapt to their stations, and within five seconds the first gun had roared its brass-coated shell at the British machine. It went wide. The officer corrected the aim, and a second shot was nearer. Another correction, and a shell burst fifty yards in front of the two-seater. Another word of command, and the four guns began firing salvoes as fast as the gunners could feed them.

Tiny sparks of yellow flame, followed by mushrooming clouds of white smoke, appeared round the Bristol, the pilot of which began to swerve from side to side as he realized his danger.

Biggles was torn between desire to watch the frantic but methodical activity of the gunners—for he had seldom stood at the starting end of archie—and the machine, but he could not tear his eyes away from the swerving two-seater; knowing from bitter experience just what von Stalhein was going through, he felt almost sorry for him. A shell burst almost under the fuselage and the machine rocked.

'He's hit,' cried the General excitedly.

'No, sir, it was only the bump of the explosion, I think,' declared Biggles.

Another shell burst almost between the wings of the Bristol, and its nose jerked up spasmodically.

'He's hit now, sir,' yelled Biggles, clutching Algy's arm.

A silence fell on the little group of watchers; the roar of the guns and the distant sullen *whoof—whoof—whoof* of the bursting shells died away as the Bristol lurched, recovered, lurched again, and then fell off on its wing

430

into a dizzy earthward plunge. Twice it tried to come out, as if the pilot was still alive and making desperate efforts to right his machine; then it disappeared behind a distant hill.

A hush of tense expectancy fell as every man held his breath and strained his ears for the sound that he knew would come.

It came. Clear-cut through the still morning air, far away over the German side of the lines, came the sound as if some one had jumped on a flimsy wooden box, crushing it flat: the sinister but unmistakable sound of an aeroplane hitting the ground.

Biggles drew a deep breath. 'Well,' he said slowly, 'that's that.'

Chapter 22
Biggles Explains

That evening a little party dined quietly in the Head-quarters Mess; it consisted of the General, his Aide-de-Camp, Major Raymond, Algy, and Biggles, who, over coffee, at the General's request, ran over the whole story.

'And so you see, sir,' he concluded, 'the unravelling of the skein was not so difficult as one might imagine.'

'But when did you first suspect that von Stalhein and El Shereef were one and the same?' asked the General.

'It's rather hard to say, sir,' replied Biggles slowly. 'I fancy the idea was at the back of my mind before I was really aware of it—if I can put it that way,' he continued. 'I felt from the very beginning that von Stalhein was more than he appeared to be on the sur-face.'

'Why did you think that?'

'Because he was so obviously suspicious—not only where I was concerned but with any stranger that came to the camp. "Why should he be?" I asked myself, and the only answer I could find was, because he had more to lose than any one else on the station. After all, a man is only suspicious when he has something to be suspicious about. Something was going on behind the scenes. What was it? When I saw him dressed as an Arab—well, that seemed to be the answer to the ques-tion.

'He never appeared in that garb in daylight, and I

432

am convinced that only a few people at Zabala knew what he was doing; he didn't want them to know; that's why he used to send the aeroplane to the far side of the aerodrome and slip out after dark when no one was about. The Count knew all about it, of course; he had to, and if you ask my opinion I should say that he wasn't too pleased about it—hence his attitude towards me.'

'But why should he feel like that?'

'Because he was secretly jealous of von Stalhein. He wanted all the kudos. Von Faubourg was vain and inefficient and it annoyed him to know that a subordinate had ten times the amount of brain that he had; he had sense enough to recognize that, you may be sure. And von Stalhein knew it too. He knew that nothing would please the Count more than to see him take down a peg. I will go as far as to say that I believe the Count was actually pleased when von Stalhein's plans went wrong. Take the business of the Australian troops, for example. Von Stalhein put that over to try to trap me; he merely wanted to see what I would do in such a case. When I got back and reported that the Australians were at Sidi Arish the Count was tickled to death because von Stalhein's scheme had failed; I could tell it by his manner. He was so pleased that he came round to my room to congratulate me. That showed me how things were between them, and I knew that I had a friend in the Count as long as I didn't tread on his toes; the more I upset von Stalhein—to a point—the better he was pleased.

'Take the business of when I dropped my ring near the waterworks. That was a careless blunder that might have cost me my life; even the Count couldn't overlook that, but he was quite pleased when I cleared myself for no other reason than that von Stalhein had told him that he had got me stone cold. If the Count had made the discovery it would have been quite a different matter. Von Stalhein sent Leffens out to watch me. Leffens was, I think, the one man he really trusted; he used to fly him over the lines until I killed him, and after that he used Mayer. He never knew what happened to Leffens, but he thought he did when he found one of his bullets in my machine. I've got a feeling that he tipped Leffens off to shoot me down if he got a chance, and that was why he daren't make much of a song when he found the bullet.

'I had already thought a lot about Sterne, who as far as I could make out was playing pretty much the same game for the British, and there were two things that put me on the right track there. First, the shadow on the tent, and secondly, the fact that some one—obviously in sympathy with the Germans—arranged my escape. Who could it be? Who had access to British posts? Mind you, sir, at that stage the association was nothing more than a bare possibility. I could hardly bring myself to believe that it might be remotely possible, but once the germ was in my mind it stayed there, and I was always on the look-out for a clue that might confirm it. That's why I went to von Stalhein's room. I hardly admitted it to myself but I knew I was hoping to find a British uniform—or something of the sort. As a matter of fact I did see a Sam Browne belt in the wardrobe, but I could hardly regard that as proof; it might easily have been nothing more than a souvenir. But then there was the British hat in Mayer's machine! It may sound easy to put two and two together now but it wasn't so easy then. Would you have believed me, sir, if I had come to you and said that Major Sterne was von Stalhein? I doubt it.

'Von Stalhein's scheme for the capture of El Shereef

434

was a clever piece of work, there's no denying that; it shook me to the marrow. At first it took me in, and I'll admit it. But he overreached himself. He made one little slip—took one risk, would perhaps be nearer the truth—and it gave the game away. Then I saw how simple the whole thing really was.'

'Do you mean when you went and saw Sheikh Haroun?' put in the Major.

'No, I got nothing out of him,' declared Biggles. 'He behaved just as one would expect a well-bred Arab to behave in such circumstances. He closed up like an oyster at the bare thought of the British suspecting him to be a traitor, and he would have died with his mouth shut if I hadn't butted in. No, it was what I saw in your tent that gave the game away.'

'What was it?'

'The ring. Those rings are few and far between. They daren't leave spare ones lying about: it would be too dangerous. Yet they knew that one of those rings found on the Sheikh would be sufficient evidence to hang him. There was only one available; it was Leffens', and I recognized it—as, indeed, I had every reason to. That set me thinking, and I reconstructed the crime—as the police say. Yet I had to act warily. One word and we shouldn't have seen von Stalhein—El Shereef—call him what you like—for dust and small pebbles.'

'But he sent you over to try to rescue El Shereef,' exclaimed the General. 'What was his idea in doing that?'

'It was simply another try-on; he wanted me to confirm that El Shereef had been arrested, and at the same time he hoped I'd make a boob. He had nothing to lose. Suppose I had managed to "rescue" El Shereef— or rather, Sheikh Haroun. The Huns would have asked for nothing more than to have had him in their hands.'

'Yes, of course, I quite see that. And by reporting that he had been shot you led him to think that we had been completely taken in.'

'Exactly, sir. I went on playing my own game, and as it happened it came off, although he made a clever move to get rid of me. He never trusted me; he was no fool; he was the only one of the lot of them who spotted that things started going wrong from the moment I arrived. It might have been coincidence, but von Stalhein didn't think so.'

'How do you mean?'

'Well, first of all the waterworks were blown up; then Leffens failed to return; then the Arab raid went wrong; then Hess got killed! Mayer crashes and gets his leg smashed—oh, no, sir, he wasn't going to believe this was just a run of bad luck. Something was radically wrong somewhere and he knew it. Whether it was anything to do with me or not, he would have felt happier if he could have got me out of the way. That's why he tried to get me pushed into the ground.'

'When?'

'The day I came over here to confirm that you had captured El Shereef.'

'What did he do?'

'He followed me over in the Pup—dressed as Major Sterne. He simply walked along the tarmac, told the flight-sergeant to put my machine in the shed and put another in its place—one which, of course, had no distinguishing mark on the top plane.'

'You assume he did that?'

'I assumed it at the time; I know it now.'

'How?'

'I've asked the flight-sergeant about it and he told me just what happened; he obeyed the Major's orders unquestioningly, as he was bound to. Then von Stalhein went back and sent out the Pfalz crowd to intercept me on the way home. It was clever, that, because if I had been shot no one would have been the wiser. I should just have disappeared, and that was all he wanted. But I knew things were rapidly coming to a head, and that's why I played a big stake to end it one way or the other; but all the same, I thought I'd bungled things badly when I landed here and found he wasn't in the back seat of that Halberstadt. I never even thought of his going over the side by parachute. After that there was one chance left, for if once a hue and cry had started we should never have seen him again, you may be sure of that. Von Stalhein had set plenty of traps, so I thought it was about time I set one, with what result you know.'

'And what do you propose to do now?' asked the General.

'I am going to submit an application to you, sir, to post me back to my old unit, number 266 Squadron in France, and I hope you will put it through, sir.'

The General looked hurt. 'I hoped you would stay out here,' he said. 'I could have found you a place on Headquarters Staff—both of you.'

'I'm sorry, sir—it's very kind of you—but—well, somehow I don't feel at home here. I would prefer to go back to France if you have no objection.'

'Very well, so be it. I can't refuse, and I need hardly say how grateful I am for what you have done during your tour of duty in the Middle East. The success of the British Army in Palestine may have rested on you alone. Naturally, I am forwarding a report on your work to the Air Board, and doubtless they will ask you to do the same. And now I must get back to my work— pray that you are never a General, Bigglesworth.'

'I should think that's the last thing I'm ever likely

to be, sir,' smiled Biggles. 'A Camel, blue skies, and plenty of Huns is the height of my ambition, and I hope to find them all in France. Good-bye, sir.'

'Good-bye—and good luck.' The General watched them go and then turned to his Aide-de-Camp. 'If we had a few more officers of that type the war would have been over long ago,' he observed.

BIGGLES
IN THE ORIENT

Chapter 1
Outward Bound

With the serene dignity of a monarch bestowing a favour, His Majesty's Flying-boat *Capricorn* kissed the turquoise water of the marine aircraft base at Calafrana, Malta, and in a surge of creamy foam came to rest by her mooring buoy, setting numerous smaller craft bobbing and curtsying in a gentle swell that was soon to die on the concrete slipways. Through the sparkling atmosphere of the Mediterranean dawn every detail of the rockbound coast stood revealed with a clarity unknown in northern isles.

In the cabin, Squadron Leader Bigglesworth, more commonly known to his friends (and, perhaps his enemies) as 'Biggles,' yawned as he stood up and reached for the haversack containing his small-kit that rested on the luggage rack above his seat.

'I've had a nice sleep,' he announced inconsequently, for the benefit of the several officers of his squadron who were pulling on shoes, fastening tunics, and the like, preparatory to disembarking.

It was the same little band of hard-hitting warriors that had fought under him during the Battle of Britain, in the Western Desert, and elsewhere, and more than one carried scars as perpetual souvenirs of these theatres of war. That none had been killed was, admittedly, a matter of wonder. There were some who ascribed this to astonishing good fortune; others, to leadership which combined caution with courage. Other reasons put forward were superb flying, straight shooting, and close co-operation—which is another way of saying that sort of comradeship which puts the team before self. The truth was probably to be found in a combination of all these attributes.

There were the three flight commanders: Algy Lacey, fair and freckled; Lord 'Bertie' Lissie, effeminate in face and manner, for ever polishing an eyeglass for no reason that anyone could discover; and Angus Mackail, twelve stone of brawn and brain, with heather in his brogue and an old regimental glengarry on his head. All wore the purple and white ribbon of the D.F.C.*

The rest were flying officers; like the flight-lieutenants they were all long overdue for promotion, but as this would have meant leaving the squadron (wherein there was no establishment for senior ranks, and consequently no chance of advancement) they had forgone promotion to remain in the same mess. There was 'Ginger' Hebblethwaite, a waif who had attached himself to Biggles and Algy before the war, and who had almost forgotten the slum in which he had been born; 'Tex' O'Hara, a product of the wide open spaces of Texas, U.S.A.; 'Taffy' Hughes, whose paternal ancestor may have been one of those Welsh knifemen that helped the Black Prince to make a name for valour; 'Tug' Carrington, a Cockney and proud of it, handy with his 'dukes,' hating all aggressors (and Nazis in particular) with a passion that sometimes startled the others; Henry Harcourt, a thin, pale, thoughtful-eyed Oxford undergraduate, who really loathed war yet had learned how to fight; and 'Ferocity' Ferris, who, born in a back street of Liverpool, had got his commission, not by accident (as he sometimes said) but by sheer flying ability.

* Distinguished Flying Cross.

442

This strange assortment of humanity, which could only have been drawn together by the vortex of war, formed Number 666 (Fighter) Squadron, R.A.F. More usually it was referred to in places where airmen meet as 'Biggles' Squadron.' And this was the literal truth, for on the formation of the unit, to Biggles had been sent—with his knowledge, of course—pilots of peculiar temperament, men with only two things in common, utter fearlessness and a disinclination to submit to discipline—two traits that often go together. Nevertheless, by example, by the force of his own personality, and by a strange sort of discipline which appeared to be lax, but was, in fact rigid, Biggles had moulded them into a team with a reputation that was as well known to the enemy as to the Air Ministry. The result was a third common factor—loyalty; loyalty to the service, to the team, and above all, to their leader.

'There's a cutter coming out, presumably to take us ashore,' observed Algy, from a seat that commanded a view of the port. 'Now we shall know what it's all about. I must confess to some curiosity as to the whys and wherefores of this sudden rush to Malta.'

'It isn't customary for an Air Commode* to turn out to meet new arrivals,' remarked Ginger. 'There's an Air Commodore in the stern of that cutter—I can see his scrambled eggs** from here.'

'Maybe it's a new regulation. Welcome to your new home, gentlemen, and all that sort of thing—if you see what I mean?' suggested Bertie, brightly.

A minute later the Air Commodore stepped aboard. He went straight to Biggles, who by this time was

* Slang: Air Commodore.
** Slang: those of the rank of Group Captains and above making reference to the gold braid on the service cap.

looking a trifle surprised at this unusual reception.

"Morning, Bigglesworth,' greeted the Air Commodore.

"Morning, sir,' answered Biggles.

'Everything all right?'

'Why not?' queried Biggles.

'Oh, I don't know,' returned the Air Commodore. 'The Higher Command seems to be particularly concerned about you. You'll find breakfast ready in the mess. Better not waste any time—you've only got an hour.'

The puzzled expression on Biggles' face deepened. 'An hour for what, sir?'

'To stretch your legs, I suppose.'

'But I don't quite understand,' murmured Biggles. 'I was ordered to bring my squadron here. Naturally, I assumed it was for duty on the island.'

'I don't know anything about that,' returned the Air Commodore. 'My orders—by signal received last night—were to give you breakfast and push you along to Alexandria. The aircraft leaves the water in an hour. My tender will take you ashore. You might as well leave your kit where it is.'

'Very good sir.'

The Air Commodore walked forward to speak to the pilot.

'Well, stiffen me rigid!' exclaimed Ginger softly. 'What do you make of that?'

Biggles shrugged. 'I don't make anything of it. We've got our orders. Alex it is, apparently. Let's go ashore for a shower and a rasher of bacon.'

Eight hours later the *Capricorn* touched down in the sweeping bay of Alexandria. Biggles stood up and reached for his haversack.

'Just a minute,' said Ginger. 'There's another brass-hat* in that cutter coming out from station head-quarters.'

Biggles looked through the window. 'You're right,' he confirmed. 'It looks as though the Near East is littered with Air Commodores. Unless I'm mistaken that's Buster Brownlow. He's a good scout. He commanded Ten Group in the Battle of Britain.'

The Air Commodore came aboard.

'Hello, Biggles!' he greeted. 'Get cracking—you've only got an hour.'

Biggles started. 'What, *again?*'

The Air Commodore raised his eyebrows. 'What do you mean—again?'

Biggles laughed shortly. 'Well, last night, out of the blue, I got an order instructing me to hand over my equipment and take the squadron by road to Pembroke Dock, where the *Capricorn* was waiting to take us to Malta. We made our landfall at dawn, after a comfortable trip. The A.O.C., Malta, pushed us along here. Now you're telling us—'

'That you're not stopping. Quite right. There's a Wimpey** on the tarmac waiting to take you to Baghdad, so you'd better get ashore.'

'Do you happen to know what this is all about?' questioned Biggles curiously.

'I know no more than you,' answered the Air Commodore, and returned to the motor-boat.

'Join the Air Force and see the world,' murmured Ferocity Ferris, with bitter sarcasm.

'That's it. The service is living up to its jolly old reputation, what?' remarked Bertie.

---

* Slang: a staff officer, also referring to the gold braid on his service cap.
** A Wellington—Twin engine heavy bomber made by Vickers.

The sun was setting behind the golden domes of Khadamain, the most conspicuous landmark in the ancient city of the Caliphs, when the Wellington rumbled to a stand-still on the dusty surface of Hinaidi airfield, Baghdad.

Biggles stood up. 'Now maybe we shall get the gen* on this circus,' he asserted.

The cabin door was opened and an officer wearing the badges of rank of a Group Captain looked in. 'Get weaving, you fellows,' he called breezily. 'A head wind has put you ten minutes behind schedule. You're moving off in fifty minutes. Leave your kit where it is and stride along to the mess for dinner.'

Biggles frowned. 'What is this—a joke?'

'Joke?' The Group Captain seemed surprised. 'Not as far as I know. What gave you that quaint idea?'

'Only that it's customary for officers to know where they're going,' answered Biggles. 'This morning we were at Malta.'

'Well, by to-morrow morning you'll be in India,' returned the Group Captain. 'My orders are to push you along to Karachi. Someone may tell you why when you get there. See you presently.'

Biggles looked over his shoulder at the officers who, with their kit, filled the cabin. 'You heard that?' he queried helplessly. 'We're on our way to India. The Air Ministry, having decided that we need a rest, is giving us a busman's holiday. If this goes on much longer we shall meet ourselves coming back.'

'I don't get it,' muttered Tex.

'Presumably none of us is supposed to get it,' replied Biggles. 'No doubt we shall though, eventually, if we keep on long enough.'

* Slang: information.

446

The stars were paling in the sky when, the following morning, the aircraft landed at Drigh Road airfield, Karachi.

'This, I should say, is it,' said Tug confidently.

'I wouldn't bet on it,' murmured Henry Harcourt, moodily.

The pilots stepped down. As they stretched their cramped limbs two jeeps came tearing across the sun parched earth. After they skidded to a stop a Wing Commander alighted.

''Morning Biggles,' he greeted. 'Get your fellows aboard and I'll run you to the mess. Coffee is waiting. You haven't long—'

'Okay, okay, I know,' broke in Biggles impatiently. 'We've only got an hour, then you're pushing us along to—where is it this time?'

'Dum Dum. Our best Liberator* is waiting to take you. Say thank you.'

'Thank you my foot,' snapped Biggles. 'We've been careering round the globe for forty-eight hours. I'm getting dizzy.'

'I thought Dum Dum was a kind of bullet,' grunted Taffy.

'So it is,' answered Biggles. 'It also happens to be an airfield about two miles from Calcutta, on the other side of India. They say that in the old days the first dum-dum bullets were made there. I could use some, right now. Let's go. Even if we're condemned to chase the rainbow we might as well eat.'

It was late in the afternoon when the Liberator landed its load of pilots at Calcutta. Biggles was first out, fully prepared to see a duty officer with a fresh movement order in his hand. Instead, his eyes fell on

* A four engine bomber made by Consolidated USA.

447

the last man he expected to see. It was Air Commodore Raymond, of Air Intelligence, who, as far as he knew, seldom left the Air Ministry.

'Hello,' greeted the Air Commodore with an apologetic smile.

Biggles shook his head sadly. 'I should have guessed it,' he said wearily. 'Was all this rushing from here to there really necessary?'

'You can decide that for yourself, after we've had a chat,' replied the Air Commodore seriously. 'Do you want a rest, or shall we get down to things right away?'

'Is the whole squadron included in that invitation?'

'No. I'd rather talk to you alone in the first place. You can tell your fellows about it later on—in fact, you'll have to. But the Air Officer Commanding, India, and the G.O.C* land forces, are here, waiting to have a word with you. That'll give you an idea of the importance of the matter that caused you to be rushed out.'

'All right, sir. In that case we'd better get down to brass tacks right away. What about my officers?'

'They can go and get settled in their new quarters. Everything is arranged. You've got your own mess.**'

'Then this really *is* the end of the trail?'

'I don't want to seem depressing, but it's likely to be the end of the trail in every sense of the word. We're up against it, Bigglesworth, and when *I* say that you can guess it's pretty bad.'

'So you send for me,' said Biggles plaintively. 'We were supposed to be due for a rest.'

'I didn't send for you,' denied the Air Commodore. 'The A.O.C.*** fixed that with the Ministry.

* General Office Commanding.
** Place where the men eat and relax together.
*** Air Officer Commanding.

Admittedly, I mentioned your name. See what comes of having a reputation. Matter of fact, I wasn't pleased myself at being hauled out here—I've been here three days.'

Biggles turned to speak to Algy. 'Take over,' he ordered. 'I'll join you later.'

Without speaking, the Air Commodore led the way to station headquarters, where, in an inner office, the two generals were waiting.

'Sorry to rush you about.like this, Bigglesworth, but there were reasons,' explained the Air Officer, holding out his hand.

Biggles nodded. 'I've been in the service long enough to know that things don't happen without a reason, sir,' he said simply.

'We brought you out here as we did, for two reasons. The first was speed, and the second, security. The fewer people who know you are here, the better. The Japanese High Command knows all about you, so if they learned that you were on the way out they'd put two and two together.' A note of bitterness crept into the Air Marshal's voice. 'They might even have prevented your arrival. Of course they are bound to find out sooner or later, but by that time you'll be on the job—I hope. Take a pew.' The A.O.C. sat down, mopping perspiration from his forehead with a large handkerchief, for the air was heavy and hot. 'Raymond, I think you'd better tell the story,' he suggested.

Chapter 2
Haunted Skies

With cigarettes lighted the four officers sat at a table that was entirely covered by a map of Eastern Asia.

'In this war of wars,' began the Air Commodore, looking at Biggles, 'from time to time one side or the other is suddenly confronted by a new weapon, or device, which, for a while at any rate, seems to defy counter measures. The result is a temporary advantage for the side employing the instrument. Hitler's magnetic and acoustic mines were typical examples. We have given *him* some hard nuts to crack, too. After a while, of course, the mystery is solved, but while it persists the Higher Command gets little sleep. Here, in our war against Japan, we have bumped into something that is not only lifting our casualties to an alarming degree, but is affecting the morale of pilots and air crews, and, indirectly, the troops on the ground in the areas where we are unable to provide adequate air cover.'

'That's unusual,' murmured Biggles.

'Unusual but understandable, as I think you will presently agree,' resumed the Air Commodore. 'British fighting forces are rarely perturbed by odds against them, or any new method of waging war, provided they know what they are fighting against: but when a man is suddenly confronted by the unknown, by something that kills without revealing itself—well, he is to be pardoned if his nerves begin to suffer. As you know, as well as I do, in such circumstances weak characters try to find Dutch courage by ginning-up, drinking more liquor than they can carry; already we have had one or two bad cases. To put the matter bluntly, we have run into something very nasty, and to make matters worse, we haven't the remotest idea of what it is. Of course, the Oriental mind works on different lines from ours, but not even our Eastern experts can hazard a guess as to what is *going* on. And now, before we go any farther, I'll tell you what *is* going on.' The Air Commodore stubbed his cigarette.

'The trouble first occurred on our air route between India and Chungking, in China,' he continued. 'You've probably heard something about that particular line of communication. When the Japs crashed into Burma, and put the Burma Road out of commission, we had to find a new way of getting war material to China. Our answer was a new life-line up the Himalayas to Tibet, and across the Tibetan plateau to China. At first coolies did the work, manhandling the stuff on their backs. But it was slow. To make a long story short we developed an air service, one that kept clear of the northern extremity of Burma, and possibly Japanese interference. For a time all went well; then, for some unaccountable reason, machines failed to get through. Not all of them. Occasionally one went through on schedule, and this only deepened the mystery. Perhaps I had better make the point clear. Naturally, when our machines first started to disappear we assumed that the Japs had got wind of the route and had established an advanced base from which fighters could operate. And that may in fact be the case. But the astonishing thing is, pilots who *have* got through have invariably reported a clear run. They didn't see a single enemy machine the whole way. That's hard to explain. If the Japs know of the route, and are attacking it, it seems extraordinary that some machines should be allowed to pass unmolested. In a nutshell, our machines either got through untouched, or they didn't get through at all. There was nothing in between. What I am trying to make clear is, the machines that failed, disappeared utterly. There has not been a single case of a pilot fighting his way through. In the ordinary course of events one would expect machines to arrive at their destination badly shot up, to report that they had been attacked by enemy fighters. But that has not happened. As I say, once in a while a pilot makes an uneventful flight. The rest just vanish.'

'That certainly is odd,' murmured Biggles. 'What is the position on the route now?'

'Between ourselves, we are temporarily suspending operations. We must. The surviving pilots are getting the jitters, and the commanding officer is jibbing at sending men to almost certain death. In the last few days a number of pilots have volunteered to rush through with some badly needed medical stores. None of them arrived. We can't go on like that.'

'But surely,' interposed Biggles, 'surely with radio a pilot could report the menace the moment it appeared? Whatever the trouble was, he would have warning of it, if only for a few seconds—time enough to flash a signal.'

The Air Commodore nodded. 'I was waiting for you to say that. You've put a finger on the most inexplicable part of the whole business. No such message has ever been received. In every case the radio has gone dead on us. We once sent a machine out with instructions to report to base every five minutes.'

'What happened?'

'The signals came through like clockwork for an hour. Then they just faded out.'

'Good Lord!' Biggles looked amazed. 'No wonder your pilots are getting jumpy. Tell me this. Does the interference apply to both ends of the route?'

'That's another astonishing thing. It doesn't. No machine has ever had the slightest difficulty in getting through from China to India. It's the India-China service that has been cracked up.'

'That certainly is a poser,' muttered Biggles, slowly. 'It doesn't seem to make sense. Have you tried operating at night?'

'We have,' asserted the Air Commodore. 'That was the first counter-measure we tried. It made no difference. Machines disappeared just as regularly as by day.'

Biggles shook his head. 'I don't wonder you're in a flap.'

'But just a minute,' went on the Air Commodore. 'There is worse to come. The same rot has now set in elsewhere, in the regular service squadrons. At the moment four stations are reporting abnormally high casualties without being able to offer the slightest explanation. In each case the casualty is a complete disappearance. The second place to suffer was right here, at Dum Dum. The third was Trichinoply, Madras, halfway down the coast, and the fourth, Ceylon, at the tip of the peninsula.'

'From which we may suppose that the Japs, perceiving that they are on a winner, are developing the thing, whatever it is,' put in Biggles grimly.

'Precisely,' interposed the Air Marshal dryly. 'I need hardly point out that if it goes on we soon shan't have any Air Force left in this part of the world. We're relying on you to get to the bottom of it.'

Biggles looked startled. 'But if your technical experts have failed, sir, what do you think I can do about it?'

The Air Marshal shrugged. 'I haven't the remotest idea. We're floored, stumped. Do what you can.'

'But that's all very well, sir,' protested Biggles. 'As far as I can see, to send my pilots out looking for nobody-knows-what, would merely be to send them for a Burton* to no useful purpose.'

'You're our last hope, Bigglesworth,' said the Air Commodore, with something like despair in his voice. 'We can't just suspend air operations—we might as well pack up altogether as do that.'

'If you go on losing pilots and machines at the rate you are evidently losing them it will come to the same thing in the end.'

The Air Marshal stepped in again. 'See what you can do, Bigglesworth. You can have *carte blanche*, a freelance commission, have what equipment you like, do what you like, go where you like—*but this thing has got to be stopped*.'

Biggles tapped a cigarette on the back of his hand. 'Very well, sir. I don't mind going out myself, but it isn't going to be very nice to have to ask my boys to virtually commit suicide. They'll go if I tell them to *go*, but I'd like you to know how I feel about it. This business of watching one's officers go one by one—'

'That's just how four other station commanders are feeling at this very moment, Bigglesworth,' broke in the Air Commodore wearily.

Biggles pulled forward a scribbling-pad and picked up a pencil. For a little while he made meaningless marks. Then he asked: 'What about altitude? Does that make any difference?'

'None,' answered the Air Commodore. 'In desperation we tried sending machines to their ceiling before

* Slang: to be killed.

454

leaving the airfield. They disappeared just the same.'

'I see. What is the longest period you have maintained radio contact with an aircraft that subsequently disappeared?'

'Four hours. That was on the Chungking run. It's a thousand miles.'

'No intermediate landing-ground?'

'None.'

'And what is the shortest period before you lost touch with a machine?'

'An hour.'

Biggles shrugged. 'The thing becomes uncanny. The time interval between one and four hours, translated to distance, is six or seven hundred miles. How can one even start looking for a thing that can strike over such an enormous area? You say that all the machines which disappeared, vanished into the blue. Am I to understand that not one of these crashes has ever been found?'

'That, unfortunately, is so,' answered the Air Commodore. 'You've flown over the Himalayas, and the Burmese jungle, so you know what it's like. It would be easier to find a pin in a cornfield.'

'These crashes, then, always occur over enemy-occupied country?'

'Either that or over the sea. From here we operate over Burma. From Madras and Ceylon most of the flying is done over the Indian Ocean.'

'There has never been an unexplainable crash in India itself?'

'There have been one or two crashes—not more than one would expect in the ordinary course of flying routine. These crashes were, of course, examined—but you know what such a crash looks like?'

'No unusual features emerged at the courts of inquiry?'

'None. In each case the pilot was killed, so he couldn't tell us anything, even if there was something to tell. There was a crash on this aerodrome two days ago. The pilot tried hard to say something before he died—but there, that could happen anyway.'

'Had he been over enemy territory?'

'Yes.'

'What about the machine?'

'There was nothing wrong with it, as far as could be ascertained.'

'How long had this pilot been in the air?'

'About twenty minutes. He left a formation and turned back.'

'Why?'

'We don't know. There was nothing very remarkable about that. Machines occasionally turn back for one reason or another.'

'What I'm trying to get at is this,' explained Biggles. 'Has there ever been an instance of an aircraft, or a pilot, affected by the new weapon, crashing on our side of the lines?'

'Not as far as we know—unless the pilot I just mentioned was a case. That seems most unlikely though, as he was one of a formation of ten. Had he been attacked, surely the others would have been attacked, too.'

'Tell me about this particular show,' invited Biggles.

'It was the last big raid we attempted from this airfield,' replied the Air Commodore. 'The rot had already set in, you understand, so the pilots and air crews taking part were keyed up for trouble. Actually, there are four squadrons here, not counting yours; two bomber squadrons and two fighter. Incidentally, you have been posted here as a communication squadron. Two days ago, one of the bomber squadrons took off soon after dawn with every machine it could raise—ten Blenheims—for a raid on the enemy-occupied airfield at Akyab. The distance to the objective, by the direct route across the Bay of Bengal, is about four hundred miles. Actually, the raid was timed for dawn, but there was still some mist about so the take off was postponed till it cleared.'

'And you say the pilots were aware of the mysterious weapon?'

'Yes. All personnel were very much on the alert.'

'Go on, sir.'

'About twenty minutes after the take-off one of the Blenheims was seen coming back. It was fairly low, gliding, in a manner which might be described as unsteady.'

'Which implies that the pilot was having trouble?'

'Yes—but then, had he not been in trouble he would not have left the formation.'

'Did he speak over the radio?'

'No.'

'So you have no idea what the trouble was?'

'Not the remotest. Shortly after passing over the boundary of the airfield the aircraft stalled, and crashed, with what result I have already told you. At the Court of Inquiry, which went into the evidence very carefully, it was decided that such an accident could occur quite apart from any secret weapon. In fact, it was that sort of accident that could occur, and does occur, regularly.'

'What was the name of this pilot?'

'Cratton.'

Biggles made a note. 'What happened to the rest of the formation?'

'The flight ended in disaster,' said the Air Commodore heavily. 'An hour after taking off, one of the nine remaining machines, before enemy opposition was encountered, without warning went into a spin and fell into the sea. Just before reaching the objective, in precisely the same conditions, another machine went down. One was shot down in combat over the target area. The six survivors dropped their bombs and turned for home. On the return journey four more went down at irregular intervals. Only two got back safely, both perfectly all right beyond being shaken by the tragedy of their comrades, and the strain of flying with the same fate impending.'

'There was absolutely nothing wrong with them physically?'

'Nothing.'

'And what about the machines?'

'They were all right, too.'

'And the surviving pilots could offer no explanation as to why the others went down?'

'None. The story was the same in every case. The stricken machine flew badly for a moment or two and then appeared to fall out of control. Sometimes the engines were cut, sometimes, the machines hit the water with the motors running.'

Biggles lit a fresh cigarette. 'I understand what you mean about pilots becoming unnerved. Anyone would freeze to the stick with that sort of thing going on round him. As far as a solution to the mystery is concerned, inevitably one thinks of death rays, so called, which I believe have often been used in fiction, but never in fact. Scientists say that such a ray is not possible—but then, scientists are not always right.'

'You think there may be something in the death ray idea, then?' suggested the Air Marshal. 'We've considered it, of course.'

'Frankly, no,' replied Biggles. 'And I'll tell you why.

If such a device was being used one would suppose that once they were within the sphere of influence all machines would be affected. In a daylight raid most aircraft keep a tight formation. I mean, if the thing could strike down one machine surely it would be able to strike down the others? We can hardly suppose that some machines are vulnerable while others are not. How was it that two came back? They were in all respects identical with those that fell. Then again, why the interval of time between the falling out of the last machines?'

The Air Marshal spoke. 'Our experts assert positively that the death ray is not yet a practical proposition, but there may be a beam device which could affect the electrical installation of an aero engine. For want of any other explanation we are inclined to accept that view.'

'I'm not,' returned Biggles bluntly.

'Why not?'

'In the first place, because the failure of its power unit doesn't necessarily cause an aircraft to go down out of control. The pilot would automatically put the machine into a glide, and while the machine was gliding he would have ample time to send out a signal. Then again, air crews wear parachutes. If the aircraft was vitally affected the men in it would bale out. To me it looks more as if machines are being sabotaged on the ground.'

'You can rule out sabotage,' said the Air Commodore. 'Those Blenheims were inspected and tested down to the last detail before they left the ground. With all this going on you can be quite sure that close watch is kept on equipment.'

Biggles thought for a moment. 'The one incontestable fact is that something is going wrong. If the trouble isn't caused in the air, then it must start on the ground. Against trouble in the air is the absence of anything like structural failure, which would certainly be spotted by the other machines in the formation. I still think it is extraordinary that none of these crews baled out, or tried to bale out.'

'It isn't always easy to abandon an aircraft that is falling out of control,' remarked the Air Commodore.

'And in the case of Blenheims the Bay of Bengal was underneath, don't forget,' put in the Air Marshal. 'The bay is infested with sharks.'

'That may have been the reason,' agreed Biggles. 'For all we know, the crews of some of the machines that were lost on the China route *may* have baled out. Even if they got down alive, I imagine they'd find it impossible to get back on foot.'

There was another short silence. All eyes were on Biggles' face as he pondered the problem.

'Tell me,' he went on presently, 'was there any rule about the number of pilots in these lost machines? I mean, has disaster ever overtaken a machine with two pilots in the cabin?'

The Air Commodore answered. 'I'm not quite sure about that. Out here we have to be economical with pilots, so in most cases—it was on the China run—when two pilots were lost together.'

Again silence fell. Biggles chewed a matchstalk reflectively. Outside, the brief tropic twilight was passing, but the sultry heat persisted. The Air Commodore switched on a light. A large white moth flew in through the open window and fluttered round the globe with a faint rustling sound as its wings beat with futile effort against the glass.

'Any more questions, Bigglesworth?' asked the Air Marshal anxiously.

Biggles looked up. 'No, sir.' He smiled wanly. 'You've given me plenty to think about. I'd like to sleep on it.'

'Then you'll—er—take the matter in hand?'

'I'll do my best with it, sir.'

'It's urgent—desperately urgent.'

'That's about the only aspect of this affair that's really obvious, sir,' answered Biggles. He got up. 'I'll go now and have a word with my officers. Between us we may get on the scent of the thing. If we do I'll report to the Air Commodore. I take it that no one on the station will be told the real reason why we have come here?'

'I'll see to that,' promised the Air Commodore. 'Even the station commander, Group Captain Boyle, supposes you to be an ordinary communication squadron, sent out here for special duty.'

'He's not likely to interfere with us?'

'No. I've told him that you will come directly under the Higher Command for orders. The presence here of the A.O.C. will confirm that.'

'Very good, sir. By the way, are you staying on here?'

'For the time being, at any rate,' answered Air Commodore Raymond. 'You can regard me as a sort of liaison officer between you and the Air Officer Commanding. Call on me for anything you need.'

Biggles saluted and withdrew. Deep in thought, and not a little worried, he made his way along the silent tarmac to the quarters that had been allocated to the squadron.

Chapter 3
Biggles Briefs Himself

The buzz of conversation died abruptly as Biggles walked into the ante-room and closed the door behind him. Only the radio went on, unheeded, relaying swing music from London. A short, stoutish, olive-skinned, middle-aged man, dressed in white duck trousers and mess-jacket, wearing a beaming smile, was standing by a low table on which rested a brass tray bearing a coffee-pot and cups.

Biggles called to him. 'Hi!, you; that'll do,' he said curtly.

'Plenty coffee, sahib. You like some, mebbe?' answered the steward.

'When I want anything I'll let you know,' returned Biggles. 'Pack up now.'

'Velly good, sahib.' Still beaming, the steward picked up his tray and departed.

Biggles looked at Algy. 'Who's that?'

'Lal Din.'

'Who's he?'

'One of the waiters from the canteen. He's all right.'

'I don't doubt it,' replied Biggles. 'But it's better not to talk in front of staff. They gossip.' He indicated the radio with a thumb. 'Turn that thing off, somebody.'

Angus complied.

'What's cooking, chief?' asked Tex eagerly.

'A dish with a nasty smell and a worse flavour,' replied Biggles quietly. 'Gather round, everybody, and I'll tell you about it. By the way, has anybody been

462

out on the station?'

Several voices answered. 'I had a look round to see what machines we had on charge,' said Algy. 'Some of the others took a stroll to get their bearings.'

'In that case you may have heard something?' suggested Biggles.

'I didn't hear anything, but there's a sort of grey atmosphere in the central mess,' put in Ginger. 'There were only a few chaps there, but they looked at me as if I were something blown in off a dunghill.'

'I ran into Johnny Crisp on the perim*,' said Algy. 'You remember him—he picked up two bars to his D.F.C. in Wilks' squadron? He's a flight-loot** in 818 Squadron now. He told me a little. Ginger is right about the atmosphere. It's sort of—brittle, as if everyone was waiting for an unexploded bomb to go off. Johnny has aged ten years since I last saw him, a few months ago.'

Biggles nodded. 'I'm not surprised. I'll tell you why.'

He devoted the next twenty minutes to a résumé of the sinister story he had just gathered at headquarters. No one interrupted. All eyes were on his face. When he concluded, still no one spoke.

'Well, has nobody anything to say?' queried Biggles.

'What is there to say?' asked Ginger.

'Sure, I guess you're right, at that,' put in Tex, blowing a cloud of cigarette smoke at the ceiling. 'Looks like we've come a helluva long way to find trouble. So what?'

'Has anybody an idea about this thing?' demanded Biggles.

No one answered.

* Slang: perimeter
** Slang: Flight Lieutenant

'Stiffen the crows!' exclaimed Biggles. 'You are a bright lot. Do I have to do all the thinking?'

'What's the use of us trying to work it out if you can't?' murmured Tug.

'What do you think about it yourself, old boy?' asked Bertie.

'Frankly, I can't even begin to think,' admitted Biggles. 'We have one single fact to work on. Something is affecting our machines, or the pilots. We don't even know which. That's the first thing we've got to find out.'

'You tell us how, and we'll get right on with it,' asserted Ferocity.

'That would be easier if I knew what we were looking for,' went on Biggles. 'One thing is certain. We shan't find it by sitting here. We've got to go out—where the others went. That will mean . . . casualties. And that's putting it nicely. We aren't the only suicide squadron on the station, but that doesn't make it any easier from my point of view. I've never yet asked a man to do a show I wouldn't do myself, so I shall make a start. After that it will be a job for volunteers. If anyone would like to fall out, he may. Now's the time.'

Nobody moved.

Biggles glanced round. 'Okay, if that's how you feel about it,' he said softly. 'Now you know what's likely to happen, let's get down to it. I shall make a start in the morning by going up to Jangpur, the Indian terminus of the China run, to have a look round. I am planning to take an aircraft over the course.'

'You mean—go to Chungking?' cried Algy.

'Yes.'

'But that's daft, mon,' protested Angus. 'How can ye find a thing when ye dinna ken what ye're looking for?'

'Has anyone an alternative suggestion?'

There was a chorus of voices offering to go out, but Biggles silenced them with a gesture. 'Don't all talk at once, and don't let's have any argument about who is going out. You'll all get your turns. I shall do the first show. That's settled. If I don't come back Algy will take over. If he fades out, too, the others will carry on in order of seniority until the thing is found, or until there is no one left to look for it. That's all quite simple. What machines have we got, Algy?'

'A mixed bunch,' was the reply. 'It looks as if Raymond has got together anything he thought might be useful. There's a Wimpey, a Beaufighter, a Mosquito, three Hurricanes, three Spits* and a Typhoon. If you've made up your mind to go out why not take the Beau, and have somebody else with you? Then, if anything went wrong, the second pilot could bring the aircraft home.'

'From what I understand, flying two pilots together is just an easy way of doubling the rate of casualties. Two go instead of one. Whether the new weapon affects the men or the machine, the whole outfit goes west.'

'That doesn't entirely fit in with what Johnny Crisp told me,' declared Algy.

'What did he tell you?'

'Well, it seems that some fellows are either extraordinarily lucky, or else they—or their machines— are unaffected by the new weapon.'

'What do you mean by that, precisely?'

'Johnny tells me that he has made eleven sorties since the trouble started and has never seen or heard anything to alarm him. But he has seen others go down, seen them dropping like shot birds all round him—

* Spitfire fighter

that's how he put it. He told me that what with this ropey spectacle, and expecting his own turn to come every minute, he froze to the stick, with fright. Once he was the only one of five to return. Another chap, a pilot officer named Scrimshaw, has been out nine times, and has got away with it.'

Biggles regarded Algy with a mystified look in his eyes. 'That certainly is interesting,' he said slowly. 'What squadrons are these chaps in?'

'They're both in 818, flying Hurrybombers*. There are only five of them left in the squadron, although they have had replacements several times. Some chaps went west on their first show.'

'I suppose it must be luck, but it seems strange,' muttered Biggles. 'There can't be anything unusual about their machines—they're all standardised.'

'They haven't always flown the same machines, anyway,' volunteered Algy.

'Then obviously we can't put their luck down to their equipment. Yet the fellows themselves must be flesh and blood, like any other men. It *must* be luck. I don't see how it can be anything else.'

'If this new weapon is so hot, why haven't the Japs handed it on to their partners, the Nazis?' inquired Henry Harcourt.

'Ask me something easier,' returned Biggles. 'All the same, Henry, I think you've got something there. So far the trouble is localised in the East. One would suppose that the Japs would pass it on to the Nazis. All I can say is, God help us if they do.'

'Maybe the Japs don't trust the Nazis,' contributed Ferocity, practically. 'They may be windy of having the thing turned on then, if ever they fell out with their

* Hurricane fighters modified to carry bombs under the wings.

466

partners.'

'That may be the answer,' acknowledged Biggles.

'How about gas?' suggested Henry. 'Have you thought of that?'

'It passed through my mind,' averred Biggles. 'But there are several arguments against it. The first is, you can only get gas in quantity to a great height, by carrying it, or shooting it up, and nobody has seen any sort of vehicle or missile capable of doing that. Then again, what about formations? If a trail of gas *could* be laid across the sky, why are some pilots affected and not others? And how are we going to account for the irregular intervals of time between the machines falling out? I can't believe that the Japs could plant gas all over the place, at different altitudes, without being spotted. Finally, if gas were used, what is there to prevent the Japs themselves from flying into it, bearing in mind that the locality would not be constant? The wind, upcurrents and sinkers, would blow the stuff all over the place. Still, we'll bear the possibility in mind.'

'It was just an idea,' murmured Henry.

'Let's get back to the question of action,' suggested Biggles. 'We've got to find this hidden horror before we can do anything about it, and no doubt some of us will do that. Plenty of others have found it,' he added significantly, 'but unfortunately they couldn't get the information home. In other words, without mincing matters, it seems that the man who finds the thing, dies. Our problem is to find it and live—or live long enough to pass back the secret. It means going out, and I shall make a start, beginning in the area where the thing struck first—that is, on the Jangpur-Chungking route. The rest of you will stay here till I get back. That's an order. On no account will anyone go into the air; nor will anyone refer to the fact, either here or anywhere else, that we have been sent out specially to hunt this thing down. At all times you will pretend that we are what we are supposed to be, a communication squadron scheduled for co-operation with forces inside India. You needn't be idle. Give the machines a thorough overhaul. I shall go up to Jangpur in the Typhoon. Algy, I'd like you to get a list of all persons outside Air Force personnel who work on the station, or have permits to visit the airfield for any purpose whatsoever. There are certain to be a lot of men of the country; there always are on Indian stations. For the benefit of those of you who haven't been to India before, we don't use the expression *natives*. It's discourteous. Raymond probably has such a list already made. That would be the first thing he'd do, I imagine, in checking up for possible saboteurs. If anyone asks where I've gone you can say I'm doing a test flight—which will be true enough. Now let's get some sleep.'

Chapter 4
Biggles Makes a Wager

The following morning, the first glow of dawn saw Biggles in the air, in the Typhoon, heading north for Jangpur, the Indian terminus of the China route. He had not far to go—a trifle more than a hundred miles. As he landed and taxied to the wooden office buildings he noted a general absence of movement, an atmosphere of inactivity. The duty officer, a pilot officer, came to meet him. His manner was respectful, but listless, as if his interest in everything about him was perfunctory. He told Biggles that the station commander, Squadron Leader Frayle, was in his office.

And there Biggles found him, looking as though he had not been to bed for a week. His eyes were heavy from want of sleep; his hair was untidy and his chin unshaven. The desk was a litter of dirty cups, plates and glasses.

Biggles did not appear to notice this. 'Good morning,' he greeted cheerfully. 'My name's Bigglesworth.'

The squadron leader's eyes brightened. 'So you're Biggles? I've heard of you. Take a seat. Can I get you anything?'

'No, thanks,' answered Biggles. 'At this hour of the morning I work better on an empty stomach.' He pulled up a chair and lit a cigarette.

'What in the name of all that's unholy brought you to this God-forsaken, sun-blistered dustbin?' inquired Frayle curiously.

'I'm told you've had a spot of trouble here,' replied

Biggles. 'I've been sent out from home to try to iron it out.'

'Go ahead,' invited Frayle bitterly. 'The airfield's yours—and you're welcome to it. I've lost four officers and four machines in four days—the last four to go out, in fact. That should encourage you to keep your feet on something more solid than the floor of a fuselage. I've three officers left out of eighteen. Not bad going, eh?'

'I heard the position was pretty grey,' said Biggles sympathetically.

'Grey! It's blacker than a black-out.' Frayle's voice took on a quality of bitter resentment. 'Grey, they call it. It's hell, that's what it is. Can you imagine what it's been like for me, to sit here day after day sending out lads who I know I shall never see again?'

'I can imagine it,' answered Biggles quietly.

'There's another one going this morning,' went on Frayle. 'I didn't order him to go. Not me. I've finished picking the roster with a pin to decide who was to be the next man to die. He just told me was going. There's a load of medical stores urgently needed in Chungking. To-morrow I shall be down to two pilots.'

'You haven't tried doing the run yourself?'

'No. As I feel that would suit me fine. My orders are to stay on the carpet. They say my job is on the station. Well, to-morrow I'm going, anyway, orders or no orders. I can't stand any more of this.'

'It's no use talking that way, Frayle,' said Biggles softly. 'You know you can't do that.'

'But I—I—' Frayle seemed to choke. He buried his face in his hands.

'Here, take it easy,' said Biggles gently. 'I know how you feel, but it's no use letting the thing get you down like this. Get a grip on yourself. Can't you see that by

470

cracking up you're only helping the enemy? What about this lad—has he gone off yet?'

'No, they're loading up the machine.'

'Good. Stop him.'

Frayle looked up. 'But this stuff is supposed to go through.'

'I know. Never mind. Stop him.'

'But what shall I tell headquarters?'

'You needn't tell them anything. I'll take the stuff.'

'*You'll* take it?'

'Yes.'

'You're out of your mind.'

Biggles smiled. 'You may be right, but I'll take this stuff to Chungking just the same. Send for the lad who was going. What's his name?'

'Bargent. He's a flying officer—a South African. You'll find him as amiable as a rhino that's been shot in the bottom with a charge of buckshot.'

'I'll have a word with him. You snatch a bath, treat your face to a razor blade, and have something to eat; you'll feel better. I'll fix things while you're doing it.'

Frayle gave the necessary order. Presently Bargent came.

'Now what's boiling?' he demanded in a hard voice.

'You're not doing this show,' said Biggles.

'And who says so?' questioned Bargent hotly.

'I say so,' replied Biggles evenly.

Bargent flung his cap on the floor, which was to Biggles a clear indication of the state of his nerves.

'And if you start throwing your weight about with me, my lad, I'll put you under close arrest,' promised Biggles, in a voice that made the flying officer stare at him.

'But I *want* to go, sir,' said Bargent, in a different tone of voice.

471

Biggles thought for a minute. 'All right. You can come with me if you like.'

'With you?'

'That's what I said.'

The South African laughed shortly. 'Okay. The machine is all ready.'

Biggles turned to Frayle. 'How many machines have you got left?'

'Two, able to do the run.'

'What are they?'

'Wimpeys.'

'And one's loaded?'

'Yes.'

'Did that arrangement appear in last night's orders?'

'Yes.'

'In the ordinary way the other machine would stand in a shed all day?'

'Yes.'

'Have you a duplicate set of these medical stores?'

'We've a hundred tons, all overdue for delivery.'

'Where are they?'

'In store.'

'Locked up?'

'Yes.'

'Who's your storekeeper?'

'Corporal Jones.'

'That's fine,' declared Biggles. 'I'm going to try being unorthodox. For a start we're going to unload this loaded machine, and take every package to pieces. Then we'll take the machine to pieces.'

'You're wasting your time.'

'What do you mean?' asked Biggles quickly.

'We've tried that a dozen times. You suspect sabotage? So did we. The first action I took was what you propose doing now, supposing that someone was

472

sticking a time bomb in the load. We've never found such a thing, or anything like it.'

Biggles thought for a little while. 'H'm. I was bound to try that,' he asserted. 'But if you've already done it there doesn't seem to be much point in repeating it, so we'll proceed with the second part of the programme. I want you to go and tell Corporal Jones, privately, to prepare a second load. Tell him to keep it out of sight. Swear him to secrecy. In a minute or two I'll bring the spare machine over and we'll load it ourselves.'

'What shall I do with the first load? The machine is waiting to go.'

'For the time being leave it just as it is. Put a guard over it.'

'This all seems a waste of time to me, but I'm willing to try anything,' said Frayle heavily.

'Then go and talk to Jones. Tell him to get a move on. Then I'd advise you to have a clean up. You may be sick, but it does no good to advertise it.'

Frayle went off.

Biggles turned to Bargent. 'You don't fancy your chance of coming back from this trip, do you?'

'Not much. Do you?'

'Yes. I think we've quite a good chance.'

'What leads you to think you are any different from anyone else?' Bargent couldn't keep sarcasm out of his voice.

'I didn't say I was different. But I've done quite a lot of flying, and I've never yet seen in the air anything capable of knocking a machine down without showing itself. I doubt very much if there is such a thing. So far, anything I've seen I've been able to dodge. It may sound like conceit, but I fancy my chance of going on doing that.'

'Would you like to bet on it?'

Biggles hesitated, but only for a moment. 'I don't go in much for betting, but I'd risk a hundred cigarettes.'

'I'll take that,' declared Bargent. 'Just what is the bet?'

'The bet is, by lunch-time I shall be in Chungking, and back again here for dinner to-night.'

'You hope,' muttered Bargent. 'I'd say you're on a loser.'

Biggles laughed. 'Well, you can't win, anyway.'

Bargent started. 'Why not?'

'If I lose—that is if we don't get back—I doubt if I shall be in a position to pay you and you'll be in no case to collect your winnings. We shall both be somewhere either on the mountains or in the jungle between here and China.'

'I'm nuts. I never thought of that,' said Bargent, grinning, and then laughing aloud.

'That's better,' remarked Biggles. 'While you can keep a sense of humour you've got a chance. Come on, let's go and get the Wimpey.'

Ignoring the machine that had been detailed, with its little crowd of loaders, they walked over to the hangar in which the spare machine was parked. Biggles climbed into the cockpit. 'You stay where you are,' he told Bargent. 'Walk beside me when I taxi over to the store. If anyone tries to get within ten yards of this machine throw something at him. If you let anyone touch you, my lad, you're not getting into this aircraft. I'm standing to lose more than a hundred cigarettes on this jaunt and I'm not taking any chances. Understand?'

'Okay.'

Biggles started the engines and taxied slowly through the glaring sunlight to the store shed. On the way, some of the porters that had been working on the other machine came hurrying across, but Bargent waved his arm, and yelled to them to keep away. He picked up and hurled a stone at one man who came on after the others had stopped. He retreated.

Frayle, in a bath wrap, appeared at the storehouse door.

'Is the stuff ready?' shouted Biggles.

'Yes, it's all here.'

'Help us to get it on board. Tell Jones to punch on the nose anybody who tries to get near us.'

'You do have some quaint ideas,' said Frayle, as he complied.

'Maybe that's why I'm here,' murmured Biggles.

In ten minutes the big machine was loaded to capacity with bundles of British and American stores, labelled CHUNGKING.

'What about something to eat before you go?' suggesting Frayle.

'No, thanks,' refused Biggles.

'It's a long trip.'

'We can manage.'

'Not even a last drink?' queried Bargent.

'Not even a last drink,' decided Biggles firmly. 'I make a point of doing one thing at a time, and the thing at the moment is to get this pantechnicon to China. Get aboard. So long, Frayle. I'm aiming to be back for tea.'

'I'll have it ready,' promised Frayle.

'Put a guard on my Typhoon. Don't let anyone touch it.'

'Okay.'

Before Bargent had properly settled himself in his seat Biggles had opened the throttle, and the big machine was bellowing across the airfield.

'Have you made this trip before?' asked Biggles, as

475

he throttled back to a steady cruising speed of just over two hundred miles an hour.

'Four times.'

'You must be lucky.'

'Maybe so. But I reckoned it couldn't go on. No sense in riding your luck too hard.'

'I suppose that's why you were trying it on again to-day?' said Biggles smoothly.

'Pah! It had to come sooner or later, and after seeing the others go, I thought the sooner the better.'

'Desperate fellow,' murmured Biggles. 'Well, we shall see. Keep your eyes skinned.'

'I suppose you realise that we're flying without gunners in the turrets?' said Bargent suddenly. 'That's asking for trouble, isn't it?'

'I have a feeling that we shan't need guns on this trip.'

'Why not?'

'Put it this way. Guns couldn't save the other crews. If guns can't stop this rot what point was there in bringing gunners? In the event of things going wrong we should only push up the casualty list. My gosh! That's pretty rough country below.' Biggles was looking below and ahead at a terrible yet magnificent panorama of mountain peaks that stretched across the course from horizon to horizon.

'It's like that pretty well all the way to China,' asserted Bargent. 'Where it isn't mountains, it's what the books call untamed primeval forest. Anyone going down in it wouldn't have a hope. They say it's unexplored.

'Let's hope we shan't have to explore it,' returned Biggles. 'Let me know if you see anything strange, in the air or on the ground.'

After that the two pilots fell silent. The Wellington

droned on, devouring space at a steady two hundred and twenty miles an hour. Mountains, groups and ranges and isolated peaks, many crowned with eternal snow, rolled away below. Valleys and depressions were choked with the sombre, everlasting forest.

'It's about time we were bumping into something,' said Bargent once, after looking at the watch. 'We must be half-way.'

'Begins to look as if this trip is going to cost you a hundred cigarettes, my lad,' said Biggles slyly, with a sidelong glance at his companion.

'If I don't lose more than that I shan't grumble,' murmured Bargent.

Two hours later the airport of Chungking came into view.

'That's it,' confirmed Bargent. 'What's the programme when we get there?'

'We'll sling this stuff overboard and start straight back,' replied Biggles.

'We're not stopping for lunch?'

'We're not stopping for anything.'

Bargent shook his head. 'You certainly are a strange bird,' he muttered.

'So I've been told. But never mind the compliments. As soon as we're in, jump down and keep the crowd away from this machine. I don't want anybody to touch it. I'll push the stuff out. They can collect it after we've gone. I shall leave the motors running.'

'Okay.'

As soon as the Wellington was on the ground a crowd of Chinese surged towards it; but Bargent held them off, gesticulating furiously. Biggles was throwing the stores out.

A Chinese officer came forward, speaking English.

'That's close enough!' shouted Bargent. 'Here's your

stuff. Some more will be coming through.'

'You in great hurry,' said the Chinaman impassively.

'We've got to get back,' answered Bargent.

'No want any petrol?'

Bargent looked at Biggles.

'No!' shouted Biggles. 'We've got enough to see us home.'

'You no stay to eat?' questioned the Chinaman.

'Not to-day, thanks,' returned Bargent. 'I've got a date with a girl in Calcutta, and she'll jilt me if I'm not back on time.'

The Chinaman grinned. 'Me savvy.'

'Okay, Bargent!' shouted Biggles. 'Get aboard. We're on our way.'

The South African picked his way through the pile of bales that Biggles had thrown out of the aircraft, closed the door and resumed his seat. The engines roared, and the machine swung round, scattering the crowd, to face the open field. In another minute it was in the air again, India bound.

'Get those cigarettes ready,' said Biggles.

Bargent laughed. 'I'll help you smoke 'em.'

'Oh, no, you won't,' declared Biggles. 'I reckon I shall have won 'em.'

There was no incident of any sort on the home run. There was no flak; no aircraft of any type, friend or foe, was sighted. As they glided in to land Bargent swore that he had never felt better in his life.

Frayle, in uniform, greeted them. 'So you got back?' he cried in a voice of wonder.

'If you think this is a ghost plane, try walking into one of the airscrews,' invited Biggles. 'You'll find it hard enough, I'll warrant.'

'Well, that's a mystery,' said Frayle.

'Not quite so much of a mystery as it was,' returned

478

Biggles.

'What are you going to do now?'

Biggles glanced at the sun, now low in the west. 'I want to get back to Dum Dum before dark, but I've just time for a snack.'

'You think it's safe to use the route now?'

'I didn't say that,' answered Biggles quickly. 'The Chinese now have a little to go on with, so you can afford to keep everything on the ground till you hear from me again. Yes, I know we got away with it this time, but that trick may not work again. By changing the planes at the last minute we slipped a fast one on the enemy. More than that I can't tell you for the moment. I want you and Bargent to keep your mouths shut tight about this show. If you talk it may cost you your lives. Keep the machines grounded. I'll be back. Now let's go and eat.'

An hour later, in the crimson glow of the Eastern sunset, Biggles landed at Dum Dum and walked quickly to the mess, to be met by an enthusiastic squadron.

'I say, old boy, that's marvellous—absolutely marvellous,' declared Bertie. 'Don't tell me you've been to China?'

'There and back,' answered Biggles. 'Let's get inside. I've got to talk to you chaps, and I don't mind admitting that I'd rather curl quietly in a corner and go to sleep. I seem to have done a lot of flying lately.'

'If you're tired, why not leave it until to-morrow?' suggested Algy.

'Because to-morrow morning I shall be just as busy—and so, perhaps, will you.'

'The point is, did you spot the secret weapon?' demanded Ginger.

'Not a sign of it,' returned Biggles, with a ghost of a

smile. 'Serious, now, everybody. Lock the door, Ginger. To-day I carried out what we might call an experiment,' he went on, when everyone had settled down. 'It leads, as most experiments do, to another. To-morrow morning I'm going to do a sortie over Burma.'

'Alone?' queried Algy, looking askance.

'I hadn't thought of taking anyone,' admitted Biggles.

'At least take someone with you,' pressed Algy. 'There may be something in this double pilot idea.'

'It isn't that I'm trying to run the show single-handed,' asserted Biggles. 'It's just that I want to avoid casualties if it is possible. There's no point in using more men on a job than it calls for. One machine can do what I have in mind to-morrow morning. Why risk two?'

'Then why not take the Beau*, or the Mosquito, and have someone with you for company?' suggested Algy.

'Yes, I might do that,' agreed Biggles.

There was a chorus of voices offering to go, but Biggles held up a hand. 'There's only one way to settle this, and that's by drawing lots,' he declared. 'That doesn't apply to flight commanders, though; they'll get their turns if I don't come back. Algy, write six names on slips of paper and put them in a hat.'

'Aren't you going to tell us what happened to-day?' queried Tex, while Algy was doing this.

'There's really nothing to tell,' answered Biggles. 'Nothing happened: that's a fact.'

Algy came forward with a hat in which lay six slips of paper, folded.

'Shake 'em up,' ordered Biggles.

Algy shook the hat.

* Beaufighter—twin engine two-seater day and night fighter.

480

Biggles closed his eyes and put out a hand. His fingers closed over a slip. He raised it. In dead silence he unfolded it and glanced at the name. He took it to Tug and smiled.

'You're it, Tug,' he announced.

'Whoopee! That's a corker,' cried Tug. 'That's the first time I've ever won a draw in my life.'

'Unless it's your lucky day it's likely to be the last,' joked Biggles grimly.

'I'll risk it,' flashed Tug, grinning. 'What time do we leave the carpet?'

'We'll decide that when we see what the weather is like,' returned Biggles.

'Do we wear brollies*?'

Biggles shrugged. 'In this affair they don't seem to make much difference, but I suppose we might as well. Don't mention this sortie to a soul, neither in nor out-side the mess. Should anyone ask what we are doing you can say we're browning off waiting for orders. That's all. Let's go in to dinner.'

* Slang: parachutes

Chapter 5
Suicide Patrol

It was still dark, but with that faint luminosity in the sky that heralds the approach of the Eastern dawn, when Biggles was awakened by the sudden bellow of an aero engine. This is not an unusual sound on an airfield, and he turned over with the intention of snatching a final nap, supposing that the noise was created by a motor under test. But when a second, and then a third engine opened up, he sprang out of bed and strode to the window. In the eerie light of the false dawn he could just discern the silhouettes of what he thought were Hurricanes, moving slowly on the far side of the airfield. For a moment or two he stood gazing, sleep banished, a frown puckering his forehead; then he slipped a dressing-gown over his pyjamas and picked up the telephone.

Two minutes later Algy arrived, also in pyjamas. 'What's going on?' he asked tersely.

Biggles hung up the receiver. 'Take a look outside,' he invited. 'Those five survivors of 818 Squadron are going off on a bomb raid in the danger area. My God! They've got a nerve.'

Algy nodded. 'Yes, I remember now. Johnny Crisp told me last night that there was some talk of a final do-or-bust show in the hope of finding the thing that killed the others.'

'They'll do that, no doubt—or some of them will,' returned Biggles, in a hard voice.

'Johnny said they were going crazy, just sitting on

the ground doing nothing. He, being the only remaining flight commander, will lead the sortie. Personally, I think he's right. You know how it is; when a fellow's nerves start slipping he has only one chance of saving himself—if he ever wants to fly again; and that's to get in the air.'

'Maybe. But these chaps are practically committing suicide, and they must know it.'

'Johnny, and the other fellow I told you about, Scrimshaw, have always got back,' reminded Algy.

'So far. But there's such a thing as pushing your luck too hard.' Biggles started. 'Just a minute! Yes, that's it. I'm going to hook on to this raid, to watch what happens. All the evidence we have up to now is hearsay.'

Algy's eyes opened wide. 'But—'

'Don't stand gibbering. Go and get Tug out of bed and tell him to meet me on the tarmac in five minutes.'

'What about breakfast?'

'There'll be more time for that when we get back.'

'You mean—*if* you get back,' said Algy, with gentle sarcasm. 'Okay.' He departed.

Five minutes later, when Biggles went outside, Tug was there, waiting, parachute slung over his shoulder. The rest of the squadron was there, too, grim-faced, silent. The five Hurricanes were just taking off, sending clouds of dust swirling across the parched airfield.

'Look at 'em,' said Biggles in a low voice. 'There they go. That's guts for you. Come on, Tug; we'll catch 'em in the Mosquito.' It did not seem to strike him that he was doing the same thing. He glanced round the ring of anxious faces, and smiled the strange little smile they all knew so well. 'So long, chaps; keep your tails up.'

'I say, old boy, watch out what you're up to, and all

that,' blurted Bertie.

'May I follow in a Spit?' cried Ginger huskily.

'No,' answered Biggles shortly.

'But—'

'You heard me. Come on, Tug. Let's get cracking, or we'll lose sight of those crazy Hurry-wallahs.'

In a few minutes the Mosquito, probably the best and fastest long-range medium bomber in the world, was in the air. It carried no bombs. Biggles was at the control column, with Tug sitting beside him instead of adopting the prone position which the special structure of this type of aircraft permits. Both wore the regulation parachutes. The five Hurricanes were mere specks in the fast-lightening sky, but the Mosquito began slowly to overhaul them.

Below, looking eastward, like an army of black snakes, was the pattern of waterways that comprise the delta of the river Ganges. Rivers, streams, and irrigation canals, lay asprawl a flat, monotonous terrain, cutting it into a vast archipelago before emptying themselves into the Bay of Bengal. Here and there a village nestled in a verdant bed of paddy-fields, or clung precariously to the fringe of one of the numerous masses of forest that had invaded the fertile land from the east. By the time these had given way to the more sombre green of the interminable Burmese jungle the sky was turning from lavender to blue, with the Mosquito about a mile astern and two thousand feet above the Hurricane formation.

'What's their objective—do you know?' queried Tug.

'Apparently there's a bridge over the Manipur River which the army is anxious to have pranged*, to interrupt the Jap lines of communication.'

* Slang: to bomb a target successfully.

484

'Do you know where it is?'

'Not exactly, but it's somewhere north-west of Mandalay; you'll find it on the map.'

Tug unfolded the map on his knees and studied it closely for a minute. 'Okay, I've got it,' he remarked.

'We must be pretty close to enemy country, even if we're not actually over it,' said Biggles presently. 'Let me know at once if you see anything suspicious. You might get down and have a squint below, to see if you can spot any sign of ground activity.'

Tug dropped to the prone position and for a little while subjected the landscape to a searching scrutiny. Then he climbed back to his seat. 'Not a blessed thing,' he stated. 'All I can see are trees and rivers. No sign of any trenches, or anything like that, to mark the no-man's-land between our troops and the Japs.'

'What with jungle and camouflage. I didn't expect to see much,' returned Biggles. His eyes were on the Hurricanes.

'Listen, Tug. We'd better have some sort of a plan. I'll watch the formation. You watch the sky. If you see anything, *anything*, let me know. Let me know, too, if you feel anything. If I see or feel anything unusual I'll let you know. It may sound silly, but if I start behaving in a manner that strikes you as odd, you take over and get back home straightaway.'

Tug grinned. 'Okay. Funny business, this waiting for something to go pop.'

'I don't think funny is the right word,' argued Biggles. 'I'd say it's dashed uncomfortable. We must be well over enemy country now, so something may happen any time. Hello—that tells us where we are.'

A few wisps of black smoke had appeared in the sky round the formation, which went on without altering course.

'That's ordinary flak*,' declared Tug.

Biggles had a good look at it before he answered. He even flew close to a patch, studied it suspiciously, and then dispersed it with his slipstream. 'I think you're right,' he agreed. 'Just ordinary flak.'

It soon died away and no more came up. A quarter of an hour passed without incident. The Hurricanes roared on with the Mosquito keeping its distance.

'I'll bet those boys are wondering what this Mossy is doing, trailing 'em,' chuckled Tug. 'They seem to be all right so far.'

'So do we.'

'Maybe it'll turn out to be a false alarm after all.'

'Maybe.' Biggles was noncommittal. Not for a moment did he take his eyes off the Hurricanes.

Another twenty minutes passed and the formation began to lose height, at the same time opening out a little.

'What are they doing?' asked Tug.

'It's all right. That bridge over the river ahead must be the target. They're going down to prang it. Keep your eyes skinned for enemy aircraft—or anything else.'

Nothing happened—that is, nothing out of normal routine. The Mosquito held its altitude, circling wide, while the fighter-bombers went down and did their work. Pillars of white smoke leapt skyward in the target area. Biggles noted one direct hit and two near misses, and made a note in the log he was keeping. There was no flak, no enemy opposition of any sort. The Hurricanes, their work done, turned away, closing in again to the original formation, and headed for home, taking some altitude.

* Exploding anti-aircraft shells.

'Well, that's that,' mused Biggles. 'I didn't see anything unusual, did you, Tug?'

'Not a thing,' muttered Tug. 'I don't get it.'

'One would have thought that if the Japs *could* have stopped them, they'd have done it on the way out, before the bombers reached their target,' said Biggles pensively. 'The thing gets more and more inexplicable. Keep a sharp look-out, we aren't home yet.'

'They're still flying pretty,' observed Tug after a glance at the Hurricanes.

'So are we if it comes to that,' answered Biggles, glancing at the watch on the instrument panel and making another note.

Fifteen minutes later he observed that one of the Hurricanes had moved slightly out of position, so that its opposite number had to swerve slightly to avoid collision. Biggles stiffened, staring, nerves tense, but aware that this might have been the result of a moment's carelessness on the part of the pilot. But when the same machine swerved, and began to sideslip, he uttered a warning cry.

'Look! There goes one of them!' he shouted. 'By heaven! Yes, he's going down!'

Tug did not answer. Both pilots watched while the Hurricane maintained its swerve, getting farther and farther away from the formation, which held on its course. At the same time the nose of the straying machine began to droop, until presently the aircraft was plunging earthward in a dive that became ever steeper.

'Pull out!' yelled Tug—uselessly. He began to mutter incoherently.

The Hurricane, still running on full throttle it seemed, roared on to a doom that was now only a matter of seconds.

'Why doesn't he bale out?' cried Tug in a strangled voice.

'No use, Tug. He's finished,' said Biggles through his teeth, and pushing the control column forward he tore down behind the stricken aircraft. A swift glance revealed the other four machines still in formation, but nose down, racing on the homeward course, which, in the circumstances, Biggles realised, was the wisest action they could take. Long before he could overtake the doomed aircraft it had crashed through the tree-tops and disappeared from sight like a stone dropping into opaque water.

Tug caught his breath at the moment of impact, and then cursed through bloodless lips. His face was pale and distorted with fury; his eyes glittered.

'No use swearing, Tug,' said Biggles evenly. 'That doesn't get anybody anywhere.'

He went on down and circled over the spot where the Hurricane had disappeared, revealed at short distance by fractured branches. Nothing could be seen. 'The crash hasn't taken fire, anyway,' he muttered, and then looked at his own instrument dials, in turn. 'We seem to be still okay,' he added. 'Do you feel all right, Tug?'

'More or less—just savage, that's all,' growled Tug.

'Keep watch up topsides,' warned Biggles.

Still circling, without taking his eyes from the scene of the tragedy he climbed back up to two thousand feet.

'Listen Tug,' he said crisply. 'I'm going to bale out.'

'You're *what*!'

'I'm going down.'

'What's the use? The chap in that kite hadn't a hope.'

'I know that, but I'm going down to try to find out

488

just what happened. Unless someone examines one of these crashes we may never know what causes them. This is my chance.'

'You'll get hung up in the trees.'

'That's a risk I shall have to take.'

'What about Japs? There may be some down there.'

'I've got a gun in my pocket.'

'But don't be crazy. How are you going to get home?'

'Walk, if necessary.'

'But we must be a hundred miles from the nearest of our troops. I can't pick you up. There ain't an open patch as big as a handkerchief within seeing distance.' Tug spoke in a shrill, protesting voice.

'All right, don't get excited,' returned Biggles. 'There is one way you can collect me, when I've seen what I want to see. Take a look at that river, about a mile away to the left.'

'What about it?'

'I don't know how deep it is, but if it has any depth at all it should be possible to put down a seaplane or flying-boat on it. Now listen carefully. After I bale out I want you to return to base, going full bore. Tell Algy what has happened. Tell him to find Raymond and get him to requisition a marine aircraft of some sort from anywhere he likes. I believe the Calcutta Flying Club used to have some Moth seaplanes—but I'll leave that to Raymond. Whatever he gets, you come back in it and pick me up. And when I say you I mean *you*. Algy will probably want to come, but he's in charge at base and my orders are on no account is he to leave. This is tricky country, and having seen the spot you should recognise it again. Is that clear so far?'

'Okay. Where do I pick you up, exactly?'

'I shall be waiting by the river, on this bank, as near as I can get to the larger of those two islands you can see. They stand in a straight reach of river so it ought to be all right for landing. That island is the mark. Take a good look at it before you go because they may be similar islands higher up or lower down the river.'

'Okay, skipper. Is there some way you can let me know if you get down all right?'

'I've got my petrol lighter. I'll make a smoke signal. If you see smoke you'll know I'm on the carpet. Take over now, and glide across the crash. There doesn't seem to be any wind to speak of.'

They changed places and Biggles opened the escape hatch.

Tug throttled back and began a run, at little more than stalling speed, towards the spot where the Hurricane had crashed.

'Keep her as she goes,' said Biggles. 'That's fine. See you later.' He disappeared into space.

Tug pushed the throttle open and having brought the aircraft to even keel banked slightly to get a view below. The parachute was floating down almost directly over the objective. He watched it sink lower and lower until eventually it remained stationary on the tree-tops.

'My God! He's caught up!' he muttered through dry lips. He continued to circle, watching, and saw the fabric split as a broken branch poked through it. But he could not see Biggles. He could only suppose that he was suspended by the shrouds somewhere between the tree-tops and the ground. It was several minutes before a thin column of smoke drifted up.

Tug drew a deep breath of relief, and blipped* his engines as a signal that the smoke had been seen. He

* To change the rhythm of the engines, by closing and opening the throttle.

490

turned to the river. For a minute he cruised up and down making mental pictures of the island from all angles. Then, banking steeply, he raced away on a westward course.

Chapter 6
Rendezvous With Death

Tug's fear that Biggles' parachute would become caught up in the tree-tops was fully justified; it would only have been remarkable had it been otherwise. Biggles knew this, so he was not surprised when he found himself swinging in his harness below tangled shrouds and torn fabric some thirty feet above the fern-carpeted floor of the jungle. He was not unduly alarmed, being well satisfied that he himself had escaped injury. By pulling on a line to increase his swing he managed without any great difficulty to reach a bough. In five minutes he had slipped out of his harness and made a cautious descent to the ground, leaving the parachute in the trees, where, he realised, it was likely to remain. A party of monkeys, after chattering at the intrusion, swung quietly away.

Perspiring profusely in the stagnant atmosphere from his exertions he mopped his face with his handkerchief, and after listening for a little while for sounds that might indicate danger, he made the smoke fire as arranged. His petrol lighter, an old letter from his pocket, and some sere undergrowth, provided the means. He heard Tug's answering signal, but he did not move until a fast-receding drone told him that the Mosquito was homeward bound. The sound died away and silence fell—a strange, oppressive silence, after the vibrant roar which had for so long filled his ears. Bracing himself for his ordeal, for he had no delusions about the harrowing nature of the task before him, he made his way to the crash. He had not far to go.

The Hurricane was much in the condition he expected. Both wings had been torn off at their roots. One hung from a splintered bough a short distance from the wreck; the other, fractured in the middle and bent at right angles, lay near the fuselage. The blades of the airscrew had folded up and the boss had bored deep into the soft leafmould. The fuselage was the right way up, more or less intact. The only sound was a soft drip-drip-drip, as liquid escaped from radiator, tank, or a broken petrol lead. Moistening his lips he walked on to the cockpit.

The pilot, whom he did not know, a lad of about twenty with flaxen hair and blue eyes, was still in his seat. He was dead. No attempt had been made to use the parachute. A head wound, where his forehead had come into contact with the instrument panel at the moment of impact, was alone sufficient to have caused death, which must have been instantaneous.

Biggles lifted the limp body out, laid it on the ground and removed the indentification disc. THOMAS GRAFTON MOORVEN, R.A.F., it read. He then took everything from the pockets—cigarette case, wallet, personal letters, some snapshots and some loose coins—and having made a little bundle of them in the handkerchief, put it on one side. This done, he paused again to mop his face, for the heat was stifling. It may have been the anger that surged through him, causing his fingers to tremble, that made the heat seem worse than it really was. Accustomed though he was to war, and death, there was something poignant about this particular tragedy that moved him strangely, making his eyes moist and bringing a lump into his throat. After months of training and eager anticipation the boy had travelled thousands of miles to meet his death without firing a shot. He had not even seen the enemy who had killed him, the weapon that had struck him down. Fully aware of the risks he was taking he had gone out willingly to seek the thing that had killed his comrades, only to meet the same fate, to die alone in the eternal solitude of a tropic forest. There would be no reward, no decoration for valour. Those at home would not even know how he died. This, thought Biggles, as he stood looking down on the waxen features, was not war. It was murder—and murder called for vengeance. His hand, he decided, would exact retribution, if the power were granted him. He drew a deep breath and set about the task for which he had descended.

First, he examined the body thoroughly, but could find no wound, no mark that might have caused death, apart from those that were obviously the direct result of the crash. There was no sign of burning, such as might have resulted from an electrical discharge of some sort. He examined the eyes closely, and noticed that the pupils were dilated. This struck him as unusual, but neither his technical nor medical knowledge could help him to associate it with a cause of death. He made a mental note of it, however.

He next turned to the aircraft, starting with the wings. He did not expect to find anything there, for had they in some mysterious way been fractured in the air he would have seen it before the machine crashed. They told him nothing, so he turned to the fuselage, beginning with the motor, paying particular attention to the ignition system. All electrical equipment seemed to be in perfect order. From airscrew to rudder he subjected the machine to such an inspection as he had never before devoted to any aircraft; yet for all his efforts he found nothing, no clue that might remotely suggest a solution to the mystery. Again mopping his face, and brushing away the mosquitoes that were attacking him, he returned to the cockpit. He had already been over it. He went over it again, methodically, but found nothing except normal equipment on both side, even smelt it. He was turning away when a small object on the floor, under the seat, caught his eye. He picked it up. It was a slip of paper, pink paper of the sort that is called greaseproof, about three inches square. There was printing on one side: WITH THE COMPLIMENTS OF CHARNEYS, LTD., LONDON. NOT FOR SALE. SUPPLIED FOR THE USE OF H.M. FORCES ONLY. He raised the paper to his nostrils. It smelt faintly of mint. Smiling wanly he screwed the paper into a ball, tossed it aside and resumed his search.

Finally, reluctantly, he gave up, no wiser than when he began. There was nothing more he could do, he decided. Tug might return at any time now, so he had better be making his way towards the river.

One last problem, one that had been in the background of his mind all along, now demanded solution. The aircraft, of course, would have to be burnt, to prevent it from falling into the hands of the enemy. But what about the body? He had no implement with which to dig a grave. There seemed little point in carrying it to the river, even if this were possible. The undergrowth was so thick that he alone, with both hands free, would find the operation difficult enough. Even if he succeeded in carrying the body to the river there would be the question of transport to the base. In any case it would involve prodigious labour and delay, which would jeopardise his life, and Tug's, for no reason outside sentiment. On the other hand he did not like the idea of leaving the body there to become the prey of creatures of the forest. He could think of only one method of disposing of it, and that was the way chosen by some of the greatest warriors of the past, the way of the Romans, the Vikings, the Indians. All reduced the bodies of their chiefs and warriors to ashes, burning their weapons, their warhorses, and their hounds with them. After all, many good airmen, including some of his best friends, had gone out that way, he reflected.

Having steeled himself for this last grim ceremony, he was moving forward when voices at no great distance brought him to an abrupt halt, in a listening attitude. There was no doubt about the voices; with them came a trampling and crashing of undergrowth. Very soon it was clear that those responsible for the disturbance were approaching.

Biggles drew back and found a perfect retreat among the giant fronds of a tree-fern. In doing this he was actuated by more than casual curiosity. It seemed possible, indeed it seemed likely, that the Hurricane had been seen to fall, in which case enemy troops would be sent out to locate it. There was just a chance that these men were part of the team that operated the secret weapon. If that were so they would be worth capturing for interrogation.

The voices and the crashing drew nearer. The men seemed to be in a carefree mood. Biggles could not speak a word of Japanese, but he was in no doubt as to the nationality of the newcomers. He took out his automatic, examined it, and waited. The voices continued to approach.

In a few minutes a man burst from the undergrowth. He stopped when he saw the crash, and then let out a shrill cry. A second man joined him.

Biggles was disappointed. They were ordinary Japanese soldiers, infrantrymen, dirty, with the usual twigs attached to their uniforms for camouflage purposes. Both carried rifles and were smoking cigarettes.

496

No other sounds came from the forest so it was fairly certain that they were alone.

Their immediate reaction to the spectacle before them was not unnatural. They broke into an excited conversation as they walked on to the fuselage. When one of them pointed at the dead pilot and burst out laughing, after a momentary look of wonder Biggles frowned: friend or foe, to European eyes the sight was anything but funny. When one of them kicked the body every vestige of colour drained from his face. His lips came together in a hard line; his nostrils quivered. Still he did not move. But when one of the men, with what was evidently a remark intended to be jocular, bent down and inserted his cigarette between the dead pilot's lips, and then, shouting with laughter, stepped back to observe the effect. Biggles' pent-up anger could no longer be restrained.

'You scum,' he grated. The words were low, but distinct.

The two Japanese spun round as if a shot had been fired. They stared in goggle-eyed amazement, no longer laughing, but fearful, as though confronted by a ghost—the ghost of the body they had violated. Superstitious by nature, they may have believed that.

Biggles spoke again. 'You utter swine,' he breathed.

This spurred the Japanese to movement. With a curious cry one of them threw up his rifle. Biggles fired. The man twitched convulsively. Again Biggles' automatic roared. The man's legs crumpled under him; the rifle fell from his hands and he slumped, choking. The second man started to run. Quite dispassionately, without moving from his position, Biggles took deliberate aim and fired. The Jap pitched forward on his face, but crying loudly started to get up. Biggles walked forward and with calculated precision fired two more shots at point-blank range. His lips were drawn back, showing the teeth. 'You unspeakable thug,' he rasped. The man lay still.

As the echoes of the shots died away a hush fell, sullen, hot, heavy. The only sound was the hum of innumerable mosquitoes. For a few seconds, breathing heavily, the smoking pistol in his hand, Biggles stood gazing at the man he had shot. Then he walked quickly to the dead pilot, snatched the cigarettes from his lips and hurled it aside.

'Sorry about that, Tommy,' he said quietly. 'Sort of thing one doesn't expect,' he added, as if he were talking to himself.

Pocketing his pistol he picked up the body, placed it gently in the cockpit and closed the cover. Then, lighting a slip of paper he dropped it by a leaking petrol lead. Fire took hold, spreading rapidly. In a moment the forepart of the aircraft was wrapped in leaping flames.

As Biggles stepped back his eyes fell on the Japanese. 'We've no dogs, Tommy,' he murmured; 'These hellhounds are a poor substitute, but they'll have to do.' Having confirmed that both were dead he dragged the bodies across the tail unit, which had not yet been reached by the flames, afterwards backing away quickly, for the ammunition belts were exploding their charges and bullets were flying. Picking up the handkerchief containing the dead pilot's belongings he walked to the edge of the clearing. There he turned and stiffened to attention. His right hand came up to the salute.

'So long, Tommy,' he said quietly. 'Good hunting.' Then, without a backward glance he strode away through the jungle in the direction of the river.

Behind him, to the roll of exploding ammunition, the

smoke of the funeral pyre made a white column high against the blue of heaven. He realised that it might be seen by the enemy and bring them to the spot. He didn't care. He rather hoped it would. He was in the sort of mood when fighting would be a pleasure.

It took him the best part of an hour to reach the river, and he was dripping with sweat when the turgid water came into view. The only living things in sight were a small crocodile, lying on a mudflat, and a grey heron, perched on a dead limb overhanging the water. There was no sign of Tug. He was some distance above the island that he had chosen for the rendezvous, and it required another twenty minutes of labour, working along the river bank, to bring him in line with it. There was still no sign of Tug, so choosing the crest of a small escarpment for a seat, he lighted a cigarette and settled down to wait. There was nothing else to do. The mosquitoes were still with him. He brushed them away with a weary gesture and mopped his dripping face, which was still pale, and set in hard lines. The strain of the last two hours had been considerable.

He passed the next half-hour in silent meditation, pondering over the events of the morning, and the problem which they had done nothing to elucidate, before he heard the sound for which he was waiting— the drone of an aircraft. But because his ears were attuned to the nicer distinctions between aero engines, at first he was puzzled. Very soon, though, he solved the mystery. There were two engines, of different types. The main background of sound was provided by the deep roar of a high-performance motor, but against it, quite distinct, there was the busy chatter of a lighter type. It seemed unlikely that there could be two light planes in that particular theatre of war, so he was not surprised when a Gipsy Moth float-plane swung into view, tearing low up the river. Behind it, weaving in wide zigzags but definitely keeping it company, was a Hurricane.

Biggles smiled faintly as he stood up and waved. The ill-assorted pair needed no explanation. Tug had returned in a marine craft as arranged, and it had brought an escort. Biggles' immediate reaction was one of relief, not so much on his own account as because, in spite of the secret weapon, Tug had obviously managed to get home, and make the return trip. He had been gone a long time, and Biggles had just begun to fear that the nameless peril had claimed him.

Tug evidently saw him at once, for he cut his engine and put the machine straight down on the water. Without waiting for it to finish its run he came round in a swirl of creamy foam to that point of the river bank where Biggles was now waiting. Biggles waded out through two feet of water and six inches of mud to the aircraft, and climbed aboard.

'Good work, Tug,' he greeted. 'have any trouble?'

Tug grinned. 'Not a trace. I saw a bunch of Zeros*, high up, as I went home, but they didn't see me. Did you find anything?'

'No.'

'Who was it—Grainger, Larkin, or Moorven?'

Biggles started. 'What do you mean?'

'All three failed to get back. The others say the hoodoo got 'em all.'

'The others? Do you mean that Johnny Crisp and Scrimshaw got back *again*?'

'They did. I left Johnny stamping and cursing on the airfield, and Scrimshaw roaring round in circles looking for somebody to shoot. Odd, ain't it?'

* Japanese fighter aircraft.

During this brief recital Biggles had remained still, half in and half out of the spare seat, staring at Tug's face. 'Odd! It's more than that. It's more than that. It's uncanny. It can't be luck. It *can't* be. But we'll talk about that when we get home. Who's in the Hurricane?'

'Angus.'

'Who told him he could come?'

'Algy.'

'Algy, eh? I like his nerve.'

Tug grinned again. 'Algy's in charge, don't forget, during your absence. Don't blame him. The whole bunch wanted to come and Algy had his work cut out to keep them on the carpet. They reckoned someone ought to come to keep an eye on me while I was keeping an eye open for you. In the end Algy agreed to let one of the flight commanders go. Angus and Bertie tossed for it. Bertie lost. I left him trying to rub a hole through his eyeglass.' While Tug had been speaking he had eased the throttle open a trifle and moved slowly to deeper water.

Biggles was looking up at the Hurricane. 'What the . . . ! What in thunder does Angus think he's doing?' he asked sharply.

Tug looked up and saw the fighter coming down in a shallow swerving dive as if it intended pancaking on the river. 'He's giving you the salute,' he said, slowly, in a voice that did not carry conviction.

Biggles did not answer at once. He stared, while the Hurricane continued its downward swoop. 'You're wrong,' he forced through dry lips. 'Angus has bought it. Look out!'

The warning was no mere figure of speech, for the Hurricane was coming in dead in line with the Moth. Tug realised it, and shoved the throttle open with a lightning movement of his hand. 'Hang on!' he yelled, as the engine roared and the light plane shot forward. He was only just in time.

The Hurricane's port wing-tip missed the Moth by inches. It struck the water with a mighty splash that drenched the Moth with spray and set it rocking violently. It bounced and splashed again, this time to disappear except for a swinging rudder.

Tug tore to the spot. 'I told him not to come!' he cried wildly. Then again, 'I told him not to come. I told him—'

'Shut up,' snapped Biggles. 'Watch for me,' he added, and dived overboard.

When, a minute later, he reappeared, gasping, with Angus in his arms, Tug was out on a float, on his knees, waiting. He took Angus first, and then helped Biggles to get astride the float. The weight tipped the plane at a dangerous angle, and Tug leaned away to the other float to counteract the list. Angus was dead or unconscious—it was not clear which.

'Help me to get him into the spare seat,' ordered Biggles.

'How is he do you think?'

'I don't know, but he must be in a bad way. He's got a broken leg, if nothing worse. We can't do anything for him here. His only chance, if he is still alive, is hospital.'

'But this machine won't lift three—there's no room, anyway.'

'I know it,' answered Biggles curtly. 'You get him back. I'll wait. I shall be all right here. You ought to be back in a couple of hours if nothing goes wrong. Better 'phone Algy from the slipway to let him know what's happened—and tell him to keep everybody on the ground till I get back. That's an order.'

'Okay,' grunted Tug.

After some delay, and with no small difficulty, Angus' limp body was lifted into the spare seat. As Biggles had said, there was no question of doing anything for him on the spot.

'Run me close to the bank and I'll get off,' said Biggles. 'There are crocs in this river.'

Tug taxied close to the bank and Biggles waded ashore.

'Okay – get cracking,' ordered Biggles.

Tug waved. The engine roared. The little plane swung round and raced away down the river. Biggles watched it until it was out of sight and then resumed his seat on the escarpment. Automatically he felt for his cigarette case. The cigarettes were, of course, soaking wet, so very carefully he laid them out on the rock to dry.

Chapter 7
Biggles Investigates

Biggles waited, waited while the sun climbed over its zenith and began its downward journey. In the low ground through which the river wound its sluggish course, the air, heavy with the stench of rotting vegetation, was still. The heat was suffocating. The swampy banks of the river steamed, the slime at the water's edge erupting gaseous bubbles. Biggles sweated. Once, a flight of three Mitsubishi bombers droned overhead on a westerly course; a little later six Zero fighters, flying at a great height, passed over, heading in the same direction, towards India.

'They must know our machines are grounded, so they're getting cocky,' mused Biggles.

It was clear that if the secret weapon was still in operation the enemy planes were not affected, which proved that the thing was under control, and discounted anything in the nature of poison gas which, once released, would be uncontrollable, and would—unless the Japanese pilots wore respirators—affect both friend and foe alike. If a beam, or ray, were being used, it could not be a permanent installation, for this also would operate against all types of aircraft regardless of nationality. Had enemy planes been insulated against such a ray the insulating material would have been discovered by technicians whose work it was to examine the enemy aircraft brought down on the British side of the lines. Not the least puzzling aspect of the new weapon was the distance over which it was effective—

or so it would seem from the immense area in which British machines had been brought down. It suggested that the instrument was highly mobile, or else there was a number of them installed at points throughout the entire forest. Yet if this were so, why had the Hurricanes been allowed to reach their objective? Had it been possible to stop them, then they would most certainly have been stopped. The fact that the Hurricane formation had reached its objective that morning suggested that the weapon had its limitations. Thus mused Biggles, sweltering on his lonely rock.

It was getting on for three hours before Tug returned. Biggles was glad to see the Moth, for apart from the delay, and the wearisome nature of his vigil, the danger of flying in the area had been demonstrated.

'You've been a long time,' greeted Biggles.

'I had to snoop around a bit,' answered Tug. 'There are bandits* about, poking their noses close to India—taking advantage of our machines being grounded, I suppose.'

'How's Angus?' asked Biggles anxiously, as he climbed aboard.

'He's alive, but that's about all. They took him to hospital. I didn't wait for details.'

'Did he recover consciousness?'

'No.'

'You spoke to Algy?'

'Yes. I 'phoned him.'

'What did he say?'

'Oh, he got a bit worked up—wanted to send the gang out, for escort. I told him what you said about staying put. He just made noises.'

'Where did you get this Moth, by the way?'

* RAF code for enemy aeroplanes

505

'Raymond fixed it. It was up a backwater the other side of Calcutta. Raymond lent me his car to get to it. It used to belong to an air taxi company. That's all I know. It flies all right—and that's all I care.'

'As we can't land at Dum Dum we shall have to go back to the place where you got it.'

'I reckon so.'

'Is Raymond's car still there?'

'No, we shall have to get a taxi.'

'Okay,' said Biggles as he settled himself in his seat. 'Better keep low: we don't want to run into a bunch of Zeros.'

The flight to Calcutta was uneventful. On several occasions enemy aircraft were seen, mostly flying high, but the Moth, skimming the tree-tops, escaped observation. By the time it had been moored, and a taxi found, and the trip made to Dum Dum, the sun was low in the western sky. Without stopping to wash or remove the mud from his clothes Biggles walked straight to the mess. The others were waiting.

His first question was, 'How's Angus?'

Algy answered. 'I've been to the hospital—just got back. They wouldn't let me see him—not that there would have been any point in it. He's still unconscious, and likely to remain so. He's badly smashed up—broken arm, broken leg, three ribs stove in and concussion. If he gets over it, it will be months before he's on his feet again. We can reckon him off the strength as far as this show's concerned.'

Biggles shook his head sadly. 'Poor old Angus. Tough luck. Still, it's something that he is still alive. I suppose it was expecting too much to hope that he might have come round. I wanted to talk to him. He might have been able to tell us something—what happened, and how he felt. As far as we know, he's the

506

first victim of the new weapon who has survived, or who has got back.'

'Then you don't know what hit him?' said Bertie.

'I haven't the remotest idea,' admitted Biggles. 'The machine just dived into the drink as if the controls had jammed, or as if he had done it deliberately. That's how it struck me. What do you think, Tug? You saw it.'

'Same as you.'

The others were crowding round. 'You didn't see anything break?' queried Ginger.

'Not a thing,' answered Biggles. 'When the machine hit the water, as far as one could see, there was absolutely nothing wrong with it.'

'What about Moorven's crash?' asked Algy. 'Did you find anything there?'

'Nothing. I'll tell you all about it later, after I've had a bite and a clean up. I really only looked in to get the latest news about Angus. I shall be busy for a bit, making out a written report on Moorven's crash, handing over his effects, and so on. I also want to have a word with Johnny Crisp and Scrimshaw. There's something unnatural about the way they always get back. It can't be luck. There must be a reason, and if we can put our finger on it we shall be half-way towards getting this thing buttoned up.'

At this point Air Commodore Raymond came in. 'I heard you were back.' he announced. 'What happened?'

'Just a minute, sir,' protested Biggles. 'I haven't had anything to eat to-day yet, and blundering about in the jungle was a dirty business—as you can see. Give me a few minutes for a bath and a bite and I'll tell you all about it. Wait here—the others will want to hear the story too. I'll be back.'

In rather less than half an hour he returned, his material needs satisfied. 'Let's sit down,' he suggested.

He then told his story. Narrated in his usual concise manner, it did not take long.

'Then we still haven't got anywhere,' said the Air Commodore despondently.

'I wouldn't say that exactly,' argued Biggles, 'Certain broad aspects are beginning to emerge. When I've had time to think about them I may be able to get a line on the thing.'

'What are you going to do next?'

'It's dark, so there's nothing more we can do in the air. I'd like a word with Crisp and Scrimshaw. There's a bit of a mystery about the way they keep getting back. Of course, it may be luck, but if it isn't, then they, or their machines, must be immune from the thing that's causing the mischief. I'd also like to have a chat with the last man who touched Moorven's machine before he got into it.'

'I've already made inquiries about that,' said the Air Commodore. 'It was a sergeant named Gray. He went over all the machines just before they took off. He seems to be terribly cut up about the three machines going west—somehow feels that they were his responsibility.'

'But that's silly.'

'That's what I told him.'

'What sort of chap is the sergeant?'

'He's a fellow of about thirty, with ten years' service. Exemplary record, and a first class all round fitter-rigger. Before the show, knowing what might happen, he went over every machine, and every engine.'

'I see. Well, we'll leave him till later. Let's get hold of Crisp and Scrimshaw.'

'Where shall we see them—in my office?'

Biggles thought for a moment. 'No. Let's make it informal. I can imagine how they feel. They'll be more likely to open up here than in your office. And I'd like to ask the questions, if you don't mind.'

'Very well,' assented the Air Commodore. 'Get one of your chaps to fetch them. He'll probably find them in the bar at the central mess.'

Biggles raised his eyebrows. 'Drinking?'

'Scrimshaw, who normally doesn't touch anything, is beginning to spend too much time in the bar. It's understandable. After all, these two have watched a squadron wiped out, and some of them have been together since the Battle of Britain.'

Biggles nodded to Ginger. 'Slip along and fetch them,' he ordered.

Ginger went. The others continued the debate for the next few minutes, when Ginger returned with the two officers.

'Sit down, chaps,' invited Biggles quietly. 'Pull up a couple of chairs.'

Crisp and Scrimshaw sat down. Biggles took a quick glance at them in turn as he offered cigarettes. They were both in the condition he expected, for he knew only too well the symptoms resulting from nerve strain, shock, and impotent anger. Scrimshaw's face was flushed and his eyes unnaturally bright. He smoked his cigarette in quick short puffs, tapping it incessantly whether there was any ash on it or not. Crisp was pale but steady; his eyes were a little bloodshot in the corners. The fingers of the hand that took the cigarette shook; the forefinger was yellow with nicotine stain.

'We're trying to get to the bottom of this business,' began Biggles casually.

'Getting time somebody did something about it,' rapped out Scrimshaw.

'No one is likely to argue about that,' replied Biggles gently. 'All is being done that can be done. The Japs have slipped a fast one on us, and the only way we shall get it buttoned up is by keeping our heads. To let it get us on the floor would be playing into their hands.'

'I hear you went down and looked at Moorven?' snapped Scrimshaw.

Biggles looked up. 'Who told you that?'

'I don't know—I heard it.'

'Where did you hear it?'

'In the mess, I expect.'

Biggles glanced round. 'Have you fellows been talking?'

'I don't think anybody has spoken outside this mess,' said Algy. 'In fact, apart from my visit to the hospital I don't think anyone has been out.'

'I remember. It was Lal Din told me,' said Scrimshaw.

Biggles looked at Algy. 'Has Lal Din been here?'

'Yes.'

'When?'

'He served coffee after lunch.'

'I told you not to discuss this thing in front of the staff,' rasped Biggles.

There was an uncomfortable silence.

It was broken by Scrimshaw. 'Pah! What does it matter?'

Biggles ignored the question. 'Let's get on,' he resumed, looking at Crisp and Scrimshaw. 'So far you two fellows have been lucky—'

He winced as Scrimshaw laughed—a harsh, jarring sound.

'Is that your idea of luck?' sneered Scrimshaw.

'All right, Let's say it wasn't luck,' said Biggles

510

imperturbably. 'Let us say there may be a reason. If we are right in that assumption we soon ought to get the thing pranged.'

'Then you didn't find anything at Moorven's crash?' asked Crisp.

'I found a couple of Japanese soldiers,' returned Biggles.

'What did you do with them?' demanded Scrimshaw.

'I shot them,' answered Biggles evenly.

Scrimshaw let out a yell. 'By thunder! I wish I'd been there. I'd have—'

'Maybe you'll get a chance to do even better later on,' interrupted Biggles curtly. 'I baled out over Moorven's crash to-day hoping to find out whether the new weapon strikes at the man or the machine. Unfortunately there was no indication. What I'm trying to find out now is, what you two fellows did that Moorven did not do. Conversely, what he did that you did not do. It may have been something that happened in the air or on the ground. I should have liked to put this same question to one of my flight commanders, who bought it this morning, but unfortunately he is not yet able to speak. Johnny, I want you to think very carefully and tell me everything you did from the moment you got up this morning.'

'Where's that going to get us?' demanded Scrimshaw, lighting a fresh cigarette from the one he already held.

'It may get us nowhere,' admitted Biggles. 'But let's look at it this way. Only one thing is quite certain. Either our machines are being attacked by something we can't see, or the pilots in them. I'm going to deal with both possibilities in turn. Right now I am working on the personal aspect. Go ahead Johnny.'

'I got out of bed,' began Crisp. 'I took off my pyjamas

511

and dressed.'

'Didn't you wash or have a bath?'

'No.'

'Go on.'

'I then went over to the mess, where I stood by the big table and had some coffee and biscuits.'

'Was anyone else there?'

'Not when I got there. The others came in later.'

'And what did they do?'

'They joined me at the table.'

'And had coffee and biscuits?'

'Yes.'

'You're sure of that?'

'Scrimshaw's here, ask him.'

'That's right,' said Scrimshaw shortly. 'We all had coffee and biscuits. Nothing funny about that, was there?'

'Nothing at all,' agreed Biggles calmly. 'And this coffee all came out of the same pot?'

'Yes,' Crisp answered.

'What about the biscuits?'

'We all helped ourselves from the same plate.'

'And there was nobody else in the room all this time—I mean staff?'

'Nobody. The stuff is put out and anybody who wants can help himself. That's the usual arrangement.'

'Go on,' invited Biggles.

'The five of us then walked over to the machines together.'

'Did you smoke after finishing the coffee?'

'Sorry—yes. I forgot that. I had a packet of cigarettes in my pocket. Being finished first I had one, and passed the packet.'

'Then you all smoked cigarettes from the same packet?'

'What's all this?' snapped Scrimshaw. 'Are you trying to make out—'

'Take it easy,' interrupted Biggles. 'I'm not trying to make out anything. I'm asking for facts. Go ahead, Johnny.'

'That's all. We got into our machines and took off.'

'You didn't touch anything else?'

'No.'

'Did you speak to anyone?'

'Yes, I spoke to the sergeant—Sergeant Gray.'

'What about?'

Johnny looked uncomfortable. 'About the change-over.'

'What change-over?'

'Well, you see, I swopped planes with Moorven.'

'You *what?*'

'Changed planes.'

'Why?'

'Well, I reckoned perhaps somebody was tinkering with the machines, but for some reason or other mine was always left alone. We decided to change kites to see what happened. If I went west*, and Moorven got back, it would begin to look as if there was some peculiarity about my machine that was saving me all the time. It was because of this that I feel so rotten now. If poor old Moorven had stuck to his own machine he would have got back.'

'You mean—he *might* have got back,' said Biggles softly. 'I understand, Johnny. What you really did was to take a big chance of going west yourself. That was pretty noble of you. I'm glad you mentioned this because it rather goes to prove that the machine doesn't make any difference, and that's important. Sergeant

* Slang: got killed.

513

Gray knew about this change?'

'Yes.'

Biggles turned to Scrimshaw. 'Did you speak to anybody?'

'Not a soul.'

'And in the air neither of you did anything beyond controlling the aircraft?'

Scrimshaw laughed mirthlessly. 'What else was there to do?'

'I don't know,' answered Biggles. 'That's what I'm trying to find out. You say you both did nothing, so that settles that. And neither of you at any time heard or felt the slightest thing, no noise, no jar, nothing unusual?'

'Nothing at all,' said Johnny.

'That goes for me too,' added Scrimshaw.

'Not even when Moorven fell out of position?' queried Biggles.

'No.'

'You saw him go, of course?'

'Yes, we both saw him go,' confirmed Johnny.

'Moorven didn't say anything over the radio?'

'Not a word.'

'Did you speak to him?'

'Yes. I called him, and asked him what he was doing.'

'Didn't he answer?'

'No.'

'And the others went down in similar circumstances?'

'Yes. Grainger fell about ten minutes after Moorven wer.t, but Larkin lasted nearly all the way home. He went down about five miles inside the Jap lines.'

'I see—thanks.' Biggles looked at the Air Commodore. 'Any questions you would like to ask?'

The Air Commodore shook his head. 'No. I think

you've covered the ground pretty thoroughly. There's just one thing, though.' He looked at Crisp and Scrimshaw. 'What are you two fellows going to do? Your squadron is washed out for the time being. Would you like a spot of leave?'

'Not for me, sir,' answered Scrimshaw. 'Leave is the last thing I want.'

'And me,' added Johnny. 'We'll go on flying till we hit the deck or get to the bottom of this thing, one or the other.'

'It won't do either of you any good to go on living in an empty mess,' suggested the Air Commodore gently. 'Bigglesworth has to-day lost one of his flight commanders. Crisp, why don't you let me attach you, temporarily, to his squadron, to fill the gap? I'm sure he'd be glad to have you. And you, too, Scrimshaw. You'll work better if you have someone to talk things over with.'

'Yes, why not?' put in Biggles quickly.

The two pilots looked at each other.

'That suits me fine,' said Johnny. 'That is, if Scrim. will come over?'

'I'll come anywhere.' muttered Scrimshaw. 'It's all the same to me.'

'It may be, but it isn't all the same to me,' said Biggles coldly. 'The boys in this squadron have covered a lot of sky since the war started, and it wouldn't be fair to them to turn in more risks then they normally take. Frankly, Scrimshaw, we haven't much confidence in fellows who grab a bottle when things get sticky.'

Scrimshaw flushed scarlet. 'Who said—'

'I said,' broke in Biggles without raising his voice. 'And what I say I mean. The sooner you understand that the better. Oh, I know how you feel. I've been through it myself, more than once. I was going through

515

it when you wore safety-pins instead of buttons, but I got over it—if I hadn't I shouldn't be here now. If you go on ginning-up you'll be no use to yourself or anyone else. We needn't say any more about it—but think it over. Make a party with my fellows after dinner and take a trip round the town. They'll do anything you want to do, but they don't brood and they don't booze—those are the only two things we bar. We've too much to do. That's all for now.' Biggles got up.

8

Death Marches on

As the officers dispersed, talking over the mystery quietly among themselves, Biggles turned to Air Commodore Raymond. 'I think I shall go along right away and have a word or two with Sergeant Gray, sir,' he announced. 'There's just time before dinner.'

'Do you mind if I come with you?' asked Johnny Crisp. 'It's partly my pigeon. Gray is in A Flight—my flight.'

'Come by all means—only too glad to have you along, invited Biggles. 'He'll probably say more to you than to strangers. That'll be enough, though, we don't want a crowd.'

Biggles, the Air Commodore and Johnny, left the officers' quarters and walked along to the sergeants' mess, where they learned that Sergeant Gray was out.

'Any idea where he is?' Biggles asked the flight sergeant who had come to the door.

'I think I heard him say something about going down to the flight shed, sir,' returned the flight sergeant. 'He wanted to have another look at those two machines that got back this morning.'

'Thanks,' acknowledged Biggles. 'Maybe we'll find him there.'

'I hope he isn't going to let this thing prey on his mind,' remarked Johnny, as they walked on to the hangar in which the two surviving A Flight machines were parked. 'He's a good chap. He's been in the squadron pretty nearly since it was formed at Kenley years ago.'

The hangar was in darkness. The Air Commodore switched on a torch. The beam fell on the two Hurricanes, but there was no one with them.

'Anyone about?' called Biggles.

There was no answer.

Biggles saw a narrow crack of light half-way down and on one side of the building. 'That must be him, in the flight office,' he observed.

They walked on to the door. Biggles opened it. He stopped. 'Take a look at this,' he murmured dryly.

Lying on the floor, breathing stertorously, was a sergeant.

'That's Gray,' said Johnny. 'Drunk as a lord, by the look of it.'

'You seem pretty sure of that,' challenged Biggles.

'He's done it before. The same thing happened last week. If I'd put him on a charge he'd have lost his stripes, and I hate doing that to a good airman. I made him promise he wouldn't do it again.'

'Does he make a habit of doing this sort of thing?' asked the Air Commodore.

'Not as far as I know,' replied Johnny. 'I think he's only taken to it lately. Pity.'

Biggles shook the sergeant by the shoulder. 'Come on, snap out of it,' he ordered peremptorily.

The sergeant did not move.

'Get up, Gray,' snapped Johnny irritably.

The sergeant lay still, snoring.

Biggles pommelled him, and in the end slapped his face.

The sergeant grunted, but did not move.

'He certainly has got a skinful,' muttered Johnny. 'He sort of went to pieces when I told him that Moorven and the others had gone west, but I didn't think he'd take it like this.' He shook the sergeant again.

'It's no use,' said Biggles quietly. 'We shan't get anything out of him in that state. There's only one thing that might bring him round. Slip over to the mess, Johnny, and get a jug of black coffee, hot.'

Johnny went off at a run.

While they were waiting, the Air Commodore spoke to Biggles. 'What do you really make of all this?'

'It's fantastic—that's the only word for it,' replied Biggles. 'What beats me is, the thing is so infernally inconsistent. To-day, Tug made three trips well into enemy country and got away with it every time. Why? How? There must be an answer to that, if only we could hit on it. There were a lot of enemy machines about; I saw them, yet they weren't affected. They flew as if they had nothing to fear. Very strange. I have a feeling, not based on anything concrete, that—'

Johnny came in, slightly breathless from his run. 'There was no black coffee on tap, so I ordered some,' he announced. 'Lal Din says he will bring it over right away.' He looked at the sergeant. 'Silly fool, letting the flight down like this.'

A minute or two later the steward came in. His habitual smile broadened when his eyes fell on the sergeant.

'He catch plenty whisky,' he chuckled. 'Here coffee, sahib. Velly stlong.'

Biggles took the coffee-pot, a small copper one, from the tray, and walked over to the sergeant. 'What part of the world do you come from, Lal Din?' he asked casually. 'You don't talk like a man of this country.'

'Me Burmese. I blong Mandalay,' was the answer.

'You don't look much like a Burman,' said Biggles without looking up, as he dropped on his knees beside the unconscious N.C.O*.

* Non-Commissioned Officer eg a Sergeant or Corporal.

'Father Burman, but he dead long time. Mother, she Chinese. Bling me up China fashion,' said Lal Din.

Biggles forced the N.C.O.'s teeth apart, not without difficulty, and poured coffee into the mouth.

The sergeant spluttered. Biggles looked over his shoulder at Lal Din, who was still standing just inside the door. 'What are you waiting for?' he asked sharply.

'I wait for coffee-pot, sahib. Canteen ploperty. Maybe someone else want coffee.'

'You can fetch it later on. We may be some time.'

'Velly good, sahib.' Lal Din went off.

'What's the matter with him? Don't you trust him?' asked the Air Commodore.

'In a show like this, the only people I trust are those I know,' answered Biggles, pouring more coffee into the sergeant's mouth.

Again the sergeant spluttered, chokingly. His head lolled from side to side. His eyes opened.

'Come on Gray; pull yourself together,' rapped out Biggles tersely.

'Wash-washer matter?' gasped the sergeant.

'You're drunk,' said Johnny bitingly.

The sergeant was indignant. 'Thash a lie. Not drunk.'

Biggles gave him more coffee.

'He says he isn't drunk,' said Johnny, looking at Biggles and the Air Commodore in turn.

'Of course he does.' The Air Commodore laughed lugubriously. 'Did you ever know a drunken man admit that he was tight? I didn't.'

'If you tell him he's drunk he'll spend the rest of the night trying to prove that he isn't,' put in Biggles wearily.

The sergeant's eyes were clearing. 'Wash wrong?' he demanded in a dazed voice, and was then violently sick.

'Tight as an owl,' muttered Johnny. 'You won't get any sense out of him till he's slept it off.'

'I'm afraid you're right,' agreed Biggles sadly. 'What a nuisance.' He shook the sergeant again. 'Listen to me, Gray. Can you hear what I say?'

'Yes—shir.'

'That's better. We'll talk to you later.'

'Don't wanner talk—hic. Those swine killed my officers. I wanner get at 'em. You hear me? I wanner—'

Biggles stood up. 'Yes, we know. You go to your bunk and sleep it off.'

'Schleep what off?' slurred the sergeant drowsily.

'You're all ginned-up,' put in Johnny, who was getting more and more angry. 'You promised me you wouldn't touch the stuff.'

'Drunk! Hark at him,' pleaded the sergeant. 'Says I'm drunk. I was never drunk—in my life—no shir.'

'We'll settle that argument later,' averred Biggles, arranging a packed parachute under the sergeant's head. 'Have a sleep. Here, you might as well finish the rest of the coffee.'

Without assistance the N.C.O. took the remainder of the coffee at a gulp. 'Thash berrer,' he declared sleepily. 'I just wanner be alone,' he rambled on. 'I only came here to be alone. Sat here, chewing the thing over, thas all. I may be sick, but I ain't drunk—no shir.'

'Silly ass,' muttered Johnny.

'I wouldn't be too hard on him,' said Biggles as they went out. 'His nerves are probably in rags. You say he's been with the squadron a long time? Well, now he's seen the squadron washed out. He ought to be sent home for a rest.'

'I'll get him posted,' promised the Air Commodore.

They went to the mess and had dinner. Later, after listening to the news on the radio, they sat in a corner with Algy and Bertie discussing the mystery from all angles, without, however, coming any nearer to solving it. Biggles said little. Eventually he looked at his watch.

'Eleven o'clock,' he announced. 'I think I shall turn in, and leave Sergeant Gray until to-morrow.'

'I'll just walk down and make sure he's all right,' offered Johnny.

'Be as well,' agreed Biggles.

The Air Commodore got up. 'I'll be getting along, too,' he decided. 'See you in the morning.' He nodded to the others and departed.

Johnny went off. Biggles stood for a minute or two talking to Algy and Ginger, who wanted to know if he had made any plans for the following day. He told them he wanted to do some more thinking before he decided on a definite programme.

He was walking along the path that led to the officers' sleeping quarters when an airman overtook him.

'Excuse me, sir, you're wanted on the 'phone,' said he.

'Which 'phone?' asked Biggles.

'The one in the hall, sir.'

Biggles turned back. 'Where have you just come from?' he asked.

'I was on duty in the kitchen, sir.'

'I see.' Biggles stepped into the hall and picked up the telephone.

'Is that you, Biggles?' said a voice. 'This is Johnny here. I'd like you to come down to the flight shed.'

'Something wrong?' queried Biggles.

'Yes, it's the sergeant.'

'Is he still there?'

'Yes.'

'Is something wrong with him?'

'Plenty,' said Johnny. 'He's dead.'

'Stay there,' said Biggles tersely. 'I'll be right down.'

Biggles ran to the shed. Johnny was there, alone, bending over the sergeant, who was lying on his back on the floor, the position in which they had left him. One glance at the open mouth and staring eyes was enough.

'He's a goner all right,' said Biggles in a hard voice. He shook his head. 'I don't get it. He was coming round fast when we left him. Well, there goes my hope of learning anything from him. I wonder why he died? You've had a look at him I suppose?'

'Of course. Can't find a thing. Not a wound, not a mark of any sort. Can't make it out. He must have passed out in a drunken stupor.'

'Well, there's nothing we can do except send for the doctor,' said Biggles.

'I wonder if he did himself in, in a fit of remorse?' suggested Johnny.

'I imagine it is very difficult to commit suicide without leaving some sign of it,' returned Biggles. 'Go and fetch the M.O.*'

Johnny departed on his errand.

After gazing at the body for a moment or two Biggles looked round the little room, his eyes taking in everything. Nothing had been disturbed. The room appeared to be precisely as when he had last seen it. The coffee-pot and the tray were still there. He went to the pot and picked it up. It was empty. Thoughtfully, he put it down again. For a while he did not move from where he stood; then his eyes stopped on a tiny object that lay on the floor near the waste-paper basket. A quick

* Medical Officer.

523

step took him to it. Stooping, he picked it up. It was a round pellet of paper, pink. Slowly he unfolded it and found in his hand a slip of grease-proof paper, about three inches square. There was printing on one side. He read it: WITH THE COMPLIMENTS OF CHARNEYS LTD., LONDON. NOT FOR SALE. SUPPLIED FOR THE USE OF H.M. FORCES ONLY. With a frown lining his forehead he raised the paper to his nostrils. His eyes switched to the dead N.C.O. He went over to him, and dropping on his knees, looked into his eyes.

There came a sound of quick footsteps and the M.O. entered, followed by Johnny. Ignoring Biggles the doctor went straight to the body. Silence settled in the death chamber while he examined it. After a while he stood up. 'I'll get him over to the mortuary,' he said.

'What do you make of it?' asked Biggles.

'I'd rather reserve my opinion till after the post-mortem examination,' replied the doctor.

'There'll be an autopsy?'

'Of course.' The doctor looked at Johnny. 'He was in your flight, wasn't he?'

'Yes.'

'Can you offer an explanation of this?'

'We found him here, drunk, about three hours ago,' answered Johnny. 'We left him in the same state. He was badly cut up about the casualties to-day.'

'Have you known him to get drunk before?'

'Yes. I had him on the mat for the same thing about a week ago. But surely, Doc, booze doesn't *kill* a man?'

'In the East, in the sort of weather we've been having lately, it can induce heat stroke, which does. More often, though, the man runs amok. In that condition he often tries to commit suicide. You'd better go, now. I'm going to lock the door till the ambulance comes to collect the body.'

They went out. The M.O. locked the door.

'Where are you going now, Johnny?' asked Biggles.

'I think I shall push along to bed.'

'Me too,' said Biggles.

'Mind if I tell Scrimshaw about this?'

'Not in the least,' answered Biggles. 'I'll see you in the morning. Good night. Good night, Doc.'

Biggles walked on alone. He did not go straight to his quarter, but walked slowly to the sergeants' mess, where he sent for the mess secretary and the barman. He took them outside.

'Sergeant Gray has just been found dead,' he announced quietly. 'He looked as though he had been drinking. Did he have anything here before he went out?'

'I didn't see him at the bar,' said the mess secretary—a warrant officer.

'Yes, he came, but he didn't stay,' volunteered the barman. 'I served him with an iced lemonade—I think it was. I know it was a soft drink because someone pulled his leg about it. Then he said he was going down to the sheds. I recall that because the flight sergeant told him it didn't do any good to mope about.'

'Did Gray seem at all agitated or upset?'

'No, sir, I can't say that he did. I didn't take much notice of him, but from what I remember he was quieter than usual.'

'Thanks,' said Biggles. 'That's all I wanted to know.'

Deep in thought he turned away and went to his quarter. For a long time he sat on his bed, thinking, smoking cigarettes. Then he undressed and got between the sheets.

Chapter 9
Biggles Plays Fox

The following morning Biggles was up early. Before doing anything else he called the hospital on the telephone to inquire about Angus. He learned that his condition was the same; he was still unconscious.

Before he had finished dressing there was a tap on the door and Air Commodore Raymond came in. He looked worn with worry. 'I've just heard about Sergeant Gray,' he said in a tired voice. 'This is awful. What do you suggest we do?'

'For a start, sir, I'd advise you to ask the doctor to give you something to help you to sleep, or you'll be the next casualty.'

'How can I sleep with this horror hanging over my head?' said the Air Commodore. 'What do you make of this business of Gray?'

'I have an uncomfortable feeling that we're partly responsible for that,' returned Biggles, without looking round. He was washing out his shaving kit.

'What on earth do you mean?'

'We were too ready to take it for granted that he was drunk.'

'Wasn't he?'

'No. At least, I don't think so, unless he got the stuff outside somewhere. The indications are that he didn't leave the station.'

'How do you know that?'

'I made it my business to find out.'

'If he wasn't drunk, then what was the matter with

526

him?'

'Why waste time guessing? The M.O. is holding an autopsy. Presumably it will be this morning, since it is customary here to bury people on the same day as they die. We shall soon know the truth—I hope.'

'There's a rumour about the station that it was suicide.'

Biggles flicked his tie angrily. 'How did *that* start? Rumour—rumour—rumour . . . always rumours. If people only knew the harm they do. I'd like to know who started this one.'

'You're not suggesting that it was started deliberately?'

'That wouldn't surprise me. Rumour is a weapon in this war.'

'You don't believe this one, evidently?'

'I prefer to keep an open mind until after the autopsy.'

'If he didn't die from natural causes then it must have been suicide.'

Biggles put on his tunic. 'It doesn't seem to have occurred to you that it might have been murder.'

'Murder!' The Air Commodore looked aghast.

'That's what I said.'

'But what possible motive could anyone have for murdering a harmless fellow like Gray?'

Biggles lit a cigarette. 'The same motive that cost Moorven and the others their lives.'

'I don't understand.'

'The man who was responsible for Moorven's death wanted Japan to win the war. It may be that the man who killed Gray—if Gray was, in fact, murdered—was actuated by the same desire.'

'But why Gray?'

'You seem to forget that Gray was A Flight fitter;

that he was the last man to look over the three machines that were lost yesterday, and that we were waiting to interrogate him. If Gray could have talked he might have told us something, something that might have put us on the track of the secret weapon. If that were so, then there was ample motive for killing him.'

'I didn't think of that,' murmured Raymond.

'Don't breathe a word of it to anyone,' adjured Biggles. 'I mean that seriously and literally. It's only my opinion. Let's wait for the result of the autopsy before we start barking up what may turn out to be the wrong tree.'

'I shan't say anything,' said the Air Commodore heavily. 'I've another worry now.'

'What is it this time?'

'The rot has started at another station.'

Biggles turned sharply. 'Where?'

'Darwin, Australia. They lost five machines yesterday out of one formation—all down in the sea. It's clear that unless we can stop it, the thing will spread over the entire Pacific. We've got to work fast. Bigglesworth.'

'You flatter me,' returned Biggles curtly. 'The whole Intelligence Branch has been working on this thing for weeks yet you expect me to produce results in twenty-four hours. Have a heart.' He finished dressing and picked up his cap.

'Where are you going now?' asked the Air Commodore despondently.

'To get some breakfast. It's a good thing to eat, sometimes.'

'And then?'

'I'm going to take out a patrol.'

'Good God, man! You can't do that!' objected the

Air Commodore in a startled voice.

'Why not?'

'Because you're our one hope now. If anything happens to you—'

'It'll be worse for me than it will for you,' interposed Biggles dryly. 'The thing won't come to *us*. We've got to find it.'

'Are you taking the whole squadron out?'

'No.' Biggles smiled faintly. 'I'll leave some for tomorrow—in case.'

Algy came in. He saluted the Air Commodore and looked at Biggles. 'What's the programme?'

'I'll tell you over breakfast. I'll be across in a minute. Do something for me.'

'What is it?'

'I'm smoking too much. Walk along to the canteen and buy me a packet of chewing-gum.'

'Okay.'

'What am I going to tell Darwin?' asked the Air Commodore.

'I may be able to suggest something later in the day,' answered Biggles, putting his map in his pocket. 'Meantime, I'll push along.'

At the door they parted, the Air Commodore returning to headquarters and Biggles walking over to the dining-room, where he found the rest of the squadron, including the new members, Johnny and Scrimshaw, already gathered, drinking coffee and munching biscuits from a large plate. Before joining them he rang the bell.

Lal Din, smiling, obsequious, answered it.

'Listen, chaps, this is the programme for this morning,' announced Biggles. Then, noticing the steward, he said, 'Bring me a packet of cigarettes.'

'Yes, sahib.' Lal Din went out.

Biggles poured a cup of coffee, spread his map on the table and looked at it for a minute or two. 'We're going to do a sortie,' he went on. 'I shan't be going myself. I'm not sending the whole squadron—just two machines. Johnny and Ginger can go. One reason for that is I don't want a mixed formation. We'll use two Hurricanes. You, Johnny, will fly X M, which leaves X T for Ginger. The others, for the moment, will have to stay on the ground. This will be the course. After taking off the two machines will head east for an hour. That will take them into the area where the machines were lost yesterday, and not far from where Angus went down. They will then turn north for fifteen minutes, after which they will return home.' Biggles looked at Johnny and Ginger. 'Is that clear?'

They nodded.

'All right, then.' Biggles looked at his watch. 'You will leave the ground in twenty minutes. Finish your coffee. There's no immediate hurry.' He looked round. 'Where's that man with my cigarettes? Ah! There you are, Lal Din. Thanks.' Biggles took the cigarettes from the proffered tray and signed the chit.

The steward went out.

Biggles lit a cigarette and sipped his coffee. Then he beckoned to Algy and took him on one side. 'Did you get that chewing-gum?'

'Yes.' Algy produced the tiny package and handed it over.

Biggles glanced at it and dropped it in his pocket. 'I've got a job for you,' he said in a low voice. 'Don't say a word about it to anyone, either here or anywhere else. I want you to go first of all to the M.O. and ask him to give you something guaranteed to make a man sick. If he jibs, go to Raymond. But if you tell him it's for me I think he'll let you have it—he knows I'm on a special job. You will then borrow the reserve ambulance, and driving it yourself, take it to the practice landing-ground at Gayhar. That's a little place among the paddy-fields about six miles north of here. You'd better push off right away, because I want you to be at Gayhar inside an hour.'

Algy's eyes had opened wide while Biggles was giving these instructions, but he did not question them. 'Have you got a line on something?' he breathed.

'I think so,' answered Biggles softly. 'This is really an experiment to test a theory.'

'What am I to do at Gayhar?'

'Nothing. Just sit on the edge of the field and wait.'

'Wait for what?'

'For me. Push off now.'

Algy went out, and Biggles returned to the others who—probably to conceal their real feelings—were making joking remarks about the two pilots detailed for the patrol. He sat down and finished his coffee. Some minutes later he again looked at his watch.

'All right, you chaps, you'd better get along now. I'll walk down with you and see you off. The rest will stay here till I come back. I may need you.'

With Johnny and Ginger he walked towards the machines, which were being wheeled out on to the tarmac. 'What a grand day,' he remarked. 'I think I'll come with you, after all. I'll fly a Spit.'

'You will!' cried Ginger delightedly.

'Yes.'

'I'm glad you've changed your mind,' remarked Johnny.

'As a matter of fact I haven't,' returned Biggles evenly. 'I intended coming all along.'

Johnny stared. 'Then why didn't you say so?'

'Because I am getting nervous of letting too many

people know my movements,' declared Biggles. 'I want you two fellows to remember what you're doing and keep your wits about you. The moment either of you feels anything happening to you, let me know—if you can.'

'You mean, when we get into enemy country?' queried Johnny.

'No. We're not going into enemy country. We're going to stop this side of the lines.'

Johnny pulled up dead. 'Then what's the idea of this sortie?'

'The idea is,' replied Biggles, 'if either of you falls out I'd rather it were where I can get at you.'

Johnny looked astonished. 'But what *can* happen, this side of the lines?'

'You may be surprised,' answered Biggles vaguely.

'But what about you?' put in Ginger. 'You talk as though something might happen to us, but not to you.'

'If my guess is right, I don't think it can,' answered Biggles. 'That's enough questions. We're not going far—only to Gayhar landing field. When we get there we shall land, and just sit in our seats for a couple of hours, leaving the engines running. Conditions will then be the same as if we were up topsides, only our wheels will be on the carpet. I'm afraid it's going to be rather boring, but it may be worth it. Let's go.'

The three machines, two Hurricanes and a Spitfire, took off in formation, with Biggles heading due east for a time, as if they were bound for Burma. But as soon as he had satisfied himself that they were out of sight of the airfield he swung round, and in a few minutes had the flight circling over the practice landing-ground.

532

Ginger spoke over the radio. 'What's that blood-wagon* doing down there?'

Biggles answered: 'I suppose somebody thinks it may be needed. That's enough talking.'

He continued circling for a little while and then went down. The three machines landed as they had taken off, and finished within a short distance of each other. And in that position they remained, the motors throttled back, the airscrews ticking over.

After an hour had passed Biggles got out and walked over to Ginger's machine. Having climbed up on the wing he asked, 'Are you still feeling all right?'

'Right as rain,' answered Ginger.

'Stay where you are,' ordered Biggles, and went over to Johnny.

'Are you still feeling all right?' he inquired.

'I'm getting a bit browned off, otherwise okay.'

'Stay where you are.'

Biggles returned to his Spitfire and resumed his seat in the cockpit.

Another hour—a long, weary hour—passed. Again Biggles got out and went over to Ginger. 'Still feeling all right?'

'Never felt better,' declared Ginger. 'This is a slow game, Biggles. How long is it going on?'

'Stay where you are,' commanded Biggles, and went on to the other Hurricane, increasing his pace when he noted that Johnny's head was sagging on his chest as if he were asleep. He jumped on a wing. 'Johnny!' he shouted.

Johnny did not answer.

Biggles touched him. Johnny lolled, limply.

Biggles moved fast. He switched off the engine and

* Slang: ambulance

533

dashed back to Ginger. 'All right!' he shouted. 'Switch off. Johnny's bought it. Come over and help me to get him down.' Then, turning towards the ambulance he raised his arms above his head, beckoning. As soon as the vehicle started forward he ran back to Johnny's Hurricane, and, with Ginger's help, got the unconscious pilot to the ground. By the time this had been accomplished Algy had brought the ambulance to the stop, and had joined the little party.

'Bear a hand, Algy. Let's get him into the blood-cart,' said Biggles tersely. He had turned a trifle pale.

They lifted Johnny on to one of the stretchers.

'Did you get that stuff from the doctor?' Biggles asked Algy.

'Yes. He says it would make an elephant heave its heart out.'

'Let's have it—quick.'

Algy handed him a bottle.

Biggles tore the cork out with his teeth and coaxed a little of the liquid the bottle contained between Johnny's pallid lips.

Johnny spluttered. He gasped. He retched. Then he was sick.

'Okay,' said Biggles softly. 'Keep that blanket over him to keep him warm.'

Johnny was sick again. Panting, he opened his eyes. They were dull, with the pupils dilated. He was sick again.

'Pass the water, Algy,' ordered Biggles. He wiped Johnny's face and bathed the temples. 'There should be some smelling-salts in that first-aid cabinet,' he told Ginger.

Ginger brought the bottle.

Johnny gasped as the pungent fumes struck his nostrils, but they hastened his recovery.

'What—what was it?' he gasped.

'Take your time, old lad—you'll soon be okay,' said Biggles soothingly.

Johnny's eyes cleared, and he was soon able to sit up.

'Feel well enough to tell us what happened?' asked Biggles.

'Yes, I think so. My God! It was awful.'

'Lucky your wheels were on the floor, eh?'

'If they hadn't been—I should—have come a crumper.* Is this—what got—the others?'

Biggles nodded. 'Tell us what happened.'

Johnny had another drink of water. 'Well, I just sat there for what seemed a long time,' he explained. 'Then I felt a queer sort of feeling coming over me. At first I thought it was the heat; then I realised it wasn't. But by that time I was too far gone to do anything about it. It was hell. Phew! Does my head rock! It feels as if there were a couple of pistons inside it.'

'That'll pass off,' said Biggles. 'Go on with the story.'

'I thought I was dying,' continued Johnny. 'Everything round me was all distorted. I had a feeling I was flying upside-down. The instruments were all heaped in a pile. I tried to move, to call you on the radio, but I couldn't. My bones had all gone to jelly. Then I couldn't make out what things were—they sort of flowed about into each other, as if they were liquid. They turned all colours.'

'But you were still conscious?'

'I can't say I knew what was happening. The pain in my head was terrible. It felt as if my brain had split into two parts. One part was mad, and the other part a sort of spectator. I couldn't do anything—couldn't

* Slang: crashed

535

make a sound. That's the last I remember. I suppose I must have passed out. The thought of that happening in the air makes my skin curl. What was it? Do you know?'

'I think so,' answered Biggles. 'I fancy it was the piece of chewing-gum you ate.'

Johnny stared at Biggles' face. 'Chewing-gum?' he ejaculated. 'What chewing-gum?'

Biggles' expression changed to one of questioning surprise. 'Didn't you find a packet of chewing-gum in the pocket of your instrument panel, and put a piece in your mouth?'

'No. I hate the stuff, anyway.'

Biggles looked incredulous. 'Are you *sure*?'

A smile, faintly sarcastic, curled Johnny's lips. 'Dash it all! I may look dumb, but I'm not so cheesed that I don't know when I chew gum. I tell you, I never touch the stuff.'

Biggles bit his lip, looking really crestfallen. 'If that's the case I'm on the wrong trail after all. I still don't understand it though. Are you absolutely positive that there was no gum in your cockpit?'

'Not to-day.'

'What do you mean by that, exactly? Does it imply that you have had some gum in your cockpit on other occasions?'

'There usually is a piece. It's a free issue, you know. Might almost call it normal equipment.'

'You find it in the machine when you get in?'

'Yes.'

'Who puts it there?'

'Sergeant Gray used to. He sort of did the round before the show.'

'But there was no gum in your machine to-day? Why not, I wonder?'

'Probably because I told Gray yesterday morning that he was wasting his time putting it in.'

Biggles looked at Ginger. 'Wasn't there any gum in your machine, either?'

'No.'

An expression of baffled bewilderment came over Biggles' face. He shrugged his shoulders helplessly. 'This is a bone-shaker,' he said in a disappointed voice. 'Everything turned out just as I thought it would, except that I expected Ginger to be the one to crack up. I've gone wrong somewhere—or else the devils have been too smart for me. I would have bet my life that I was on the right track. I'd more or less proved it—as I thought—this morning. I offered you a piece of chewing gum—Algy had got it for me from the canteen. You refused. I offered Scrimshaw a piece. He refused, too—told me he never touched the stuff. I was suspicious of chewing-gum, and when I discovered that neither you nor Scrimshaw touched the stuff it seemed to confirm my theory—that the stuff was phoney. I was convinced that you and Scrimshaw always got back because, by a lucky chance for you, neither of you chewed gum. By passing out this morning, Johnny, you've knocked my theory sideways.'

'What set you on this chewing-gum line of argument?' asked Ginger curiously.

Biggles took a small square of pink paper from his pocket and showed it to Johnny. 'This is the stuff the gum is packed in, isn't it? Really, I needn't ask you, because I bought a packet this morning.'

'That's right,' agreed Johnny.

'I found a piece of this paper in Moorven's machine. That told me he had been chewing-gum in the cockpit. I paid no attention to it at the time—after all, there was nothing remarkable about it. But when, last night,

537

I found a piece of the same paper in A Flight office, where Gray was lying apparently drunk, I began to think. When I learned from the sergeants' mess that Gray had had nothing to drink there, I thought still harder. I thought I was on the track. When, this morning, as I have said, I learned that you and Scrimshaw, the survivors of a squadron, never touched gum, my surmise began to look a certainty. Now it looks as though the gum has nothing to do with it . . . but I still think there's something queer about it.'

'Since Gray is dead, he couldn't very well put gum into any of the machines this morning,' Algy pointed out.

'That's true enough,' admitted Biggles. 'And I'm afraid that settles the argument. There was no gum—yet Johnny passes out. Obviously, it wasn't gum that did the trick.' He sat down on the end of the stretcher and lit a cigarette.

'Well, there was certainly no gum in my machine,' declared Ginger. 'If there had been I should probably have nibbled a piece. I was getting pretty browned off, sitting there doing nothing.'

For a little while Biggles sat with his chin in his hand, deep in thought. Then he got up. 'Stay where you are,' he ordered. 'I'm just going to have a look round these machines.' He went off, climbing first into the cockpit of Johnny's machine, and then treating Ginger's in like manner. He was not long away. 'All right,' he said briskly when he returned. 'We may as well get back to Dum Dum. Don't mention this business to anyone, nor even speak of it among yourselves in the mess. I don't think you're quite fit to fly yet, Johnny, so you'd better trundle back in the blood-wagon. Do you feel well enough to drive it?'

'Yes, I'm all right now,' answered Johnny. In spite

of his assurance he still looked somewhat shaken.

'Fine. Algy will fly your machine home. Let's go.'

Biggles walked over to his aircraft, and after waiting for Algy and Ginger to get into position, took off.

Chapter 10
The Blitz That Failed

When Biggles landed at Dum Dum, and taxied in, he observed with mounting curiosity that the airfield was, to use the common Air Force expression, in a state of flap. Airmen were running about, orders were being shouted, and engines roared as aircraft were dispersed all round the perimeter of the airfield. Having stepped down, he was gazing with mild surprise at this spectacle, when Air Commodore Raymond, followed by Group Captain Boyle, the station commander, came hurrying to him.

'Thank heaven you're back,' began the Air Commodore in a tense voice. 'You're the very man I want to see.'

'What the dickens is going on here?' asked Biggles.

'We're in for a pasting, I'm afraid—and Calcutta, too, no doubt,' asserted the Air Commodore, pulling a wry face. 'We've just had a signal from our forward observers to the effect that the biggest formation of Jap bombers seen in this part of the world is heading in this direction. Ninety-eight of 'em. We suppose they're taking advantage of the situation created by the secret weapon to have a really good smack at us. They know we are powerless to stop them.'

'You mean, they *think* we are,' returned Biggles grimly. 'How far away is this formation?'

'They'll be here in twenty minutes.'

'What are they?'

'Mitsubishi bombers.'

'Any escort?'

'No. They have good reason for thinking they don't need one.'

'What are you doing about it?'

'We're sending up six fighters to intercept them.'

'Six! What do you suppose six machines are going to do against that mob? Why only six? There are more fighters than that on the station.'

'I know, but we daren't leave ourselves without a reserve. With this secret weapon operating I don't suppose we shall see any of our machines again.'

Biggles pointed at a pathetically small formation of Spitfires just taking off. 'Are those the six?'

'Yes.'

'Stop them. Call them back.'

'But—'

'I know what I'm doing, sir. Recall them.'

The Air Commodore hesitated. 'But if Calcutta is bombed—'

'You're going the right way to get it bombed,' broke in Biggles impatiently. 'Look, sir, we've no time to waste in argument or explanations. If you'll leave this operation to me I promise you won't regret it.'

'But think—'

'I've never let you down yet, have I?'

The Air Commodore decided. 'All right.' He turned to the Group Captain. 'Recall those machines.'

The Group Captain hurried off, and in a few seconds the flight could be seen returning. Algy and Ginger had landed. Biggles waved to them, beckoning urgently. Then he turned again to the Air Commodore. His voice was brittle.

'Will you let me handle this?'

'Yes, but if things go wrong—'

'I know—you'll be held responsible. I'm afraid that's

a risk you'll have to take, sir. I know how many fighters I've got, but how many others are there available on the station? I'm including the two Hurricanes belonging to Crisp and Scrimshaw in my outfit.'

'Apart from those we've seven—all that are left of 910 Squadron.'

'As Crisp isn't back yet, that means we can put up fifteen, all told, if we include my Beaufighter.'

'But are you going to leave the airfield without a single fighter on it?' cried the Air Commodore aghast.

'What are fighters for if not to fight? They'll never have a better opportunity than this, nor is there ever likely to be a greater emergency.'

'But suppose none of them get back?'

'That'll be your worry—I shan't be here,' answered Biggles curtly.

Algy and Ginger came running up. 'What goes on?' asked Algy quickly.

'There's a big formation of Jap bombers on the way,' Biggles told him without emotion. 'We ought to be able to hit them a crack. Algy, I want you to get every fighter on the station lined up—including those Spits that are just landing—with the pilots on parade behind them. Jump to it. Ginger, turn out the squadron. It will line up with the rest. Make it snappy.'

'You're sure you know what you're doing, Bigglesworth?' asked the Air Commodore, in tones of acute anxiety.

'No, I'm not sure,' answered Biggles frankly. 'How can anyone be sure of anything in times like these? I'm hoping, that's all, but that doesn't mean I'm guessing. Sorry I haven't time to talk any more now. See you later.' He walked briskly to where the machines had been mustered in line, with their pilots in a group behind them. He beckoned to Algy. 'Keep those fellows together until I join you; I want a word with them. I shan't be long.'

'Okay.'

Biggles walked on to the end of the line of machines. In a few minutes he was back, facing the line of pilots, officers and sergeants, who were fidgeting at the delay.

'Listen, everyone,' he said loudly. 'You all know what's been going on here—I mean, this secret weapon scare. Forget it. If anyone goes for a Burton to-day it will be from some other cause. Here is your chance to get your own back for what the enemy has done to those messmates who are no longer with us. There are a hundred Japs for you to carve at, so you can help yourselves. There's no escort so it should be a slice of cake. Scrimshaw, last night you seemed to have a load of dirty water on your chest. Now you can get rid of it. My crowd will remember what happened to Angus yesterday.'

'Here comes Johnny Crisp,' said someone.

Looking round Biggles saw Johnny running like a hare across the field.

'Hey! What's going on?' yelled Johnny.

'There's a big Jap formation on the way,' Biggles told him.

'Gimme an aircraft—gimme an aircraft!' bleated Johnny deliriously.

Biggles smiled. 'Sure you're fit to fly?'

'Watch me; oh boy, just watch me!' cried Johnny hysterically.

'All right—take the Beaufighter.' Biggles turned back to the waiting pilots. 'That's all. Give these perishers everything you've got. We haven't far to go. I shall lead in the Typhoon. Let's get weaving.'

There was a rush for the machines.

Biggles started for his aircraft. Pointing eastward, he

shouted to the Air Commodore, who was standing by, 'Get in your car and head up the road that way. You might be in time to see something worth watching.'

The Air Commodore waved understandingly, and ran towards his car.

Biggles climbed into his machine, settled himself in the seat and felt for the throttle. Engines roared, and the mixed formation moved forward, swiftly gaining speed, sending clouds of dust swirling high into the air behind it. Heading eastward, Biggles eased the control column back for altitude.

Five minutes later, at fifteen thousand feet and still climbing, he saw the enemy formation, composed of Mitsubishi bombers as the Air Commodore had stated, strung out like a great dragon across the sky, at an estimated height of twelve thousand feet. He smiled mirthlessly as he altered course a trifle to intercept it. He spoke in the radio.

'Tally-ho, boys! Tally-ho! There they are. We've got 'em. Bertie, get me that leader. Ginger, Tug, stay up to pick off stragglers. Here we go!'

Biggles launched his attack from the starboard quarter, aiming at the neck of the dragon. He went down in a steep dive, with the rest opening out as they streamed down behind him. In an instant the air was being cut into sections by lines of tracer shells and bullets. He picked a Mitsubishi on the near side of the enemy formation, the pilot of which was showing signs of nervousness. Being nearest to the descending tornado he was edging away, forcing others inside the formation to swerve, and lose position in their efforts to avoid collision. To Biggles this was as old as war flying itself. There is usually one such machine in a big formation, and it becomes as much a menace to its own side as to its opponents.

544

Biggles planned to aggravate the trouble. He held his fire. Tracer flashed past him, but he paid no heed to it, even if he saw it. But when bullets began splashing off his engine cowling he frowned, and pressed a foot gently on the rudder-bar, but without taking his eyes off the bomber he had marked down. He took it in his sights, and at three hundred yards jammed hard on the firing button. The Typhoon shuddered a little as the guns flamed, concentrating a cone of bullets on the Mitsubishi, which swerved wildly, causing others to do the same. The first result of this was not immediately apparent, for the Typhoon had roared over its target to zoom steeply on the other side.

Turning on the top of the zoom Biggles saw that the onset had achieved all that he had hoped of it. The dragon had cracked across the middle, and the formation was now in the shape of a dog's hind leg. Four bombers were going down in different directions and at different angles, one in flames, one smoking. Two others, one of which, Biggles thought, was the swerver, had their wings locked—the prelude to disaster. As he watched they broke apart, one, minus half a wing, to fall spinning. The crew of the other baled out. A Hurricane was also going down, leaving a plume of black smoke to mark its trail. The pilot scrambled out on the fuselage, to be swept off instantly into space by the tearing slipstream.

A look of puzzled astonishment came over Biggles' face as he made out another Hurricane boring along up the middle of the enemy formation blazing a berserk path with its guns. Such madness, far outside the range of recognised tactics, was at all events effective, and the enemy machines were thrown into confusion. But it was also suicidal. Biggles recognised Scrimshaw's machine.

'Scrimshaw, come out of that, you fool,' he snarled into the radio.

Whether Scrimshaw heard the order or not Biggles never knew. He may have tried to obey. At any rate, the Hurricane, all the time under the fire of a dozen enemy gun turrets, whirled round, and then zoomed high. For a moment it hung in a vertical position, its airscrew flashing; then its nose whipped down viciously, dead in line with a Jap. Without altering its course it plunged on, and struck the Mitsubishi just aft of the centre section. There was a blinding explosion, which must have been felt by every aircraft within half a mile. Several other bombers in the immediate vicinity were hurled aside as dead leaves are swept up by a gust of wind. Pieces of the machines that had collided flew far and wide.

'There goes Scrimshaw,' muttered Biggles to himself, as he raced down to plaster the disturbed bombers before their pilots could regain control. At the same time he tried to keep an eye on what was happening. 'Strewth! What a scramble,' he murmured.

The air was now so stiff with milling machines at various altitudes that it was impossible to watch the end of any one incident. It was not easy to avoid collision. The battle resolved itself into a number of fleeting, disjointed impressions. Machines, fighters and bombers, were everywhere, banking, zooming, turning, diving, some unloading bombs. Through this fearful whirlpool bodies were falling, some suspended on parachutes, others dropping sheer. Black, oily smoke, formed ugly streaks against the blue. Only one thing was clear. This big formation had been broken into pieces. It was no longer a cohesive fighting unit. Here and there one or two of the bomber pilots had managed to keep together, and these were being harried by the fighters. Below, bombs were exploding everywhere among the paddy-fields. The smoke of crashed machines rose in mighty pillars. In one place a wood was on fire.

Biggles made no attempt to call off his pack. He realised that no order he could give could make things worse for the bombers. It had to be a fight to the finish. He grabbed a little more altitude to try to get a clearer picture of the entire combat, to see how things were going; at the same time he edged towards the west to cut off any bombers that might still be trying to get through. Ginger and Tug were there—Tug with his undercarriage wheels hanging at a lop-sided angle—circling, sometimes darting in, guns grunting, at bombers that were swerving about in an attempt to get clear of the general mêlée. It was now apparent, however, that although the bombers might have an alternative target, they had given up hope of reaching the original one. In his earphones Biggles could hear Japanese voices. He called Ginger and Tug to him.

'Let's give em what we've got left!' he shouted, knowing that his ammunition, and probably that of the others, was getting low.

In that last wild onslaught he got one bomber for certain, in flames, and two probables. He had a narrow escape. He flinched instinctively as a shower of bombs, flung off by a machine far above him, went sailing past at a curiously oblique angle. A Japanese pilot nearly fell on him, too, as he hurtled earthward with his parachute still packed. Then a sudden reek of glycol told Biggles that his radiator had been damaged, so he turned to the west, calling repeatedly on all pilots to rally.

The surviving bombers were now specks in the sky, most of them heading eastward. The fighters, too, were scattered; on those that were near he focused his eyes, in an endeavour to identify them. He saw Johnny's Beaufighter, looking considerably the worse for wear, limping along on one engine. Other machines, Spitfires and Hurricanes, closed in. In a few minutes, strung out in a line across the sky, they were following.

Biggles' motor packed up just short of the airfield boundary, but he managed to scrape in. Jumping out he watched the Beaufighter circle twice with its under-carriage retracted, and guessed the trouble. Johnny couldn't get his wheels down. At the end of the third circuit, with the ambulance chasing it round, the Beau-fighter made a pancake landing, to finish cocked up on its nose. Biggles smiled when he saw Johnny take a flying leap out of the cockpit and scuttle for a short distance before turning to look at the mess he had made. No one moves faster than an airman leaving an aircraft that is likely to burst into flames. Johnny got a lift on the ambulance, and the driver ran on to pick Biggles up.

'What a party—what a party!' yelled Johnny, who seemed wild with excitement. He appeared to be unaware that his nose was bleeding copiously, the result of his crash landing.

'I think we sort of discouraged them,' said Biggles, grinning.

As they travelled slowly towards the tarmac Biggles checked the machines coming in. He counted eleven. 'Eleven out of sixteen—not bad,' he remarked. Then he saw another machine, flying low, that he had over-looked. 'Twelve,' he corrected.

The station commander was waiting. 'How did it go?' he asked tersely, anxiously.

'We gave them a pasting all right,' answered Biggles. 'Those that are left won't come this way, I'll warrant.

A lot of them unloaded their bombs over the fields, so presumably they'll go back home.'

'How many did you get?'

'I can't tell you that till we've checked up,' replied Biggles. 'We intercepted just this side of the lines, so confirmation ought to be easy, by counting the crashes. The troops on the ground must have had a grandstand view.'

'No trouble with the secret weapon?'

'None at all,' asserted Biggles. 'Excuse me a minute, sir,' he added quickly, 'I'm anxious to find out who's missing. I know Scrimshaw has gone, for one. He either collided with, or deliberately rammed, a Mitsubishi. Something of the sort was pretty certain to happen; he was out for blood.'

The pilots who had landed were now getting out of their machines—all except one. It turned out to be a sergeant pilot of 910 Squadron with a bullet through his shoulder. An ambulance rushed him to hospital.

A quick check revealed that the missing pilots were Ginger, Henry Harcourt, Scrimshaw, and a pilot officer of 910 Squadron. One or two of those that returned had received minor wounds. All the machines showed signs of punishment. Bertie had had a remarkable escape. A cannon shell entering through the side of the cockpit had torn the sole off his boot without touching the foot, and then remained transfixed near the root of the control column without exploding.

'Did anybody see what happened to Ginger?' asked Biggles sharply. 'I was with him just before the finish. He seemed all right then.'

Nobody answered. Apparently nobody had seen Ginger go down.

'He may have baled out,' said Biggles. 'That goes for all of them—except Scrimshaw. He went for a

Burton in a big way.'

'I'm not sure, but I fancy Henry got it in the first dive,' put in Tex. 'I didn't see him after that, but I noticed a machine going down, and it looked like his.'

'Well, we shall have to wait.' Biggles turned to the Group Captain. 'Where's the Air Commodore?'

'He went off up the road and hasn't come back yet,' answered the Group Captain. 'Good show, you fellows. That's a load off my mind, I can tell you. I wonder why the Japs didn't use their secret weapon?'

'There was probably a reason,' remarked Biggles softly. 'This looks like the Air Commodore coming now. He's got someone with him. Who is it?'

'It's Henry,' said Algy, as the car drew nearer.

The car did not stop, but raced on to the medical hut.

'That means Henry's hurt,' observed Biggles. 'Phew! Is it hot, and am I dry! Let's go and get a drink.'

Before they reached the mess the Air Commodore joined them. He was smiling. 'Great show, Bigglesworth—absolutely terrific,' he complimented. 'I never saw such a scramble. At one moment I counted five Mitsubishis all falling at once.'

'What about Henry?' asked Biggles.

'Nothing very serious, but I'm afraid he'll be off your strength for a bit. One of the bullets that set his machine alight slashed his arm badly. He baled out, but hit a tree and damaged his leg. I fancy it's broken.'

Biggles lit a cigarette. 'Bad luck. Did you see anything of Ginger?'

'Oh, dear! Isn't he back? No, I didn't see him. That's not surprising, though. Machines were falling all over the sky. There is this about it though; if he baled out he'll be on our side of the lines.'

Biggles nodded. 'How many bombers do you reckon

we got? We haven't checked up yet.'

'I counted twenty-three hit the ground, but there must be a lot of others that won't get back. I noticed several making off, shedding bits and pieces, and they've a long way to go over that forest to their nearest airfield. Funny there was no sign of the secret weapon.'

'Very odd,' agreed Biggles, smiling faintly. 'I'm going in for a drink—I'm as dry as an old boot. I want a word with you later, sir, but I shall have to see about combat reports first, while the thing is fresh in everyone's mind. You might send someone up to the lines to ask the troops if they saw where our machines fell. It's not much use looking for them from the air, with all that mess about, unless we have some definite information to go on. You'd better arrange for a party to go out and collect the loose Japs, too; I saw a lot of them bale out.'

'I'll do that,' promised the Air Commodore. 'See you presently.'

Followed by the others Biggles walked on to the mess.

Chapter 11

Biggles Sums Up

It was shortly after lunch when Air Commodore Raymond walked into the ante-room, to find the officers of 666 Squadron sitting about, or reclining, for it was the hottest time of the day and the heat was intense. Conversation still centred on the morning's big dogfight, concerning which fresh details were being remembered and narrated, some humorous, some tragic.

'Any news of Ginger, sir?' asked Biggles, when the Air Commodore entered, and the others gathered round him.

'Not a word. By the way, have you heard how Mackail is getting on?'

'I rang up the hospital about half an hour ago,' returned Biggles. 'He's about the same—certainly no worse. I'm more worried about Ginger at the moment.'

'All units near the line are being questioned,' stated the Air Commodore. 'So many machines came down in a small area that it's hard to trace any particular one. How many bombers do you reckon you got, now you've made a check?'

'We make it twenty-six certain, ten probables, and at least thirty damaged.'

The Air Commodore smiled. 'Your fellows are too modest. There are thirty-one down on our side alone; several others were observed to be losing height as they made for home.'

Biggles nodded. 'Good. If we don't hear something about Ginger pretty soon we'll take what machines are serviceable and try to locate his aircraft. Has the M.O. made his report yet about Sergeant Gray?'

'Yes.'

'What has he to say about him?'

'He's a bit puzzled, because the state of the body presents some unusual features; but he can't find anything to account for death, which he has ascribed to heart failure. The strange thing is, he says Gray had not been drinking.'

'I could have told him that,' murmured Biggles. 'No sign of poison?'

'None. Nor were there any signs of a self-inflicted wound.'

'There wouldn't be,' said Biggles grimly.

'Why not?'

'Because Gray was murdered.'

The Air Commodore stared. 'Are you serious?'

'This isn't exactly an occasion for mirth.'

'You speak as though you are certain Gray was murdered.'

'I'm convinced of it—now.'

'But who on earth would kill Gray?'

'We've already discussed this, you remember? Any enemy agent would kill him. He was killed to prevent him from talking. I think I know who did it, but I'd rather not mention names until I have proof. I hope to have that very soon.'

'You astound me,' said the Air Commodore, looking shaken. 'You haven't wasted your time.'

'I've none to waste—life is too short. Besides which, India in the hot season isn't my idea of heaven. I want to get this job tied up so that I can go home.'

'What about the secret weapon? From the way you behaved when you took off to intercept the Jap formation I gathered you had an idea about it.'

553

'I've more than an idea,' answered Biggles. 'I know what it is. Only it isn't a weapon. I'd call it a trick.'

The Air Commodore looked thunderstruck. 'Are you telling me that—you have—actually got to the bottom of the thing?'

'Let us say almost. I'm far enough into it to see the bottom, anyway.'

'But this is wonderful!' cried the Air Commodore. 'I'll tell the Air Marshal that we've got the thing buttoned up.'

'I didn't say that,' disputed Biggles. 'Let's put it like this. When I tackled the job it seemed to me that there were two angles to it. The first was to find the thing, and learn how it did the mischief; the second was to put a stop to it. The first part has been done, but the second part is still very much in the air. We've got to be careful. If once the enemy realises that we've rumbled his game he'll slide away like a ghost on roller skates, maybe to start again somewhere else with a variation of the racket. We've got to bait the hook and strike our fish before he realises that we're after him. As it is, I'm a bit worried that he'll smell a rat.'

'Why?'

'Because of what happened this morning. He'll know how many machines we put up, and how many came back. In other words, he'll know that for once his secret weapon went off at half-cock. True, he may think that was partly due to luck, or to the fact that it was a short show. That's what I'm hoping. But he *may* guess the truth. It is even possible that he saw me spike his guns, so to speak.'

'You actually did that?'

'On this very airfield—right in front of your eyes.'

The Air Commodore looked at Biggles suspiciously. 'Are you pulling my leg?'

554

'Have a heart, sir. What have I ever done to create the impression that I'm an irresponsible humorist?'

'Where is this weapon?'

'In my pocket. Would you like to see it?'

'I certainly would.'

In dead silence Biggles put his hand in his pocket and produced a small bar of chocolate. 'That's it.'

No one spoke. In an embarrassing silence the Air Commodore looked at the chocolate, then at Biggles, whose face was expressionless. 'Are you out of your mind?' he asked coldly.

'You would be, if you browsed for a little while on this particular sample of confectionery.'

Understanding began to dawn in the Air Commodore's eyes. A mutter of amazement came from the assembled officers.

The Air Commodore's eyes came to rest on Biggles' face. 'Would you mind explaining?'

'I'm going to tell you the whole story, so far as I know it,' returned Biggles. 'I think it is my duty to do so, although the tale is not yet complete. In this detective line of business it was the practice of that prince of sleuths, Sherlock Holmes, to keep his clues and whatnots under his hat until he had the whole thing nicely rounded off, and then explode the solution with a rousing bang under the startled noses of his baffled associates. That technique, I regret to observe, has been maintained by the more humble members of his profession who have followed him. I say I regret it because it's stupid, it's selfish, and for all practical reasons, pointless. Had Holmes been knocked down by a cab, or otherwise accidentally been sent for a Burton, his secret, the result of his investigations, would have gone west with him, and the villains would have got away with it after all. In our case I'm not going to risk that happening. If the skunk who is operating on this airfield didn't mind killing Gray, he would, if he knew I was after him, be delighted to stick a knife in my ribs. In case that should happen you will be able to carry on, so here's the gen as far as I've got. It's a bit of a mouthful, but by the time I've finished you'll know exactly what's been happening and how things stand right now. Taffy, go over to that door and don't let anyone come near it. Tex—Ferocity, you take the windows and do the same thing. Sorry to be dramatic, but I'm not taking any chances of being overheard. The rest of you make yourselves comfortable. We've got the afternoon in front of us, and it's too hot to do anything, anyway. Moreover, I'm not quite ready for the next move. This is the story, so far.' Biggles sank into an easy chair and lit a cigarette.

'The first thing that struck me about this weapon was that the Japs had invented it,' he began. 'The Japanese don't invent things—at least, not mechanical devices. They're good at copying other people's. They'll copy anything—they even copied their language from China. It would be a strange thing, you must admit, if they had produced a mechanical device, like a death ray, for instance, that has baffled Western scientists. For this reason I worked on the assumption that the hidden death was not a mechanical instrument. The next outstanding feature was the peculiar inconstancy of this alleged weapon. The machines on the China run that did get through, got through without any interference. Why? If this weapon was as efficient as it appeared to be on one occasion, why should it fail utterly on the next? The locality of the aircraft, the weather conditions, in fact, all conditions, were precisely the same. Yet obviously something was different. What could it be? There was another factor, a curious one, but to me, significant. Only machines flying from west to east were lost. Machines flying from Chungking to India got through. Again, why? A ray, or beam, or any other weapon, would surely work the same whichever way the aircraft was travelling. One was forced to the conclusion that whatever was happening was the result of something that started on the ground, not in the air. Clearly, the thing did not start at Chungking. There was no intermediate landing-ground, so it looked as if the trouble was at Jangpur. And whatever was happening there was happening, broadly speaking, to the aircraft.

'Now, an aircraft in flight consists of three parts— the airframe, the motor, and the pilot. The failure of any of these must result in the failure of the whole. Therefore, should any one of these be affected the result would be the same—the machine would not get through. The question was, which was it? I resolved to tackle the three things separately, in turn. Frankly, I suspected that either the airframe, the engine, or the pilot, was being sabotaged—and in the end I was not far out. It was, I suppose, a natural assumption—the first thing that would strike anybody. The problem was to find out *what* was being sabotaged, and how.

'I could think of no other way of testing this than by actual practice, so I decided to fly from Jangpur to Chungking. It was not what you'd call a fascinating experiment, because I like living as much as anybody, and I was staking my life against an opinion. I made the trip, taking Bargent, the original pilot, with me. Nothing happened. Why didn't anything happen? The answer, according to my line of surmise, wasn't hard to find. Nothing happened because until I climbed into the aircraft no one, except Frayle, the C.O., Bargent, and myself, knew that particular machine was going to

557

make the run. I took precautions to make sure nobody knew. In any case, the decision was taken so suddenly that there could have been no time for anyone to interfere with the machine. Another aircraft had been detailed, and I'm pretty certain that had I flown it, it would not have got through. Anyhow, there was lesson number one. I had proved that an unexpected pilot flying an unexpected aircraft could get through. This was in accord with my theory, and the implication was obvious. A saboteur was at work at Jangpur, a man who was in a position to know which machine was next on the schedule to make the run. It seemed safe to assume that what was happening at Jangpur was also happening here. I didn't risk a second trip at Jangpur. Oh, no. It might not have come off a second time.' Biggles lit another cigarette.

'So for my second experiment I came here,' he continued. 'It confirmed my opinion. Officially, we are a communication squadron, so nobody—I mean the saboteur—would expect our Mosquito to suddenly take off and head for Burma. Again I got away with it—for that very reason. Angus' arrival on the scene was not in my programme. He came up the river on his own account. But mark this! I understand there was some discussion in the mess as to who was going to escort Tug. This must have been overheard by the saboteur, who had time to sabotage Angus' machine before it took off. All this was supporting my theory.'

'But Tug Carrington went back up the river,' reminded the Air Commodore. 'Why was his machine not tampered with?'

'For the very obvious reason that he did not take a machine from this station. He flew a seaplane, and had to go some distance to get it. The saboteur, even if he knew about it, would have no time to get to it.'

'Of course, I'd overlooked that,' said the Air Commodore.

'Sergeant Gray, poor fellow, unwittingly provided the next link in the chain,' resumed Biggles. 'And a startling one it was. I told you that when I landed in the forest beside Moorven's crash I found nothing. That was not strictly true. I did find something, but at the time it suggested no sinister purpose. In fact, I threw it away and thought no more of it. It was a little square of pink paper, bearing the name of a British confectionery manufacturer. When I found just such a piece in A Flight shed, when Sergeant Gray was there, drunk, as we thought, I began to wonder. There was something else in that room that aroused my suspicions. It was a coffee-pot. On the occasion of my first visit I sent for coffee. Gray drank it all.

'When I went back, hours later, the coffee-pot was still warm. I could find only one explanation of that. Somebody had been to Gray with a fresh pot of coffee. Gray was hardly in a state to fetch it. Had he wanted it, it is far more likely that he would have gone across to the canteen. The person who took that coffee, took it because he wanted an excuse for going there, in case he was seen. He had good reason for caution. He went to kill Gray, for fear Gray would talk. Gray, had he lived, would have insisted that he was not drunk. He could have proved it. This would have led to the question, were the other cases of drunkenness on the station—there had been some, you know—really that, or were the men the victims of a mysterious malady? The saboteur did not want that sort of talk, we may be sure. With one thing and another I began to get a glimmering of the truth. You see, after Johnny told me that on the day Moorven was killed they had swopped planes, I suspected that it was the pilot, not the aircraft,

559

that was being tampered with.

'Now let me come to my first flight of this morning. I set a trap. In the mess I briefed two machines and two pilots to go out over Burma—Ginger and Johnny. I said nothing about going myself, although I intended going.' Biggles paused to smile. 'I wanted the saboteur to work on the other two machines, but not on mine. Actually, there was very little risk, because I had not the slightest intention of letting Johnny and Ginger go anywhere near Burma, nor, for that matter, be in the air long enough for the secret weapon to work. We landed at Gayhar, and sat there on the ground with our engines running. Things did not pan out as I expected them to, and I don't mind admitting that I got a shock when Johnny passed out. I thought it would be Ginger. Bearing Sergeant Gray in mind I was prepared to find one of them in a state *resembling* drunkenness, but actually in a condition of coma, the result of being drugged.'

'Hey! I like that,' cried Johnny. 'How did you know we weren't going to be poisoned?'

Biggles laughed at Johnny's indignation. 'Had the stuff been poison it would not have been necessary to murder Sergeant Gray, would it? No, he would have died anyway. I was pretty sure that the stuff was a powerful narcotic rather than a poison. There were strong arguments against the use of poison, as I shall presently explain. I had worked it out, from the discovery of the pink paper, that the dope was being administered in chewing-gum, which would occasion no surprise if it were found in an aircraft. It would be a simple matter to get the stuff into machines briefed for flights over enemy country. Judge my chagrin and alarm when Johnny, after we brought him round, swore that he had not touched any chewing-gum. Nor, in fact, was there any in his machine. I was flabbergasted. It looked as if I was wrong. But when I inspected Johnny's machine, and found on the floor the wrapping of a bar of chocolate, I knew I was right. This wrapping-paper, I may say, bore the same name as that on the chewing-gum wrapping—Charneys, London. Only the method had been changed. Chocolate was now being used instead of gum. I found a piece of the same brand of chocolate in Ginger's machine; as it happened, he hadn't touched it. If he had, he would have passed out, too. If Johnny had had a grain of common sense he would have told me that he had eaten chocolate.'

'I like that,' protested Johnny vehemently. 'I'm not a thought reader. You were talking about chewing-gum.'

'It's all confectionery,' declared Biggles. 'The next question was, why had the saboteur suddenly switched from gum to chocolate? That puzzled me for a little while. Then I hit on what I think is a reasonable explanation. The saboteur had realised that Johnny always got back *because he didn't like chewing-gum*, so to get him he baited his machine with chocolate. And he got him. Had Johnny gone out over Burma in that machine he wouldn't be here now.'

'But what about your machine, old boy?' put in Bertie. 'Wasn't there any chocolate or chewing-gum in that?'

'No.'

'Why not?'

'Because, my poor chump, I gave no indication that I was going on the sortie. The only person who knew I was going, was me. I took good care of that. Supposing that I was staying on the ground, the dope merchant did not bait my machine. Only machines briefed for operations received that sort of attention, otherwise the wrong people might have got hold of the bait, with awkward consequences. That, of course, is what happened to Sergeant Gray. Johnny never touches gum. A week ago he came back with a piece of gum still in the pocket of the aircraft where it had been planted. Gray, looking over the machine, as he was bound to, found it. He chewed it, and passed out. Everyone thought he was drunk. He wasn't. He was doped. The same thing happened yesterday. I would wager that when Johnny came back from the sortie when Moorven and the others were lost, he had a piece of chewing-gum on board. Am I right, Johnny?'

'Now you mention it I recall seeing a packet.'

'Exactly. Gray found it. The same performance was repeated. Dash it, poor Gray almost *told* us what had happened. He said he had been sitting there *chewing* the thing over, but no one took him literally. He became unconscious. It was known that we were waiting for him to come round to ask him questions. That hadn't happened on the previous occasion. It was realised that he might mention the chewing-gum to us. So he was quietly murdered. We now know why Johnny and Scrimshaw always came back. Neither of them touched chewing-gum.'

'What a devilish scheme,' muttered the Air Commodore.

'But horribly effective,' returned Biggles. 'What has been happening is now plain enough. A pilot takes off. Sooner or later he discovers a piece of chewing-gum in the aircraft. He chews it. The narcotic takes effect. By that time it is too late for him to do anything about it. Johnny has told me how everything suddenly swam before his eyes. He lost the use of his limbs. The machine falls, crashes, and the pilot is killed. Very simple, but as I just said effective. The mysterious

562

interval of time between the falling out of the machines is now explained. Naturally, the time when a machine went down would depend on when the pilot found the dope. Yesterday, three pilots died like that. Moorven was the first to find the gum. He was the first to fall. After he had put a piece of the stuff in his mouth he dropped the wrapping paper on the floor, where I found it.'

'Frightful,' muttered the Air Commodore.

Biggles went on: 'To some people, this putting stuff in the cockpit of an aircraft might seem a haphazard sort of scheme. Actually, it was more likely to succeed in its purpose than a bomb. One would notice a bomb—but not a piece of chewing-gum. The more you think about it the more devilishly cunning it appears. Nothing could look more natural than gum, nothing more harmless. Scores of pilots chew gum regularly when in the air; we've all done it and we've all left odd packets in our machines. On a long flight a fellow would be almost certain to find the stuff: and having found it, ninety-nine out of a hundred would sample a piece. Of course, there would be occasional exceptions, like Johnny and Scrimshaw. I'm sorry about Scrimshaw. In his fury he lost his head—practically threw his life away. Yet even the exceptions like Johnny and Scrimshaw wouldn't escape indefinitely. As we have seen, chocolate could be substituted for gum. If it turned out they didn't like chocolate, no doubt in course of time they would have been tempted with biscuits, popcorns, or acid drops. Sooner or later their turn would have come.'

'A grim thought,' put in the Air Commodore.

Biggles continued: 'The devilish scheme had one big snag. Once put into action, it could not be allowed to fail. Had the dope got into wrong hands people would

563

have started falling about all over the airfield, and the game would have been up. There is no doubt that this did happen once or twice. When I first arrived I was told that there had been several cases of drunkenness. These men weren't drunk; like Gray, they were doped; but who was to guess it? But too much of that sort of thing would have led to questions. We can see why dope was used instead of poison. Had these men, who were supposed to be drunk, died, there would have been trouble. That would have meant an investigation and the scheme might have been discovered. The after-effects of a narcotic are not unlike those of alcohol—which is, in fact, a narcotic.'

'Do you know what drug they are using?' asked the Air Commodore.

'Not yet. It doesn't matter much, does it? The East is rotten with drugs—opium, hashish, bhang, charas, qhat, and heaven only knows what else. The next problem is to find the devil who dishes out the stuff.'

At this point Taffy, who was still at the door, let out a yell. 'Here comes Ginger, look you!' he shouted. 'By Davy! Is he in a mess!'

A moment later Ginger appeared in the doorway. He was hatless, perspiring freely, mud-plastered from head to foot with a layer of grey dust over the mud. But he was smiling.

'What cheer, everybody,' he greeted, and then flopped on the nearest settee. 'Blimey! What a climate . . . what a country,' he murmured with intense feeling.

Chapter 12
The Oriental Touch

Ginger was welcomed with boisterous enthusiasm.

'Where have you been all this time?' demanded
Biggles, when the babble had abated.

'Walking, mostly,' was the weary reply. 'I've walked
miles and miles and miles. Eventually I got a lift on a
bullock cart to a road, where I was lucky enough to be
picked up by a jeep on the way to Calcutta.'

'What happened to you?'

'Nothing astonishing.' Ginger made a gesture of
chagrin. 'I blotted my copy book,' he confessed. 'I got
a brace of bombers and went out for the hat trick. One
of my little ambitions has always been to get three
birds with one stone, so to speak. Unfortunately I
hadn't much ammo left, so to make sure I went in
close.' Ginger smiled lugubriously. 'I went too close. I
thought the rear gunner was looking the other way,
but he couldn't have been. As soon as I opened up he
handed me a squirt that nearly knocked my engine off
its bearers. I had to bale out.'

'Did you get *him*?' demanded Ferocity.

Ginger shook his head sadly. 'That's the irritating
part of it. I don't know. I couldn't hang around long
enough to see.'

There was a titter of mirth.

'I got down all right—in the middle of a thousand
acre paddy-field. The rice was growing in mud. I never
want to see rice again. That's all. What's going on
here—a mother's meeting?'

'Not exactly,' returned Biggles. 'Go and have a clean up and you'll be in time for tea.'

'I suppose I might as well,' murmured Ginger, rising. 'What a life.'

After he had gone the debate was resumed.

'We must get on with this,' averred the Air Commodore. 'I'm anxious to hear the rest. When Ginger came in you were saying something about the enemy agent who has been, and presumably still is, working here. You had previously said you thought you knew who it was. Whom do you suspect?'

'The genial Lal Din.'

'That moon-faced steward!' The Air Commodore looked incredulous.

'Yes.'

'But he has no business near the machines.'

'He may have no business, but as he is so well known it is doubtful if anyone would comment if he was seen strolling round. From what Johnny tells me it seems—ironically enough—that the culprit handed the stuff to Sergeant Gray to put in the machines. Very cute. Gray, of course, had no idea what he was doing. Lal Din—or whoever it is—would probably pass it over with a remark to the effect that the stuff was a regulation issue, or a free issue, from the people at home. Such a statement would not be questioned. It becomes still plainer to see why Sergeant Gray had to be silenced. Had we been allowed to question him it would have emerged that the only thing that passed his lips was chewing-gum. He would have remembered where he got it, how it got into the plane, and who gave it to him.'

'If we keep watch, we ought to be able to catch the scoundrel red-handed,' suggested the Air Commodore.

'If we keep watch,' argued Biggles, 'we shall be more

likely to start the whole station talking. One word, and our dope merchant will take fright. I'm pretty sure it's Lal Din. He's not what he says he is, anyway. He tries to make out he's a Burmese Chinaman, and he talks English like one—up to a point. But his accent is a bit *too* pronounced for a man who has lived his life in Burma, and has been in British service. I'd say he's got Jap blood in him. Anyway, I started working this morning on the assumption that Lal Din was an enemy agent. I made sure he was present when I briefed the flight in the mess, by ordering a packet of cigarettes. He stood by with them on his tray while I was giving my orders. So at any rate he knew, or thought he knew, which machines were going out. I deliberately gave him time to do his dirty work. The same sort of thing must have happened before. As a mess waiter Lal Din would hear talk, and perhaps see Daily Orders on the notice-board. He was in this mess when Angus asked Algy's permission to escort Tug, when Tug was coming to fetch me in the seaplane. Incidentally, it may interest you to know that nearly all the machines which took off this morning to intercept the Jap formation were planted with dope—including the Spitfires I asked you to recall. I went to each aircraft before the sortie and collected the stuff. That's what I meant when I said I'd spiked the secret weapon under your nose.'

'I wondered what you were doing, dashing from plane to plane,' put in the Air Commodore.

'Now you will understand, too, what I meant when I spoke of the saboteur smelling a rat. It would probably be easier to get the dope put in the aircraft than recover it from them when they came back. He's probably puzzled as to why so many of our machines *did* come back. He'll be still more puzzled if he ascertains that the doped confectionery was apparently eaten—or at any rate, discovers that it has disappeared. We must be careful that he does not learn the truth. It was for that reason that I did not take the rather obvious course of putting a guard on the machines after they returned. This saboteur, whoever he is, is cunning, and once he spotted that the machines were being watched, not only would he keep clear, but he might fade away altogether. There are other ways of discovering who he is. I prefer to give him enough rope to hang himself—and other people. Assuming that the operative on this airfield is Lal Din, it doesn't follow that he is the instigator of the scheme, or that he is working alone. It is more likely that there is a big organization behind him. Similar men are on the same job at Jangpur, Ceylon, and elsewhere. We don't know who they are. We must find out before we can hope to rope in the whole network. When we strike we've got to make a clean sweep and pull in the brains behind the show. We've got to find out how the dope is getting into the confectionery. We can be quite sure that it doesn't come out from England like that. Charneys, the manufacturers, are a big, old-established British firm, quite above suspicion. Clearly, someone is getting hold of the stuff at this end and putting the dope into it. Not all of it, of course; but a certain quantity which is kept handy for use as required. Someone has access to this stuff when it arrives from England. He must be found, otherwise, if it becomes known that the chewing-gum and chocolate racket has been rumbled, we may have all sorts of foodstuffs being doped. That would mean scrapping thousands of tons of perfectly good food which would become suspect.'

'Yes—er—quite so,' said the Air Commodore, in a strange voice.

Biggles looked at him questioningly. 'Is something

the matter?'

'No.' Raymond smiled—a funny, twisted smile. 'You've shaken me to the marrow, that's all. Not so much by the nature of this thing as by the way you've rooted it out.'

'We haven't finished yet,' declared Biggles, shaking his head. 'We're only half-way. Before we make our next move there will have to be some careful planning. The first question to arise is, what are we going to do about the other stations that are affected? Of course, it would be the easiest thing in the world to get in touch with the commanders of those stations and tell them to order their pilots to lay off the confectionery. But if we did that it's a dead cert that the enemy would hear about it. A safer plan would be to keep all machines grounded—except in case of dire emergency—for the time being. If we aren't ready to strike in twenty-four hours then I'm afraid we shall have to let the other stations know what is causing the trouble. But give me a few hours before you do that.'

'It seems to me,' said the Air Commodore, 'that the first thing we've got to do is to establish beyond all doubt that Lal Din is our man.'

'And then what?'

'We'll arrest him and make him talk.'

'Suppose he doesn't talk? We shall have stumped ourselves. Remember, if he's what we think he is, he's our only link with the enemy organization.'

'But I'm thinking about the urgency of the matter,' returned the Air Commodore. 'If it turned out that he was our man, and could be made to tell us the name of his employer, we could strike immediately and clear the whole thing up.'

Biggles shook his head. 'It's risky. Of course, if it came off it would be fine, but if it failed we should be worse off than before.'

'I think it's worth taking a chance,' decided the Air Commodore. 'Could you devise a means of finding out right away if Lal Din is the culprit?'

'That should be easy,' replied Biggles. He shrugged. 'We'll try it if you like, but if it fails, don't blame me.'

'Try it,' advised the Air Commodore.

'All right,' agreed Biggles, without enthusiasm. 'Algy, go to the 'phone, ring up the central canteen, and ask the manager to send Lal Din over here with some cigarettes.'

Algy went to the 'phone.

'When Lal Din comes in, you fellows at the door and windows keep on your toes in case, when he realises that the game is up, he tries to make a break,' ordered Biggles.

Presently Lal Din came, beaming as usual. 'Cigarettes?' said he, looking round the room.

Biggles, from the easy chair in which he was seated, put up a hand. 'Over here.'

Still beaming, Lal Din approached, and handed over the cigarettes. He was turning away when Biggles called him back.

'By the way, Lal Din,' he said, 'do you like chocolate?'

The Oriental did not start. His walk seemed to freeze to a standstill. He looked back over his shoulder—still beaming.

Biggles tossed a bar of chocolate on a small table in front of him. 'Try that,' he suggested.

Lal Din did not move. His broad smile became fixed, the humour gone out of it. The atmosphere in the room was electric.

'What's the matter?' said Biggles evenly. 'Don't you like chocolate?'

570

Very slowly the steward reached out and picked up the bar. 'Me eat after work,' he said.

'Eat it now,' ordered Biggles. He spoke quietly, but there was an edge to his voice.

The steward did not move. His eyes were fixed on Biggles' face, as if he would read what was going on behind the impassive countenance.

'Eat it,' snapped Biggles.

Very slowly the steward looked round the circle of faces. Then, like an automaton actuated by a hidden spring, he moved. He streaked to the far side of the room, and as he ran he drew from somewhere a small narrow-bladed knife. In front of the fireplace he dropped on his knees.

Biggles was on his feet. 'Stop him!' he shouted.

But he was too late. With a calm, but swift deliberation that was horrible to watch, the steward drove the blade into his side, and dragged it across his stomach. Gasping, he fell forward on his face.

The breathless hush that followed was broken by Biggles. 'Call the ambulance, somebody,' he said bitterly. 'Let's get him out of this.' He looked at the Air Commodore. 'That should settle any doubts about his nationality. Only a Japanese would commit hara-kari. Well, there goes our link with the enemy organization. We might have guessed he'd do something like that when he saw the game was up—and he knew it was up the instant he saw that chocolate. That would tell him why the big blitz failed this morning, and why so many of us got back. He'd never dare to tell his boss that he'd failed. That would mean losing face, which is worse than death to a Japanese. So he took a short cut to eternity. Pity, but there it is. One can't be right all the time.'

Chapter 13
Fresh Plans

The ambulance came, and went, taking the body of the treacherous steward. Also the bloodstained hearth-rug.

'Yes, it's a pity about that,' said the Air Commodore uneasily. 'It was my fault. I should have left you alone.'

'We found out what we wanted to know and a fat lot of good it has done us,' replied Biggles moodily. 'But there, the damage is done, and it's no use moaning about it. We tried a scheme that might have saved us a lot of trouble. It didn't work. Now we must think of something else.'

'I'd better leave you to it,' murmured the Air Commodore contritely. 'When I butt in I do more harm than good. You've done marvellously, Bigglesworth. Keep it going.' He went out.

Biggles dropped into a chair.

'That was a dirty business,' remarked Algy.

'It was really my fault. I should have insisted on playing the game my own way. Still, let's be charitable. Raymond is nearly out of his mind with worry; he must be desperately anxious to get the business buttoned up.'

'What are you going to do next?' asked Algy. 'Is there anything you can do?'

'Oh, yes,' answered Biggles readily. 'There are plenty of things; the question is, which is the best? We've no time to lose. As it is, I'm scared that the return of nearly all our machines this morning will have made the whole enemy organization suspicious.

Now, on top of that, comes this business of Lal Din slicing himself in halves. When his boss hears about that—'

'But will he?' interposed Algy.

'If he doesn't hear about it he'll soon know that Lal Din is no longer here; or if he is, that he is not on the job.'

'I don't see why he should know.'

'Of course he will. Look at it this way. What will be the reaction of the chief enemy agent in India to the wiping out of the big Jap formation this morning, followed by the return of nearly all our machines? The first thing he'll do is try to get in touch with Lal Din, the man on the spot, to demand an explanation.'

'Yes, I think that's a reasonable assumption,' agreed Algy.

'He will then discover that Lal Din isn't available, and you can bet your life it won't take him long to find out why. That's why we've got to move fast.' Biggles thought for amoment. 'I'll tell you what. Let's go to the canteen to find out if anyone has already been making inquiries about Lal Din. I think it's an angle worth watching. Did you get that list of personnel I wanted?'

'Yes.'

'Who's the manager of the canteen?'

Algy took a sheet of paper from his pocket and ran an eye over it. 'Ali Mansur,' he answered. 'He's an ex-Askari, a retired sergeant of the King's African Rifles— twenty-four years' service. Got the D.C.M.* and the Long Service Medal.'

'That should put him above suspicion, anyway,' declared Biggles. 'Let's go and see him.'

* Distinguished Conduct Medal

They found the manager in his office. He was an elderly, dark-skinned, heavily moustached man, with a soldierly bearing, wearing his medal ribbons on the lapel of a spotless white jacket. He had not yet learned of the fate of his assistant, and after dwelling for a moment or two on the need for secrecy, Biggles told him the truth, which in any case could not long be concealed—that Lal Din was dead by his own hand.

'This man was a Japanese spy,' said Biggles. 'He could not face defeat. The chief Japanese secret agent will soon want an explanation of the decisive blow we struck this morning against the enemy bombers. What I am anxious to know, sergeant, is this. Has anyone been here making inquiries for Lal Din?'

'Not today, sahib,' replied the sergeant.

'You're sure of that?'

'If such a one had been here I should know of it.'

'Has Lal Din been out, or asked for time off?'

'No, sahib. He could not leave the station without my permission.'

'What exactly did you mean when you said, not today? Have inquiries been made for him on other occasions?'

'Yes, sahib.'

'By whom?'

'His brother, or a man calling himself a brother, comes to see him.'

'Have you seen this brother?'

'No, sahib.'

'How's that?'

'I rarely leave the station, and the brother has no permit to enter. So we have not met.'

'What happens, then?'

'The brother, or any stranger, must go to the main gate. There he speaks to the N.C.O. of the guard, asking for Lal Din. The N.C.O. rings me on the telephone, and if it is possible I allow Lal Din to go to the gate. You must understand, though, that there were days when Lal Din took time off. Then, doubtless, he left the station, although where he went I do not know. I can only tell you of what happens when the brother comes asking for him when he is on duty.'

'This has sometimes happened?'

'Often, sahib.'

'But it has not happened today?'

'No, sahib.'

'Thank you, sergeant. You have told me just what I wanted to know.' Biggles turned to Algy. 'We're lucky. No one has been here yet, but in view of what happened in the air this morning I think someone *will* call. Of course, it may be that the chief saboteur is waiting for Lal Din to report to him with an explanation. When he doesn't show up someone will be sent to find out why. That may take time. I can't afford to wait. I've another line of approach up my sleeve, and I'd like to tackle it right away.' Biggles turned back to Sergeant Mansur. 'There is another matter I would like to discuss with you. Who gave Lal Din his job at this station?'

'I did, sahib. As mess caterer I employ my own staff—with the approval of the adjutant*, of course.'

'How did you get in touch with Lal Din?'

'There was a vacancy, sahib, and he came to me on a recommendation.'

'From whom?'

'Messrs. Tahil and Larapindi.'

'Who are they?'

---

* An officer specially appointed to assist the commanding officer with all official correspondence and administrative duties.

'Shippers' and merchants' agents, sahib. They represent many British firms in India. Much goods imported go through their hands. They have a big warehouse at the docks, in Calcutta, and offices in many Eastern towns.'

'Does this firm supply stuff to our canteen?'

'Yes, sahib.'

'Things like chocolate, chewing-gum . . .'

'Yes, among other things, sahib.'

'When is this stuff delivered, and how?'

'When we need supplies I ring up Tahil and Larapindi, and they send the goods up in one of their cars.'

'And what happens when the stuff gets here?'

'It is unloaded and put out for sale.'

'Who unloads it?'

'Sometimes I check it in, sahib; sometimes Lal Din, or one of the other assistants, might do it.'

'Anyway, the stuff is taken to the canteen and made available for the troops?'

'Yes, sahib.'

'And this firm recommended Lal Din?'

'Not the firm exactly, sahib. Mr. Larapindi rang me up on the telephone and asked me to find work for a very good man he knew.'

'I see,' said Biggles slowly. 'What sort of man is this Larapindi—have you seen him?'

'Many times, sahib. He is Eurasian, but of what precise nationality I do not know. He is a small man, with a brown face, and wears very large spectacles.'

'I am told there has been a free issue of chocolate and chewing-gum. Is that so?'

'Yes, sahib.'

'How long has it been going on?'

'It is not a regular thing. We had the first case sent up not long ago. It came with other goods from Tahil and Larapindi.'

'Was this after Lal Din arrived?'

'Yes, sahib.'

'And he dished the stuff out?'

'Yes, sahib—he offered to do it.'

'Thank you, sergeant. You have been most helpful.' Biggles turned to Algy. 'This is worth following up.' he said quietly. 'I've half a mind to abandon my alternative scheme, which was to slip up to Jangpur to try to nab the fellow there who is doing what Lal Din was doing here. If I could get my hands on him I might make him speak.'

At this moment Air Commodore Raymond came hurrying into the canteen. 'I've been looking everywhere for you,' he told Biggles.

'Now what's wrong, sir?' queried Biggles.

'The Higher Command says we simply must get this China route in full operation again. The Chinese doctors are having to perform operations on their wounded without anaesthetics. Not only are medical stores urgently needed, but several senior officials are waiting to go through. Now we know what caused the trouble I thought perhaps you could do something about it, if it isn't upsetting your plans.'

'No. As a matter of fact it fits in with my plans quite well,' returned Biggles. You can reckon that the route will be functioning again to-morrow. I'll slip up right away to see Frayle. All you have to do is send him some machines, and pilots to fly them.'

'And you don't think there will be any more risk?'

'I don't think so, sir—at any rate, not if my plan succeeds.'

'Then I can tell the A.O.C. that the route will be open with effect from to-morrow?'

'It will—unless you hear to the contrary from me or

Algy.'

'Good.' The Air Commodore hurried away.

Biggles turned back to Algy and the sergeant. 'Now this is what I want you to do, Algy. You keep in touch with Sergeant Mansur. If anyone comes asking for Lal Din the sergeant will let you know. You will go to the gate and see the man. Tell him that Lal Din is sick. Don't let him suspect the truth. When the man goes off to report to his boss, as it seems pretty certain that he will, you'll follow him and watch where he goes. Make a note of the place and return here. I shall have to go to Jangpur, but I'll get back as quickly as I can. It may be late to-night or early to-morrow morning. If the route is to open to-morrow I've got to pick up the man who is putting the dope in the machines.'

'Why not tell the fellows up there straight out not to touch any confectionery they find in their machines?'

'Because in five minutes everyone of the station would know what was in the wind—including the spy. He'd escape, and warn his boss in Calcutta. No, I've got to catch him. We're not ready yet to broadcast the story. I'd better warn Frayle that I'm coming.'

Algy's eyes went round when he heard Biggles, on the telephone, tell Squadron Leader Frayle that he was coming right away to take another load of medical supplies to Chungking. Biggles continued: 'I want you to start loading the machine at once—yes, in the ordinary way. I don't mind who knows about it. I shall take off as soon as it's ready. By the way, I may be staying at Jangpur for a day or two, so you might fix me up with a room and a bed.'

To this Frayle apparently agreed, for as Biggles hung up he said with a smile, 'That's okay.'

Said Algy: 'Are you really going to Chungking?'

'No fear. I've too much to do here. But I'd like the

gent at Jangpur who hands out the dope to *think* I'm going.'

'Ah,' breathed Algy. 'I get it.'

'I'll be getting along,' decided Biggles. 'You watch things at this end. I hope I shan't be long away.'

In a few minutes, having ascertained that the radiator had been repaired, Biggles was in the air, in the Typhoon heading north on the short run to Jangpur. A haversack containing his small-kit went with him.

Squadron Leader Frayle and Flying Officer Bargent met him on the tarmac, Frayle to say that the transport plane was ready, and Bargent to ask if he could go as second pilot. Biggles refused, gently, but firmly. 'I have reasons of my own for making this trip alone,' he said. 'With luck you should be able to take a machine through yourself, to-morrow.' Turning to Frayle, Biggles asked, 'Did you fix me up with a room?' On receiving an assurance that the room was available he walked over to look at it, and leave his haversack.

Bargent had wandered off, so Biggles was able to speak privately to the station commander who, without asking questions, nevertheless made it clear that there was something about this projected trip that struck him as phoney.

Biggles decided to take him into his confidence. 'The facts, briefly, are these, Frayle,' he said quietly. 'This route has got to start functioning again to-morrow. There's nothing phoney about that. More pilots and machines are being sent up to you. Unfortunately you've got an enemy agent on the station. You can't operate while he's about, so I'm here to nab him. If I succeed, you should have no further trouble. That machine standing out there ticking over has been tampered with—or at least, I hope it has. I've given the saboteur plenty of time to do his dirty work. Now then:

579

after I have taken off certain things will happen that may surprise you. My subsequent behaviour, for example. But whatever happens I want you to carry on as though everything was normal. And see that your officers do, too. Don't let there be any discussion. Show no surprise, and leave me alone. That's all. I'll push along now.'

'It's your funeral,' murmured Frayle simply. He was too good an officer to argue.

Leaving his small-kit in his room, in mellow evening sunlight Biggles walked across to where the Wellington was waiting. There were several airmen and native porters standing about, watching with interest, but they said nothing. Appearing not to notice them Biggles climbed into his seat, tested his engines, waved the attendant mechanics away, and took off.

As soon as his wheels were off the ground he put the aircraft on a course that was practically due east, for Chungking, and when he settled down he examined the contents of the locker. Conveniently placed, he found a packet of chewing-gum. Smiling grimly he put it in his pocket.

The aircraft roared on through the fading light. The time, by the watch in front of him, was a quarter to six.

Chapter 14
The Trap

Precisely half an hour later, in the silvery light of a full moon, Biggles roared back to the airfield at Jangpur and landed. The return of the aircraft caused minor sensation. Mechanics appeared, running, and there was some brisk conversation when the transport machine was identified. The few remaining officers on the station, mostly ground staff, but with Frayle and Bargent among them, came out to see what was going on. In the clear moonlight this did not take them long.

Biggles climbed out. He seemed to be not quite steady on his feet, and after swaying for a moment rested a hand on an airman's shoulder as if for support.

'What's the matter?' asked Frayle anxiously. 'Why did you come back?'

'Engine—giving trouble,' answered Biggles in a dull voice. 'Getting a—lot of—vibration—starboard side. Thought I'd better—turn back . . . not risk—forced landing.'

'I should think so,' agreed Frayle, looking at Biggles with a curious expression on his face. 'Are you feeling all right—yourself, I mean?'

'No. Feel sort of—odd,' replied Biggles, holding his head in a dazed sort of way. 'Must have got—touch of sun. Twinge of fever—maybe.' He staggered and nearly fell.

The audience of airmen and porters whispered among themselves. There was a titter of laughter when a voice was heard to say, 'Tight as an owl.'

'I think you'd better go to your room and lie down,' suggested Frayle.

'Yes,' muttered Biggles thickly. 'Best thing—I think. Head's sort of—swimming. Must be—fever. Seems to be getting—worse.'

Frayle made a signal and the ambulance came out to meet the party. Biggles allowed the station commander to help him into it.

'Shall I send the M.O. along to see you?' offered Frayle.

'No, thanks. I'll be—all right. Go—sleep.'

'As you like,' returned Frayle.

The ambulance took Biggles to the sleeping accommodation that had been prepared for him—a small room in the station commander's bungalow, which was an extension of the officers' quarters. Most of the officers went back to the mess, but Frayle and Bargent, having removed Biggles' tunic, helped him on to the bed and took off his shoes. He appeared to fall asleep immediately.

Said Bargent, looking down at the recumbent figure: 'I've got a nasty feeling there's something fishy about this. If I hadn't done a trip with him I'd swear he was three sheets in the wind.'

'He half prepared me for something unusual,' replied Frayle. 'He said that whatever happened I was not to worry him, but leave him alone. I don't like leaving a fellow in this condition, but I suppose we shall have to.' They went out, leaving the electric light on.

As soon as they had gone Biggles raised himself on an elbow, listened intently for a minute, and then got off the bed. Moving quickly he switched out the light, locked the door, drew the curtains aside and arranged the window so that it could be opened easily. For a little while he stood surveying the airfield, a clear view

582

of which the window commanded, while pale blue moonlight flooded the little room. Leaving the window he took out his automatic, examined it, and put it in a side pocket of the slacks he still wore. The time, he noted, was twenty minutes to seven. Then, apparently satisfied, he settled himself on the bed in a sleeping position facing the window, and half closed his eyes.

Time passed. For a while there were occasional sounds outside—footsteps of airmen going on or off duty, and voices as they talked or called to each other. But as the night wore on these sounds died away and silence fell. After a short interval the orderly officer* could be heard making his first round. More time passed. Once, far away, a dog or a jackal yelped. A cock crowed in a distant village, apparently misled by the brilliant moonlight into thinking that dawn was at hand. Biggles did not move a muscle. Only his chest rose and fell with his deep breathing. The difficulty, he found, was to do this without actually falling asleep, for he was beginning to feel the strain of working at high pressure, and he was really tired. His eyes, half closed, were on the window. Not for a moment did they leave it.

He lost count of time, but he estimated roughly that it was about nine-thirty when he saw that for which he had so long waited. There was no sound, but a shadow moved slowly across the square of moonlight framed by the window. Within a minute it was back, stationary, close by the window. All this Biggles saw quite clearly through half-closed eyes. Moonlight flashed on the glass of the window as inch by inch it was opened. Still there was no noise, and as the man crept into the room Biggles marvelled that anyone could move with

* The officer on duty for the day

583

such a complete absence of sound. Standing close against the window, the visitor made no more noise than the vague shadow he appeared to be. Biggles could not make out any detail. Beyond the fact that the visitor was naked except for a loin-cloth, and carrying in his left hand a strip of rag, he could see nothing of him.

Like a black wraith the marauder appeared to float towards the bed. Again he stopped and listened, before bending over the prone form on the bed as if to examine it. His breathing was just audible. Then, taking the strip of rag in both hands he pressed it firmly over Biggles' lips and nostrils.

As the rag touched his face Biggles' hands shot up and seized his assailant by the throat. With a convulsive jerk the man broke free, and Biggles knew that he had made a mistake; for the throat was slimy with oil, and his fingers could not maintain their grip. The man streaked like a panther to the window. Launching himself from the bed Biggles got him by the legs: but they, too, had been oiled, and although the man fell, he was free again before Biggles could take advantage of the fall. The body slid through his hands like an eel. In a flash the man was on his feet. Biggles, too, was getting up. He caught the gleam of steel and flung himself sideways, but a sharp pain in the upper part of his left arm told him that the knife had found a billet. After the first stab there was no more pain; only a feeling of nausea.

By this time his assailant had turned, and had again reached the window. Biggles, by this time aware of the futility of trying to hold the body, grabbed at the loin-cloth, and tried to drag the man back into the room. But either the stuff was rotten, or in two pieces, for the part he had seized came away in his hand, with the result that he went over backwards. By the time he had recovered himself, although he was still on the floor, the man was half-way across the sill, a black silhouette against the moonlight. It was obvious that in another second he would be gone.

Now Biggles' plan had been to catch the man alive, for which reason he had so far refrained from using his pistol; but seeing that the man was about to escape, and aware that if he succeeded in this it would be fatal to his plans, he snatched out his pistol. There was no time to take aim. He fired from the hip. The weapon roared. The flash momentarily blinded him, so that he could not see whether he had hit his man or into. Vaguely conscious of hot blood running down his arm he scrambled to his feet and dashed to the window. One glance told him all he needed to know. A figure lay asprawl on the brown earth. Panting, for the last few minutes had been strenuous, Biggles backed to the bed and sat down heavily, to recover his breath and his composure.

Outside, voices shouted. Footsteps approached, running, both inside and outside the bungalow. A fist banged on the door. Before Biggles could answer, or get to it, it was forced open with a crash. Someone blundered into the room. The light was switched on. Frayle, in pyjamas, stood there.

'What happened?' he asked sharply. 'Who fired that shot?'

'I did,' replied Biggles laconically.

'Good God, man! You're wounded.' Frayle's eyes were on the bloodstained sleeve of Biggles' shirt.

'It's only a scratch,' returned Biggles. 'Give me a drink—water will do.'

Frayle obliged.

'Thanks.' Biggles drank, and drew a deep breath.

'That's better. Send for the M.O., Frayle, to have a look at that fellow outside. Tell him to bring his needle and cotton—my arm may need a stitch.'

Bargent entered through the window. 'I say!' he exclaimed, in a perturbed voice, 'You've killed the fellow.'

'I'm sorry about that—in a way,' replied Biggles. 'I wanted him alive. Who is he—do you know?'

'Of course I know. It's Kong Po, our *dhobi-wallah**.'

'What was his nationality?'

'We always supposed he was a sort of Chinese.'

Frayle spoke: 'He's Chinese according to his station identity card.'

'Alter it to Japanese,' cried Biggles.

Presently the M.O. came in. 'There's nothing I can do for that fellow outside—he's dead,' he announced. 'What about your arm?' He looked at the wound. 'Narrow, but rather deep,' he went on. 'You'd better have a stitch in it.'

'Go ahead,' invited Biggles. 'Don't be long; I've got to get back to Dum Dum. Give me a cigarette, Frayle.'

'Before you go, perhaps you won't mind telling me why you came here to bump off my *dhobi?*' Frayle's voice was soft with sarcasm.

'I didn't come here to shoot him,' replied Biggles evenly. 'I came here to get him, but he knifed me and I daren't let him get away. Too much was at stake.'

'Why did you want him?'

'Because,' answered Biggles, flinching as the M.O.'s needle pricked his skin, 'he was your own pet secret weapon. He came to this room to strangle me. I thought he would come. I hoped he would. One of our airmen

* Indian military term for laundryman. From Hindustani *dhob* = washing.

at Dum Dum, a sergeant named Gray, was murdered in precisely the same circumstances and for the same reason. I planned for a repetition of the incident, and it came off. Your precious Kong Po was afraid I might put two and two together, and talk about it, when I came round from what he supposed was a stupor brought on by a drug.'

'But I don't understand,' said Frayle impatiently. 'How does this hook up with the secret weapon?'

'I'll tell you in plain language,' decided Biggles. 'Keep the story to yourself though, for the time being. There isn't a secret weapon—or not the sort you probably have in mind. The enemy has planted agents on certain of our airfields. With so many Orientals about that wasn't difficult. The master-brain behind the racket had enough influence to get these men jobs. In our case, at Dum Dum, the spy was a mess waiter. The real work of these men was simple. All they had to do was arrange for a small supply of chocolate or chewing-gum to be put in each operational aircraft just before it took off. These sweeties were not the sort you'd give to the baby to suck. They had been treated with a powerful narcotic. It needs little imagination to visualise what happened in the aircraft. During the course of the flight the pilot finds the confectionery and has a bite, with the result that he loses the use of his limbs and his brain and crashes. It was always on the boards, however, that the stuff might fall into the hands of someone other than the man for whom it was intended. The sergeant I mentioned just now got hold of a piece. During the night, while he was still under the influence of the drug, he was murdered to prevent him from talking. I didn't know how it was done, but I do now. Strangulation was the method employed; I imagine it isn't hard to strangle an unconscious man without leaving a mark. This evening I set a trap. I took off but returned, ostensibly with engine trouble. There was dope in the machine. When I landed I acted as though I had fallen for it. Some of your fellows thought I was drunk. Only the spy, who was pretty certain to investigate, would know the truth—or what he thought was the truth. That I had been drugged. It was up to him to see that I didn't come round, so he came to do me in. I was waiting, with the result that he got it, not me. That's all. Now he's out of the way there won't be any more doped confectionery in your machines, so with effect from to-morrow the route will operate in the normal way. But to be on the safe side— you needn't say why—you can issue a secret order to your pilots forbidding them to touch any sort of food while in the air. In any case, I'm aiming to clean up the whole gang in the next few hours. Meanwhile, for obvious reasons, you will say nothing of this to anyone. Should someone come here inquiring for Kong Po— and that may happen—just say that he has met with an accident and is not available.'

'Well, stiffen my benders!' muttered Bargent. 'I never heard such a tale in my life.'

'The East is the home of strange stories.' returned Biggles dryly, as he tried moving his arm, which the M.O. had now finished bandaging.

'What beats me is, how you got on the trail of the thing,' said Frayle, in a voice of wonder. 'It was so simple, yet so subtle—'

'The Oriental mind works on those lines. I've been in the East before,' murmured Biggles as he stood up. 'I'll just have a look round this *dhobi-wallah's* bedroom and then get back to Dum Dum.'

As Frayle led the way to the room Biggles asked: 'How did you come to employ this man—Kong Po?'

'A fellow in Calcutta rang me up and asked me if I had a vacancy for a good man. He said Kong Po had worked for him, so he could recommend him. The chap was out of work and he wanted to help him. So I took Kong Po on.'

'You knew this man who rang you up, I presume? I mean, he wasn't just a stranger?'

'Oh, no. I've met him several times. As a matter of fact he's a wealthy merchant who has often made presents to the mess. I wish there were more about like him.'

A ghost of a smile hovered for a moment round Biggles' lips. 'Was his name by any chance Larapindi?'

Frayle started. 'Yes. What on earth made you say that?'

'Only that he has showed an interest in Dum Dum, too,' replied Biggles casually.

The room turned out to be a tiny cubicle near the kitchens. A systematic search revealed only one item of interest—a small cardboard box containing several loose bars of chocolate, wrapped, and packets of chewing-gum. The box bore in large type the usual confectionery manufacturer's announcements, under the heading: CHARNEYS GOLD MEDAL CHOCOLATES. LONDON. AGENCIES AT CALCUTTA, CAPE TOWN, SINGAPORE AND SYDNEY,

'Very interesting,' murmured Biggles. 'As the stuff is loose we may assume that the box is merely a receptacle for the present contents which, I imagine, have been doctored. I doubt if the man had any hand in the preparation of the dope; the chocolate and gum would be issued to him in this form, ready for use. Better burn the stuff, Frayle, to prevent accidents.'

A corporal medical orderly came in. In his hand he carried a packet of notes, brand new. 'I thought you'd better take charge of this, sir,' he said, speaking to his station commander. 'I found it tied up in Kong Po's loin-cloth. There must be close on a thousand rupees — a lot of money for a man like that to have about him.'

'Too much for an honest *dhobi-wallah*,' said Biggles softly. 'I'll take charge of that, Frayle, if you don't mind; I have an idea it will tell us something. Well, there doesn't seem to be anything else; I think I'll be getting along.'

'Sure you feel fit enough to fly?' queried the M.O.

'I'm all right, thanks,' answered Biggles. 'Arm's getting a bit stiff, that's all — but I don't fly with my left hand.'

In twenty minutes he was back at Dum Dum. The time was just after ten o'clock. He went straight to Air Commodore Raymond's quarter. The Air Commodore was there, writing a report.

'I thought it would ease your mind to know that the Chungking run is okay now, sir.' reported Biggles. 'The regular service will be resumed in the morning. Things are moving fast, and may move faster before dawn. While I'm talking to my chaps I want you to do something for me.'

'Certainly.'

Biggles took from his pocket the notes that had been found on the dead *dhobi-wallah*. 'From the condition these are in it seems likely that they were issued recently,' he surmised. 'I want you to find out which bank issued these notes, and to whom.'

The Air Commodore looked dubious. 'At this hour? People will have knocked off work.'

'Then tell them to knock on again,' requested Biggles. 'This business won't wait. You ought to be able to get the information on the 'phone.'

'I'll try,' promised the Air Commodore. 'I take it

590

you've got the enemy agent at Jangpur ear-marked?'

Biggles was at the door. He looked over his shoulder, smiling grimly. 'I ear-marked him all right—with a forty-five pistol slug. See you later.'

He went on to the mess. Algy and the rest were there, waiting. Some were dozing, but there was a quick, expectant stir, when Biggles entered. He spoke to Bertie.

'Get some coffee and see that it's strong. I'm dog tired, but we're going to be busy for a bit. You might scrounge some sandwiches or biscuits at the same time.' He turned to Algy. 'Did you have any luck?'

'It worked out as you expected,' replied Algy. 'A man calling himself Lal Din's brother rolled up, asking for him. I told him Lal Din was sick. He went off and I followed him.'

'Good. Where did he go?'

'To the docks, to the warehouse of Tahil and Larap-indi. I hung around for some time but he didn't come out, although there seemed to be a fair amount of activity.'

'There'll be more, presently,' promised Biggles. 'I fancy that warehouse is the target for to-night. I'm just waiting for confirmation. I shall be glad when this show is over; I'm missing my beauty sleep. Ah—here's the coffee.'

'What happened at Jangpur?' asked Ginger. 'The others have told me what happened here.'

Biggles gave a brief account of events at Jangpur. He had just finished when the Air Commodore came in.

'I got the information you wanted,' he announced. 'I'm afraid you'll be disappointed; the money seems to have been issued in the ordinary course of business.'

'It would be,' mutter Biggles cynically.

591

'It's part of a pay-roll issued by the Peninsular and Oriental Bank, to—just a minute.' The Air Commodore fumbled with a slip of paper.

'Tahil and Larapindi?' suggested Biggles.

The Air Commodore stared. 'That's right. How the deuce did you guess that?'

'I wasn't guessing,' returned Biggles. 'Thanks, sir. You can go to bed now. I may have some good news for you in the morning.'

'Are you going out?'

'We are.'

'Can I come?'

Biggles shook his head. 'You'd be better advised to keep out of the way. What 666 Squadron is going to do, or may have to do, to-night, is entirely unofficial. There's no place for an Air Commodore.'

'All right. I'll leave you to it.' The Air Commodore looked at Biggles suspiciously. 'Be careful.' He went out.

'Are we really going down to this warehouse place?' asked Tug.

'Probably. It depends. I have a call to make first.'

'But I say, old boy, it's a bit late for making calls, isn't it?' queried Bertie.

'Not too late, I hope.'

'Say! Suppose there's nobody at the warehouse?' put in Tex. 'How shall we get in?'

'It was never my intention to ring the front-door bell,' said Biggles. His manner became brisk. 'Algy, see about transport. Better get a light truck, one we can all get in. And in case there's an argument you'd better all bring guns. On the other hand, there may be nothing for you to do. We shall see. Ginger, you're about the best fitter in the party. Put a few tools in a bag in case we have to do a spot of housebreaking.

592

Which reminds me; I think it would be a good idea if everyone wore tennis shoes, or something with a sole that won't make a noise.'

'Where do we go first?' asked Algy.

Biggles went to the telephone directory, looked up a number and made a note. 'I want you to drive me first to Mimosa Lodge, Razlet Avenue. If I remember, that's one of those wide streets in the European quarter east of the Maidan. I'll guide you.'

'What are you going to do there?' asked Algy.

'I'm only going to make a call.'

'On whom?'

'A gentleman by the name of Larapindi,' answered Biggles.

Chapter 15
Biggles Makes A Call

Algy drove the car, a light, covered service lorry, to Calcutta. Biggles sat on one side of him, with Ginger on his left.

On the short drive in Biggles said: 'I can't tell you exactly what I'm going to do because I'm not sure myself. The business has reached that touchy stage when anything can happen. I'm a bit scared of the plan I have in mind, but our hands are being forced. We've got to move fast, before the enemy learns what has happened to his operatives at Dum Dum and Jangpur. I'm pretty sure this fellow Larapindi is in the racket, and if he's not actually the head man, he's pretty high up. The broad idea, if I find Larapindi at home, is: first, to allay his suspicions, if they are aroused; and secondly, to get him to do something that will give us the necessary evidence to hang him.'

'Couldn't we get the police to raid his premises, both his home and the warehouse?' suggested Algy.

'We could, and that is what the police would probably do if they knew what we know. But I don't think it would do the slightest good. It's ten to one they wouldn't find anything. Spies aren't such fools as to leave incriminating evidence lying about when they know the police are on the job. Police actions are governed by regulations. They have to announce their intentions by knocking at the door. If we asked for a police raid the chances are we should do more harm than good, by exposing our hand for nothing. I've always

594

taken the view that when one is dealing with tricksters the best plan is to play tricky. So I'm going to try unorthodox tactics. If I slip up there will be an awful stink—a question asked in Parliament, perhaps. We shall get a rap over the knuckles, and perhaps lose some seniority.'

'That should worry us,' remarked Algy sarcastically.

'We'll stop the car a little distance from the house,' went on Biggles. 'Here's the Maidan. I believe that's the Avenue Razlet, over there. Pull up against the kerb when I give the word.'

In view of the lateness of the hour—it was nearly eleven o'clock—there were few pedestrians about, and very little traffic. The night was fine and hot. The Hugli River wound like a monstrous black snake through the resting city.

'You'll do,' said Biggles sharply. As the car pulled up he continues: 'Tell the boys to keep quiet while I'm away. If I'm not back in an hour you'll know something's gone wrong, so you'd better come looking for me. If you do, remember that unless my suspicions are all cock-eye, this Larapindi is as cunning as a jackal and as deadly as a cobra. Sit fast and keep your eyes on the house. I may be some time.'

Biggles walked on up the avenue. A policeman directed him to Mimosa Lodge, a magnificent house standing in its own spacious garden. A fine pair of wrought iron gates gave access to a short drive that ended at a sweeping flight of steps. The gates were not locked, and in a minute Biggles was pressing the bell.

The door was opened, as he expected it to be, by a servant, quiet, efficient, in spotless white. The man looked a trifle surprised when he saw the visitor, but in reply to Biggles' inquiry said that Mr. Larapindi was at home. Biggles presented his card, and was then asked to wait in a hall, the furnishings of which were so fine, so rare and so costly as to give him a twinge of uneasiness. The house appeared to be the residence of a millionaire rather than that of an enemy spy. While the servant had gone to deliver his card his eyes roamed from one object of Oriental art to another, with rising misgivings. Then he realised that as a partner in the great firm of Tahil and Larapindi, the man whom he had come to see probably was a millionaire several times over.

The servant, walking with soft, easy steps, returned. 'This way, sahib,' said he.

Biggles followed him through a sumptuously furnished library to a door at the far end. On this the servant knocked before opening it. 'Enter, sahib,' he invited, with a little bow. 'Mr Larapindi awaits you.'

As Biggles accepted the invitation he took in the scene at a glance. The room, not a large one, was fitted out in a manner that was something between a private sitting-room and a study. Again the furnishings were impressive. Pieces of priceless Oriental porcelain, objects in carved ivory and exquisite work in precious metals, occupied the shelves. Behind a large lacquer writing-desk the owner was standing to greet his visitor. He was a small man immaculately dressed in European clothes. Large gold-rimmed spectacles, slightly tinted, almost concealed his eyes.

'Please to be seated, sir,' said Larapindi, in faultless if rather suave English, at the same time indicating a heavily-carved chair that had already been pulled towards the desk in readiness. Having seen his visitor seated he himself sat down behind the desk.

'Thank you,' said Biggles.

'You wish to see me?' went on Larapindi smoothly. 'I do not think we have met before?'

Biggles smiled awkwardly. 'No. This is hardly the time to call, I'm afraid, but when I have explained the reason I hope you'll forgive me. It happened that in passing your house I remembered, or it may have been that your house reminded me, of something my canteen manager once told me. But before I go any further I should explain that I am the temporary Mess President at Dum Dum airfield. Some time ago, Sergeant Mansur, our canteen manager, informed me that you have been good enough to recommend a man for work in the canteen. His name is Lal Din—or perhaps you don't remember him?'

'I recall him perfectly well,' said Larapindi, in an expressionless voice. He pushed towards Biggles a massive gold cigarette box. 'Please to have a cigarette, sir.'

'Thank you.' Biggles accepted the cigarette. 'This man Lal Din has turned out to be a most excellent steward—always cheerful, willing and obliging. We shall miss him.'

Larapindi's chin dropped a trifle so that he could survey his guest over his large glasses. 'Do you mean, he has—gone?'

'Not exactly,' returned Biggles. 'But the day before yesterday he complained of not feeling well. Yesterday he was obviously very ill, so I sent the Medical Officer to see him. It turns out that the poor fellow has smallpox.'

Larapindi drew a deep breath. 'Oh, dear! That is very sad.'

Biggles thought he caught a suspicion of relief, or it may have been understanding, in the way the words were spoken.

'Of course, it hardly needs me to tell you what an outbreak of infectious disease means on a station like

597

Dum Dum,' he went on. 'Lal Din, poor chap, has been put in an isolation ward, and there, I'm afraid, he'll remain for some time. Which brings me to my point. We're going to miss him. To-morrow morning I shall have to see about getting a new steward. In the ordinary way I should have advertised for a man, but this evening I had to come into the city, and in passing your house it struck me suddenly that as your first recommendation had turned out so successfully you might know of another fellow. I don't expect you to produce another Lal Din off-hand, so to speak; but you might know of someone who could take up his duties right away. We shall be short-handed without Lal Din, and the sooner I have someone to replace him the better. In the ordinary way that might take two or three days. Now you know the reason I hope you will pardon me for breaking in on you at so late an hour.'

Larapindi made a deprecatory gesture. 'Do not speak of it,' he protested. 'Call on me at any time. If I can be of service the honour will be mine. It happens that you have called at a most fortunate moment. Only to-day my business manager came to me telling me of a man who has applied to us for work, a most excellent man. I should be glad to employ him myself, but I shall account it an honour if you will allow me to send him to you. I forget his name for the moment, but he is a Burmese from Rangoon, one of those unfortunate creatures who had to fly to India before the invasion of these hateful Japanese. He has been a house servant, and has had experience as a waiter. When would you like me to send him to you?'

'First thing in the morning,' requested Biggles. 'The sooner he takes up his duties the sooner will the pressure on our overworked staff be relieved.'

'I shall see that he is there,' promised Larapindi.

'Thank you. That is really most kind of you,' said Biggles gratefully. 'By the way, on my last tour of duty in India I believe I once had the pleasure of meeting Mr. Tahil, the senior partner of your firm. I trust he is in good health?'

'Alas, no,' sighed Larapindi sadly. 'Evidently you did not hear of his tragic accident?'

'Why, what happened?' asked Biggles, who was genuinely surprised, and not a little interested.

'Poor Mr. Tahil died from snake-bite,' explained Larapindi. 'It happened on a golf links, of all places. His ball fell in the rough. Stooping to pick it up he accidentally touched a *krait** that must have been lying beside the ball. Unfortunately, we were some way from the club-house. I ran all the way, but it was no use. Before a doctor could arrive with serum he was dead. It was a lamentable affair, and caused something of a sensation in Calcutta, because Mr Tahil was a noted philanthropist, besides being a good servant of the government.'

Biggles' eyes were on Larapindi's face. 'What a terrible shock it must have been to you. I take it you were playing together?'

'We were. It was indeed a shock. I've hardly recovered from it.'

'And a blow, too, I imagine,' murmured Biggles sympathetically. 'I mean, his death must have thrown a lot of extra work on your shoulders, since it would leave you in complete charge of the business.'

Larapindi shrugged. 'These things happen; we must face them. I am doing my best to carry on single-handed.'

---

* A small but extremely poisonous Indian snake. Its bite is usually fatal in a few minutes.

Biggles shook his head. 'I am very sorry to learn of this.'

Now, during the latter part of the conversation his eyes lifted to a framed photograph that hung on the wall behind his host. Actually, there were several such photographs, most of them portraying the various offices of the firm of Tahil and Larapindi throughout the Orient. But one photograph in particular claimed his attention, for it was a picture of an aircraft, a civil marine aircraft—or to be more precise, a Gull. It was moored on a river, off the end of the slipway, with a private hangar bearing the name of the firm in the background. The aircraft, which carried the Indian registration letters VTT-XQL, also bore on its nose the name of the firm.

'Pardon my curiosity, Mr. Larapindi,' said Biggles, 'but the photograph behind you arouses my professional interest. I see your firm operates its own aircraft?'

'It did, until the war put an end to private enterprise,' answered Larapindi, swinging round in his chair to glance at the photograph. 'We try to be progressive, you know. Our interests in the East are so widespread that the adoption of the aeroplane as a means of transport was almost automatic. We bought a machine, a Gull, and established a repair and maintenance depot a few miles higher up the river. It would have been developed had not the war put an end to our plans— only temporarily, I hope.'

'Of course,' said Biggles quietly. 'No doubt you had to ground the machine when the war started.'

'Yes, the government asked us to, and, naturally, we were only too anxious to oblige. We shall need pilots when the war is over, so if ever you abandon the service as a career I hope you will come to see me, to our

600

mutual benefit.'

'I'll bear it in mind,' promised Biggles. 'But I must be on my way. I'm glad to have had this opportunity of meeting you.' He got up.

'I hope we shall meet again, sir,' said Larapindi, also rising.

'I'm sure we shall,' replied Biggles evenly. 'Meanwhile, I shall expect your man first thing in the morning.'

'He will be there.'

Larapindi saw his guest to the door, where they parted.

Biggles returned to the lorry.

'How did you get on?' asked Algy.

'I got what I went for,' answered Biggles. 'Now listen, everybody. I've told Larapindi that Lal Din is down with smallpox, and asked him to send us a man to replace him. He has promised to send one along first thing in the morning. That means he's got to get busy, to-night, finding a man, giving him instructions, and supplying him with a stock of doped confectionery. I doubt if he'll risk talking over the telephone. Unless I've missed my mark he'll attend to the business in person. We'll watch from here. If he goes out, we'll follow.'

Hardly had he finished speaking when a man, in the attire of an Indian servant, appeared at the iron gates, and walked briskly down the avenue.

'What about him?' asked Ginger.

'He's probably part of the organisation, but we've got to go for bigger game,' answered Biggles. 'That chap has been sent out on an errand—probably to fetch the fellow Larapindi has in mind to replace Lal Din. We're all right. Either the man will be brought here, in which case we shall know it, or he will be taken somewhere else. If he is taken somewhere else, Larapindi will have to go out to see him. Ah! What's this?'

A servant had appeared at the gates and opened them wide. A minute later an expensive touring car crept through. The gates were closed. The car cruised away down the avenue.

'After him,' ordered Biggles crisply. 'Keep the car in sight, but don't get too close.'

'What about the Tahil part of the partnership?' asked Algy, as they followed the car. 'Aren't you interested in him?'

'Tahil is dead,' answered Biggles slowly. 'He was bitten by a snake while playing golf with Larapindi. Since it must have suited Larapindi remarkably well to be left alone in charge of the business, I have a feeling that there were two snakes on the links that morning. But let's discuss that presently.'

Five minutes later it was clear that the car was heading for the dock area.

'It looks as if he's going to the warehouse,' said Algy. 'This is the direction, anyway.'

This surmise turned out to be correct. The car stopped before the main entrance of the establishment of Tahil and Larapindi. The lorry had also stopped, some distance away, but close enough for Biggles to see Larapindi alight and enter the building. The car was driven back a little way, revealing that it had a chauffeur in charge, to be parked in a narrow turning, one side of which was entirely occupied by the warehouse.

'It looks as though he's going to be some time, otherwise the car would have waited at the front entrance,' remarked Biggles. 'It's a bigger building than I expected,' he added, taking stock of the warehouse and its position. Not that much could be seen. The building, a vast square pile, stood alone, separated from similar warehouses which lined that side of the road by narrow streets. It fronted the main road. The rear part, which seemed to be much older than the front, which was obviously modern, overlooked the broad, turgid, Hugli River.

'When I saw it in daylight, the place gave me the impression of being a very old building with a new front stuck on it,' said Algy. 'It's pretty ramshackle at the back.'

'Most warehouses are, or those I've seen,' answered Biggles. 'Hello, here's another car stopping. It's a taxi.'

The taxi pulled up at the front entrance, deposited two passengers and drove on.

'We're doing fine,' murmured Biggles. 'One of those fellows is Larapindi's servant, the one we saw leave the house. The other must be the man he went to fetch— the man Larapindi is going to send along to replace Lal Din. Brought him in a taxi eh? Must be in a hurry. This is how I hoped it would pan out. If I'm right, Larapindi is going to give that fellow his instructions. Instructions wouldn't be much use without the dope, so it must be kept here. This is where we take a hand. Listen everybody. Algy and Ginger will come with me. We've got to get into that building somehow. Bertie, you'll take charge of the rest of the party. Leave someone here to look after the lorry. Post the others round the building to see that no one gets out. If you hear shots, or anything that sounds like a row, break in and lend a hand.'

'Why not wait for this new assistant to come out and grab him with the goods on him?' suggested Johnny Crisp.

'I'm not interested in him,' answered Biggles. 'The man I want is Larapindi, and we've got to catch him

603

handling the dope, or he'll slip through our fingers like a wet fish. Come on, Algy. Come on, Ginger—bring your bag.'

In a minute they were on the pavement, at a corner of the big warehouse. Biggles set off down a side turning, looking at the windows. 'We've got to get in without making a noise,' he said quietly. He continued walking until they had nearly reached the river, and then pulled up by a door, a side entrance to the building. As a matter of course he turned the handle, to find, as he expected, that the door was locked. He turned to Ginger. 'What have you got in that bag?'

'I've got a hacksaw, a file, some tyre levers; a drill—'

'Good. The drill ought to do the trick,' interrupted Biggles. 'Make a hole near the handle, and cut out a piece of wood big enough to get a hand through. The key will probably be in the lock on the inside.'

This conjecture proved to be correct, but ten minutes were occupied in cutting the hole. Ginger did the work while Biggles and Algy kept watch. As it happened no one passed through the little street, so the work was not interrupted. As soon as the hole had been made Biggles inserted a hand, and with an exclamation of satisfaction brought out the key. He inserted it in the lock on the outside. As the door swung open, the warm, aromatic aroma of mixed Indian merchandise, tea, spices, jute, oilseeds and grain, poured out to greet them. Without a sound they stepped inside. Biggles closed the door. There was a faint snick as he switched on his torch. Its beam stabbed the darkness.

Chapter 16
The Green Idol

Not until he was inside the building did Biggles realise fully the size of it, and the problem this presented. It was apparent, however, that they were in that part devoted to the storage of merchandise, and by the character of it, the export department. Cases of tea, sacks of grain, bales and boxes stood stacked in orderly array from floor to ceiling, with narrow corridors between to permit the passage of those whose business it was to handle these goods. To Biggles, it seemed unlikely that Larapindi would conduct his affairs in that section of the building; it was almost certain that he would be somewhere in the administrative department, and with the object of finding this he set off, moving quietly but quickly along a corridor that ran parallel with the narrow street outside, in the direction of the front entrance. Algy and Ginger followed close behind. The reek of the goods was not unpleasant, but it was almost overpowering in its pungency.

After a little while, however, this smell began perceptibly to change, and the reason was soon evident. There was a break in the ranks of merchandise, and on the far side of the passage thus made the type of produce changed abruptly. Here, now, were wood and cardboard boxes bearing the names of British and United States manufacturers; clearly, the import department. Once Biggles stopped, and without speaking pointed to a large notice stencilled on one of the cases. The words were CHARNEYS, LONDON. CONFECTIONERY.

Biggles continued to walk forward, and presently perceived that he was nearing his first objective—the administrative block. The merchandise ended, to give way to numerous passages, with wood-partitioned offices, some large, some small, bearing the names of wholesale and retail departments and the names of their managers. Biggles' progress became slower and more cautious.

So far not a sound of any sort had broken the tomb-like silence of the warehouse; but now, passing an unpretentious staircase there came from somewhere in the distance, high above, no louder than the rustle of dry leaves, a murmur of voices. Biggles hesitated for a moment and then went on. He did not go far, being brought to a halt when the passage ended at swing doors, panelled with panes of frosted glass, through which came a feeble but steady light. Switching out his torch, and laying a finger on his lips for silence, he made a stealthy reconnaissance. Then, with infinite care, he allowed the door to sink back into place and turned to the others.

'It's the main hall,' he breathed. 'There's a man on duty inside the front door. We can't go any farther this way without being seen. We shall have to go back.' He retreated as far as the narrow stairway, and after listening for a little while to the distant sound of talking began a discreet ascent.

The staircase, after making two right-angle turns, ended in a corridor on the first floor, lighted by a single electric bulb. The corridor extended for some distance on either side, with doors at frequent intervals. All were shut. It was now possible to distinguish a single voice, a voice of authority it seemed, speaking rapidly. It still came from above. Biggles explored, and half a dozen paces along the corridor found another staircase leading upwards. It was precisely the same as the first, and for practical purposes a continuation of it. It mounted to the second floor, to another corridor identical with that of the floor below. The voice still came from above. Another advance took Biggles and his companions to the third floor. Still the voice came from higher up. It was now fairly clear, but after listening for a moment Biggles shrugged his shoulders. He could not identify the language, much less make out what was being said.

Farther upward progress was now barred by a door on which a single word had been painted in white letters in several languages. One of the languages was English. The word was PRIVATE. Biggles tried the door. It opened readily, revealing another staircase. But this one was different. On the floors below the boards had been left bare; here they were covered by a thick red carpet. After a slight inclination of his head Biggles went on up to the next floor, into an atmosphere altogether different from those down below. Gone, now, was any impression of a warehouse or business office. The appointments were those of a luxury hotel, or a suite in a block of expensive flats. The staircase ended in what might best be described as an outer hall of some size, richly furnished and carpeted. Around this hall, opposite the intruders as they stood at the head of the staircase, were four doors. One stood ajar. The room to which it gave entrance was lighted, but it was not from here that the voice came. It was the room next to it.

Biggles looked at the others with a puzzled expression on his face. He did not speak, but by a gesture indicated what he was thinking. Indeed, something was now explained that had puzzled Ginger all the way up the stairs—the loudness of the voice inside the room. It did not speak in an ordinary conversational tone, but was pitched high as though it were reading aloud to an audience. No explanation of this being forthcoming, after a little grimace to indicate his lack of understanding, Biggles crossed the hall to the open door, and without touching it, peeped in. A faint click of the tongue, denoting surprise, brought the others to his side. Very slowly he pushed the door wide open so that the whole interior of the room could be seen. Strictly speaking it was not a room. It was a laboratory.

After a swift survey of the scene Biggles paid no attention to the scientific apparatus that stood about, or the rows of jars and bottles that occupied the numerous shelves. He went straight to a bench on which had been accumulated an assortment of objects, a curious assortment—curious because they were not what one would expect to find in a laboratory. Most conspicuous were two cardboard boxes, bearing in bold type a name, and certain announcements, which to Biggles were becoming familiar. The name was Charneys. Both boxes had been broken open and part of their contents strewn on the bench. In one case it was chewing gum; in the other, chocolate. Near these was a pile of loose wrapping-papers, some pink, some brown, that had obviously been torn carelessly from the products named on the boxes. The contents of the wrapping-papers, however, were not there. Close at hand, in two separate boxes, were identical wrapping-papers, but these were brand new. There were only two other objects on the bench, but they were significant. One was a small glass jar half filled with an oily, colourless liquid, and the other, a case across which lay a hypodermic syringe.

It needed less time to observe these things than to describe them, and after a long penetrating stare

Biggles said softly: 'This is it. We're in the dope shop. Larapindi didn't lose any time preparing samples for the new man to distribute at Dum Dum. This little collection tells the whole story. He takes the stuff as it arrives from England, unwraps as much as he needs, gives each sample a shot of dope with the needle, and rewraps it in a new paper. He can't inject much dope into a solid bar of chocolate, but no doubt one drop would be ample to knock out anyone not used to the stuff. I knew a fellow who once chewed a piece of charas—the dope that's most popular in India. To be on the safe side he nibbled a piece only half the size of an orange pip, but he went out as if he'd been hit on the head with a rolling-pin. We may assume that the stuff in that bottle is highly concentrated. I'd like to make Larapindi drink the lot. That's him talking in the next room; I recognise his voice, although what he has to shout about I don't know. We've enough evidence here to hang him, so let's see what he has to say about it. There may be some slight argument when he sees us, so have your guns handy. Algy, you stay here and don't let anybody touch this stuff. I'd like Raymond to see it just as it is. Come on, Ginger,' as he finished speaking Biggles took his automatic from his pocket and slipped into his right sleeve, so that it was held there by his fingers.

Leaving Algy by the bench, followed by Ginger he returned to the hall and walked on to the door through which the voice still came. 'He seems to have a lot to say,' he murmured. 'I shall try to open the door—assuming it isn't locked—without being seen, but I don't think there's much hope of that. I've no idea of how he'll behave when he sees us, but you'd better be ready to move fast. Hold your hat—here we go.'

Biggles' fingers closed firmly over the handle of the

door. Very slowly he turned it. The door moved. A slit
of light appeared between door and frame. He released
the handle: but instead of the door remaining open
only a few inches, as he intended, it continued the
opening movement—slowly, but quite definitely.

The result was inevitable. The movement was seen.
But before that happened Biggles was granted three
seconds' grace to absorb the picture presented to his
gaze. It was enough, although what he saw not what
he expected. Far from it. He had thought, indeed, he
had convinced himself—unwisely, as he later confessed—that there would not be more than three persons in the room; Larapindi, the steward who was to
replace Lal Din, and perhaps the servant who had
fetched him. Instead, there were not fewer than seven
or eight people present. He did not count them. There
was no time for that. Not that it mattered much. These
men were seated round a large mahogany table, so that
the proceedings had the appearance of a board meeting;
a strange one, perhaps, because the centre of the table
was occupied by a green stone idol. Larapindi was
standing at the head of the table, unfortunately for
Biggles, at the far end, because in that position he was
facing the door. The heads of his disciples, or assistants,
or agents, or whatever they were, were bowed in the
direction of the idol in reverent adoration.

Now, had this been all, Biggles might have been
embarrassed, for he would have been the last man to
interrupt a devotional ritual, whatever religion was
involved. But it was not all. In front of each man,
looking absurdly out of place on account of its blatantly
European character, was a little heap of the packets
Biggles had come to know so well; packets of chewing-
gum and chocolate. This told him all he needed to
know. The fact that several agents, instead of one, were

610

being instructed in their duties, and that these agents were obviously being bound to their murderous tasks by a religious ceremony, made no difference to the broad situation. He had, as he had planned, caught the plotters red-handed. That was the dominating factor. Whether he and Ginger would be able to apprehend so many was another matter. They had at least the advantage of surprise.

Larapindi was the first to observe the open door. He must have seen Biggles at the same time. His voice broke off abruptly. And thus, for a long second, the scene remained, immobile, frozen, as it were, like a screen play suddenly arrested. Then, as if wondering at the sudden cessation of sound, the bowed heads were raised. The agents looked at their chief. They saw his fixed expression and noted the direction of his stare. With one accord they turned.

Biggles' gun slid into his hand and came up like the head of a striking cobra. 'Don't move, anybody,' he snapped. He would have avoided bloodshed had it been possible.

It was not. Perhaps the agents did not understand. Be that as it may, the words broke the spell. The order was ignored. Movement returned, and it returned with a rush. With a unanimous gasp of alarm, and a crashing of overturning chairs, the agents sprang to their feet in panic. In doing this they came between Biggles and Larapindi, who was not slow to seize the opportunity this human cover provided. He sprang to the wall, and on the instant the room was plunged into darkness.

Three streams of orange sparks leapt across the room. They started at the muzzle of Biggles' gun and ended at the spot where he had last seen Larapindi. Loud cries of fear accompanied the reports. There were answering shots from different points of the room, to be followed instantly by the thump of falling bodies. A little light entered through the open door from the hall, but it was not sufficient to enable Biggles to see clearly what was happening, except that all was in confusion. Men were staggering about, colliding with each other and falling over the chairs. It was a situation for which he was not prepared, and one that seemed to defy immediate remedy. He had no desire to perpetrate a massacre. Realising that he could serve no useful purpose by remaining inside the room, and that there was a chance of his being knocked down in the mêlée, he backed into the hall. It seemed to be the wisest course, particularly as he had only to keep the door covered from the outside to prevent anyone from escaping. On the spur of the moment he assumed this; and it was no doubt a natural assumption; but in the event it turned out to be another mistake. He took up a position in the lighted hall on one side of the door, few paces from it, and shouted at Ginger to take up a similar position on the other side.

'Plug anybody who tries to get away,' he ordered grimly.

'What a mess,' muttered Ginger in a disgusted voice, as he obeyed. He side-stepped briskly as a little brown man darted out, blazing wildly with a small automatic.

Biggles fired and the man went down. 'I'm afraid we've started something,' he said, with a worried frown, as from somewhere in the lower regions there came a crashing and banging, with a few sporadic shots.

'That must be our crowd breaking in—they've heard the rumpus,' opined Ginger. 'Why not lock the door, and keep Larapindi and the rest inside until the police come to collect them?' he suggested, indicating the room, from which now came an excited muttering.

'That's an idea,' agreed Biggles. He went to the door, and having taken the key from the far side, slammed it. He turned the key.

While this brief operation was in progress other things were happening. Algy put his head round the laboratory door and demanded to be told what was going on. Biggles gave him a brief idea of what had happened, and ordered him to remain where he was. Voices were shouting somewhere below. Feet thumped on stairs.

'Bigglesworth! Where are you?' called one voice.

'That sounds like Raymond,' said Ginger. 'What's he doing here?'

'He must have followed us—like an old hound that won't be left out of the hunt,' answered Biggles, smiling. 'Perhaps it's as well. I'll hand this mess over to him.'

Tug, gun in hand, appeared at the head of the stairs. There was blood on his face and on the front of his tunic. 'Have you got 'em?' he asked excitedly.

'Not exactly,' replied Biggles. 'What have you been up to?'

'I met a bloke on the stairs,' explained Tug. 'He tried to stop me coming up. We had a row about it and he got the worst of it.'

Air Commodore Raymond, panting heavily, was the next to arrive. 'What on earth are you doing here?' he demanded.

'I might ask you that,' returned Biggles curtly. 'I told you to keep out of it, so that—'

'I know. So that if things went wrong you could shoulder the blame. I'm not having that. I brought you out, so if anyone is going to get a rap it will be me.'

'It may come to that,' declared Biggles. 'Larapindi is a big bug in this part of the world, and he may be able to pull enough strings to cause serious trouble in India. But we can talk about that later. Larapindi is the boss of the local spy ring—I've got all the evidence I need to prove that. He's in that room with some of his gang.'

'Then let's have him out,' said the Air Commodore bluntly.

'Okay,' agreed Biggles. 'But someone's liable to get hurt. I wanted to avoid that. I'm by no means sure of the nationality of some of these fellows, and we don't want to have a political issue made out of it. Still . . .' He went to open the door, turned the key, and pushing the door open, stepped inside. 'Come out of that,' he ordered. 'The place is surrounded. You can't get away.'

There was a brief pause. Then, one by one, four men came out.

'These men may be dressed like Hindus, but if they aren't Japs I'll eat my buttons,' swore the Air Commodore.

'Where are the rest?' said Biggles. The beam of his torch cut a wedge into the darkness of the room. He ran in and switched on the light. Three men were lying on the floor. Larapindi was not among them. Biggles' eyes flashed round the room. There was only one possible hiding-place—a large safe that stood open. He went to it and looked inside, but the man he sought was not there.

'He's got away,' he rasped. 'There must be a secret way out of this room—probably a lift. It's no use looking for it now.' He turned to the Air Commodore. 'I'll leave you to take care of things here, sir. Algy's in the next room with some things you ought to see. Tug, you stay here with Ginger and give the Air Commodore a hand to clean up the mess. He'll need some help.'

Biggles made for the stairs.

Chapter 17
The End of the Trail

Biggles went down the stairs three at a time, not a little annoyed at the turn the affair had taken—annoyed with himself, that is, for not having taken more direct action in the room upstairs. He should, he thought, have foreseen the possibility of the move Larapindi had made; for should the chief enemy agent escape, the coup he had planned would have to be accounted a failure. There was a chance that Larapindi might still be somewhere in the building, and if that were so, by posting the rest of the squadron to cover the exits, his escape might be frustrated.

He nearly fell over a body that lay at the foot of the second-floor staircase—presumably the man Tug had shot on his way up. Biggles turned his torch on him, and caught his breath sharply when it revealed a Japanese Air Force tunic. It was not until later, though, that he grasped the full significance of this. At the moment he was simply astonished that an enemy airman should wear uniform in such a place and at such a time. Without giving the matter serious thought, it flashed into his mind that the Japanese might possibly be one of those who had baled out in the combat, and had made his way under cover of dark to the warehouse, knowing that Larapindi would provide him with a hiding-place. The man still clutched in his hand a Japanese general service pattern revolver.

Biggles ran on down to the main hall. The first thing he saw was a man in native dress—the hall porter, he thought—lying on his back on the floor. A knife lay beside him. Taffy Hughes, as pale as death, sat in a chair, one foot in a pool of blood, with Johnny Crisp, on his knees, twisting a tourniquet round his leg.

'What's happened here?' asked Biggles sharply.

Johnny answered: 'Taffy and I bust the door in when the shooting started. Taffy was first. This guy—' Johnny indicated the man on the floor '—stuck a knife in him.'

'Look after him,' ordered Biggles. 'Have you seen a man go out through this door?'

'No one has gone out this way,' replied Johnny.

'Where are the others?'

'Outside, I suppose. Only Tug followed us in, and he went on up the stairs.'

Biggles went out into the street. The lorry was there, with Ferocity, alone, in charge.

'Have you seen a man come out of the building?' asked Biggles tersely.

'Not a soul,' returned Ferocity.

'Where's Bertie and Tex?'

'They went down the side street to grab Larapindi's car.'

'Okay. Stand by,' commanded Biggles. 'Taffy's been knifed, but Johnny is with him. If it turns out that Taffy is badly hurt you'll have to run him to the hospital. If not, wait for the others.'

Biggles ran on down the side street. Larapindi's car was still there. Tex, gun in hand, was standing beside it. The native driver cowered against the wall with his hands up.

'Have you seen anybody come out, Tex?' asked Biggles.

'Sure,' answered Tex. 'A little feller in European clothes shot out of the side door. When we shouted to him to stop he had a crack at us and then bolted towards the river. Bertie went after him.'

Biggles raced on down the street. It ended abruptly at the river, but to the right there was a long wharf, flanking the rear of the warehouse. 'Bertie! Where are you?' he shouted.

The answer was two pistol shots in quick succession. The reports came from the far end of the wharf, which was occupied by cranes, conveyors, trollies and similar dock equipment. Biggles ran towards the sound. More shots guided him as he ran. Then came another sound, one that spurred him to a sprint. It was the throbbing hum of a powerful motor-boat. He came upon Bertie taking long distance shots at a long low craft that was tearing the surface off the water as it headed up-stream.

'The blighter's got away,' muttered Bertie. 'Sorry, old boy.'

'Was he a little fellow in European clothes, wearing spectacles?'

'Yes. I lost sight of him in all this clutter. Next thing I saw was the boat.'

'Are there any more boats?' asked Biggles.

'I haven't seen any. I shouldn't think there are two like that.' Bertie pointed to the fast disappearing speed-boat. 'Let's follow in the car,' he suggested. 'The blighter's got to come ashore somewhere sooner or later,'

Biggles clicked his fingers. 'My gosh!' he muttered, aghast. 'I've just remembered something. I'll bet I know where he's making for. He's got an aircraft up the river. He's going to pull out.' Biggles went on quickly. 'We've still a chance. Bertie, go into the main hall and call Dum Dum on the 'phone; tell them to bring a Spit out and have it started up. I shall be there in five minutes.'

Without waiting to see if Bertie followed Biggles

617

raced back to Larapindi's car. 'Look out! I want this car,' he told Tex in a brittle voice. 'Take your prisoner inside and hand him over to Johnny. Tell Johnny to call an ambulance from the airfield to pick up Taffy. Then join Ferocity in the lorry and try to overtake a motor-boat that's heading up-stream. Larapindi's in it. He's got a hangar somewhere up the river, with a machine in it. Try to stop him from getting away. If the hangar is this side of the river you may have a chance.'

Biggles was moving as he spoke, and by the time he had finished he was in the driving-seat. The car shot forward, and in another minute was racing along the road to Dum Dum.

In the short drive that followed Biggles took risks which in the ordinary way he would have considered unjustifiable. The driver of a belated bullock cart, which he missed by inches in avoiding a careless pedestrian, would doubtless have agreed with him. But everything depended on speed. He reached the airfield without mishap, and after skidding to a standstill at the main gate to announce his identity, went straight on across the landing-field to where a Spitfire was standing, its engine idling.

'Is she all right, flight-sergeant?' he shouted to the N.C.O. in charge, as he jumped out.

'Okay, sir,' was the answer.

Biggles climbed into the cockpit. An instant later the engine roared and the Spitfire moved forward. In five seconds it was in the air, swinging round in a wide turn towards Calcutta. The river came into view. Biggles eased the control column forward. On reaching the river he turned steeply, and roared up-stream with the floor of his fuselage not more than fifty feet above the water. He noted several cars outside the warehouse as he flashed past. Ahead, all he could see was that the placid surface of the river had been disturbed. There was no sign of the motor-boat. He tore on for three or four minutes, annihilating distance. Before him the moon gleamed on the broad surface of the water. He had always realised the futility of trying to make any sort of search in the dock area, which stretches for miles, but he hoped that somewhere above it, where there was less congestion of vessels, he would see either the motor-boat, or the aircraft. He saw neither. Doubts assailed him. It was only assumption that Larapindi would try to effect his escape by air. The enemy agent had asserted that the Gull was grounded for the duration; and so, undoubtedly, it had been—officially, Biggles reflected. But that would not prevent Larapindi from keeping it in an airworthy condition if he thought there was a chance that he might need it.

Biggles zoomed. Banking gently, his eyes probed the deep blue void through which he moved. He began to circle, extending his range with each turn. There was no sign of the aircraft he sought. Moodily he began to wonder if he had been wise in rushing into the air; and he was still wondering, torn by indecision, when during a turn he saw two bright sparks of light on the ground, winking at him. He took the lights to be the headlamps of a car, on the far bank of the river. With quickening interest he realised that this might be a signal to him, bearing in mind that the lorry would be able to judge his position by the sound of his motor.

Making for the lights he nearly collided with the Gull, and thereby had what must have been one of the narrowest escapes of his career. He did not know it was the Gull. He barely saw it. He was concentrating his attention on the winking headlights, trying to make out if the flashes formed a signal in Morse, when the thing happened. To say that a shadow appeared in the darkness would convey only a poor impression of the actual event. When two high-performance aircraft are approaching each other head-on, even in broad daylight, from the moment they become visible to each other, to the moment of contact, is a very short time indeed. At night the time factor is lessened, in ratio with reduced visibility. The black shape of the Gull did undoubtedly approach, but from the time it came into sight, to the moment of passing, was a split second. Biggles hardly saw it. Rather did he become aware of it. He acted without conscious thought. It was one of those occasions, and there are many in every pilot's career, when there is literally no time for thought. Life depends on perfect co-ordination of brain and limb. The two things, actuated by an impulse which is akin to instinct, must operate simultaneously, or all is lost. Biggles' right hand and foot jerked. The Spitfire reacted convulsively, like a horse startled from sleep. The two shadows seemed to merge. Then they flashed past each other. The danger was averted. Again Biggles moved. His nerves were rigid from shock, the sensation as when we say our heart stands still; but he moved. The control column was back in his thigh, and the Spitfire had whirled round almost in its own length. Then for the first time he really saw the Gull, and recognised it.

The rest was comparatively easy. Glancing down to see where he was he observed that by an ironic twist of fate the Gull was just passing over the eastern boundary of the airfield, from which the enemy agents had sent so many British pilots to their deaths. He waited for a moment and then fired a short burst past the Gull's cabin. He assumed that the civil machine would be unarmed, and he resolved to give the pilot a chance to land should he prefer surrender to death, although it would probably come to the same thing in the end. He did not think his enemy would accept the invitation. And he was right. The Gull jinked, and then, to Biggles' surprise, someone in the cabin opened fire on him with a machine-gun, presumably a mobile weapon. He hesitated no longer. Swinging round to the off-side quarter of the fugitive he closed in, took careful aim, and fired. Tracer flashed across the intervening distance. The apex of the cone of fire struck the Gull amidships; the machine appeared first to crumple, and then break across the cabin. Pieces broke off and whirled away astern. The nose of the stricken machine dropped. It dived. The motor was cut, but still it dived, in an ever-steepening swoop earthward. With expressionless face Biggles watched it strike the edge of a paddy-field. He circled twice and then turned away, not feeling inclined to risk a night landing near the wreck, although the country was open. In any case, he knew that there was nothing he could do for whoever might be in the machine. So he cruised back to the airfield and landed, taxi-ing on to the ambulance station.

'I've just shot an enemy machine down, not far from the road, about two miles east of the airfield,' he announced. 'I fancy there are casualties. I'll come with you.'

'I thought I heard shooting, sir,' answered the driver, as Biggles got in beside him.

There were two bodies in the wreck. One was Larapindi. The other, obviously the pilot, was unknown to him. The ambulance returned to the airfield and the bodies were taken to the mortuary. Biggles went back to Larapindi's car, which still stood where he had abandoned it, and drove quietly back to the warehouse.

Things were different from when he had left. A line of police cars occupied the kerb outside the main entrance, from which he gathered that the Air Commodore had considered it advisable to call for assistance. He found a little crowd in the hall; it included most of the members of the squadron, and the Air Commodore. His arrival caused a stir.

'What about Larapindi?' asked the Air Commodore urgently, anxiously.

'He won't give any more trouble,' answered Biggles.

'Where is he?'

Biggles took out his cigarette case. 'What's left of him is in the station mortuary,' he replied.

'How did that happen?'

'He'd got an aircraft parked up the river, apparently with a tame pilot standing by. He must have kept the machine there for just such an emergency.'

'We've found five Japanese airmen here so far, hiding in different parts of the building,' put in the Air Commodore. 'This must have been a rendezvous for enemy pilots who were forced down on our side of the lines. It seems that that was another of Larapindi's activities. The search is still going on. I take it you shot him down?'

'I had to, or he'd have got away. He was heading east. That's all there was to it. What's happened here?'

'Nothing very exciting, since you left. We're still cleaning up. We've taken everybody into custody. That stuff in the laboratory was interesting, but not so interesting as the contents of Larapindi's safe. You caught him on one foot, so to speak; otherwise, if he had had time, no doubt he would have destroyed everything. As it is, we've got particulars of the dope operatives on the other stations, to say nothing of other agents, and where they are working. They are being rounded up. By dawn the whole organization should be wiped out.'

'Was Larapindi a Jap,' asked Biggles.

'I haven't been able to get to the bottom of that yet,' answered the Air Commodore. 'He was a Fascist, anyway. He was a wealthy man, but that wasn't enough. He wanted power, which is an obsession with a certain type. I found a document in the safe, a sort of agreement, promising him a high political position in India should the country be taken by Japan. He played for a big stake, and lost.'

Biggles nodded. 'Have you found any indication as to whether this dope business was his own idea, or whether he was put up to it by Japan?'

'We don't know yet. We may never know—not that it's important.'

'What's the position of the firm?' queried Biggles.

'Oh, it was genuine enough, originally, there's no doubt of that,' asserted the Air Commodore. 'Larapindi was the crook. With Tahil out of the way it provided a wonderful background for espionage. The firm has agents and branches everywhere, and the top floor of this warehouse must have been an ideal meeting-place for enemy agents. Tahil died from snake-bite, you know.'

'So Laripindi told me. I should say Larapindi was the snake that bit him.'

'Old Tahil was a good fellow. It must have suited Larapindi to have him out of the way. Young Tahil, the old man's son, is at Oxford. I imagine he'll come back and take over the firm. Well, you've done a good job, Bigglesworth. I'll see you get credit for it.'

'You mean, you'll see that the squadron gets credit for it,' corrected Biggles.

The Air Commodore smiled. 'Of course—that's what I meant. I suppose you'd like to get back to England now? If you go right away I'm afraid you'll leave

Mackail and Harcourt here.'

'How are they? Have you heard lately?'

'Yes, I rang up the hospital this evening. Harcourt is doing fine—he wasn't seriously hurt. Mackail has come round, and the M.O. says he'll recover, but it will be some time before he flies again.'

'Good. What about Taffy? The last I saw of him he was sitting here bleeding like a pig. One of Larapindi's men had knifed him.'

'It's nothing serious,' stated the Air Commodore. 'In fact, Crisp, who went back with him in the ambulance, tells me that the M.O., after putting a stitch or two in him, has let him go to his quarters.'

'Bertie and Tex saw Larapindi take off,' put in Ginger, who was one of those standing by, listening to the conversation. 'They went with Ferocity in the lorry. they couldn't do anything to stop him because they were on the wrong side of the river.'

'Absolutely,' declared Bertie. 'All I could do was wink my jolly old headlights at you, to show you where we were.'

Biggles smiled. 'I saw them; and I was so interested in them that I nearly flew into Larapindi. If he was more scared than I was he must have died from shock. I shall have a nightmare to-night—the thought of collision always did give me the jitters.' He yawned. 'Which reminds me, a spot of sleep wouldn't do us any harm. Let's get back. I want to have a little wager with Taffy.'

'What is it?' asked Algy.

Biggles laughed. 'I'm going to bet him that the hole in my arm is deeper than the one in his leg. Come on. Let's go, before the Air Commodore thinks of another tangle for us to straighten out.'